# MAN'S BEST FRIEND

## THE DOGMOTHERS - BOOK SIX

# roxanne st. claire

## Man's Best Friend
THE DOGMOTHERS BOOK SIX

ISBN Ebook: 978-1-952196-09-6
ISBN Print: 978-1-952196-10-2

COVER ART: The Killion Group, Inc.
INTERIOR FORMATTING: Author E.M.S

# Critical Reviews of Roxanne St. Claire Novels

"Non-stop action, sweet and sexy romance, lively characters, and a celebration of family and forgiveness."

*— Publishers Weekly*

"Plenty of heat, humor, and heart!"

*— USA Today* (Happy Ever After blog)

"Beautifully written, deeply emotional, often humorous, and always heartwarming!"

*— The Romance Dish*

"Roxanne St. Claire is the kind of author that will leave you breathless with tears, laughter, and longing as she brings two people together, whether it is their first true love or a second love to last for all time."

*— Romance Witch Reviews*

"Roxanne St. Claire writes an utterly swoon-worthy romance with a tender, sentimental HEA worth every emotional struggle her readers will endure. Grab your tissues and get ready for some ugly crying. These books rip my heart apart and then piece it back together with the hope, joy and indomitable loving force that is the Kilcannon clan."

*— Harlequin Junkies*

"As always, Ms. St. Claire's writing is perfection...I am unable to put the book down until that final pawprint the end. Oh the feels!"

*— Between My BookEndz*

Before
**The Dogmothers…**
there was

## The Dogmothers Series

Hot Under the Collar (Book 1)

Three Dog Night (Book 2)

Dachshund Through the Snow (Book 3 – a Holiday novella)

Chasing Tail (Book 4)

Hush, Puppy (Book 5)

Man's Best Friend (Book 6)

*And more to come!*

For a complete guide to all of the characters in both The Dogfather and Dogmothers series, see the back of this book. Or visit www.roxannestclaire.com for a printable reference, book lists, buy links, and reading order of all my books. Be sure to sign up for my newsletter on my website to find out when the next book is released! And join the private Dogfather Facebook group for inside info on all the books and characters, sneak peeks, and a place to share the love of tails and tales!

www.facebook.com/groups/roxannestclairereaders/

# Acknowledgments

Hugs of gratitude to the experts who backed me up on this one. Much love to Associate Veterinarian Christine Horne (with certifications in Canine Rehabilitation, Acupuncture and Spinal Manipulation or Chiropractic). She helped me heal Judah, so I named a character after her. Also, Silver James, retired member of the fire service and law enforcement, who has stepped in on so many occasions when I've written a firefighter hero, making sure I've got it all right. And finally, air kisses to beta reader Lorie Humpherys, who not only talked me off the ledge but actually came out there with me to guide me back with great ideas and a gentle touch. Shout out to my developmental editor Kristi Yanta and copyeditor Joyce Lamb, part of the amazing team behind me on every book. Y'all rock.

# Chapter One

*Twenty Years Ago*

"To Declan Mahoney," Evie said as she raised a paper cup of pilfered Jameson's, "my friend who is like a banana."

Declan snorted and rolled his eyes. "Ah, boy. Here it comes."

"'Cause he's so…" She leaned closer to whisper, "A-peeling."

He groaned, but a smile lifted his lips as he raised his glass. "To Evie Hewitt, the *punniest* person I know."

They put the cups to their lips, but Evie didn't take a sip. Instead, she gazed right into dark eyes so familiar and comforting, she couldn't bear to look away.

"Drink it up, buttercup."

She shook her head. "No, I want to do a better birthday toast. No jokes this time." She lifted the paper cup again. "Here's to my best friend since, wow, life began?"

"Since you got bumped up to third grade from second because you're so smart."

"On our birthday!"

1

Declan shook his head but couldn't help smiling. "You waltzed into Mrs. Burley's classroom and announced it was *your* birthday. On *my* birthday."

She threw her head back with a hearty laugh. "And my mom used glitter frosting to add your name to my pink Care Bears cake because that's all she had."

"Totally wrecked my playground cred for the rest of the year." His eyes sparked with humor.

She leaned back to look at him, wanting to drag out the toast as long as possible. For the whole night, actually. Because there was no better way to spend their shared birthday than alone in the mountains at midnight, a teeny bit tipsy, looking into each other's eyes.

"Here we go," she said. "The real toast. To my best friend."

"You sure about that now?"

"Well, except for the time he unfairly beat me—some might say he actually *cheated* me—out of a win in the seventh-grade Bitter Bark spelling bee—"

"Come on, E," he said on a laugh. "You missed duffel, fair and square."

"I did not *miss* it." She reached over and brushed a lock of his dark hair off his forehead, something she didn't normally do with her friends, but tonight... everything was different. Even the view over the lake where they always camped was different, but that was because Declan had driven to the opposite side to a far more secluded and private section than the one they'd always gone to.

And she knew why. Tonight, they were so ready to step outside the comfort of their friendship and find...a different kind of comfort. The kind that required seclusion.

"Where was I?" she asked, a little lost.

"Griping about the spelling bee when you flubbed duffel."

"Because the second spelling in the dictionary is D-U-F-F-*L-E*," she informed him. "And the only reason they gave it to you was because half the people in the auditorium were named Mahoney or Kilcannon." She added a jab to his shoulder, loving how hard firefighter training had made his muscles. "How could I fight the Irish Mafia of Bitter Bark?"

"Says the last remaining direct descendant of Thaddeus Ambrose Bushrod. The girl who literally waves from the lead convertible in the Founder's Day parade every stinking year."

She looked skyward. "Oh God, please let me have a midterm on October 22 this year so I can avoid the parade."

"What? Big Bad Thad would roll over in his grave if you don't represent the first family of Bitter Bark." He inched a fraction closer, giving her the faintest whiff of his indescribably masculine scent, as intoxicating as the Blue Ridge Mountains air and the golden liquid in their paper cups. "Plus, I get a secret thrill when that car goes by."

And she got a secret thrill when his voice got low and sexy like that.

"Did you know…" He brushed some hair back from her face now, hooking it over her ear, holding her gaze one heartbeat past what a friend would do. "I always get there early so I can get a Prime Evie Viewing Spot on the top stair of town hall."

"Then you're crazier than I thought."

"Yup." He shrugged. "Are you finished toasting? Or are you going to dredge up the time I backed into your dad's brand-new Mercedes while trying to navigate the Gloriana House driveway in reverse?"

3

"Just smashed right into it. *Oof.* He was mad." She chuckled at the memory, then inhaled that scent again, still lost. "So, where was I?"

"Setting the record for the longest birthday toast in history."

She slipped her lower lip under her teeth and sat up a little straighter. "Okay, fine."

"Bring it home now, E."

On one more sigh, she lifted the cup again. "To the boy who shares my birthday, the kid who can spell but can't drive in reverse, and the man…" *I am dying to kiss.* "Who can now legally purchase this stuff so we won't have to steal your Gramma Finnie's stash." She tapped her Dixie cup to his. "Happy twenty-first, Dec."

He pinned those chocolate eyes on her and never looked away while they knocked back their shots, which made her choke on the whiskey burn.

"There's my little lightweight."

She managed to get the liquor down her throat. "Shut up. You were raised on this juice."

He poured two more shots, but hers barely covered the bottom of the cup. Of course he didn't want her to get hammered up here on their annual birthday camp-out. Declan was always looking after her. "My turn, birthday girl?"

She shuddered as the whiskey hit her belly. "Your turn." She lifted her cup. "Hit me with your best toast, baby."

He cleared his throat and looked into her eyes again and, once more, she was gooey right down to her toes. How did this happen? When did every thought about Declan go from whether they'd play a game of pickup basketball to whether they'd…*make out*?

"Okay…" He made a face. "I'm trying to think of a worthy pun."

"I know it's a challenge for you." She winked at him. "But you try, and I love that."

"Here's to Evie…as intoxicating as this whiskey."

"Not bad." She dipped closer. "A for effort *and* the nicely buried compliment."

"Right?" He lifted the drink. "Okay, let's go with, here's to the girl who proved to Bitter Bark High that you can be hot *and* make an endless stream of bad jokes."

"You think I'm hot?" Nothing *buried* about that compliment.

He just snorted as if the question was too dumb to answer. "I raise my glass to the future Doctor—"

"If you say Dolittle, I'm gonna pour this over your head."

"Doctor Evangeline Hewitt, destined to become a world-class veterinary neurologist."

"Oh." The seriousness of the toast surprised her, but not the pride in his voice. He always sounded like that when he talked about her dream career. "As soon as I finish ten *more* years of vet school, specialty training, rotations and residencies, *and* certification."

"Which you have mapped out like the ambitious creature you are. Anyway, it'll be worth it, Evie. I'll just be a small-town firefighter—"

"Pffft. By the time I finish school and training, you'll be captain, like your dad is." She lifted her brows. "And then on to the pinnacle, *Chief* Mahoney."

"And you'll be a literal brain surgeon."

"*Animal* brain surgeon."

"No less amazing." He lowered his cup a bit. "You, Evie, are amazing."

5

"Aww. Is that your toast? To my amazingness?"

"Yes. To your unparalleled amazingness." He touched his cup to hers. "And the hope that this is the year…" She saw him swallow and then inhale slowly. "That we're not friends anymore."

Her hand froze on the way to her lips. "Oh. That's not a joke."

"No, it is not."

So this was it. Tonight. "I'll drink to that."

He smoked her with a look that was somehow sexy and suggestive without having to say a word before tossing back his shot.

She took a tiny sip that did little more than wet her lips. She didn't need it. She was drunk on possibilities. "It's been different this summer," she said on a whisper.

"Yeah, it has."

Ever since she'd returned to Bitter Bark at the end of her junior year at NC State, their friendship had intensified to something new and physical and humming with tension.

Casual touches had been more frequent. Hugs goodbye had lasted longer. Their conversations, always honest, had gotten deep and thoughtful and adult, especially when they talked about why neither of them was in a relationship. And this afternoon while they were swimming in the lake? All that unnecessary and electrifying body contact had only made this freakishly hot August day even hotter.

In fact, it seemed like the whole summer had been leading up to this, their annual birthday camping trip when they'd be alone all night, with no friends, families, or parents expecting them home before sunrise. Tonight, no one even knew where they were.

Her head buzzed with a mix of anticipation and desire and maybe a little of Gramma Finnie's Jameson's, making her fall back on the rough blanket, still warm after the sweltering day.

"How many times do you think we've come up to this lake on our birthday?" she asked.

"Oh, I don't know. First time, we were really young. Maybe when I turned twelve and you were eleven? You came with my family when my brothers and I were each allowed to bring a friend."

"I remember that. I was so honored to be the friend you picked. And your dad brought those big inner tubes, and your sister was practically still a toddler, making your mom so nervous every time she got near the water."

"Smella Mahoney. Making mothers crazy since 1988."

Evie closed her eyes and remembered how fun it had been as an only child to be with that big family. "You think we'll come back in the future, Dec?"

"Sure." The total lack of hesitation made her smile.

"Like when I'm finally a vet and you're the fire captain?"

"Of course."

"How about when we're really old?" she asked. "When I'm wrinkled like my Grandmama Penelope?"

"And I'm gray and fat enough to play Santa at the fire station." He patted his stomach, which was anything but fat. She fought the temptation to reach over and explore the muscles he'd developed while hauling hoses and lifting ladders at BBFD.

He held her gaze, his smile fading, his eyes intense.

"What?" she asked with a half-smile.

"You ready to play?" he asked.

7

Heat curled through her. "Is that what you call it?"

He laughed and poked her in the side, making her giggle. "The Birthday Game. What did you think I meant?"

"Umm...the We're Not Just Friends Anymore Game?" She added a flirtatious smile.

"That's not a game, E. That's serious business."

Her whole body grew heavy at the husky tone in his voice. "Okay." She rolled onto her side and propped her head up. "Birthday Game, then. You go first."

He slid down next to her, matching her position so they were face-to-face. "Best movie this year."

"Hmm. Tie between *Erin Brockovich* and *Dinosaur.*"

"The kids' movie, *Dinosaur*? You saw that?" he asked.

"Twice. It got me through finals last semester. Also a few long calls with a certain firefighter when things were slow at the Bitter Bark station."

That made him smile. "Well, you're nothing if not eclectic. I'm going with *Gladiator*."

"You're nothing if not predictable. Biggest personal victory?"

"Probie graduation." He tapped her nose. "Thanks again for coming back for it."

"Wouldn't dream of missing your big day. My biggest victory was getting the job at your uncle's vet office this summer. I can't believe how much I'm learning. Dr. Kilcannon is a brilliant vet, and your cousin Molly? She's young, but I love working with her. On our lunch breaks, we plan the vet practice we're going to open together someday."

"They love having you there. Okay. Let's get the bad one over with. Worst day of the past year?"

"I hate this one," she said, making a face. "This past

year? I guess when I took that B-minus in microbiology. Gah, that hurt."

"The brain trust takes a B."

"*Minus*."

He grinned at her. "Unheard of."

"It should be. What was your worst day of the past year, Dec?"

"That fire out on Red Oak Road," he answered without a second's hesitation. "First real big one for me, and man, if my dad hadn't been leading me into that warehouse and watching out for me every step of the way, I'm not sure I'd have made it out."

She put a hand on his arm, and this time it wasn't just a sly way of touching him. "You be careful in that job, Dec."

"I am," he promised her. "What's next? Happiest moment of the year?"

"I think…" She narrowed her eyes at him. "When I finished the semester, drove like a maniac from Raleigh to Bitter Bark, and you were in your truck in my driveway, waiting for me."

He gave her one of those slow, crazy-cute Mahoney smiles that made her stomach flutter and her knees weak. "I couldn't wait for you to call, E. I was counting the damn minutes until you got back home."

Yes. *Everything* was different this summer. "So now what was your very best moment of the year?" she asked. "The big one, the highlight, the moment that made the year worth living."

He didn't answer for a long time, but never took his eyes from hers. She could feel the heat, the sparks, the magnetic pull between his body and hers as he leaned over her. "Hasn't happened…yet."

For a few seconds, she couldn't breathe. He had to hear her heart hammering. Or maybe that was his. They were close and getting closer. It was hard to separate him from her. And she didn't want to.

"But we could make the best moment of this year…" He closed the space between them, his lips almost, but not quite, touching hers. "Right now."

*Oh yes, please.* Silent, she reached up and slid her hand around his neck, easing his mouth to hers for their first real kiss.

They'd kissed before. At an eighth-grade graduation party during a game of spin the bottle. At the post-prom party during a big group date and after a few drinks, but they'd just laughed about it the next day. And when she'd gotten her college acceptance, but that was an accident when their lips brushed.

But they'd never kissed like *this*. Long. Sweet. Intentional.

He scooted closer without breaking contact. His soft lips tasted hot and peppery, like the stolen whiskey.

With a moan that came from deep in his chest, he angled his head and added pressure, making her dig her fingers into his shoulders. He rolled her onto her back, and with each breath, they got closer, more intimate, and she could feel every firefighter-toned muscle, and one very impressive bulge she'd *never* felt before, pressing right where she wanted it.

This was Declan. This was insane. This was *perfect*.

He drew back for one second, his eyes closed, his lips parted. With another moan of pleasure, the next kiss grew more explosive when their tongues touched and they both seemed to want *more*. She bowed her back and spread her legs around his hips and forgot everything in the world but the new and thrilling sensations knotting her up.

"Evie," he murmured, splaying his hands over her ribs, his grip tight, like he was forcing himself not to touch her everywhere. "You feel so good."

"You have no idea how good I feel." She rocked against him, nearly crying out from the shock of raw pleasure.

"You're sure?" His fingers worked their way down to her T-shirt hem, inching it higher.

She eased him back enough so she could study his expression. "It's going to change us, Dec." It wasn't a question.

"About damn time, if you ask me."

Instead of answering, she looked into eyes she knew as well as her own. She knew every gold fleck and long dark lash. She knew how to read the expression in those eyes. She'd seen them red from smoke when he got off a terrible shift, and she'd seen them sleepy in an eight a.m. algebra class. And lately, she'd noticed his eyes were constantly on her. And not always on her face.

Just the thought of how his heated gaze had coasted over her body when she walked to his truck tonight made her ache.

Silently, she sat up and pulled the T-shirt over her head.

"Oh." His gaze dropped down to her lacy black bra. "Pretty fancy for camping."

"I had a feeling…"

"You did?" He pressed his hand to her breastbone, his palm grazing the lace. "Probably the same feeling I had when I packed some, uh, extra gear."

He'd brought a condom.

Biting her lip, she looked up at him. "I've always hoped it would be you."

His whole body went still, eyes widening. "This is your first time?"

"Don't you think I'd have told you if I'd slept with someone?"

"Um…I didn't tell you."

She started to respond, then closed her mouth. She couldn't be surprised at that. Declan was twenty-one, super cute, and a Mahoney, for God's sake. Girls were always floating around him and his younger brother Connor. Plus, she'd spent most of the past three years at NC State, three hours away. Up until tonight, they'd simply been the best of friends and she'd had no claims on his body. Yet.

"Well, I haven't," she admitted. "Does that make a difference?"

He considered that, silent as he so often was when his wheels were turning and he wanted to make the right decision.

"Like you said, everything is going to change. But you being a virgin?" He took a shaky breath. "I'm not sure—"

"Declan." She fisted his T-shirt. "I waited for something. Someone. *You.*"

"I'm not sure anything has ever made me happier," he finished, putting a hand on her cheek. "I won't hurt you," he whispered, his breath already tight. "We'll take it slow and easy and—"

She pulled him down for a blistering kiss on the mouth.

"And like that." He chuckled into the kiss, sliding his hand around to unclip her bra. "Happy birthday to us, E."

"Happy birthday to us, Dec."

# Chapter Two

When the sun came up and bathed the world in a soft golden glow, Declan awoke deep in the sleeping bag they'd hardly needed for the oppressive summer night, his arms painfully empty, his whole body on fire with an unfamiliar sensation. What was that ache, other than what he woke up with every morning?

He blinked into the light, then squinted at a silhouette down on the dock, where Evie stood peering over the rolling hills and navy blue water of the lake.

Evie. *That* was the feeling pressing on his chest. Evie, when she lost control, and when he was finally deep inside her, and when they fell asleep, knotted together.

His navy BBFD T-shirt skimmed her bare thighs, which were long and lean, and holy God, he'd never known anything could be that insanely smooth.

He took a full minute to drink in the sight of her, still reeling from the discovery that the girl he considered his closest friend was now the woman who'd given him everything last night.

And then he knew what that unfamiliar burn was. Declan Mahoney was completely, totally, and undeniably in love with Evie. She had everything he wanted—a wacky sense of humor, a brain like a damn computer, a body that drove him absolutely crazy, and she was the best friend he'd ever had.

Did Evie know that this was it? Game over? It was them, together, forever and ever, a-*freaking*-men. She would, eventually.

"Hey, gorgeous." His voice came out sleepy and gruff. "Come back to…bag."

She turned, silent for a long moment, but he couldn't see her expression with the rising sun behind her.

"You okay?" he asked when she didn't say anything, pushing up to his elbows.

"Yeah, I'm good." She walked over the wooden dock and to their campsite hidden in the trees, finally reaching the blanket. She dropped to her knees next to him, her blue-fire eyes too bright for her to have just awakened. "Was that weird? Last night?"

*Weird?* "I'd use a lot of words to describe what happened in this sleeping bag, E, but 'weird' would not be one of them."

She pulled her long black hair back to look hard at him. "I mean…we had *sex*, Declan."

"Oh, is that what we did? Good addition to the birthday traditions, don't you think? Gives new meaning to pin the tail on the…" He let the joke go and put a hand on her bare thigh. "Please tell me you're not having second thoughts or morning-after regret."

She didn't answer right away, and that made his chest clench. "Can we still be friends?" she finally asked.

"What kind of question is that? We'll be friends forever. Best friends. I tell you everything."

She lifted a brow. "Apparently not."

14

"Everything that really matters. I haven't been with that many girls, if that's what you're thinking. And no one was…" He shook his head. "There's only you now. There's only ever been you, honestly. And there only ever will be—"

She quieted him with a finger to his lips. "You *do* realize what's ahead of me, right? Like, *eons* of school, graduate school, specialty training, residencies, and rotations. I don't want to be a country vet, Declan."

"I know. You want to be a veterinary neurologist, a surgeon, a top-notch specialist, because you have the blood of Thaddeus Bushrod in your veins, and you don't do anything halfway."

She narrowed her eyes at him. "Are you making fun of me?"

"Not this time. I totally respect what you want to do with all those brains God gave you and those talented hands." He inched back. "And whoa, they are—"

"Declan, I'm serious."

"So am I," he shot back. "But does all that talent and ambition leave no room for a future for us?"

"It's daunting for me to think about the future," she whispered. "I want…all that, but I can't really think about our relationship."

"You've never had to think about our relationship," he countered. "It's like…breathing."

"After last night?" she challenged.

"Heavy breathing," he joked. But for once, she didn't laugh, her eyes downcast, her pretty mouth nowhere near forming the smile he expected.

"Hey." He lifted her chin, forcing her to look at him. "We don't have to…do that again." Which would be a damn shame. "Our friendship isn't contingent on sex or anything else, to be honest. We'll be friends for the rest of our lives. I will always be there for you, in whatever capacity you want. You believe that, right?"

"I believe it, but you have a lot to do, too. Make captain by the time you're thirty, then chief when your dad retires. We have plans, Dec."

He took her hand and rubbed her knuckles. "I know this is who you are, Evie Hewitt. You aren't happy if you don't have a schedule and a long-term plan and short-term strategy and lists of pros and cons."

"True, but that long-term plan is *long*. Would you really wait all those years?"

"For you? Of course."

She gave a dry, disbelieving laugh. "You're going to wait, like, a decade? Declan Mahoney, one of the best catches in Bitter Bark?"

"You say that like I'm a fish and girls are casting their hooks at me."

"Well?"

"I won't bite." He inched closer and took her chin between his fingers, holding her pretty face steady. "Unless you want me to."

"Declan."

"Listen, I'd wait until I'm ninety, and then I'd come right back up here on this mountain and play the Birthday Game in a sleeping bag with you." He closed the space and put his lips against hers. "Maybe by then I'll get that whole pun thing right."

He felt her sigh against his lips before returning the kiss. But when they parted, he could still see doubt darkening her blue eyes.

"Hey, I have an idea," he said, snapping his fingers. "Do you have any paper?"

"I have index cards in my backpack left over from school."

"Get me one with no organic-chem notes on it."

"No promises." She pushed up and grabbed her bag, fishing out a rubber-band-wrapped pack of index cards, taking one out. "A pen, too?"

"Yes, please."

She came back with both, folding down next to him. "What are you doing?"

"I'm putting my money where my mouth is, as my Irish granny likes to say. I'm writing a, I don't know, a pact? A guarantee. An index-card contract. Something you can hold on to and believe in when I'm not around."

At the top, he wrote *DECLAN'S PROMISE* in all caps, staring at it for a minute. Taking a deep breath, he started filling in the narrow blue lines with tiny printed words. "I, Declan Joseph Mahoney…" He hesitated, then looked at her. "Not sure what to say."

"How about 'being of sound mind and body'?" She leaned forward and ran her finger down his bare chest. "I mean, it was pretty sound last night."

He smiled. "Don't distract me, woman." He kept writing, saying the words out loud to be sure he got them right. "Do hereby swear that I will wait for Evangeline May Hewitt…"

"Don't say forever," she whispered. "There's nothing worse than a broken promise."

He gave her a look. "Fine. For…twenty years," he added as he wrote.

"That feels like forever."

"And anytime in between," he added, "I promise to be whatever she needs me to be."

"Nice and vague," she teased.

"You want specifics?" he asked. "Okay." He continued to write. "I will be her friend, lover, husband..." He looked up to see her reaction, which was wide-eyed.

"Husband?"

"I said anything you need. Confidant, partner, provider..." He scribbled the words. "What else?"

This time when he looked up, there were tears in her eyes. "No." He stroked her long hair and pushed it back. "You shouldn't be crying."

"You already are everything, Dec."

He leaned closer to kiss her for that. "What else, then?" he whispered. "Chauffeur?"

"But not in reverse, because that's the way the Mercedes bends."

"And she's back, ladies and gentlemen." He chuckled, tapping her nose with the pen. "Okay, how about chef, traveling partner, fellow camper, and...handyman?" He leaned closer. "'Cause I nailed you last night."

She snorted. "There's hope for you yet, Mahoney."

Laughing, he kept writing. "And father to our..."

She put her hand over his, making the pen pause and giving him a serious expression. "I get the idea."

So he just signed his name and gave her the card. "Keep that. We can revisit it on every birthday for the next twenty years and see what I've missed."

She reread it, smiling, then handed it back to him. "You keep it safe for us. You can wave it under my nose whenever I have doubts or have to run off to school or an animal hospital."

"Fine." He took it, giving her a look he hoped she understood while he folded it in half. "Now, will you get in this bag so we can seal this deal?"

"Oh yeah. Wait! What time is it? We have a twelve-year-old mastiff with bladder stones coming in for a procedure at nine. A sick mastiff, Declan." She bit her lower lip and made what he thought of as her *an animal needs me!* face. "I have to be there to hold his big paw."

"Of course you do, Dr. Dolittle." But wasn't her tender heart for sick animals one of the many things he loved about her? He slipped the index card into the side of his backpack. "Looks like I lose to bladder stones."

"Hey, you just promised—"

"Kidding." He leaned in and kissed her. "I respect the bladder. So much that I'm headed into the woods right now."

"Declan." She took his hand. "I don't go back to school for a week. When's your next night off?"

"Since my dad did me a favor by taking my twenty-four-hour shift because *someone* wanted to camp on our actual birthday…"

"That's part of the tradition," she said.

"True, but I'll have to make it up on Thursday. So, I'm on duty until Friday. Why?"

"Let's come back here." She lifted his hand and kissed his knuckles. "We can start making next year's best-of list."

He kissed her again, wanting so much to tell her he loved her, but knowing it would send her on an *I have a million years of school ahead* rampage.

"It's a date, E." He gave her one more kiss.

They didn't talk much on the way back to Bitter Bark, but held hands and listened to Tim McGraw because "My Best Friend" was her favorite song. And it sure felt right for this moment.

It wasn't until he turned the corner onto his street that Declan reached over to turn off the music.

"Did I forget a Kilcannon event or something?" he asked, skimming the additional cars on the street and recognizing Aunt Annie's van and his cousin Liam's truck. Uncle Daniel was here, too. "Didn't you say there's a mastiff surgery this morning?"

"Yeah. Dr. K should be at the office."

The first spark of something worrisome flickered in his chest and then flared when the front porch door opened, and Gramma Finnie walked out.

"She doesn't look happy," Evie said, leaning forward to better see the sixty-something woman, whose graying hair looked wild and her face blotchy. "Think you're busted for stealing her booze?"

"I don't know." He scanned the cars again, seeing his younger brother's Jeep parked in the driveway, but not Dad's Tahoe. And his shift had ended three hours ago.

As he got out of the truck and reached into the back for his pack and the sleeping bag, he saw Gramma Finnie dart back inside, the screen door slamming. What was going on?

Evie came around the truck to get next to him, giving him a questioning look and reaching for his hand. "Looks like your entire family is here."

His gaze moved to Dad's empty spot in the driveway. "Not all of them."

Just then, Uncle Daniel stepped outside, and right behind him, Aunt Annie. Instantly, Declan let go of Evie's hand and hurried toward his uncle, who he could see, even from fifty feet away, was...not right.

"Hey, Uncle Daniel," Declan called, forcing his voice to be steady even though his throat was closing against his will.

Where was Dad?

"Declan." He saw his uncle take a deep, steadying breath, his broad shoulders squaring as if he were about to go into battle. Or deliver some kind of bad news. "I need to talk to you, son."

Declan stopped mid-step, staring at the man coming toward him, trying to read his expression, which looked…ravaged.

"Is everyone okay? Mom? Ella? The boys?" But even as he went through his family, he knew. Deep in his gut, he knew. He *knew*.

*Where the hell is Dad?*

His aunt hung back a few steps, her permanent smile gone, her face swollen from crying.

Uncle Daniel reached him, holding out both arms. Declan didn't move as he could almost feel parts of his brain start to shut down.

His uncle put his big doctor's hands on Declan's shoulders, squeezing lightly as he closed his red-rimmed eyes. "There was a call last night. A house fire."

Declan stared at him, the thrumming of blood in his head so loud it sounded like the words were spoken underwater.

"And something…went wrong."

*Oh God.*

Declan had never seen Daniel Kilcannon cry. That was the only thought that could register as his uncle's entire face seemed to fold as he started to weep. "We lost him, son. We lost your father."

*What?* He mouthed the word, but nothing came out. No sound. No breath.

"I'm so sorry." Uncle Daniel folded strong, sizable arms around him, but Declan couldn't hug back. He stood stiff and immobilized as more parts of him shut down.

His thoughts. His heart. His feelings. One by one, everything froze. It was the only way to keep from throwing his head back and howling in agony.

"Dec, I'm so sorry."

"Dad." He managed to croak the word, pulling back. "What happened?"

His uncle didn't answer right away, glancing instead to Evie. God, Declan had forgotten she was there. Suddenly, Aunt Annie came to Evie's other side, sliding an arm around her waist.

"Gloriana House," Uncle Daniel whispered.

Evie gasped, but Aunt Annie squeezed her. "Your family is fine," she said. "Your parents and grandparents got out safely."

"And Taddy?"

"Yes, they got the dog," Aunt Annie assured her. "The house is only partially damaged."

*Gloriana House?* Dad died saving Evie's family home? Declan felt himself taking steps backward, dropping his pack and the sleeping bag, trying—and failing—to process the world coming down around his shoulders.

"Why…why didn't you come and…" His voice trailed off. He knew why. Because he'd picked the most secluded, secret spot on the mountain where *no one could find them.*

"Liam and Shane drove all over the campground, son, as soon as we heard around four in the morning. But they couldn't find you."

He closed his eyes, imagining his cousins looking for him last night. Then, he shook off the thought and forced his brain to work like a firefighter's. "Are they still at the site, doing S&O?" No way that salvage and overhaul would be done by eight on a fire that started in the middle of the night. "I need to—"

"You're not going there," Daniel said, his voice leaving no room for argument.

"How did it start?"

"No idea yet. It was contained quickly, though."

Not quickly enough. "But what happened?" How could his father, a skilled and vigilant firefighter, not walk out the way he'd walked in?

"All we know is a second-floor overhang collapsed on him, and he…" Daniel swallowed. "They haven't even started the investigation, son."

"Anyone else?" Declan asked, his voice tight.

"George Rainey, his partner, managed to…" He heaved a sigh. "He got out in time."

But Dad *didn't*?

How was this possible? Declan closed his eyes, seeing flashes of white behind his lids as he bent over and let out a silent scream.

*No.* Not possible. Not Dad. Not Joe Mahoney. Not his hero, his mentor, his whole world. His *father.*

"Oh, Dec. I'm so sorry." Evie draped over him, but her body felt heavy and hot, and he couldn't bear the weight of her grief on top of his.

He eased her off, standing straight, digging deep for reason and sense and the ingrained responsibility that his father had carved into his heart. If *he* was broken, what about the rest of his family?

"Where's Mom?" he asked on a ragged whisper, looking at the porch where Gramma Finnie stood arm in arm with his cousin Molly.

"She's inside," Uncle Daniel said. "Everyone's waiting for you."

Waiting for him to come back from the mountains, where he'd been having sex with Evie while his father had been…covering his shift. And dying for him. And saving her family.

On their *birthday*.

No. This didn't happen. It didn't. How? *Why?*

He turned to Evie, but her face was soaked with tears and red from the same agony whipping through him.

"Dec." She pressed her hands to her mouth, tears flowing.

"Your family is staying with the Langleys, dear," Aunt Annie said gently, still holding Evie like she could crumble any second. "Your father's on his way now to bring you there."

"Dec," she whispered again.

He tried to answer, but stared at her, his head buzzing, sobs ready to strangle him.

He dropped his head back and endured the next wave of pain, then turned away, the emptiness that engulfed him so indescribable that he just wanted it to stop. He wanted everything to stop. He wanted to run and be alone in the depths of darkness that he knew would never, ever lift. Away from them. Away from her. Away from everyone.

But he couldn't run. He had three younger siblings who'd depended on Dad and a mother who'd lived and breathed for her husband.

"Dec, I'm so sorry." Evie managed to get hold of him and wrap her arms around him, her whole body quaking as she wept. "I'm sorry," she murmured into his chest. "I'm so sorry."

But he stood stone-still. He knew what he should do. Hold her. Hug her. They should cry on each other's shoulders.

*Didn't he just promise her all that?*

But nothing in him worked. Everything had shut down, like a plug had been pulled and the power had gone out for good.

She gazed up at him, looking desperate for something he couldn't give her. Not now. Maybe…not ever.

"I'll wait for my dad," she said. "You go. Take care of your mom. Your brothers. Ella." She broke again when she said his little sister's name.

All of them…fatherless. They were his job now. His responsibility. Not Evie. His family was *all* that mattered.

"I'm going into the house," he said, his voice thick. He didn't wait for her response, mostly because he knew he couldn't take it. He couldn't help her when she still had both parents and grandparents, and so many others would be depending on him.

Without another word, he turned and walked inside. With each step, he wondered if he'd ever feel anything except pain for the rest of his life.

# Chapter Three

*Twenty Years Later*

While her grandfather slept in the four-poster behind her, Evie stared out of one of the arched windows of Gloriana House as an early October afternoon painted the hills around Bitter Bark in the golds and russets of autumn. Her gaze took its usual path, drifting down the hill, over the upscale homes of Ambrose Acres, and then toward the brick buildings and the clock tower over town hall.

Even from here, she could spot the bronze statue of Bitter Bark's founder, Evie's great-great-*great*-grandfather, Thaddeus Ambrose Bushrod, standing sentry in the middle of it all.

The view had thrilled her as a child when she'd slip up here to her grandparents' bedroom and look out over the town. In her mind, she was a princess surveying the kingdom, part of a venerable bloodline, the sixth generation of Bitter Bark's first family. The Bushrods, then the Hewitts, were as much a part of the town's fabric as the enormous hickory tree that "Big Bad Thad" had erroneously called a bitter bark and then named the town after it.

The view had broken her heart when she was living in Raleigh, as she had for the past twenty-some years with only occasional visits to see Granddaddy Max and Grandmama Penelope. From up here, she could see the fire station, and she used to imagine Declan Mahoney hard at work, saving lives and protecting the people of this town. But never, ever picking up the phone to call his onetime best friend.

Because after the fire, there'd come *the ice*. She and Declan had entered into what Evie thought of as "the frozen years," where they remained to this day. The burned wing of the glorious Victorian mansion that Thaddeus Bushrod Jr. had built at the turn of the century had been repaired after the blaze that had started when rags soaked in chemicals combusted in the heat.

But no team of architects, historians, and contractors had come to fix the damage done to a friendship that was supposed to have lasted a lifetime.

Declan had changed the morning his father died, withdrawing from everyone but his family. Evie had tried to break through the walls grief had built around him. At the funeral, before she left for school, and many times that first year, she'd reached out to him, but all she'd gotten was…distance. Excuses. And silence. He'd never been mean or mad or even shed a tear, but he could no longer connect with her.

Did he blame her? Did he believe that if they hadn't gone to the mountains, the outcome might have been different? Did he resent her mother, whose painting rags had started the fire that collapsed the second-floor veranda and trapped Captain Joe Mahoney? Did he hate Gloriana House, or her family, or just life in general?

She didn't know, because the boy who told her

everything wouldn't share anything, so after a while, it became easier for Evie to try to forget how much she missed Declan. With the exception of the occasional unexpected and awkward encounter, neither of them had the courage or strength to break the ice that had formed around their friendship. After a decade or two, the very idea of some sort of reconciliation or revival seemed hopeless.

So now, this view made Evie feel bittersweet. At forty years old, an only child with no children of her own, Evangeline Hewitt was the last in a long line of Bushrod descendants who'd called Gloriana House home. When Granddaddy passed away, the great Victorian manor would enter a new phase, whatever that would be, with no family to live in it.

Not long after the fire, which her Bohemian mother had called a sign from the universe that they should "follow their dreams" and live on a sailboat in the Caribbean, her parents had moved. Dad didn't follow dreams, he followed Mom like a loyal lapdog, so off they'd gone. Those two had zero desire to live in a rambling, three-story, one-hundred-and-twenty-year-old mansion that still had the original oil lamps and woodwork in some of the rooms.

And Evie had made her life more than three hours away, becoming one of the top specialists in her field, now the head of the Neurology Department at the NC State College of Veterinary Medicine. So, eventually, the house would have to change hands, but no one really wanted to face that yet.

"I know what I want."

Evie turned at Granddaddy's gruff voice, surprised he was awake. "You'll take that tea now?"

"A celebration of life."

"Excuse me?" She came closer to the bed, perching on the edge to take his withered old hand in hers.

"I saw it on TV," he said. "Some old guy. Older than me, and that's old." He gave her a smile that showed he hadn't had the energy to put his dentures in today. "No funeral. I hate that Mitch Easter*crook*."

She laughed softly at the reference to the town's unpopular undertaker. "I told you to quit with this dying nonsense."

"Evangeline, dear, don't humor me. I'm ninety-two, and I can't remember the names of my body parts, let alone what they were supposed to do when they worked."

She smiled. "Your sense of humor is working just fine." She got up to adjust the Navy baseball cap that he liked to hang on the post of the bed, a reminder of his World War II service.

"I want you to be in charge of my celebration-of-life party," he continued. "I want it to be crowded and happy and right in the middle of Bushrod Square. And I want a big band to play Glenn Miller's 'Moonlight Serenade.'" He looked at her with sad gray eyes, dimmed by time, giving her an inkling of how her own pale blue gaze might look in fifty years. "Then Penny and I will be dancing together in heaven. And then you can do whatever you want with this old house. I don't care."

"Oh, Granddaddy." She sat back down next to him, knowing he did care, very much. "You know you're going to live to be a hundred. And one."

He sighed. "I promised Penny I'd hold on until…well, never mind. You'll plan that party for me, won't you?"

She knew what he was holding on for—the next generation in a long line of generations. "I'll give you a

Glenn Miller party." She patted his hand and got back up to look out the window when she heard a car door. "But don't rush it, okay? I like having you around."

A boat of a Buick had pulled into the driveway, which wasn't that unusual since Granddaddy frequently had visitors. But most of them called first, and no one had contacted her about coming by today. She hoped it wasn't some pushy tourist who wanted to see the inside of the house. It was enough that they stood on Ambrose Court and took pictures.

"Looks like you've got company. You up for a visitor?"

"Maybe. Who is it?"

She peered at a woman. "I don't know this lady. Wait, she's waiting for someone on the passenger side."

"A lady, huh?" He pushed himself up, a smile pulling. "I could use a little company. You bring her up, and I'll put my dentures in and show her my biting humor. Get it? Biting."

"Got it, and sorry I didn't say it first." She helped him out of bed, got him in his robe and slippers, and led him to the bathroom before heading down to the entryway. The closer she got to the leaded-glass front door, the better she could see the shapes of two women. Then she heard a loud bark, followed by a low growl. Guests *and* dogs?

She pulled the door open and did a double take at the sight of the Irish grandmother she'd known since childhood. She inched back as two dachshunds, one extremely stout and brown, the other tan and frisky, darted at the door.

"Oh, I wasn't expectin' you, lass!" Finola Kilcannon adjusted her bifocals as if to get a better look at Evie, while the other woman tugged on leashes to hold the dogs back. "We assumed a nurse would answer the door."

"It's me, and what a nice surprise." Evie reached out to give the tiny woman a hug, adding a smile to her friend, another octogenarian, though one who'd obviously worked hard at looking younger.

Evie let one wave of decades-old emotion wash over her as she pressed Gramma Finnie to her heart. But that was all. Just one crashing wave, then she composed herself.

Over the past twenty years, Evie had trained herself not to react to any of the large Irish clan that Declan Mahoney called family. She'd long ago learned to hide her response whenever she'd see a Mahoney or Kilcannon and bury the need to ask about him. She was warm, but cloaked in the same steel armor she wore when she performed a life-or-death surgery on someone's beloved pet. Not that she got to do many of those anymore.

"You look fantastic, Gramma Finnie," she said and meant it. The little old lady might be a few years younger than the man in the bed upstairs, but she looked as spry and alert as Evie remembered.

"Oh, lass. I'm old, but the Jameson's keeps my blood flowin'." She patted her puff of white hair while her cornflower-blue gaze danced over Evie.

Evie tamped down an ancient memory of stolen Jameson's that tickled her brain.

"And I don't think we've met," Evie said to the other woman, putting two and two together and coming up with...the Greek side of the Kilcannon family, added when Daniel Kilcannon remarried. "But I talk to Molly once in a while, so I'm guessing you are the great and powerful Yiayia."

"I am Yiayia," she said with unabashed pleasure and pride, shaking Evie's hand. "And it is so nice to finally meet you. I've heard so much about you."

"You have?" Who'd be talking about her in that family? "And who are these darlings?"

"Pyggie and Gala." Yiayia relaxed the leashes. "We hope your home is dog-friendly."

"Anywhere I am is dog-friendly," she said, bending over to greet the pups, getting a lick from the tan one and a look of pure skepticism from the darker one. He was certainly chunky enough to be called Piggy, although the name seemed a tad mean.

"Please, come in." She invited them all into the entryway, and immediately Yiayia gasped.

"Holy cra…cow. It's prettier on the inside, and that's saying something." Yiayia circled slowly, taking in the oversized two-story entry and wide red-carpeted staircase.

"Don't dig too deep, because you'll find a lot of things falling apart." Evie walked to the stair rail and rocked the round newel to prove her point.

"A problem many of us *grande dames* deal with." Yiayia let her head fall back to look up at the crystal chandelier. "My goodness. How do you clean that? Wait…no one does."

"Agnes!" Gramma Finnie put her hand on the other woman's arm. "This is the most beautiful home in Bitter Bark."

"But not necessarily the cleanest," Evie agreed, looking up at the hundreds of dangling pieces of crystal overhead. "There's a way to lower that thing, but that's above my pay grade."

"Are these real?" Yiayia pointed to one of the antique brass lanterns on either side of the dining room entry.

"The oil lamps?" Evie nodded. "Obviously, we don't use them for lighting anymore, but yes, they actually work. They're all over the house."

"What brings you home, lass?" Gramma Finnie asked, then her eyes popped. "Is Max worse? Havin' trouble?"

"He has good days and bad, and yes, he's part of the reason I'm here. I took a sabbatical this semester to keep him company and…" She lifted her hands in a way that gestured toward the house. "Help my parents figure out what needs to be done around here. Granddaddy's having a difficult time maintaining everything."

"So pleased you'll keep Gloriana House in the family," Gramma Finnie said.

"Oh, nothing is set in stone," she said, purposely vague, since no one really knew what they'd do with the house once that sad day came. "So, how are you? How's your family?"

"Everyone is fine."

"Declan is really good," Yiayia said quickly, making Evie blink in surprise.

"Oh, Agnes." Gramma Finnie clucked and slid her arm around Evie's. "I was just telling her on the way over here how you and Declan have the same birthday, only one year apart. Do you think I could see dear Max? Is he up for company today?"

"He'd love to see you." She stole a look at the other woman, her brain stuck on that unexpected mention of Declan.

"Agnes will stay here with the dogs." She could have sworn Gramma Finnie sent a meaningful look to her friend, which seemed strange. A warning? A message? Some silent communication.

"Of course. You know where Granddaddy's room is, right, Gramma Finnie?" Evie asked.

"Uh…I might need a refresher, lass. Agnes, keep the pups on leashes, but maybe you could look at the museum room with all the family treasures." Finnie pointed to the double doors of the library entrance, proving she didn't need *that* much of a refresher.

"We'll wait right in there." Yiayia gave Evie a tight, almost nervous smile and scooted her purse strap a little higher, giving off a weird vibe that Evie didn't understand. "They're good dogs," she added.

"They're adorable dogs," Evie assured her, giving both doxies a little love before she walked with Gramma Finnie up the stairs, taking the climb slowly for the older woman's benefit.

"So tell me about all the Kilcannons and Mahoneys," Evie said, glancing over the railing to see Yiayia and her dogs hustling to the room where generations of Bushrod and Hewitt antiques and heirlooms were displayed.

"Oh, there's a lot of babies," Gramma Finnie said. "Are ye really here for the whole semester, then? Through the start of the new year?"

"Yes, I am."

Finnie gave Evie a sideways look, her gray brows raised. "Any handsome man on your arm these days?"

She gave a light laugh, as used to the question as any single forty-year-old woman. "Now and again, but most of the time, I'm busy with work."

"Oh, really? Well, then, you must come out to Waterford Farm, then, and see our *whole* family."

Somehow, she doubted that would happen, but she was saved from answering when they reached her grandfather's room.

"Granddaddy? I have a wonderful surprise for you."

"I hope it's a good Cuban cigar and a bottle of brandy."

"That can be arranged," Gramma Finnie called out, smiling conspiratorially at Evie. "Though I prefer a fine Irish whiskey."

"Finnie Kilcannon!" he called out. "Come in here, you blue-eyed bombshell."

Finnie giggled and headed in, but Evie held back, a sixth sense making her want to go check on the stranger in the house.

"Go chat," Evie said. "I'll talk to your friend."

A look that could almost be panic crossed Gramma Finnie's face. "Stay with us a wee bit, lass. She's fine alone, I promise."

"He gets enough of me," she said, that sixth sense fluttering again. What were these two up to, exactly? "Go." With a pat on the older woman's back, she pivoted and headed down the hall, her footsteps soft on the hall runner as she listened to two old friends greet each other.

She slowed her step at an unexpected punch of memory.

*Two old friends.*

Hadn't Declan once said he'd wait for her until he was ninety, close to the age her grandfather was right now? An ancient sadness, dulled by decades of nudging it away, pressed on her heart, probably brought on by seeing Gramma Finnie, a woman Declan adored.

Thoughts of him were always under the surface when Evie was in Bitter Bark, knowing he could be around any corner or in any store. And that encounter would simply leave her aching for more and wondering where her best friend had gone.

Once, about six years after the fire, Evie had decided to try one last time to reconnect with him. She'd accepted a rotation at Vestal Valley College and lived with her grandparents for a few months, with hopes to rekindle the friendship she desperately missed.

But the only friendship she rekindled was with his cousin Molly, then a vet student and a single mother. Molly had invited her to Waterford Farm but, as a true friend would, had warned her Declan was seeing someone, so Evie steered clear of him that semester. All that Molly could tell her was that Declan had grown "serious" since his father's death, with family respon-sibility heavy on his broad shoulders.

After that, she'd seen him a few times, once outside the hardware store, another time passing in the square.

Then, a few years ago, she'd come to help Dr. Kilcannon with a brain-tumor surgery on his dog Rusty. The setter had healed in a week, but it had taken Evie a full month to get over the impact of seeing Declan in the vet office waiting room that day.

As she reached the bottom of the steps and headed to-ward the museum room, she heard the squeak of a hinge.

Was that...the cover for the piano keys? Did Yiayia play? Evie didn't want to be rude, but every treasure in the former library was priceless, including the Krakauer, a Victorian upright her great-grandmother had commiss-ioned exclusively for the house.

Without making a sound, Evie headed to the double doors, her eyes widening when she realized Agnes had closed them to an inch-wide crack.

Had she done that to keep the dogs from getting out? Walking closer, Evie peered through the slit at the very moment the woman slammed the keyboard lid so fast it clunked with a noisy thud that made the tan dog bark.

Evie used the distraction to enter.

"Can I share some of our family history?" Evie asked.

Yiayia whipped around, her dark eyes flickering with guilt. "Oh. Hello. Didn't hear you."

*Obviously*. Planting a smile that she doubted reached her eyes, Evie took a few steps closer, her gaze dropping down to Yiayia's bag, gaping wide open. Snooping was one thing, but had she...*taken* something?

"It's quite the room," Yiayia said, her voice tight as she gestured toward the many shelves and surfaces filled with knickknacks, photos, ceramic dishes, antique lighters, leather-bound books, and more than a few pieces of jewelry worth thousands.

"My great-grandmother Evangeline started displaying the heirlooms in here many, many years ago after her older sister, Gloriana, died. That's Glory Bushrod in the portrait." She indicated the large watercolor over the piano of a dark-haired beauty of nineteen who could have stepped off the set of *Downton Abbey*.

"Is that who the house was named for?" she asked.

Evie nodded. "And my grandmother Penelope continued the tradition of making this room a museum." She took a few steps closer, still trying to sniff out this woman's game. She didn't seem...innocent.

Evie gestured to the piano the woman had opened and closed. "Do you play?"

"No, but I heard you do."

Evie drew back, surprised. "My goodness, you've heard quite a bit about me."

The other woman crossed her arms, her dark eyes narrowing as if she was having some deep mental debate. "I have. I've heard you've known Finnie's family for a long time. That you go way back, and your family and hers—which, through marriage, is now mine—have a long…history."

Blood drained from Evie's face as she tried—and failed—to follow the ramblings. Was Yiayia chattering to change the subject from her strange activities in the room, or was she referring to the tragedy of the fire?

Would this woman be impolite enough to bring that up?

"It's a small town," Evie said, carefully dancing around the conversation. "We all have histories and intertwined pasts."

"But you and…" She swallowed and glanced at the door. "You have more than…"

Evie held up a hand to stop her. "Would you like something to drink?" She gestured toward the door. "I have some iced tea in the kitchen."

"Because you don't want me alone in this room."

Dear God, she was *blunt*. "I'd like to chat."

Her eyes tapered to slits. "You think I stole something, don't you?"

"Goodness, I—"

She huffed out a breath. "I knew I couldn't do this Finnie's way. I told her over and over that this was not the way to go about our mission. I'm terrible at subterfuge."

"Mission? Subterfuge?" Evie shook her head. "Wow, color me clueless, Yiayia."

"Oh, now I've gone and stepped in it."

"Deeply." For a long, totally confused moment, Evie

stared at her, then perched on the edge of a velvet settee. "So why don't you step out of it and explain?"

She dropped her face into her hands. "When am I going to learn to shut my big fat mouth?"

"Not now, I hope."

Yiayia sighed as she slumped in a chair. "I call things as I see them, you know? It's gotten me in trouble." She waved a hand like she couldn't be bothered with all that trouble, drawing Evie's attention to her long red nails. "But in the end, we Dogmothers usually get what we want."

"Dogmothers?"

"A nickname." She pointed at the dogs. The heavier one had already crawled under the settee to rest, but the other one inched toward Evie and looked right up at her.

She couldn't resist rubbing her little head. "This is Gala?"

"Galatea. And that's Pygmalion settling in for a snooze."

"Oh, that's where you get the name Pyggie."

"Had no idea he'd get that fat."

Evie chuckled at that and offered her palm for Gala to sniff and lick. "They're precious. And you and Finnie are the Dogmothers."

"But we're also matchmakers."

"Excuse me?" She couldn't have heard that right.

"We're quite successful, if I do say so myself." She gave a broad smile. "It's Declan's turn."

*What?*

"Listen." The woman pressed those red-tipped nails together in a prayerlike pose. "Please don't tell Finnie. Please? I promised her I'd do this her way, but her way is…" She shook her head vehemently. "You don't get two people back together on hope and a prayer, but you know Finola. 'The Irish say hope makes all things possible.'" She did a spot-on brogue, which would be funny if anything about this confounding conversation could be funny.

"Get two people back together?" That was all that stuck in Evie's head.

"You. And Declan. You belong together."

She stared at Yiayia, speechless.

"Finnie told me everything, and I do mean everything, dear. I know about your friendship and the fire—so unbelievably tragic—and she mentioned how you did surgery on Rusty, and everyone could see how affected Declan was merely to be in the same room with you."

She almost couldn't believe she was hearing this. Almost. Except, deep inside—maybe not so terribly deep—she wanted to roll up in a corner and beg the woman to share every little detail.

Declan had been affected, too? Had he suffered for weeks afterward like she had? They *belonged together*?

"He's such a wonderful man," Yiayia crooned.

No kidding.

"He's so handsome and the captain of the fire department, and everyone looks up to him so. He's set in his single ways, is all, but then Darcy Kilcannon happened to mention that she heard you were in town—"

"Agnes? Evie?" Finnie called. "Where did you girls go?"

"Oh my God!" Yiayia shot up, low-grade panic on her face that was instantly reflected on little Gala's expression. "Please don't tell her I told you. Please. Go along with her stupid plan."

"What plan?"

"Shhh! She's coming."

"Agnes?"

"In here, Finola." Her voice was reed-thin with nerves. "Chatting with this lovely lady."

Evie stood on shaky legs when Gramma Finnie came into the museum room, looking sweet and innocent and like she'd never made a "stupid" plan in her life.

Maybe it was the way Gala panted like she sensed Yiayia's stress, but something stopped Evie from asking a single question.

Maybe it was the red-tipped hand that closed over her wrist and squeezed. "So nice to talk to you, Evie," Yiayia said through gritted teeth. "What a fascinating history this room has."

Or maybe it was a bone-deep desire to let Gramma Finnie's plan...*work.*

She shot one quick look to Yiayia, long enough to silently communicate that, for whatever reason, her secret was safe.

Only then did those fingers relax.

"And, Agnes, did you, uh, get a good look around?" Gramma Finnie asked pointedly.

"Oh yes. We can leave now." She scooted her bag up on her shoulder and tugged the leashes. "Let's go, you two."

"I hate to visit and run, but we must get the dogs out." Gramma Finnie was almost to the door already. "So nice to see you, lass. And your dear sweet grandfather."

Yiayia beamed at her. "Such a beautiful woman you are, Evie. Inside and out. I can see why..." She caught herself. "Why Finnie wanted me to meet you."

Except Finnie had said she thought a nurse would be here.

"Goodbye, then." Gramma Finnie took Yiayia's other hand. "We'd best be going."

In what felt like an extremely rushed exit, the two women slipped out the front door and toddled down the drive like the two dogs between them.

The Dogmothers? Matchmakers?

The minute the car pulled away, she headed back into the museum room to try to figure out their...plan. But nothing appeared to have changed in this room. Then Granddaddy's bell rang furiously, which usually meant he needed something right away.

She headed toward the stairs, taking them two at a time, then down the hall to his room, surprised to find him standing by the window seat. "You okay, Granddaddy?"

"Oh yes. I'm wonderful. Elated. Never felt better." He turned, his color high for the first time in days. "Finnie and I had the most fascinating conversation."

"That's great. She certainly seems to have lifted your spirits."

"She did indeed."

"No more talk of a celebration of life?"

"Pffft! Too much to live for, Evangeline." He waved a hand, his eyes no longer faded with clouds but sparkling with unexpected vigor. "I'll take that tea now, if it's not too much bother. Iced, please. And maybe something to eat?"

"Of course." She eyed him carefully. "You *are* feeling better, Granddaddy."

He gave a smile. "Oh, you know what the Irish say. 'With hope, anything is possible.'"

Since when did he quote Irish proverbs? Since Finola Kilcannon came over with a *stupid* plan. But she could still hear the Greek grandmother's voice.

*You belong together.*

*Oh, sweet ladies and dear old gent. Hate to break it to you, but that ship sailed long ago...and sank.*

# Chapter Four

Declan pushed away from his desk three hours after his shift ended, the mountain of paperwork finally conquered. But then his phone dinged with a text, and he almost didn't want to look at it. Probably another reminder from Chief Winkler that staff evaluations and schedules were due on Monday.

It was a test, of course. How far could Mahoney be pushed to prove what a great chief he'd be?

*Far, Winkler. Push me right into the chief's office, where I belong.*

He picked up the phone, but the text was from his grandmother—who rarely resorted to texting to get her messages across—asking him to bring raspberry croissants to Waterford Farm for the Sunday dinner dessert. Seriously? No one else in the entire three-family clan could do that? Only the future Bitter Bark fire chief?

"Hey, bro." Connor, his younger brother and a fellow firefighter, pulled open the glass office door, looking fresh from only three hours on his shift. "Why are you still here?"

"Better question." He lifted the phone. "Why does

Gramma Finnie want *me* to stop at Linda May's before I head over to Waterford this afternoon?"

"Because you're the responsible Mahoney who cares if everyone's needs are met." He grinned. "Sorry to miss Sunday dinner with the crew, but *someone* scheduled me to work two weekends in a row. Thanks, pal."

"Your schedule is golden for the rest of October." He stood, and instantly, ninety pounds of black, gold, and cream-colored fur lifted his head from a bed in the corner and stared at Declan, an expression of pure dejection on the poor dog's face.

The Alaskan Malamute and Siberian Husky mix had looked that way since the moment Declan had arrived at work earlier this week and found him sleeping outside the station's back door.

Surrendered, abandoned, or merely lost, the poor guy they called Lusky, since his breed blend was called an "Alusky," had attached himself to Declan. When he wasn't curled in a corner, he lumbered around the station, eating without enthusiasm, and letting out the occasional howl that would be heart-wrenching if it wasn't such a funny-sounding wail.

"Lusky's gonna blow," Connor said, watching the creature lift his girth and then drop it into a classic downward dog.

"Any second," Declan agreed.

Connor opened the door a little wider. "Sorry, I have to. They live for this."

Rolling his eyes and knowing what to expect, Declan closed his laptop and gathered up his papers while his brother pointed to the dog. "Don't let me down, big man," Connor whispered. "Three…two…one…"

His huge mouth opened and out came a yowl that

would make a wolf green with envy. Instantly, three jackass firefighters answered the call with howls of their own.

"Are you done having fun at this dog's expense?" Declan challenged. "Wait. Scratch that. I'm asking the man who ran his dog for town mayor."

"And won." Connor reminded him. "Why are you in a suckier mood than usual, Big D?"

"Oh, let's see, I worked twenty-eight hours, finalized three new training exercises, interviewed volunteers, revised the policies-and-procedures manual, and inspected the engine."

"Why aren't you chief again?"

"Good freaking question, Connor. I guess because we already have one."

"Who sure knows how to delegate."

Declan agreed with a soft grunt in the dog's direction. "Don't forget I've suddenly got a new best friend with no chip, no collar, and attachment issues. And to top it off, my grandmother has me doing her bakery run."

"Like I said, that's why they call you the responsible one and me the handsome one." Connor knelt in front of the dog, threading his fingers into the thick fur on his monstrous head, then stroking the distinctive widow's peak on his face. "Speaking of handsome. You're a showstopper, you know that?" He glanced up at Declan. "Who'd give this guy up, though, seriously?"

"God only knows," Declan replied.

He'd worked at this station for so many years, there wasn't a dog story he hadn't heard. For some reason, when people ran out of money, luck, or time and were too ashamed to take their pet to a shelter, they left them at the fire station. Nine times out of ten, Declan was the one to step in and take care of the poor beasts, who had no idea why they were in a strange place where sirens screamed and boneheads howled back.

"Whoever it is, they've had seventy-two hours to have a change of heart. Garrett's been running notifications and pictures, too, throughout his whole lost-dog network. Nothing left to do but take this guy to Waterford Farm today and get him into the adoption program."

"He'll go fast," Connor said. "He's too pretty not to find a home."

"But he sheds like a sheep." Declan plucked at hairs on his uniform trousers, then slung his pack over his shoulder. "Let's go, Lusky," he called, watching the dog rise slowly. "I'm going to have Molly look at him first thing. I don't think he's quite right."

"Good idea. Oh, and pro tip? Since I can't be there to guarantee a win, get on Shane's team for touch football. He's been working on plays."

Declan threw him a look. "You know I don't get on the field with those lunatics."

"You should." He pointed at his brother. "A little lunacy would help you, man."

"I don't need help."

Connor rolled his eyes and disappeared into the station, and Declan took off.

A few minutes later, he pulled his truck into the garage of the brick ranch house he called home, ready for a shower and fresh clothes. The shift had been busy, but Declan had caught enough sleep that he didn't worry much about getting the shut-eye he usually needed after twenty-four-plus hours on duty.

But instead of relaxing on a Sunday morning, listening to some classical music, drinking coffee, and catching up on the news, he responded to yet another text from Gramma Finnie. This one a reminder that Linda May invariably ran out of raspberry croissants, and no one really wanted any substitutes.

*So hurry it up, lad.*

The responsible one, huh? Well, someone in the family had to be. "Yes, ma'am," he murmured as he led the dog back out to his truck.

At the open passenger door, Lusky crouched down and refused to jump, instead letting out one of his signature wails.

"Come on, you're not that fat." Declan wrapped his arms around the dog and lifted him into the truck. "Hope Linda May lets tricolored bear-wolves in her place."

In town, he snagged one of the secret parking spots behind the bookstore that only locals knew about, since there wasn't another space to be found. No wonder his grandmother had sent him on this errand instead of going herself—the bakery was packed with the after-church crowd and leaf-peeping tourists scarfing down the world-class raspberry croissants.

When he reached the front of the line, Linda May, who wore her signature Best Baker in Bitter Bark name tag, offered Lusky a treat. "I didn't know you had a dog, Declan," she said as she bagged up the croissants.

"He was surrendered at the station. Any chance you've seen him before? We've been trying to track down an owner, if only to get some medical history and an age."

She shook her head as she handed him change. "And that's not a face you'd forget, is it?" Her gaze shifted past him as her face lit up. "And neither is that! Hello, Evie Hewitt. I heard you were in town, Doctor!"

Declan froze in the act of sliding a bill into his wallet, his mind going blank for a second. It always did during a rare Evie sighting.

Every time, he'd pray for the courage and strength to say something—*anything*—that could explain why he'd let their friendship become a casualty of that fire. But the words would never come, or the ones that bubbled up would sound hollow and pathetic, so he stuffed them back down into the emotional basement, where they'd been rotting for twenty years.

And then he was miserable for weeks.

Could this time be different? *Please, God. Please.*

"Oh, who do we have here?" Evie's voice behind him punched as effectively as a fist to his solar plexus. It was still sweet and pretty and as clear as it was on those sweaty, unwelcome nights he dreamed about her. "A Husky-Malamute mix?"

Okay, maybe God wasn't going to intervene. But…Lusky? Because who could connect with Evie better than an animal?

The dog stood a little behind him, so Evie obviously didn't know Declan was there, giving him a few extra seconds to brace for impact before he turned.

But as he did, the dog rose up and slapped his paws on her chest, howling in a way that perfectly reflected how Declan felt every single time he saw her. Overwhelmed, dazed, and full of longing, love, agony, and ecstasy. If he could bellow like this dog, Declan might be able to explain away the last twenty years.

"Oh!" Evie stumbled back, holding out her hands and laughing in surprise. "That's quite a greeting, my friend."

"Sorry." Declan managed to pull the dog back, and only then did Evie lift her gaze to look at him. And there, in that split second when she realized who he was, he saw a flash of something he remembered so well in her laser-blue eyes. That beautiful, warm, affectionate look that had been wiped away by a tragedy and time.

"Declan!" She backed away again, as if the sight of him had even more of an impact than the dog's giant paws and loud cry.

"Hello, Evie." Yes, he had the unfair advantage of preparation for the moment, but nothing ever really prepared him for her.

"Declan," she said again, barely a whisper, as he could have sworn he saw a veil of protection fall over her face.

But it didn't hide the fact that she got prettier every time he saw her. Her striking pale blue eyes still made a dramatic contrast to her nearly black hair, which now fell a few inches below her shoulders, so shiny and straight he imagined it was like raw silk to the touch.

Her face had lost its youthful softness, but that accentuated her cheekbones and the hint of a cleft in her chin that had always fascinated him. Still slender, still graceful, still stupefyingly gorgeous.

"I had no idea you were in town," he said.

"I haven't been here that long." Her gaze dropped over his face and chest, then instantly returned to his eyes. "Granddaddy had a sudden craving for a raspberry croissant." The explanation came out sounding a little nervous, as if he'd asked what she was doing at the bakery. Or as if she expected him to be cool and distant because he always was.

*Not this time. Not this freaking time.*

"Oh dear," Linda May interjected. "The next batch of raspberry is still in the oven. Will Max take strawberry or chocolate chip?"

"Here." Declan held his bag out to her, the other hand still clamped on the dog. "Take mine."

"Your Linda May raspberry croissants?" She lifted her brows. "Do you know the street value for that bag?"

He laughed, the joke so...*Evie* that it relaxed some of the tension stretched across his chest. They could laugh, right? They always could laugh.

He tipped his head toward a nearby table being wiped down. "How about we wait for the croissants together?"

She considered the offer, her eyes warm with surprise. And maybe a little happiness. She glanced down at the dog as if Lusky had the answer.

He barked once, then lowered his head to gaze upward with a sweet, submissive plea in his eyes.

"He's begging so I don't have to," Declan joked. Kind of a joke. Also kind of one hundred percent true.

As she laughed at that, her shoulders dropped, and he could see the very moment she made the decision. "Then I say yes."

"Give that dog a treat," he said, grabbing one from a small bowl on the counter.

It took a few minutes to get coffee, settle into the seats, and tuck the howler under the table with his cookie. But once they did, he took two croissants from his bag and placed them on napkins, and then they looked at each other, suddenly dead silent.

Of course. And now the obvious question. *What the hell happened to you, Mahoney?*

He swallowed. "So, how's your grand—"

"I hear you're a captain—"

They spoke right over each other, then chuckled at how awkward that was.

Evie brushed some croissant flakes from her hands. "Go ahead."

"No, ladies first."

She nodded. "Just wanted to say congratulations. I heard you're a captain."

Of course she was too classy to open with a demand for an explanation he wasn't sure he could give. "Thanks. Got the promotion a while ago," he said, lifting his coffee cup.

"Next is chief?"

"God, I hope so."

She smiled at him. "Your dream job."

The fact that she remembered that touched him. But then, he remembered her dreams. "And you, Evie? A veterinary neurologist, right?"

"I am, or, I was." She leaned back with a sigh. "A few years ago I took the job as head of the Veterinary Neurology Department at NC State."

He lifted his brows. "Wow."

"It means I haven't had a scalpel in my hand for a while. At least when I was teaching, I was also practicing at the animal hospital."

Teaching. He'd heard somewhere—from Molly, probably—that she'd taken the teaching track at her alma mater. "Never imagined you'd give up the sick animals for a room full of students," he said.

"They both need me, only in different ways." She glanced down at the pastry. "I started as a guest lecturer, then took a teaching position and some additional graduate studies to get yet another degree, and then, well, the school made it tempting to take the department-head job." She lifted a shoulder, making him wonder if there wasn't more to the story. "It's not quite the high of

52

hands-on medical work, but I thought it would be a chance to finally have control over my schedule."

"That makes sense."

Okay, small talk. Easy. Comfortable. Nothing earth-shattering. He felt some air escape with relief, even a kick of happiness. Good to know that they could be transported back for a moment to one of the many conversations they'd had about career plans, more than a few right here in this bakery.

"So..." He dragged out the word, unwilling to get too serious. This qualified as the longest, most in-depth conversation they'd had in two decades, and he didn't want to ruin that. "You like faculty work?"

"Well, I do admit I miss the unique thrill of being licked by a Saint Bernard and scarred..." She lifted her hand to show a pale white line on her skin. "By a hungry hedgehog." She fluttered long fingers that could play the piano and operate on a tiny animal's brain with the same grace.

"You never could resist an animal in need."

"I still can't, but running a department is a great job, and we have one of the best neurology programs in the country. Plus, the dean is a good friend of mine, and she gave me this semester-long sabbatical without blinking an eye."

"You're here for a whole semester?" He was the one who blinked an eye. In fact, he had to fight to keep all the reaction out of his voice. *Here for months* meant...more casual contact like this.

He might as well write off the possibility of a good night's sleep until next year.

"You don't have to look like I announced I'm moving into the fire station," she teased.

"Did I? I'm surprised and..." Ridiculously pleased at this news. "Hey, there's always an extra bunk there if your grandfather is driving you crazy."

"He's not," she assured him. "The house is a little bit of a headache, but..." Her voice trailed off, and she looked down.

Because that freaking house would always crush any chance of reconnecting.

"My parents are trying to figure out what to do with it eventually," she finished.

"They don't want to keep it?" he asked, keeping his gaze direct and his voice level.

He might have his personal reasons for hating Gloriana House, but the classic Victorian was one of Bitter Bark's most impressive landmarks, attracting tourists with all those windows and gables and a three-story circular tower.

"Well, you know Dawn Hewitt, my mother the artiste and true hippie, currently living on a forty-foot sailboat somewhere in the Caribbean, where she is quite content."

"But it's your dad's family's house, so..."

"Well, my father's wind blows whatever way Mom wants it to."

"Helpful on a sailboat," he joked.

"Good one." She pointed at him and laughed lightly, and it was like someone played a song he hadn't heard in years. His laughter and hers, at a play on words. Man, it had been a long time since he'd heard that.

"But, truth is, they'd be happy to sell Gloriana House when the time comes," she said.

Which left the obvious question. "What about you? I know you always loved the place..." He didn't know how to finish that.

She took a few seconds, sipping coffee before

answering. "I have mixed feelings," she finally said. "I do connect with the long line that came before me, including that remarkable great-grandmother I'm named after. But…" She shrugged. "My life is in Raleigh."

Her life had been in Raleigh for the past twenty years, a thought that always gave him a thud of disappointment. Maybe if they'd had more chances to talk… But when he'd shut down—and he sure as hell had shut down— she'd gone back to school and rarely returned. And he'd stayed shut down long past the statute of limitations on friendships.

"Sure, sure," he said with forced casualness.

The table suddenly wobbled as the dog pushed up, finished with the chewy treat he'd been gnawing. He plopped his head on the table, eyes on Evie, because where the hell else would anyone with a beating heart want to look?

"And you, handsome Husky, are a big gorgeous goofball." She stroked the dog's head. "When did you get him?"

"He's not mine," he said. "He was left at the station, and I'm taking him to Waterford Farm to hand him over to my cousin Garrett, who'll put him up for adoption."

"Really?"

"Are you interested? I'm sure you have a dog or six, every one of them with a special need."

"You know me too well." She gave a warm smile. "I actually don't have a dog right now," she said on a sigh. "I've lost a few a little close together, as happens when you have a weakness for the unhealthy ones, but lately…" She trailed off again. "This guy is beautiful."

Declan reached over and gave Lusky's ear a rub. "Fair warning, he's a howler."

"You are? Howl you do that, doggo?"

He shook his head, laughing. "Here come the howl puns."

She leaned closer to the dog. "Howl-lelujah, he remembers my bad jokes."

"Who could forget them?"

"Because I'm howlarious, right, bud?" They both gave the dog a head rub at the same second, their fingers accidentally brushing. And that just made Declan want to snag her hand and hold it. Which would be wrong on so many levels. And also very right.

And there was the problem that paralyzed him whenever he saw Evie.

"What did you say his name is?" she asked.

"We've been calling him Lusky at the station. One of the guys googled the Husky-Malamute mix, and they called that mix an Alusky."

"Lusky? Do you like that name?" she asked the dog.

The dog put his big gold and black paw over her hand, lifting his head a little as if he wanted to tell her something. Of course, he did because…Evie. The original dog whisperer.

Lusky opened his big jaw to let out a bellow, but Evie fearlessly covered his snout. "No howling in the bakery," she warned softly. "It'll make the cookies crumble."

And, son of a gun, he shut up. "Whoa, you're good."

"Years of training. But when you do this…" She put her hand on his snout again. "Add a little pressure right under his chin with your thumb. It mimics the bite of the pack leader." She held Lusky's head steady, looking right into the dog's eyes for a long moment. "Have you taken him to the vet, Declan?"

"I've only had him seventy-two hours, per station policy, waiting for a claim on him. But Molly's going to look at him today," he said. "Why? You see something, Doc?"

"I don't know," she said. "Something in his eyes."

He leaned forward, trying to see what she saw. "Not garden-variety abandonment?"

She stroked the dog's head and studied him some more. "Is that what's buggin' you, Lusky? Missing someone you love?"

Declan sat back to watch her work her animal magic. "You always were Dr. Dolittle."

She smiled, no doubt remembering how he'd often called her that. "What can I say? Animals talk to me, and then I slice them open. Or at least I used to. I hope Molly can do a thorough exam on a Sunday."

"She can. There's a full animal hospital at my uncle's place, almost as big as their vet office in town. In fact, you'd flip if you saw Waterford Farm these days."

"I've heard your uncle transformed it into quite the canine center," she said, still stroking the dog's head and carefully watching Lusky's eyes, gleaning information like she did. "What a wonderful tribute to your aunt. She was the biggest foster failure I ever knew. That woman could not give up a dog."

He laughed, weirdly warmed by the fact that there was no need to explain a thing to Evie Hewitt. She knew his family—immediate and extended. She knew this town, from the best croissants to secret parking spaces. And she knew him, the good, the bad, and the…damaged.

"I'm surprised Molly hasn't taken you out to Waterford Farm." Because then his whole family would have made damn sure he knew Evie Hewitt was back.

"I haven't called her yet to let her know I'm in Bitter Bark," she said, finally taking her gaze off the dog to look at him again. "Usually when I'm here, it's only to check on Granddaddy, then I have to get back to Raleigh. Like I did that time I worked on Rusty."

"I remember," he said softly, tamping down the understatement of just how much he remembered.

But she caught the understatement and held his gaze, silent for a few heartbeats, while his chest got tighter and tighter.

"Here we go!" Linda May yanked them out of the moment, plopping a pink bakery box on the table. "There are a few extras for the wait."

"Thanks, Linda May," Evie said.

"Thanks for your patience, although..." She regarded one, then the other, a smile growing. "Sure is nice to see two old friends back together." She gave Evie's shoulder a pat, then stroked the dog's head. "And I hope you get things squared away with this guy."

She turned away, leaving them both suddenly preoccupied with finishing their coffee.

"Anyway, great to see you, Declan," Evie said with what seemed like a little false brightness as they stood. "I'm sure we'll run into each other again."

He nodded, but the voice inside his head was screaming one simple, clear, undeniable word. No. No. *No.*

*No, don't leave. No, don't slip away. No, don't waste this opportunity. Not again, not this time.*

Outside on the sidewalk, he put his hand on the dog's head, trying to telepathically beg for help. *C'mon, Lusky. Help me out here, bud. Talk to Dolittle for me. Buy me some time and another chance.*

But the dog took a few steps ahead, ignoring the silent plea.

"I should probably leash him," Declan said. "But that makes him—"

"Howl," Evie finished, her attention riveted on the dog's backside. A frown formed as she followed, and her head dipped, her concentration complete. "Has he always walked that way?"

"With that little hitch? Well, yeah, since he's been at the station, but I thought it was because he's overweight."

She caught up with Lusky, ushering him to the side in front of a store and out of foot traffic. "Hey, bud." Crouching down, she put her hand on his back and slid it very slowly along his spine, working up from his flank. When she reached a point right above his shoulders, he put his head back and let out a monstrous howl.

"Now that's pain." Declan came closer, his instinct to protect the dog, even though he knew what good hands the animal was in.

"Wobbler Syndrome," she said.

"What's that?"

She looked up at him. "The technical term is cervical spondylomyelopathy, a common and not inconsequential spinal problem. I've seen it frequently, and I've performed surgery for it many times, not that we'd go straight to surgery. But we should start with an X-ray to make sure. Maybe some pain management or physical therapy, depending on how far along the disease has progressed. You don't know how old he is, do you?"

"I don't know a thing about him," he said honestly, getting down next to her. "Is he in a lot of pain, Evie?"

"Likely only when he moves his neck a certain way."

She stroked his head again, holding the animal's gaze. "You've figured out how to cover it, haven't you, buddy? Because you're beautiful *and* smart."

Exactly like the veterinarian in front of him. "There's an X-ray at Waterford," Declan said, a plan clicking into place. "Will you come with me and check him out? It sounds like something we'd want a neurologist for anyway."

She opened her mouth to respond, and he was positive she would say yes. There wasn't an animal in the world she wouldn't help. It was like breathing to her.

"Molly can do the X-ray and email me the pictures. I'll be happy to give a diagnosis and recommend treatment."

"Evie…" He stood and took her hand to guide her up, knowing that one of them had to do something to break this pattern. Lusky helped, but Declan had to close the deal. "That dog needs you." *And so do I.*

She held his gaze with the same expression she'd used on the dog, her eyes full of warmth and hope and caring. A look he remembered on the darkest nights when he went down to that emotional basement and unpacked *all* the baggage.

"Okay," she whispered on a sigh. "I'll take the croissants to Granddaddy and meet you there."

"Thank you."

She got down again and let the dog give her a swift lick on the cheek. "And we'll do what we can to get you out of your misery, mister."

And maybe, just maybe, she could get Declan out of his misery, too.

# Chapter Five

As Evie neared Waterford Farm, she admitted the truth to herself. There wasn't a snowball's chance in hell that she was going to walk away from that handsome creature making such a valiant effort to hide his pain.

Either one of them.

Lusky had Wobblers, she'd bet her professional reputation on it. And Declan? He had…something. Deep inside, she could see the spark of the boy she'd spent so much of her childhood laughing with, clawing to get out of a cage of his own making. He didn't laugh quite as easily as he used to. He didn't tease her with playful observations and inside jokes. He didn't even talk as much as she remembered, not that he was ever that talkative.

Exactly like the dog, she could see that shadow of distress when he swallowed his thoughts and tried to hide them, and she could hear the ache in his voice when he tiptoed around tough subjects the way Lusky limped on his back paws.

And Evie had only one mode when it came to animals in pain—fix them all.

On a sigh, she forced herself to focus first on the one she understood. If left untreated, Wobblers could make a dog's life absolutely wretched. And, except for a professor at Vestal Valley, there wasn't a highly qualified veterinary neurologist for miles in any direction. So she might have been wary about Declan's invitation, but she couldn't actually let that dog far from her sight.

As she drove through the white gates of Waterford Farm, she let herself sink back to the moment when she'd looked up and seen Declan Mahoney at the bakery. Her first thought?

*Good God, did the man simply get better every year?*

He'd always had that smoldery, understated appeal that had made him such a cute teenager and attractive young firefighter. But maturity, experience, a few silver threads at his temples, and a body honed to perfection by his physical work had notched him up way past *attractive*. Now he was…

Declan.

She still didn't know why he'd iced her out of his life—not exactly, anyway. Maybe it was time she did. Maybe he was ready to let go of some of that pain and grief and blame and ice. Maybe he could do a little *explaining*.

Then, could she trust him not to disappear emotionally again? His pain, unlike his dog's, wasn't something she could slice away with a scalpel or mitigate with medicine.

But, of course, Evie Hewitt would try.

She followed the long, winding drive onto the property, not surprised when the tree line broke and opened up to a gorgeous vista that spread like an emerald blanket to the horizon. Waterford Farm had always been a picturesque homestead outside of town, teeming with family and more than a few dogs.

She'd been here dozens of times with Declan, for dinners and barbecues, four-wheeling with his many siblings and cousins, and she'd come to visit Molly not long after her sweet mother, Annie Kilcannon, had died suddenly.

But Waterford hadn't been anything like this even as recently as four or five years ago. No longer a "homestead" in the country, this was a professional and welcoming paradise for four- and two-legged creatures. The old handmade outdoor stalls Dr. Kilcannon had built for his wife's constantly growing pack of foster dogs had been replaced with a cream-colored clapboard kennel building that stretched around a grassy pen she assumed was used for training and exercise.

Several other outbuildings dotting the landscape included grooming facilities, the vet office, and what appeared to be a small dormitory for trainees.

Overlooking it all, the yellow farmhouse, with its sunny wraparound porch and festive green shutters, perched on a rise that afforded breathtaking views of the Blue Ridge Mountains.

The homestead where Declan's cousins grew up and now worked had aged gracefully and managed to look even better than she remembered. Kind of like...

*Declan.*

He stepped off the porch toward the driveway, most of his face covered by a ball cap and sunglasses. The warm afternoon called for a T-shirt and worn Levi's, and from this distance, she could really stare, like she'd wanted to at the bakery.

His chest was broad, his shoulders strong, and his waist narrow.

And Evie Hewitt had no place ogling her former best friend like he was featured in a firefighter calendar. Which he surely had been by now. *Mr. August.*

Because it was hard to look at him and not remember that hot summer night when they'd fallen into each other's arms and made the journey from best friends to lovers. Thinking about it kicked up her heart rate, but she tried to will herself not to go there. It would be foolish to think he'd forgotten, but it would be crazy to fantasize that it could ever happen again.

He reached her car as she pulled behind a van she could have sworn his aunt had owned when they were younger, opening her door as she turned off the ignition.

"Thought you might chicken out." A half smile pulled at his lips, drawing her gaze there and her memory back to that night she was trying not to think about.

"Chicken?" She brushed his body as she got out of the car, then poked his chest to move him out of the way. "Nah, I'm here for a dog."

He chuckled, stepping aside. "Should have seen that one coming."

"You handed it to me," she said, looking around. "Wow, they've really transformed this place."

"It's the biggest canine training and rescue facility in the state." There was no small amount of pride in his voice.

"Speaking of canines, what did Molly say about our patient?"

"She's with him now, along with my uncle. In the vet office." He gestured toward a small building to the right of the kennels, leading her there. "Come on, I'll take you."

"Let me grab my bag from the back." As she opened

the hatchback, she said, "Before I left, I poked around the NC State online library to get the very latest on Wobbler Syndrome, including a study that was recently completed by a few of our best grad students." She reached for a leather messenger bag, but he held out his hand to carry it for her. "Oh," she said as their fingers brushed. "Thanks."

"Molly and Uncle Daniel seem to agree with your diagnosis," he said. "And they also agree you're the expert."

"Which is kind of funny, since Dr. Kilcannon gave me my first vet job." As they reached the wooden porch of the standalone veterinary hospital, a sleeping setter raised his head from the corner.

"Is that Rusty?" She went straight to the old red dog, kneeling to greet him. "How's that beautiful brain of yours, big guy?"

"Better since you removed the tumor," Declan answered.

She ran her hand over the spot, remembering the surgery and the week this awesome setter had spent under her care back in Raleigh.

"Hey, baby," she said softly, a familiar feeling welling up as he looked at her with brown eyes that she could have sworn held appreciation. "Do you remember me, fella?" She bent over and kissed his silky red head. "'Cause I sure remember you."

He poked his wet snout against her cheek, making her laugh.

She stood up slowly, unable to wipe the smile from her face as she turned to Declan. "There's nothing like it," she whispered.

"Like seeing an old friend?"

"That, too." She smiled, her heart relaxing a little at

the warmth in his eyes. Maybe the Declan she'd known wasn't completely MIA, after all. "But seeing a dog you saved?" She glanced back at Rusty. "Honestly? It makes my fingers itch to do surgery again. I miss it so much."

"My uncle said your work on Rusty was…masterful, I believe was the word he used."

She tipped her head at the compliment, but just then the door popped open, and Molly stepped out, her mahogany curls bouncing, her hazel eyes bright, her arms wide open.

"There's my favorite TA!"

Evie hugged the other woman, adding a squeeze of affection. "And my favorite student, Dr. Kilcannon."

"It's Bancroft now. The *real* Dr. Kilcannon is back with Lusky." She slipped an arm around Evie and led her into a cozy little reception area with a fish tank and a wall full of photos of Irish setters much like the one snoozing on the porch. "Only you could diagnose something as complex as Wobblers while standing on the street."

Evie glanced over her shoulder to see Declan right behind them. "Lusky was letting you know," she said. "I'm sure you would have figured out that something was wrong when you checked him out today."

"We're in here." Molly guided her into an exam room, where Dr. K stood over the dog lying on the table, holding a tablet with an X-ray image on the screen.

"Evie Hewitt." The tall, handsome country vet reached out both arms for a hug. "The woman who saved my Rusty."

She returned his embrace. "I just saw him. He's still glorious."

"He's got a lady love named Goldie and a new reason for living."

"I heard you have one named Katie." She beamed up at him. "Congratulations."

"She's definitely a reason for living." Laughter deepened the crinkles around his blue eyes, which were exactly the color of his mother's, little Gramma Finnie. "And you met Katie when you did Rusty's surgery. I hope you'll stay and see her again."

She had an excuse—Granddaddy—all ready to go. She could handle running into a random Mahoney or Kilcannon, who were always gracious. But the last time she'd seen Colleen Mahoney was at her husband's funeral, one of the saddest days of Evie's life. She wasn't quite prepared to see Declan's mother today.

"Well, let's start with our patient," she said, shifting her attention to the exam table, where Declan stood with two strong hands cradling the big dog's head.

Declan leaned over to whisper in one pointy ear, "Brought in the big guns, bud."

"He's doing better now," Dr. K said. "I gave him a little feel-good shot. Especially after I saw these." He handed her the tablet. "You can swipe to see them all."

"Yeah, whoa." She slid her finger over the screen to get to the lateral shot of his spine. "Severe compression. Jeez. He's likely had this for a while."

"Can you tell this layman exactly what his problem is?" Declan asked.

"Of course." Evie shared the image with him. "See those two vertebrae kind of crushed together? This disease is essentially compression on the spinal cord, which can, in certain positions, cause excruciating nerve pain."

He made a face and glanced at the dog. "Damn. We thought that howling was just a breed thing. I'm sorry, big guy." He looked back to the X-rays. "What causes it?"

"We don't know," Evie answered honestly. "Wobbler Syndrome has been misunderstood for so long, I think it has at least fourteen different veterinary terms. Usually, it's cervical spondylomyelopathy, which translates to... neck vertebrae smooshing the spinal cord."

Evie gave the dog a look of sympathy, but everything she'd seen now fit together in her brain and compelled her to place a soothing hand on his furry head. "Lifting his head too high can be agonizing," she explained. "And he's adopted a clumsy gait to accommodate that. Isn't that right, baby? You're trying to fix yourself."

"Oh, no wonder he whines and trips over himself." Declan turned back to the dog. "And one of those knuckleheads at the station called you an oaf. I'm sorry, bud." After a sigh, he asked, "So what do we do for this boy?"

She liked that Declan took ownership of a very sick dog he'd known for only seventy-two hours, especially when she suspected the cost and trouble associated with the treatment were why Lusky had been abandoned in the first place.

"Normally, I'd start with a program of pain relief and physical therapy, but that should have been done a long time ago. We can certainly dull any pain, but it won't solve the underlying problem."

"Surgery?"

"He'll likely need it," she said. "But I'd love to take him over to Vestal Valley and do an MRI, which will tell us so much more."

"Whatever you suggest," Declan said. "Is he suffering?"

"Not as long as he stays on a low-dose pain med," Dr. K said. "And, like Evie said, he knows how to manage his pain by not moving in certain ways."

"His activity has to be restricted, though," Evie added. "Only short walks. A collar's fine, but no leash, and we should limit his movement. He should be with someone as much as possible." She looked into Lusky's eyes, feeling the connection as their gazes met. "He's a people guy, I can tell."

"He is that," Declan said. "He whines the minute I leave a room, then gets up to follow, and that makes him howl, but now I know why. How can you know that already?"

She gave a shrug. "Gut instinct, I guess."

Dr. K put a hand on her shoulder. "Evie has always been the most tender and empathetic surgeon I know."

"Oh, thank you," she said.

"Agreed," Molly chimed in. "Every animal is like your own child."

She smiled at the compliments, turning back to the dog to get the attention off of her. "They are babies," she said. "You just need some love and attention, right? Maybe peanut butter and bacon, too."

His eyes flickered at the word *bacon*, making them all laugh. "Well, he knows what bacon is," she joked.

"Which we have plenty of at Waterford," Molly said. "And vet techs who can work overnight, too."

Evie nodded, trying to ignore the ache building in her chest as she looked into the dog's eyes. "Will he be crated?" she asked.

"I'm afraid if he's in one of our bigger kennels, he'd have a little too much freedom of movement," Dr. K said. "So we'll keep him in our holding and healing room, which actually has another patient right now, so he won't be completely alone."

"Oh, okay," she said, imagining his sad face as he rested in a cage.

Declan angled his head, looking at her. "You don't like that idea."

She laughed softly. "Am I that transparent?"

"To me."

Her heart nearly flipped in her chest. "I know you have an amazing staff here, and he'll be in such good hands," she said quickly. "We should do the MRI first thing tomorrow, if we can get into Vestal Valley."

"I have some pull there," Dr. K said, taking out his phone. "Let me make a call."

"Let me go see if I can grab our weekend vet tech you can talk to," Molly added, stepping out after her father.

"Thanks." Evie bit her lip, barely aware that she'd tunneled her fingers into Lusky's thick fur. "You'll be in good hands, love," she whispered.

"But you'd like him in your hands."

At Declan's words, and the sweet, soft way they were spoken, she looked up at him. "I do have a lot of room, and…would you mind?"

He laughed. "I don't think there's any stopping you at this point. Dog in need," he said to Lusky, "meet your new best friend. And roommate."

"Really?" She felt her whole face brighten. "You wouldn't mind if I kind of kidnapped him while we get him better?"

"On one condition," he said, his eyes glinting with a hint of that tease she'd missed.

She lifted a brow and tried to ignore the quiver that ran through her at the possibility that his condition might be…an evening together. "Anything." Because her answer would be *yes*.

As he was about to reply, Molly and Dr. K walked in.

"We're good to go at Vestal Valley," Dr. K said.

"Vet tech can stay all night," Molly added.

"Actually, Lusky's going home with Evie," Declan said. "That is, if I can also get her to perform his surgery."

*That* was his condition? So, not a date. *Chill, Evie, chill.*

"Me?" She hadn't picked up a scalpel in nearly a year. She was emotionally invested in Lusky's owner, whether she wanted to admit it or not. And she was far from the elite surroundings of NC State's facilities.

"I think it's a great idea," Molly said.

"There isn't a surgeon in the state with your skills," Dr. K agreed.

"You're all very kind," she said. "Let's look at the MRI and make a game-time decision."

"I'll take that," Declan said. "And of course he'll stay with you for as long as you like."

Molly slid her arm around Evie's. "If we get him comfortable for a few hours, can you join the family for Sunday dinner?"

"Oh, I'd love to, but I have another patient at home. And if you think ol' Lusky here can make some noise, then you can't imagine a ninety-two-year old World War II vet who wants his 'linner'—late lunch, early dinner—at exactly the same time every day. But I'll take a rain check, I promise." She gave the dog another gentle stroke. "I'd like to get Lusky home and situated as soon as possible."

"Absolutely," Dr. K. said. "Dec, can you help Evie get this boy to her house?"

Instantly, Evie's hand froze. She didn't look up, but she could feel the tension that suddenly stretched through the room.

Declan Mahoney hadn't stepped foot in Gloriana

House since before the fire that killed his father. And she would never ask him to—

"Of course," he said. "We'll take whatever supplies we need from here, meds, and a dog bed. I can bring him over in my truck. Right now, Evie?"

"I think that would be best for the dog."

As he nodded slowly, Evie could have sworn she saw one brick of his protective wall tumble to the ground. Now if she and this wobbly dog could manage not to trip over it, things would be looking up for both of them.

# Chapter Six

The great contradiction about Gloriana House was that it represented the best and the worst of Declan's life. For the first twenty years, the stately Victorian that sat at the top of the hilly residential section known as Ambrose Acres was the home of one of his favorite people on earth. Knocking on the big leaded-glass front door had meant he was moments away from Evie Hewitt and her laughter and beauty and warmth.

For the second twenty years of his life, the monster loomed, bearing down on the town, its very existence a reminder that Joe Mahoney had once roamed these streets, saving lives and doling out advice to family and strangers.

So, now, at forty-one, Declan was entering the *third* twenty years of his life, and maybe it was time that Gloriana House represented something else. Something bright and positive and constant.

Jeez, it had been a long time since he'd felt bright and positive. But that was the magic of Evie. Ever since he'd heard her voice at the bakery, something deep inside him had shifted a little.

Maybe that was his dreaded basement door opening up. Or…closing.

"What do you think, bud?" he said to the sleeping dog. "How about we change things up in our boring lives, huh?"

The dog's eyes stayed tightly closed. He was sound asleep, thanks to whatever Uncle Daniel had given him, and maybe his dog's sense that a sweet, nurturing, wonderful woman was making room in her heart for him.

"Lucky dog," Dec murmured. Could she ever make room for...a man? This man? This very man who'd once felt the earth move with love for that girl?

Because she *had* been a girl. And he'd been a boy. And life hadn't really happened yet.

It had been a long time since Declan had allowed himself to think about that night in the mountains. Forced every year to celebrate and mourn on the very same day, he'd never allowed himself the luxury of thinking about the *other* milestone of life that occurred on August 28.

The date had rolled around a little over a month ago, less difficult but no less meaningful for Declan and his whole family. Not once on that day had he thought of it as the one and only time he and Evie had sex.

But he couldn't help remembering when he saw her...and wishing it had all turned out so damn different. If they hadn't gone camping that night, if Dad hadn't taken his shift, if life had dealt them different cards, what would have happened?

He wouldn't have been killed in the fire because he'd have never been sent in first, not back then, less than a year out of probation. So...would he and Evie be married? Would Dad be retiring and helping Declan prepare to take his place as chief? Would she have moved back and started a practice here? Would they have...*kids*?

God, she'd have been a spectacular mom. And he'd have been…content.

Coming around the last corner, he looked up to the hill, forcing himself to stare at Gloriana House, trying to look at it objectively.

Painted in shades of deep yellow and creamy white, all trimmed with dark brown accents, the three-story manor stood like a monument to an era gone by. Its classic mansard roof draped over the top floor like icing on a cake, and graceful Palladian-arched windows offered maximum light and balance. Wrought-iron railings wrapped around the first and second floors, each supported by stately white columns. A single octagonal-shaped tower rose up from one corner, topped by a pointed turret. The locals liked to say that tower was built by Thad Jr. to be the closest thing to heaven in all of Bitter Bark.

Reaching out on the other side—a second-story veranda that covered a large patio underneath.

That would be the closest thing to hell.

*New perspective, Dec. New perspective.*

After all, it wasn't the same overhang that had collapsed and killed his father after rags soaked in linseed oil had combusted into a blaze on the patio underneath it. Penelope Hewitt, Evie's grandmother, had rebuilt the whole wing in keeping with the historical architecture. No doubt there was still a first-floor sunroom, once Evie's mother's painting studio, adjacent to that patio, and a bedroom above it that opened up to an upstairs veranda. But the physical structure was not the same, and Declan had to remember that.

"Plus, you'll be there," he said to the dog as he turned in to the drive. "And maybe you can keep talking to Evie for me, since I apparently suck at it."

He spotted Evie's compact SUV in the driveway. She stood next to it, looking at her phone, waiting for him, bathed in light and surrounded by that glow that always drew him closer.

No, it wasn't that he couldn't talk around her. He simply couldn't find the words that she so deserved to hear. He didn't even know what they were.

She looked up and waved, a breeze fluttering her dark hair.

How about... *You're beautiful and I loved you.*

Loved.

"Past tense, right? With a D. Right, pooch?"

Pooch didn't answer.

Declan stared at Evie, feeling an ancient and familiar kick in his gut and that ache he remembered waking up with one morning in the mountains. He'd known for sure at that moment that they were meant to be. Then...life and pain and family changed everything. Well, it changed *him*.

And he didn't have the first clue how to explain that to her, but if they were going to spend time together, he'd damn well better figure it out.

Shaking off the thought, he took a deep breath, parked, and climbed out, opening the back cab as Evie approached. "The pupper is crashed."

"Happy juice," she said, reaching in to pet him. "Any chance you could carry him?"

"Of course."

"I called Granddaddy and told him what's happening, and he insisted on dressing and coming downstairs to greet you. You'd think I was bringing home a prince."

He gestured to the dog. "You sort of are."

"Pretty sure he didn't mean the dog. Come on. I'll open the door for you and then grab the bed," she said.

"Then we'll get the rest of his stuff."

"Sounds like a plan." He leaned over to reach for Lusky, but Evie put her hand on Declan's arm, stopping him.

"Dec."

He looked over his shoulder. "Yeah?"

"I know this isn't easy."

For a moment, he didn't speak, but got a little more lost in her eyes. Were they always *that* hauntingly silvery-gray-blue with a hint of sapphire around the iris?

"And I appreciate it," she added, yanking him from his way-too-close examination of her eyes.

"You're the one doing me a favor, E," he said quickly.

Those eyes shuttered when he used the nickname he bet—he hoped—no one but him ever called her.

"What I appreciate," she said, "is you…talking. Giving me a chance. Coming up here. And…" She added some pressure on his arm. "Just you," she finished on a whisper.

How did she do that? How did she say those things so *easily*?

"S'okay." He gave her a tight smile and turned back to the dog, not trusting his voice or his ability to ever have the right words.

Once, years ago, he'd have had those words. He'd have teased her or punctuated the conversation with a tap on the tip of her nose. He might have even leaned down and kissed her once they'd broken that barrier.

But that guy disappeared a long time ago. Now, he barely managed a lame *s'okay*.

"Got him," he said, turning with his hairy bundle. She walked with him, snagging a giant dog bed from the back of her SUV and leading the way up the three steps to the front door.

It opened before she could even fish out a key.

"Well, well, well, if it isn't the good Captain Mahoney himself." Max Hewitt stood in the doorway, wearing crisp cotton pajama pants, a loose T-shirt, and a Navy baseball cap at a jaunty angle over his feathery gray hair.

Once a staple around Bitter Bark—usually when he was being feted for his generous donations, including a hefty annual sum to first responders—Max Hewitt had spent the better part of the past ten years since his wife died inside this house. That was obvious from his complexion, which was pale but for a few oddly shaped splotches the EMT in Declan recognized as purpura.

His shoulders were narrow to the point of bony, and he had a sunken chest and probably pronounced ribs. Still, he gave a big denture-heavy smile, and Declan half expected him to salute.

"Special delivery, Mr. Hewitt." Declan hoisted the dog an inch higher. "We're bringing a guest."

"I couldn't be happier," he said, stepping back into the oversize entry to allow them in.

"Let's put him here for the moment," Evie said, laying the bed to the side of the stairs. "When he wakes up and feels ready to move, I'll take him out and then let him get the lay of the land."

Declan eased the big guy onto the bed, making sure he was fully cushioned and comfortable before standing up to properly greet the older man, who instantly stretched out his arms.

"You give me a hug, Declan Mahoney."

Declan reached down to embrace a man he remembered as five-ten or so, but who'd shrunk to more like Evie's five-six.

"So great to see you, Mr. Hewitt."

"Please, son. It's Max for you."

Evie stepped a little closer, putting a gentle arm on her grandfather's shoulder. "You shouldn't navigate those stairs alone, Granddaddy."

He grunted and shot her a look. "I've been up and down those steps ten million times in my life, young lady. There are nineteen of them, the sixth one from the bottom creaks, and the second one from the top has a nickel under the carpet that I put there when I was nine." He added a toothy grin. "I didn't want to greet this important guest from my bed."

Declan smiled at him, admiring the effort that this old man had taken. "Thank you, Max. And I'm sure if he were awake, this boy, who we're calling Lusky, would thank you."

"Lusky? Not in this house."

"Oh, Granddaddy, you're not going to insist on the Thad tradition of dog names, are you?"

Declan frowned. "Did you have a dog named Thad? I remember…" He dug into his memory, coming up with a border collie Evie had adored. "Oh, yeah. Taddy."

"And Jude, Faddei, and yes, Taddy," Max said. "All of them forms of Thaddeus, which is the only name a dog who lives in this house will ever have. It was the original owner's personal rule."

Evie rolled her eyes. "Well, this dog isn't going to live here, and he doesn't look like a Thad."

Max took a few steps closer and looked down at the dog, who lifted his head a bit and sniffed. He blinked and slowly started to push up.

"Easy." Declan stepped closer, not wanting the dog to hurt himself or greet Max with paws to the chest.

"I think he's a little too hammered to jump," Evie said.

But he did manage to get up on all fours and give a quick shake. Max came a little closer, and Declan put his hand down, ready to snag him if he jumped.

"Hello, handsome," Max said. "That's quite a face you have. And a tail. And a body."

In response, the dog whipped his fluffy tail, making them all laugh.

"He needs a name as striking as he is," Max said. He put his hands on his slender hips and leaned forward, holding the dog's gaze. "You shall be Judah. That's the Hebrew form of Thaddeus, if I'm not mistaken. My grandmother Amelia had a big black dog named Judah when I was a little boy, and I loved him."

"Judah." Declan nodded. "It suits him."

"Judah it is," Evie said, giving her grandfather a gentle hug. "Now can I take you back upstairs and bring you some food?"

"Declan can walk me up," he said. "I'd like a private word with him, if you don't mind."

She looked a little surprised at the request, but Declan crooked his arm toward Max.

"It would be my pleasure, sir."

They turned to the stairs and paused at the bottom of the mountain of red. As long as he could remember, the carpet on these steps had been ruby red. Kind of garish, but it suited the house.

"Slow and easy, son," Max said. "Nineteen steps."

"With a squeak and a nickel."

He smiled as they made their way up, taking their time, but not talking until they reached the top. When they did, Declan turned and looked down at Evie, who was sitting on the floor, petting Lus—*Judah*—who'd gotten back onto the bed.

She leaned back and looked up at Declan, her eyes bright even from the floor-to-ceiling distance. "You okay?" she mouthed.

Maybe she meant with the job of trudging Max up the stairs, or maybe she was wondering about all the emotions of being in the house. Didn't matter. She just…got him. And that made him way more than okay.

He nodded and added a wink, then lost sight of her as they headed down the hall.

"I am not going to lie," Max said as they got closer to the bedroom. "I was dumbstruck when Evie called to say you were coming here."

Declan was quiet for a moment, not sure how he was supposed to respond to that.

"But then, Finola told me. She said it could happen."

He slowed his step as they reached the doorway. "Finola? My grandmother?"

"Yes, she was here yesterday."

Gramma Finnie had been here? While Declan processed that, Max released his grip on Declan's arm and crossed the room to a massive four-poster, taking off his slippers and easing his body onto the bed.

"She's a fine-looking woman, that Finnie Kilcannon."

Declan gave a quick laugh. "She's…something." Including a little *deceptive*. He'd handed her a bag of croissants a few hours ago and told her that Evie was coming to see the dog. She'd never said a word about being here yesterday.

Of course she'd understand all the emotions of this house, but it was unlike his grandmother not to at least offer up her best Irish saying to fit the situation. Instead, she'd shared a few secret looks with her partner-in-crime, Yiayia.

What the hell was she up to? Sending him to the bakery and…

"So, let me guess," Declan said as it all started to make sense. "You and my grandmother both had a sudden need for raspberry croissants at exactly the same time this morning."

He lifted his gray brows and took his time getting situated in the bed. "And what if we did?"

Declan smiled, helping him pull up the covers as he fell back on a few propped-up pillows. "Then I'd say you were both very…optimistic."

"What else is there when you're staring down the barrel of one hundred years old?"

*There's minding your own business.* But he didn't have the heart to say that. "Well, I'm not exactly sure what you think will come of this, but—"

"A baby."

Declan jerked back. "Excuse me?"

"A baby could come of this."

"A…" He couldn't even say the word.

"Oh, I know Finnie wants hearts, flowers, and a big ol' wedding, and that's fine…or not. But there is one thing my granddaughter needs, and only one thing to make her—and me, if I have to be honest—happy."

*A baby?* Declan stared at the old man.

"Good idea, huh?" Max gave a grin, obviously misinterpreting Declan's stunned response. "You could do that, right?"

He didn't even take the time to let that idea settle, instead deciding to explain something to the old man. "I know this might seem like science-fiction to you, sir, but the world is different today. If Evie wants a child, then she is quite capable of doing that by herself.

With medical assistance, obviously." Or she could adopt.

Max barked out a laugh. "It doesn't seem like science-fiction, son. It seems like balderdash. Why would she go to some clinic and have a stranger's kid with no guarantee that she's swimming in a good gene pool? You're a known quantity. Good family. Nice bones. Decent brain. Fine heart." He tapered his eyes to slits. "And I don't imagine it would *kill* anyone to try."

"Oh, Max." He shook his head, if for no other reason than to clear it. "That's not something you...offer up like...a piece of candy."

He made a face, pulling up the blankets and comforter. "Then let her be the last of one of the greatest family lines that ever lived," he murmured.

Seriously? "She doesn't have to be if—"

"She's *forty*," he said gruffly. "I don't know if she ever went to some fancy doctor to store up for a rainy day. Probably thought her whole damn life she'd marry..." He shot an accusatory gaze at Declan. "*Someone*."

The word pressed on his chest, but Declan stood stone-still, because the old guy probably wasn't *wrong* about that.

Max gave the comforter a good pat. "I'm all set now, son. Thank you for your time."

Declan took one step back, still processing. This was more than your run-of-the-mill, granny-induced romance intervention. Everyone in his family knew the two matriarchs fancied themselves as matchmakers, but this? This was way bigger than an arranged date.

"Yes?" Max asked when Declan didn't leave. "You have more to say on the subject?"

So much more. "Max, I could never...do that and not want to be part of...everything."

"That's what Finnie said. 'He's an honorable lad,'" he

mimicked. "Fine. Be honorable, then. That beautiful woman downstairs was born to be a mother."

He honestly couldn't argue with that. Evie was a natural nurturer, but she'd funneled all that into animals. Was he wrong in thinking that was enough?

"And Finnie said you've done nothing but *act* like a father for half your life." He lifted his straggly brows. "Maybe it's time you *be* one for a change."

Did he really think that was something two people could just *do*? Didn't he realize the monumental responsibility involved?

"So." Max dragged the single syllable out. "Time's a-wastin', young Mahoney. And I'm gonna kick the bucket any day." He closed his eyes. "Tell Evie I'm not hungry. And maybe bring Judah up. I think he'll be good company. Thank you, Declan."

This time, he couldn't deny the dismissal as Max closed his eyes. But had his silence meant agreement to this old man? Because he sure as hell wasn't...

A *baby*?

That would be insane. Impossible. Life-changing and rule-breaking and not the way things were done. Not to mention the fact that Evie really didn't need him in the scheme of things. And he sure as hell didn't need...

Hell. He didn't know *what* he needed. In the space of a few hours, his whole life had tilted sideways.

Max started snoring, so Declan walked out, so dazed he practically walked into Evie carrying a tray.

"He went to sleep," he told her.

"Of course he did. Well, I'll put this by his bed, and then we can finish getting Judah set up."

"He asked that we bring Judah up here." Among other strange requests.

"Really? Huh." She nodded as she went into the room and quietly set the tray on a table near the bed. While Declan stood in the doorway, she smoothed Max's comforter and tucked it around him, suddenly looking very...*maternal*.

Good God, was it really Declan's fault she didn't have her own family?

"Judah here with you? You're full of good ideas, Granddaddy," she whispered, leaning over to kiss him on the forehead.

He was full of ideas, that was for sure. Good, crazy, laughable, and *balderdash*, whatever the hell that was.

She stood, took a minute to adjust the shutters to darken the room, then joined Declan at the door.

"Don't even think about it," she said with a raised, teasing brow.

That was the terrifying thing. He was. Might not think about anything else. "Think about..."

"Leaving without telling me what he wanted to talk to you about." She tugged on his T-shirt sleeve, pulling him into the hall. "I won't rest until I know."

She wouldn't rest if she did.

It was the house. It had to be. What else could have made Declan change from the easygoing, warm, *present* man he'd been all day, to the one who suddenly seemed...*distant*?

"I guess bringing him here was a mistake," Evie said when the last of the supplies were unloaded.

"Because he needs bags of food the size of a football field?" He lowered the sack of dry food to the laundry room floor. "I doubt he'll eat it, anyway."

"I can make him plain chicken," she said. "No dog turns down chicken, and he needs to eat. And that's another reason I didn't want him crying in a crate. He'll eat once he gets comfortable here."

"You think he can?"

"Eventually." She eyed him as she leaned against the washing machine, trying to decide if honesty would make him disappear for twenty years again. Because even when he got quiet and cool, she didn't want Declan far away. "But I didn't mean him being here was a mistake. I meant you."

His broad shoulders rose and fell with a sigh. "I'm fine," he said.

Really? Because he'd changed so dramatically in the last half hour. "I guess this can't be easy for you."

"No, no, it's not that."

"Then what is it?"

He leaned over to pick up some kibble that had fallen from the top of the bag, suddenly preoccupied with cleaning up the laundry room. "Just trying to…" He blew out a breath. "Anyway, I better get back to Waterford, or I'll miss dinner completely," he said.

"You can have dinner here."

He looked at her, a storm she didn't understand brewing behind his eyes. "That's okay. You have enough to worry about."

"You can't leave until you tell me why Granddaddy wanted privacy," she said playfully, trying to lighten the mood. "He goes on these crazy kicks about things he wants to give people in his will. It won't upset me if he mentioned dying, because he says that all the time. Did he offer you his prized fishing rod or something?"

"Something," he said vaguely, looking at his watch.

"Okay, then." She pushed off the washer, the sting of his rebuff zinging up her spine as she turned to walk out. "I guess we're back to chilly exchanges and brick walls for us. Fun while it lasted, though." As she started out the door, his fingers clamped on her arm, stopping her.

"Evie."

She turned, meeting his gaze, which was…tortured. Why? The house? Granddaddy? Her? What could make him look so utterly torn? "What is it?"

"My grandmother was here."

The non sequitur—or what seemed like one—threw her. "I know. I let her in, along with her friend Yiayia."

"Do you know why?"

"Um, actually, I do. The Greek lady spilled the beans, and I understand there's some underhanded matchmaking going on."

"To say the least."

"And that's what's bothering you?" For some reason, her heart hitched. Was the very idea of them together the thing that put such torment in his eyes?

"Your grandfather and my grandmother both had a sudden craving for croissants at precisely the same time," he said.

She gave a soft laugh. "They enlisted his help? I don't know, Declan, it's kind of sweet."

"Sweet? Evie, there's more—"

She put her hand to his lips, the warm shock to her fingertips a small price to pay to end his obvious misery. She *got* it. He *hated* the idea.

"Well, don't worry about that," she said with false brightness. "It's nothing but octogenarian foolishness. I'm not interested."

"You're not?"

"Of course not, Declan."

His gaze moved over her face with a questioning look. "You're...not?"

"You need it in writing?" she asked, but as soon as the words came out, she regretted them. Did he remember—

"Don't be ridiculous," he said. "I thought you should know what they're up to."

"I knew."

"And never mentioned it to me?"

She bit back a soft laugh. "We just ran into each other this morning, and we've been a little busy with Judah. But jeez, Dec, you don't have to act like the idea is...toxic."

"It's kind of huge, don't you think?"

She stood still for a moment, torn about how best to respond. Was the idea of them together again so freaking awful that he had to look *pained* by the idea?

Well, she had to remember the history. It would always be there, like a cloud hanging over them, stealing sunshine.

"I better go check on Judah." She slipped out of the laundry room before he could stop her again, trying to will her heart to settle.

Which had no place being *un*settled. She hadn't seriously entertained any thoughts of rekindling anything with Declan, had she? Sure, she ogled his muscles and enjoyed his company and spent an extra minute or two studying his sexy lips and thinking about a friendship from long ago.

But did he have to flip out at the idea that people who loved them both wanted them to be happy? Did he have to...*shut down?* Of course he did. That, apparently, was Declan's MO.

"Hey, baby." She folded onto the floor next to Judah,

grateful he was still resting, even though his eyes were open. "Those meds making you feel better? I'll give you more when they wear off. No need for you to freak out about being in a strange place when you get sober."

"Do you want me to carry him upstairs to your grandfather's room?" Declan asked as he followed her into the entry hall a minute later.

"If he goes up there, I have to be sure he can navigate the steps," she said, pushing up. "Let's see how you handle adversity, Judah." She couldn't help sending a little glance at Declan to underscore her point.

If he picked it up, he wasn't reacting. Instead, he stared up the stairs. "Long way up there for a dog with a compressed spine," he said.

She put her hand on Judah's head and guided him toward the stairs. "You decide, Judah. Can you do stairs, big boy?"

He made his way to the bottom, looking up as if he understood exactly what she'd said. Then he lifted one paw, looked at her, then dropped his head and began to climb. After a few steps, she turned him around to be sure he could get back down, which he did quite well.

"He really does speak English," Declan said.

"And he's doing great." She led him back up, letting him stop to sniff at the top. "Probably smells all the Thads of the past," Evie said, a few steps behind him. "It's good to have a dog in this house, don't you think?"

"He won't be too far from you?" Declan asked, carrying the bed as he joined her.

"Actually, this is ideal," she said. "Not only can they keep each other company, but there's a small camera in the room linked to my phone." She pointed at him. "Do *not* tell Granddaddy."

"You spy on him?"

"I make sure he's breathing in the middle of the night," she said, ushering the dog down the hall.

"Did you listen before? When I was in there?" He actually sounded *worried*.

"No, I didn't." She headed into the room. Granddaddy was still sound asleep, wiped out from his trip down and up the grand stairs, but they set up Judah not far from the bed and closed the door.

When they were on the way downstairs, Evie resisted the urge to ask Declan to stay again. There was only so much rejection a woman could take in one day.

"I don't know how to thank you for all this," he said, a few steps behind her on the stairs.

"Please, I've missed hands-on vet work." She turned at the bottom, watching him come down. "And if you wanted to help me get him to Vestal Valley for the MRI tomorrow, I would appreciate that."

He stopped on the final step, his large hand landing on the newel, which of course rocked at the touch.

"Whoa." He pulled back. "Did I break that?"

"No, it was already loose. Like so many things in this house, it needs work. I found crown molding buckling in my bedroom upstairs, and half the windows don't open and close easily. You heard Granddaddy—that heinous red rug you're standing on is as old as he is, and the whole house is as wobbly as that dog."

"I could help you."

She blinked at him. "Excuse me?"

"I'm pretty handy," he said. "I've done a ton of work at my grandmother's Victorian. It's nothing like this, obviously, but I helped repair the basement stairs that damn near killed my sister-in-law. And I did work on some crown molding there, too. I could fix all the windows easily. I've been doing stuff like that for years, thanks to my strange work schedule."

"Would you want to do that?" Since he was acting so damn *weird*.

He angled his head. "I just said I didn't know how to thank you for the help with Judah, so yeah, I'd like to."

"But…you'd be here. In this house. With me."

He laughed softly. "You make that sound like hell."

"Well, isn't it?"

His smile disappeared. "Evie. Come on. We've got a huge bridge to cross, both of us. I would very much…" He swallowed, clearly struggling with the words. "I'd like to be friends again, despite what plots the oldsters are cooking up."

She stared up at him, letting the statement wash over her. Friends. He was offering an olive branch, and she should take it. Maybe not the offer of her dreams, but with twenty years and a million miles between them, it was better than nothing.

"I'd like that, too," she said.

"Friends?" He reached out his hand, holding it palm up.

She hesitated a second or two, then put her hand in his. "Friends."

They clasped each other's hand, and he came down the last stair, and she took a step closer, and without another word, he guided her against his chest, folding his arms around her.

As soon as she felt his heart beating against hers, she knew that, deep down, she wanted more, but probably wasn't ever going to get it.

# Chapter Seven

On his way to pick up Judah and Evie for their appointment at the college, Declan made a stop in town at Bone Appetit, the dog treat and accessory store his sister owned and ran with their mother. Judah would probably love something from Ella's array of organic dog treats, and Declan could use...someone to talk to.

His brothers were his usual go-to for advice, but Connor and Braden weren't exactly neutral on the subject of relationships anymore. They were both up to their eyeballs in love, and that colored everything from their perspectives. He needed to talk to someone who'd agree that the idea Max Hewitt had planted was dumber than dirt.

Not that Ella was an actual foundation of stability, but she was the only one of his siblings and cousins not yet married or involved. She was thirty-two now, ran a successful business, and her wanderlust appeared to have toned down over the years. He couldn't remember the last time his kid sister had the sudden urge to backpack through Patagonia or go mushing in Alaska. Plus, he loved the hell out of her sassy self.

After the sleepless night he'd had, he could use the company. And coffee, and Ella always had that fancy by-the-cup stuff at the store.

When he pushed open the glass door to Bone Appetit, he heard the bell, a dog bark, and then the musical sound of his sister's laughter as she finished up with a customer.

"Declan!" Her whole face brightened when she saw him. She came around the glass case that displayed her latest pet toys and trinkets to give him a hug. "Hello, my favorite brother!"

He nodded to the customer and a shaggy sheepdog who stepped out before he stepped in. "You say that to all the Mahoneys, Smella."

She rolled her eyes, having lived with enormous grace under the unfortunate nickname that one of her three brothers—they all tried to take credit—had hung on their baby sister when she was still in diapers.

"But this time it's true." He accepted her embrace with one of his own, unable to resist giving her short, spiky hair a rub, tousling it even more.

"You are in so much family trouble," she announced. "Why did you run off with Evie yesterday and deny us all a chance to see her?"

"We didn't run off. We took the dog back to her house, and by the time we finished getting him settled, I…" *Needed to be alone.* "I had dinner at home."

"Boring." She wrinkled her nose, which somehow only made her pixielike features even prettier. "Grannies were crushed, you know."

"Don't even get me started on those two."

She giggled and gave him a playful jab in the shoulder. "You're next, so accept your fate. Thank you so much for taking the heat off me."

"Next for what? That's the question."

"Love!" She swooped around him, returning to her perch behind the counter. On the stool, she rested her chin on her knuckles and blinked her enormous brown eyes as if *that* could distract him from the four-letter word she'd just exclaimed. "They are positively high on their success with John and Summer."

He threw his hands in the air. "Would you stop? You act like they created some kind of arranged marriage. No force of nature could have stopped that relationship, and if anyone deserves credit, it's Summer's little girl when she claimed John's puppy as her own. Can I have some coffee?"

She pointed to the station at the front of the store that had cups for customers and free kibble for their dogs. "Say what you will about the Dogmothers."

"Starting with how inane that name is."

"They sent Sadie off to run against Connor for mayor—"

"They sent her to manage his campaign, but then she ran against him." He poured a full cup of black coffee, inhaling the aroma as he looked out the front window onto one of the main streets of Bitter Bark, already bustling with tourists and locals and, of course, dogs.

"And Yiayia claimed to leave her bag at Overlook Glen so Alex would go back and connect with Grace," Ella continued.

"Pretty sure they tried to line up John for Grace, which would have been a disaster."

"And Cassie and—"

"Stop." He turned to face her. "Whose side are you on, anyway?"

Her big eyes got even bigger. "There are no sides, Dec.

94

We all want you to be happy. And Evie..." She sighed. "I remember when I was a little girl how she was always hanging around you, and she was so sweet. And funny. Quick with the lame one-liners, if I recall correctly."

"You do."

"And you were always so nice back then, so much more fun."

He was?

"And it was cool to have another girl around in that family full of testosterone."

"You always had Darcy," he said, referring to her cousin who was eternally attached to Ella. In fact, he could see through the door that adjoined this business to Darcy's grooming shop next door, proving they were still attached.

"True, but there was something special about Evie. We all thought you'd marry her."

He tried not to respond to the matter-of-fact statement and was saved when the only other customer in the store brought a pack of pawprint-covered dish towels and matching food bowls to the counter.

While Ella ran the charge and made small talk, Declan walked away, sipping his coffee and staring at a wall of dog treats, Ella's last words echoing in his head.

He thought he'd marry her, too.

When the customer left, he snagged a bag of peanut butter cookies and set it on the counter.

"For Lusky?" Ella asked.

"Evie's grandfather renamed him. He's Judah now."

"Judah?" She gave an approving nod. "Excellent name for that spectacular dog. Of course, we didn't get to see more of him since you ran away yesterday, but Molly said you're taking him in for an MRI at Vestal Valley."

"Evie and I are," he said, taking out some money. "In about an hour, as a matter of fact."

"Oh, *Evie and I are*," she mocked. "But no, the Dogmothers have no idea what they're doing."

"This time, they've gone a little too far out on a limb."

"On a limb? You and Evie?" She gave a light laugh. "I can't think of two people more meant to be in that tree. And let's face it, big guy." She reached over and ruffled his hair, much like he'd done to her. "I see a little snow on the roof. What the hell are you waiting for? Someone better than Evie Hewitt?"

He stepped back from her touch. "She has a huge job in Raleigh."

"They have fire departments in Raleigh."

And animals in Bitter Bark. "I can't leave this family."

She tipped her head and fried him with a *get real* look. "We're fine, Declan. The family in total is now the size of a small country. You actually might not be missed for a while." At his look, she gave a throaty laugh. "Kidding, obviously. But seriously, no one needs a…" She kind of shrugged. "Father figure anymore." She added a smile to temper the sting. "Even me."

He slapped his hand to his chest. "You're killin' me, Smell."

"I'm trying to make sure you don't dismiss the idea of Evie Hewitt for some dumb reason. She's not in Raleigh now. Why don't you just hang with her for a few months and see how it goes? Why does it have to be all or nothing?"

"All or…" He leaned over the counter to whisper, even though there weren't any customers around. "Do you know what they want? Or at least what her grandfather wants, so I assume those two eighty-year-old troublemakers are in on it."

She laughed. "I love that they dragged in the old guy for backup. Those two are relentless."

"Wait until you hear how relentless." He took a deep breath. "They want me to give her a...*baby*."

She gasped noisily, jerking back, her eyes as round as dark chocolate wafers. "A...holy...oh my...Declan!"

"Right? If that isn't the most—"

"Fantastic idea!"

He stared at her.

"I mean, wow. I can totally see why you'd do that."

"Ella!" He choked her name. "It's not like giving her...a necklace. Or a..." He glanced around. "*Pet*. I'm not some kind of sperm bank."

She made a face. "Ew. I hate that word."

"Well, I hate the idea, but that's practically what her grandfather implied. That I could just..." He waved his hand. "Produce a baby."

"Well, why the heck not?"

Was she serious? "For one thing, we've barely said ten words to each other in twenty years."

"Whose fault is that?"

"Mine," he said without hesitation. "I couldn't...I didn't...I had to..."

She angled her head. "Use your words, little boy."

He muttered a dark curse.

"Not that word."

"Ella, I screwed up, okay? When Dad died, I..." *I died, too.* "I struggled. And whether you like it or not, I had to hold things together for the five of us. I couldn't go running after Evie."

She rolled her eyes dramatically. "I'll have a side of weak sauce with that chicken."

"Ella."

"Come on, Declan. I get it. You broke down and freaked out. Connor became a cocky jerk. Braden buried himself in books. I…" She shook her head. "We all handled it differently. And you pulled away from the woman you closely associated with the pain."

He frowned as the words hit, and there was no way to argue with them.

"I mean, she lives in the house where Dad died. That's not an easy thing to get over."

She lived in Raleigh, to be perfectly accurate, but was Ella far from the truth? "Yeah, maybe." And why couldn't he say those words to Evie?

"But it's been *twenty years*, Dec. We've all had to move on and have lives. Dad would hate you missing out on a great thing because she *reminds* you of how he died. Or you have some weird misplaced guilt because you weren't at that fire. You think *you'd* have gone in first? A newbie like you were?"

He leaned back, eyeing her. "How'd you get so smart, Smella?"

She grinned. "I've always been the smartest one of the bunch, but so pretty…" She put her fingers under her chin and fluttered her lashes. "That y'all forgot to notice."

"I notice."

"And your smart sister says you"—she aimed her finger at his face—"are the daddiest guy I know."

"The…I don't know what the hell that means."

"It means you're a natural. You're the guy who made sure every door was locked and all lights were off when everyone went to bed."

Because that's what their father did, and someone had to do it for the Mahoney family.

"You're the one who handles the barbecue and makes sure everyone has helmets on when we go muddin'.'"

"Because no one else can make a decent steak, and hello, I'm a firefighter. Safety first."

"And I've seen you when kids crawl all over the pumper truck on field day. You love kids. Every time you're near one of the little ones in the family, your eyes light up."

"Probably because Danny's tearing my hair out."

She laughed. "True. But you know what I'm saying. There's a daddy living in that big ol' chest, and honest to God, Dec, you were more fun when Evie was around. I'm all for bringing back that Declan."

"You were twelve."

She shrugged. "And you used to make me laugh so hard I snorted milk out of my nose at the dinner table."

"You're confusing me with Connor."

All humor faded from her face. "No. I'm not. You could hold your own with Connor in the joke department. And the fun department. And the…okay, not the girl department. But probably because you were so wrapped up in Evie, you never practiced."

Was all that true? "Look, I get your point. I've changed. But back to the problem at hand. I can't be a part of…a *baby*."

"Then sign over complete custody," she suggested, like it was as easy as cashing a check. "Let her raise a baby alone."

That would be *worse*. Way worse. Unthinkably worse. "And then there would be my offspring in the world, and I'd want to know that child and be involved in their life."

She shrugged. "So do that."

"But we're not married."

"*Welllll…*" She dragged out the word and waggled her brows.

"Ella, come *on*."

"Okay, okay." She held up both hands to stop his arguments. "It's not traditional, I get it. And if you ask me, probably not what Gramma Finnie had in mind when she sent you for croissants."

He choked softly. "Nothing in this family is a secret, is it?"

"Nothing."

"Well, this is, Ella," he said sternly. "I don't need an army of my siblings and cousins and step…*things* coming at me telling me to…you know."

"*Produce.*" She cracked up. "Or I guess I should say *re*produce."

"This isn't funny."

"Only a little." She came around the counter to make her point by putting her hands on his shoulders. "Why don't you stop thinking about what *you* want and think about Dr. Evangeline Hewitt?"

"That's all I've thought about for twenty-four hours."

She gave a smug smile. "So you are thinking about her."

This time, he gave her the *get real* look.

"Dec, she's your age, right?"

"A year younger."

"So, she's forty? I mean, wanting a baby is so natural and normal. Especially for a woman who's put her heart and soul into a career. Her clock's ticking, even with modern medicine."

He huffed out a breath, more than a little irritated that he came for backup and got pushback instead. "She doesn't need me and my…" *Baggage.* "It's no big deal for a woman to have a baby on her own. Or adopt one."

"True, but maybe that hasn't worked out. Maybe she doesn't want a stranger's baby. Maybe she has her own reasons for wanting yours."

"She never said she wants mine," he told her. "This came from her grandfather."

"Why don't you talk to her?"

He looked away, scratching his neck, hating the question.

"Dec?"

"I will. I...I..." He shook his head. "There's a lot unsaid between us, Ella. We have a complicated history. It isn't like we can sit down and start...making a baby, for God's sake."

"Which is not usually done in the *sitting* position, although I suppose you could try." She bit her lip to keep from laughing.

"Why is this funny to you?" he demanded.

"Because you're so smart and capable, always in complete control, and now you're..." She twirled her finger. "Unraveling."

"I'm not..." Yeah, he was.

"Declan, listen to me." She reached out and took his hand. "I've watched you—we all have—for all these years. We've watched you close off and shut down and systematically keep every woman at a safe distance and sabotage any relationship you've ever had."

He looked skyward. "You really need to give up the dog-treat business and hang your shingle as the town shrink."

"All I'm saying is you don't have to be our substitute father anymore, sweet brother of mine. Maybe it's time you think about being a real one."

The second person in less than twenty-four hours to say that to him. He waited a beat, then lifted a brow. "Those grannies paying you?"

"Are you kidding?" She flicked her pink-tipped nails. "The longer they focus on you, the more time I have to be young, free, and single. Who'd want to be in a relationship? Ugh." She stuck out her tongue, suddenly looking like the ten-year-old pest he remembered so well. "No, thanks."

"You little hypocrite." He snagged the bag of treats and pointed it at her. "Not a word, Ella Mahoney. Not a word to anyone."

She gave a tight smile and made an X on her chest.

By the time he reached Gloriana House, he realized his sister was right about way too many things. He did need to talk to Evie, but he shuddered at the idea of a conversation like that.

A baby. Jeez.

And holy hell, he *was* thinking about it.

# Chapter Eight

There was something about the smell of the animal hospital at Vestal Valley College that put Evie at peace. It smelled like...home.

Or maybe that was the clean, masculine scent of the man next to her as they walked out of the exam room, confident that Judah was in good hands for his MRI.

"You sure he can handle anesthesia?" Declan asked, holding a door that led to a long hall.

"It's only a twilight, and he's a sturdy guy and shows no other signs of sickness," Evie said, using the same tone she would with any pet parent, then her expression softened. "But I really wanted to be in there."

"I thought they'd let you."

"Hospital policy." She shrugged. "I understand, but..." She paused at an exam room to see a vet instructing two young students on how to do an abdominal check on a big black cat.

"That's a good boy, Kittah," the doctor said, and Evie could feel her whole body pulled toward the room, wanting to check Kittah, too.

Right before they reached the reception area, she glanced into a room lined with a crate wall, nearly every cage occupied. This time, she couldn't help herself. With a quick look around, she took Declan's hand and brought him with her.

"Let's peek at the patients," she whispered, making him chuckle.

"You can't help yourself, huh?"

"Nope." Inside the room, she inched closer to the first cage to see a beautiful white Lab with a name card that said Brinkley.

"Hey, Brinkley," she whispered, getting a sigh and a flutter of his lids. "Oh, you're not feeling so hot, are you, sweetheart?"

After a minute, she stepped to the left and stroked the tiny orange paw that a kitty slipped through the wire cage. "Sleep tight, little Holly," she whispered, reading the name card. "Were you a Christmas kitten?"

She almost didn't notice the weight of Declan's hand on her back. Almost. The sick animals were riveting, pulling at her heart as they always did, striking a chord that made her ache to help and help hard.

But his touch was so soothing, and it nearly took her breath away.

"Dr. Dolittle," he whispered, making her smile.

"I should never have forced you to see that movie with me."

"But I swear you talk to them."

"But they don't talk back, sadly." She took a step to the side to check on BooBoo, a darling little Yorkie, licking the bright green gauze that wrapped his tiny leg. "Because that would be too easy, right, BooBoo? If you could tell me what's wrong, I could fix it."

BooBoo stopped licking and looked at her, silent. But she could see the absolute agony in those sweet brown eyes.

"Excuse me, can I help you?"

They both turned at the question from a vet tech who didn't look at all amused at the intruders.

"Sorry, I wanted…"

"The waiting room is right through that door." The woman, young enough to be a student, nodded to the hall, her gloved hand holding a small syringe.

"So sorry." Declan took a step forward, his hand still on Evie's back. "This is Dr. Evangeline Hewitt, the head of the Department of Veterinary Neurology at NC State."

"Declan, it's okay, I—"

"Oh, Dr. Hewitt!" The woman's eyes widened. "I've read your work in myotonic dystrophia. I'm writing my senior thesis on the subject, and your paper has been gold to me. I'm Valerie Kaufmann, by the way."

"Hi, Valerie, and…thank you. So happy the work is helping with your thesis."

"Are you lecturing at Vestal Valley? Because, oh my God, I'm there."

"Goodness, I didn't expect to be recognized." Suddenly self-conscious, she felt her cheeks warm with a light flush. "No, I'm not here as staff or faculty, though. We brought in a dog for an MRI."

"Oh, sure, sure. And jeez, I hate to be the one to boot you out, Dr. Hewitt, but that little fellow…" She nodded toward BooBoo's cage.

"Is waiting for meds," Evie said quickly. "So sorry to get in your way."

"Not at all!" She smiled at Declan. "Are you Mr. Hewitt? I can tell you're proud of your wife. She's a legend in neurology."

This time, the blush burned full force on Evie's cheeks.

"Evie's a talented doctor," he said gracefully, too classy to embarrass the young woman for the mistake.

"But I don't belong in here," Evie said. "And you have work to do." Back in the hall, she let out a noisy breath. "Nice save, Mr. Hewitt."

"That's Captain Hewitt to you," he said, lightly elbowing her. "And who knew you were famous? A legend, no less."

"Only to veterinary students." But the feeling was nice—being here, talking about things that mattered to other vets, not messing with department administrivia. "I actually like it here, back in the trenches where the real vet work is done. But I shouldn't be poking my nose in other doctors' cases."

"Come on." He nudged her toward the reception area. "You're going to crawl out of your skin with the need to heal every animal in the place if we don't at least take a walk."

"But the doc could come out at any minute."

"They'll text you." He led her to the door. "I want to talk to you about something anyway."

Finally, an explanation and apology? That she would take, gladly. "Okay."

He didn't let go of her hand as they walked out into a hall, then through some glass doors to the sunny campus of Vestal Valley College.

"There's a little coffee shop around the corner that way," she said, gesturing. "It used to have the most insane pecan pie. Super rich and gooey, and the crust could bring you to tears."

"Gotta have a crust that will make me cry."

They took a shady path that meandered through the heart of the small college campus.

"You sure know your way around here," he mused.

"I went here for a semester, remember?"

"Vaguely. During graduate school?"

"I did one neurology rotation here. Molly was an undergrad then." She eyed him as they neared the coffee shop. "You were, uh, otherwise involved at the time."

He nodded. "I recall that now."

"What was her name?"

"That I don't remember," he said, then laughed at her surprised look. "Okay, I remember, but it didn't last."

"Kept me from coming to Sunday dinners, though, when Molly invited me. I didn't want to run into what's-her-name."

"Bethany," he said softly, opening the door to the coffee shop and holding it for her. "Her name was Bethany Tate, and she worked at the fire station for a while."

"Ah." The ping of jealousy was light, fast, and not really surprising. "What happened?"

They picked an open booth by the door, sliding in across from each other. "Now *that* I don't remember," he said. "But if you ask my sister, she'll say I kept the woman at arm's length and sabotaged the relationship, because apparently that's my MO."

She had to smile at his tone, which was rich with sarcasm.

When the waitress greeted them with menus, Declan held out his hand. "Do you have any of your famous pecan pie?"

"The best in Bitter Bark," she said.

"Don't tell that to Linda May, but we'll have an extra large slice, two forks and two coffees. But don't fill hers to the top, because she likes almost half of it cream."

Her jaw loosened as a little shiver of surprise ran through her. "Declan."

"That hasn't changed, has it?"

"No, but…thanks for remembering."

He tipped his head as if to say, *How could I forget?* Which only sent a second shiver through her. So, time for a third shiver, she supposed, ready for whatever he wanted to discuss.

She put her elbows on the table and dropped her chin on her knuckles. "So. What did you want to talk about?"

He flashed a split-second deer-in-the-headlights look at her. "Um…" He shifted in his seat. "What was that thing the vet tech mentioned? Myopic…dysfunctionia?"

She laughed from the belly, the way only Declan could make her laugh. She'd forgotten how much she loved that feeling. "Myotonic dystrophia. I headed a study on it at NC State. Is that what you wanted to talk about?"

"It's really impressive," he said softly, leaning back and looking at her.

"Nah, the study had a terrific team, and all I did was give orders."

"I meant your whole career, Evie. I knew you were going to do well, but wow, you've knocked it out of the park."

"Oh please, just because one student knew my work."

"Don't be modest. You're amazing."

A thread of a memory wound its way around her heart. *To your unparalleled amazingness.*

She brushed it away, more from habit than anything else, and then the waitress returned with their order, including what looked like a quarter of a pecan pie.

"A four-Kleenex crust," Declan joked as he picked up his fork and broke off a bit of the piecrust. "Anyway, your career is what you always hoped it would be. You never let anything stop you. That's…something."

"I guess," she said, stirring the extra splash of cream into her coffee, trying to figure out where he was going with this. For some reason, it wasn't what she expected. "I've always been focused."

"Laserlike," he agreed. "Nothing ever made you want to get off that track?"

She looked up at him, not sure why he'd ask that question. Why was he dancing around that wretchedly overdue conversation?

"Not really." She curled her fingers around the warm mug and studied him while she lifted it to her mouth. "Did anything ever make you want to stop being a firefighter, or get off the track toward captain and, ultimately, chief?"

He shook his head. "It's different for a woman."

She damn near dropped the cup. "Do you need a time machine to get back to the 1950s, or can you make it all by yourself?"

He smiled and stabbed his fork into the pie with a little too much force. "I'm not trying to be some kind of chauvinist. But I do see this in firefighting. A lot of women have to, you know, make a choice. Work or…" He gave her a pleading look, but she was not helping him out of this hole he was digging harder than he was poking at that pie. "You know. A family."

She lowered the cup without taking a sip, looking down at the table, knowing it would be easy to give him grief about the old-school mind-set and keep the topic off her personally. Did he really not know why she never married and had a family? Did he really think it was because of *work*?

But how could she look across this table and say, *Work was my consolation prize.*

He gestured toward the plate. "Come on. Have some cry pie." He lifted his brows as if he expected at least a smile for that attempt.

But she couldn't smile or eat. The subject was too raw. And was he never going to *mention* that he'd created a twenty-year gap that might just be the reason they were having this conversation in the first place?

"I will." She finally took a sip of coffee, then set the cup down and leveled her gaze on him. "Why haven't *you* had a family, Declan?"

He shifted his attention to the pie. "I think I just told you. Arm's length and sabotaged relationships, or so says Dr. Smella Mahoney, my personal psychiatrist." He gave a soft laugh. "She's smart, though, and probably right."

"Why wouldn't that be true for me, then, too? Why would you assume it was work?"

He studied her for a moment, collecting his thoughts like he so often did. "I figured you wanted kids."

"I figured you did," she fired back without hesitation.

"I have oodles of nieces and nephews, and the way things are going, I'll have more."

She accepted that—and the fact that if she was going to get an explanation or apology, she'd have to ask. And she just didn't want to do that.

After a moment, she finally took a piece of the sweet and sticky pie. "I...tried," she admitted as she angled her fork into the crust. "Didn't work out for me."

He studied her intently, a hundred questions in his eyes. Did he want to know about exhaustive and stressful donor insemination attempts? About the tests that showed absolutely nothing was wrong except bad timing? About how she filled out a mountain of paperwork to adopt, but gave up after a sleepless night of sobbing because she absolutely did not want to do that alone?

Should she detail how every time she turned around, another year had passed, and she was still single and childless, but her career was skyrocketing? Or about how every time she dated someone or got intimate with a man, she ended up feeling weirdly empty and scared and lonely because that man wasn't...who she wanted him to be?

No. That was all too much angst for pie and coffee the second day they were together after a twenty-year freeze that he wouldn't even acknowledge.

"I'm a working-woman cliché," she said simply, finally bringing the fork to her mouth. "No kids for me."

"But you're the end of the line," he said quietly.

Damn it, was she never going to taste this pie without choking?

She put the fork down without taking the bite. "Now you sound like my grandfather."

"It's a noble line, that Bushrod-Hewitt family. I'm sure he wants to continue it. And your parents, too. Right?"

"My parents only want me to be happy, and my grandfather..." She narrowed her eyes, a picture she probably should have seen sooner beginning to emerge. "What exactly did my grandfather say to you yesterday, Declan?"

He paled slightly. "Oh...you know."

"If I knew, I wouldn't ask."

"Evie, come on. Eat your pie."

"Declan, come on. Answer my question."

He smiled at her. "I just had déjà vu so hard. We always used to talk that way, remember? Echo words and sentences."

"I remember." *Everything, Dec. I remember everything. Don't you?* "I also remember that you're really good at changing the subject and managing to use as few words as possible when you don't want to talk about something."

"Hey, I brought it up."

"Then answer. What did my grandfather say to you when you went upstairs with him yesterday?"

He put his fork down and pinned his gaze on her, dark, intense, and unwavering. "He said you should have a baby."

"Well, that ship has—"

"*My* baby."

All she could do was stare at him, speechless and stunned. Had he said...

"Hey." He tapped her knuckles and pointed at her phone, lighting up on the table. "Doc's texting."

She glanced at the message. "Judah's waking up," she whispered. "We should go."

"But we haven't finished—"

"Why don't you eat the pie and meet me there? I really want to check on Judah."

"I meant we haven't finished our conversation."

She closed her eyes. "Clearly, my sweet Granddaddy has lost his ninety-two-year-old marbles. So, yes, we have finished the conversation."

She slipped out of the booth and headed toward the door, more surprised at the sting behind her eyelids than the unexpected and insane turn that conversation had taken.

Sure, they could try. Might even succeed, since there was apparently no reason she couldn't have a baby.

But then what would happen when he looked at her and remembered that if it wasn't for her, he'd have a father? What would happen when she went back to her life in Raleigh, and he wanted to take the baby to Waterford Farm every weekend? What would happen when she fell head over heels in love with him, and he went skulking back into his dark place and froze her out again?

No. Of all the options for a baby she'd considered over the years, Declan fathering one as some kind of bizarre *favor* was out of the question.

Hustling toward the animal hospital, she swiped under her eyes. Well, what do you know? That pie crust really did bring her to tears.

# Chapter Nine

Jeez. She was worse than he was when it came to difficult topics of conversation. No wonder they'd gone twenty years without saying all that needed to be said. Which was so wrong for two people who used to tell each other everything.

Declan was still stinging with the frustration of that unfinished conversation when he caught up with Evie at the animal hospital. How could he find out what she wanted, like Ella suggested, if she refused to tell him?

Dr. Rafferty ushered them right into his office, launching them into yet another conversation Declan didn't quite understand. This one was spoken in the language of vets that unintentionally shut him out as they discussed *ambulatory tetraparesis* and *ataxia* and a lot of other terms that were almost as incomprehensible as, *Granddaddy lost his marbles, and the conversation is finished.*

Sure, he agreed with the first one, but did the idea have to be finished? Not even discussed? Even laughed about or toyed with? Couldn't they even think, *What if?*

Or had too much time and silence passed? Or, oh God, worse. Maybe she thought he was offering some kind of quid pro quo for all the lost years. Was that it?

"It is most definitely not cervical stenotic myelopathy," the doctor said, pulling him back into the current conversation.

"Sadly, no," Evie agreed.

Sadly? Declan leaned closer, forcing himself to focus on Judah. "It's not Wobbler Syndrome?"

"It is," Dr. Rafferty said. "But not bone-associated."

Evie turned to Declan and put a gentle hand on his arm, the way he imagined she talked to dog owners. "Judah's symptoms are disc-related, within the spine. Essentially, he has chronic bulging discs," she said. "Which could lead to a sudden herniation, if not treated. And his problems walking will only get worse."

He cringed. "That doesn't sound good."

Evie turned the medical image toward Declan. "See that circle? Imagine his spinal cord is made up of pieces of pepperoni, and this is a slice."

"Not a perfect circle," he noticed.

"Exactly. His is badly misshapen."

Dr. Rafferty leaned forward. "Judah has a more uncommon form of Wobblers, the kind we can't treat with meds and nutrition."

"Surgery?" he asked.

Evie tipped her head and looked at the vet across the table from her. "I know what I think, but I'd like your opinion, Dr. Rafferty."

"I don't think a dorsal laminectomy will work in this case. Definitely a CVS."

"So, no surgery?" Declan asked.

"No *simple* surgery," Evie explained. "We'll have to do what's called a cervical ventral slot procedure, which means we'll remove damaged discs."

"A very tricky operation," Dr. Rafferty said. "The surgeon needs to know exactly how to operate that drill."

A *drill*. Yikes.

"I've done this surgery a hundred times, and I'll gladly do it one hundred and one," Evie said. "If I'm allowed to use these facilities."

The other vet looked uncertain. "Policy says no, I'm afraid. We can only let surgeons associated with Vestal Valley College's Veterinary School operate here."

"Could you do it at Molly's office?" Declan asked. "You did Rusty's surgery there. Brain surgery. That was tricky, too."

"I'd need the scope to see in the actual spinal column," she said, then looked back at the other doctor. "I did a rotation here when I was in graduate school. Would that help my case?"

"Honestly? Your impressive credentials are probably all we need," the other doctor said. "But I have to clear it with the powers that be. That'll take a few days, though."

"Can Judah wait a few days?" Declan asked.

"He can." Dr. Rafferty pushed up. "Though I'd like to bring him back in a day or two and have Christine, our top PT, do a physical and perform some acupuncture for pain control."

"Great idea," Evie said. "I'd love to meet with her and discuss post-op therapy, too, no matter who does the surgery."

"Why don't you two discuss your options while I check on our patient and get you on Christine's schedule?"

When he left and closed the door, Declan turned to her. "I want you to do the surgery, Evie, here or wherever."

"And I want to do it. This is *not* an easy surgery, but I respect that they have to follow protocol."

"Should we take him to Raleigh and do the surgery at your hospital?"

She gave a wry laugh. "I can't do surgery there, either."

"You can't?"

"I'm on sabbatical, remember? But Dr. Rafferty will get me clearance. He just has to jump through a few hoops."

"Don't forget we have twenty-four/seven access to Waterford Farm and two of the best vets in the state in my uncle and cousin."

"I'd love to have Molly as my backup in the OR." She nodded, thinking, then lifted a brow in question. "Even if I do the surgery, the whole thing is going to be pricey. You know that, right?"

He shrugged. "I can cover the expenses. Judah's my responsibility now."

"That's very kind. I'm sure this is why his owner abandoned him," she said, closing her eyes and shaking her head, always empathetic to an animal's plight.

"No doubt," he agreed. "Medical costs are probably the number one reason people surrender animals."

She leaned in. "But then, thank God, someone like you, with a heart of gold, pays for their medical treatments."

"You think I have a heart of gold?"

"Yes." She answered without a second's hesitation, which did something stupid to his insides. Or maybe that was being less than two feet from Evie, making plans, solving problems, and talking like they used to.

"We've always been a good team, E."

"Do *you* want to be in the OR, too?" she asked with a smile.

"I'm saying that…the thing your grandfather mentioned, about the ba—"

She put her hand over his mouth. "Don't."

"I want to know if you—"

"It's off the table," she said simply. "In fact, there isn't a table. Discussion closed."

But he had to ask. He had to know. "You don't want a baby, Evie? You don't want a child of your own?"

She searched his face for a long time, silent, no doubt formulating an answer that could formally end the conversation.

"That's just it," she finally whispered. "It wouldn't be *my own*."

Of course. She was right. It would be his, too. And that was obviously a problem for her.

Who could blame her after how he'd shut her out all those years? He deserved this. And didn't deserve her.

The door opened, and Judah came galumphing in with Dr. Rafferty, reminding Declan that he already sort of had a kid now—a four-legged one. And that might have to be enough.

Granddaddy was asleep when Evie went up to get his tray and check on Judah, who was curled up and comfy in his bed, snoozing as deeply as the other guy in the room. So she took the tray downstairs, knowing the conversation she wanted to have with her grandfather would have to wait until tomorrow.

She'd had a chance earlier, but the truth was, since she'd been home from Vestal Valley College, she hadn't had the heart—or nerve—to ask Granddaddy about…

*Declan's baby.*

Why would Granddaddy suggest something like that? And why couldn't she stop obsessing about it? She'd done such a good job of putting the baby dream in a compartment she rarely opened, and now, there it was, calling her and demanding she…imagine.

No, she wouldn't go there.

Instead, she hummed to herself while she put dishes in the dishwasher and wiped off the tray, then checked the time and realized she hadn't made herself dinner yet. As she was walking to the fridge to see what she could scare up, she heard a soft tap at the front door, and her heart did a little jump.

Declan?

She tamped down the little jolt of excitement, heading to the front hall to see the silhouette of a person who was definitely a man, but that wasn't Declan's tall, commanding physique.

"Can I help you?" she called through the leaded glass.

"I'm looking for the owner of this house," a man said. "My name is James Bell. I've left a few messages with Mr. Hewitt, but I understand he's not feeling well."

Bitter Bark wasn't exactly a hotbed of crime, but she wasn't about to open the door to a stranger. Plus, it was too late for company even if Granddaddy did know the man.

"Can you leave your number and what you need? I can speak to him tomorrow and see if he can contact you."

"Sure. I'll leave my card. I'm interested in buying this house."

She inched back, eyes wide. "Really?"

"If you're not selling, ma'am, I understand. But I've been in love with this house for years. I don't want to miss the opportunity to make an offer on it, should you be accepting them."

Curiosity got the better of her, making her open the door, but she left the chain on. "It's not on the market," she said.

A man in his mid-forties, with reddish hair, wire frames, and a narrow build, stood a few feet away, wearing a button-down shirt and crisp khaki pants, writing something on a card.

"I'm giving you my office and cell numbers on here." He smiled at her and pushed back his glasses with his wrist, where lines of black ink peeked out from his cuff. Surprising for a guy who looked like an accountant. "I really hate to be this bold, walking up to the door and ringing the bell like a loon, but…God, I want this house."

A thread of something curled through her, a feeling she couldn't quite describe. Not jealousy, exactly. Not pride. Not resentment. But a bit of all three. "It's a wonderful house," she agreed. And whoever got to live in it would be very lucky.

He lowered the card and pen, and his shoulders sank. "You're not going to sell it, are you." It wasn't a question, and his disappointment was clear. "I figured it was a crazy dream."

"Actually, we might. Hang on." Someone in love with the house might pay top dollar when the time came—and with all that had to be done to bring it up to date, that could be a blessing for her parents. Mom would want to at least get a read on the guy. If they sold it without a realtor, it would be easy and fast, when the time came. Better for people living in the Caribbean, for sure.

With all that rationalization and the fact that the man seemed sincere and was not the least bit threatening, she closed the door, slid the chain, and then reopened it to have a proper conversation. "I'm Evie Hewitt," she said, extending her hand. "My grandfather is Max."

"James Bell." His fingers were cold, his grip strong. "Will you be managing his estate?"

She flinched at that. "He's very much alive and sleeping upstairs."

"Oh, sorry. God." He shook his head and pushed at those glasses again. "I know that. I do. I've done a little digging around town. In fact, I used to live near here, but now I'm in Charlotte."

"And you're looking to buy a house in Bitter Bark?"

"I run my own consulting business and can work anywhere. Truth is, my fiancée and I have driven by here a million times, and she's nuts about this place, too." He let out a little sigh and added a goofy smile. "I want to give her the house as a wedding present. I happened to be nearby on business today and thought I'd give this a try. I know, knocking on the door and asking to buy a house is a little strange, but if I get it, I want it to be a surprise for Jenny. I mean, assuming…if there's any chance…if you sell."

His nervousness was a little endearing, along with his story. "Well, we're not selling yet, Mr. Bell. We likely won't before your wedding."

"Please, call me Jim." He handed her his card. "And we can wait on the wedding. In fact…" He let out a sigh. "The house might be the very thing to make my hard-to-pin-down lady finally set a date."

"Oh, I see."

He laughed nervously. "I'm babbling, ma'am, and I'm sure you're not interested in my story. But this is the closest I've ever gotten…" He inched to one side to look past her into the house, closing his eyes with a grunt. "And of course the stairs are red. Exactly like we imagined."

Well, she wasn't going to invite him in, no matter how sweet his story or how much he hinted at it. Not to mention how sad it would make Granddaddy to know they were even talking about selling.

"I'll keep your card, Mr. Bell. If and when we're ready to put it on the market, I'll call you."

"Could I make an appointment to see it sometime? Not now, obviously. I would never be that rude. But sometime?"

"Let me think about it."

"All right, and while you're at it, turn over that card and think about that number. Please consider it a starting offer."

She glanced down.

"Go ahead, take a look. I want you to know I'm serious."

She flipped the card and stared at the seven-digit number. "Oh…" She barely breathed the word.

"I'm interested in the furnishings, too. Any and all that you'd leave. I'll take everything as is."

Which would thrill her mother.

"I want the house, ma'am."

He certainly did. "Well, thank you so—" A high-pitched howl echoed behind her, making her suck in a sudden breath. "Judah!"

"Your dog? Or a wolf?" he joked.

"Right the first time." She inched back and put a hand on the door to close it, lifting the card with the other. "Thank you, Mr. Bell…Jim."

"Think about it, please."

"I will."

Judah howled again, even louder, if that was possible, so she closed the door quickly, flipped the dead bolt, and jogged toward the stairs. She picked up speed on the third howl, not at all sure of what she'd find when she finally reached Granddaddy's door.

Rushing into the room, she came to a sudden stop...not expecting *that*.

"He wants to get on the bed, Evie." Her grandfather was sitting up, smoothing the covers next to him as if he was making space. "But every time he lifts his head, he cries."

"It's his spine," she said. "He could probably use another dose of medicine, and...do you *want* him up there?"

"More than anything, right, boy?" He patted the bed and gave a toothless grin to Judah, who stood next to the bed with nothing but longing and frustration on his face. "He's good company."

"Oh, I'm sorry, Granddaddy. I thought you were asleep."

"He woke me up. Can you put him up here?"

"Let me get a pill in him and take him out one last time. Then I'll bring him back and get him on the bed."

"Well, hurry it up, or I'll be asleep again." He beamed at Judah. "But I need some company in here."

She took care of the dog and gave him some chicken with his painkiller, then walked him back upstairs to find Granddaddy still wide awake.

"Okay, Judah." Evie wrapped her arms around him. "Up you go, big guy."

With a soft grunt and braced feet, she lifted his back half, helping him onto the bed.

He immediately walked up to get next to Granddaddy,

going right to his face to give it a grateful lick with his long tongue.

"Well, he sure likes you," she said with a chuckle.

"I like him right back. Now you settle there, Judah, and I'll tell you a story until we're both asleep."

Her heart practically folded in half as she watched the dog carefully position himself where he was comfortable and Granddaddy was safe.

"God, we don't deserve dogs," she whispered as her whole being swelled with affection.

Granddaddy patted the thick fur with his spotted, knotted hand. "Once upon a time," he started, "there was a man named Thad."

"The first or junior?" Evie asked with a smile.

"The first. I'm going to tell him the whole story of our great family line, since he's part of it now."

"Um, he's Declan's dog."

"Like I said, he's family now."

She shot him a look, but he was fully immersed in petting Judah, and the last thing she wanted to do was get him worked up over whatever he'd said to Declan. It could wait until morning.

She walked over to the window seat to settle in and listen. He started with how Thaddeus Ambrose Bushrod, a captain in the British Royal Navy, had moved to America to stake his claim and build a small town in North Carolina. From there, Big Bad Thad, as they called the man who stood more than six and a half feet, marked off the town square and opened the first business, a bar the locals still called Bushrod's.

Evie looked out the window as the evening lights of that very town flickered to life, a half moon rising over the square named after her great-great-great-grandfather.

*He said you should have a baby...my baby.*

She closed her eyes and listened to the biographies of all the Bushrods and Hewitts who'd come before her and gave up the fight.

While Granddaddy droned on, she let herself sink into a dream she thought she'd long ago given up.

# Chapter Ten

Declan had texted only, *Coming over around ten*, because texting Evie, *I can't freaking stay away*, would probably have a stalker-y tone. Let her think he wanted to check on Judah, which he did, but he'd thrown enough tools in the truck to do more than that.

He'd start with the broken stair rail, take a look at the warped windows, then work his way through the house to help with whatever it needed. It was the least he could do for how much she was doing for Judah.

And it was the best way to spend more time with her…which, face it, was all he really wanted. And maybe, with a little time, he could find a way to say the words she deserved to hear. Over the past few days, it had been all about Judah, but now, he had to man up and take whatever fury or heartache he had coming his way.

She opened the door before he made his way up the walk, locking her hands on her hips, which accentuated the narrowness of her waist and long legs in jeans, eyeing the toolbox he carried. "Bringing a screwdriver so you can loosen up?"

Laughing, he lifted the metal toolbox in his right hand. "Friends don't let friends' windows stick."

"Declan."

"Evie," he echoed, their old joke so natural it kind of took his breath away. "I told you I'd be your handyman."

Her eyes flickered at that, and an expression he couldn't quite decipher crossed her face, which looked prettier every time he saw her. "You don't have to work today?" she asked as she let him in.

"I'm off today. I have twelve hours tomorrow and twenty-four on Thursday and Friday, but then I'm free all weekend." He stepped past her, stealing a whiff of her feminine scent and letting their arms brush because it was nice.

"That's not too bad."

"Perk of being the one who makes the schedule," he said, heading right to the newel to set the toolbox on the stairs. "How's Judah?"

"Attached to his new best friend."

He turned, a smile pulling. "Max?"

"They're inseparable. They slept together last night."

He fought the urge to let his gaze travel over her T-shirt and jeans again and crack a joke about sleeping together. Nope. Too soon. "No word from Vestal Valley on the surgery yet?"

"Not yet." She joined him at the bottom of the steps, looking up at him with those bright blue eyes that always reminded him of a cut-glass perfume bottle Gramma Finnie owned. "But you might not have too much work to do after all."

"How's that?"

"A man came by here last night and made an offer on the house. As is."

"You have it on the market?" How did he not know that?

"No. But if it ever is, he wants to buy it as a surprise wedding present for his fiancée, because they've been in love with the house for years. He made a starting offer that knocked my socks off."

"Wow." He shifted his attention to the newel, rocking the solid wood back and forth in his hands to try to figure out how the original carpenter had affixed it and why it wasn't a solid piece of wood.

And why this news of hers sent a punch into his gut that he didn't understand. Not that it was hard to surmise. Once her grandfather died and she sold this house, Evie Hewitt would have no reason to ever come back to Bitter Bark.

"Wow is right. I called my parents this morning, and they were pretty psyched."

"They really don't want to keep this house?" He flipped open the toolbox.

"They really don't," she confirmed. "Plus, the offer was seven digits, and the first wasn't a one."

He let out a low whistle. "Holy…wow. That's a lot of cash for Bitter Bark."

"Seriously." She reached into the toolbox and pulled out a wrench, holding it up. "This is not a drill. Repeat. Not a drill."

"Har-har. *Nailed* it."

"Ooh, good one." She plucked through the box, picking up a wire cutter. "Unlike this guy who tried to be punny, but he just couldn't cut it."

He cracked up, swamped by a sudden rush of good feeling. "So how does Max feel about this house offer?"

"I kind of avoid the subject of the house with him,"

she admitted, putting the wire cutter down. "He knows my parents aren't leaving the Caribbean, and I can't take care of the house from three and a half hours away. Plus, who wants to talk about it when it means talking about him…" She lifted a shoulder. "Obviously, he's not going to live forever, but I personally would like to believe that he might."

"He thinks he's checking out any minute," Declan said. "But nothing is really wrong with him, right?"

"Nothing but boredom with this world and hope he'll see Grandmama Penelope in the next," she said wistfully.

He found the weak spot in the newel, bracing on the top step to work on it. "Well, it sure is a one-of-a-kind house."

She studied him for a long time, and he could practically taste the question before she asked it.

"Is it hard for you to come here, Dec?" she asked gently. "I would understand if it is."

He didn't answer right away, still using all his strength to try to jiggle the jammed but unsteady newel free. "Not gonna lie, I've never liked driving by this place. And not only because of the bad memory, but…" He looked at her. "All the good ones, too."

She smiled. "Like the time we stayed up all night doing our science projects?"

"And yours won, naturally." He shook his head, remembering what a mess his had been, while her presentation boards had been perfect. "And remember when you dared me to ride a flattened cardboard box down these stairs and your grandmother caught me?"

She laughed so hard she almost snorted, the sound like music to his ears. "Oh my God, your face when she came around that corner."

129

"I told her I was practicing for sledding season." He did snort on the next laugh. "I damn near peed my pants in fear."

"She wasn't mad, though. Mildly amused."

"You were always pulling crap like that, E. How about when Ella locked herself in the back stairs' secret hatch when we were babysitting her?"

"Oh, you freaked out."

"My baby sister was locked in a hole in the staircase landing."

"I told her it was a good hiding place to try to fool you, but it wasn't supposed to lock with her in it," she said on a laugh. "God, this house has idiosyncrasies."

"You hid my sister in a hole," he said, giving her a look.

She waved her hand. "She thought it was one grand adventure."

"She would." He worked the wooden globe from side to side again. "I may have to squirt some glue in the seam," he said. "Although you'd think this carved ball would be part of the post."

"It's always been a little loose, even when I was young. But now it feels like one good pull and—"

"Whoa!" It detached with so much force that Declan almost lost his balance, making Evie reach up to his waist to steady him. "What the hell?" he muttered, turning the thing over to see it was made like a wooden cork that fit into a carved space in the newel post. "I've never seen anything like this."

"Welcome to Gloriana House," she said. "Surprises in the woodwork. Literally."

Leaning over, he looked into the hole. "But it's… What's that?"

130

"What's what?" She popped up to peer in, her face so close to his, he could feel the warmth of her skin. "Oh my God, Declan. There's a box in there."

"Way down there, unreachable."

"No such thing as unreachable," she said, stepping back. "I need the right tool. A metal hanger? Something long and tweezerlike." She shot off toward the kitchen, leaving behind her sweet Evie scent and a vague feeling of déjà vu. And a smile *still* on his face.

"Look what I found!" She came back with a long pair of rubber-tipped tongs that she snapped near his face. "What do you call these?"

"Tongs."

"You're welcome."

He rolled his eyes. "A total stretch."

"'Cause I was *tweasing* you."

He laughed. "I walked right into that."

"The best kind."

He reached for the tongs. "Want me to do it?"

"My hand's smaller. I can get deeper." She positioned herself on the step above the newel while Declan pulled out his phone to give her light. "I can't wait to find out what it is," she said. "Grandmama Penelope used to always find treasures in the house, mostly things about Gloriana Bushrod. Amelia, her mother, was so distraught after Glory died that she would hide her things. Once, my grandmother found a letter in a broken floor board written by Amelia the day after Gloriana died. It was so sad. It's in the museum room."

"The creepy room."

She shot him a look. "It's not creepy."

"Evie. It's a room full of sad letters about dead relatives."

"Please. There's an altar to the family's Irish setters from the past in your cousin's waiting room," she reminded him. "That room has the history of this house. And this might...belong in it." She grunted and pushed harder, drawing his attention to her body as she worked, too on task to notice him appreciating the curves and angles and the way she filled out a pair of jeans.

"I got it!" Her whole face turned pink as she worked to squeeze the tongs and not drop the box as she slid it up the deep well in the newel.

She managed to pull the box out of the newel, and Declan snagged it right before it fell back in. "Good teamwork."

He handed it to her, and she dropped back on the step with a happy sigh, holding a small jewelers box in both hands. "What do you think? A ring? Brooch? Empty?"

Easing down next to her, he couldn't help but be more captivated by her beautiful expression than the treasure she'd found. "Oh, I hope not empty." Because he didn't want to see that glimmer in her eyes disappear. In fact, he wanted to see it all the damn time.

"Here goes." She lifted the lid and gasped softly at the shiny gold heart-shaped necklace inside. "It's a locket!" she exclaimed, gently taking the necklace from the box and giving him an excited look. "I bet there are pictures inside."

"Oh yeah. My grandmother had one of those and gave it to my mom."

She rubbed her thumb over the engraving on the front, her touch slow and reverent, then slowly turned it over with a soft gasp. "Gloriana and Evangeline, 1910." She gave a little shiver, chills on her arms.

"So, Evangeline's your great-grandmother?"

"Yes, Glory's younger sister." She slid her fingernail into a crack in the heart, then popped it open like a book. "Look." She held it out so they could both see that each side of the heart held a sepia-toned picture of a baby. They were so similar he could never have told them apart.

"These are their baby portraits," she said. "So, this necklace must have belonged to Amelia Bushrod."

"Okay, wait." He closed his eyes to see the family tree. "Great-*great*?"

She nodded. "The wife of Thaddeus Jr. and daughter-in-law of Big Bad Thad himself. The woman who built Gloriana House and named it for…" She tapped one side of the locket. "This little lady right here. Her first-born."

"Wow. That's something."

Leaning back, she sighed, pressing the locket to her chest. "Oh, Dec."

He tried to read her expression, surprised to see it so sad after such a great find. "What's wrong?"

"I can't sell this house," she whispered. "There's so much history and so many treasures. Who knows what else is hidden in the walls?"

"All kinds of pieces of your family."

She nodded, her mouth turned down. "My mother never really cared or connected, you know? It was Grandmama's house, and my mom and my dad lived here because…" She gave a soft laugh. "I don't even know why. Convenience and habit and because it's huge."

"And your dad really doesn't want to keep it, if only for posterity?"

"He only wants to make my mother happy, and she wants to live on a boat and paint sunsets. When I talked to her this morning, she couldn't have been more overjoyed by the prospect of a multimillion-dollar payout and no giant house to maintain."

She stared at the locket for a long time, her chest rising and falling with slow breaths. "But this family is so special," she whispered, her voice cracking. "And this house…"

"Is special, also."

She glanced up at him, looking a little surprised he would say that. "It's such a shame to…"

"Sell the house?" he guessed.

She looked up from the locket into his eyes, a storm brewing. "Would you really…" She took another breath, searching his face.

"Would I what?"

"Would you…"

He closed his hand over hers when she didn't finish. What did she want? Some work on the house or…something more permanent? Something that he woke up ten times in the middle of the night thinking about?

He took a breath and added some pressure on her hand. "Look, I know it might be hard to believe because a lot of time has passed, but, Evie, ask me what you want me to do. I can't ever say no to you."

She looked down at their joined hands. "You told me that once, you know."

He knew. He remembered. *Declan's promise*. A list of promises he smashed to kingdom come literally less than an hour after he made it.

"So go ahead, ask me."

A vein pulsed in her throat as her chest rose and fell with another breath.

"Would you…" She popped off the stairs and pointed

to the chandelier. "Go up to the attic and find the winch to lower that so I can clean that monster?" she asked, rushing the question as if she couldn't get it out fast enough.

*That* was what was causing her so much visible stress? Somehow, he doubted it. "Sure."

"And will you really fix the window sashes and also nail down the floorboards and maybe help me paint?" Again, she asked quickly, like she didn't want time to change her mind.

"That's why I'm here." One of the reasons, anyway. "Are you trying to drive the price up even further?"

"I want to honor the house, Declan. I want to return it to its original beauty. I want to do that for my grandmother and great-grandmother and…" She pressed the locket to her chest. "My great-great-grandmother who built it. The least I can do is fix Gloriana House."

"Okay," he said slowly, standing up to get close to her. "Of course I'll help you, and what I can't do, I'll help you find someone who can."

She turned to him, only then realizing they were inches apart. "I know this isn't your favorite place to spend time."

"But you are one of my favorite people to spend time with." He felt his lips lift in a smile that mirrored hers.

"Really?"

"Some things don't change, E."

"But…" She held his gaze, slicing him wide open with those cut-crystal eyes. "Then why did you freeze me out, Dec?"

There it was. The question he'd known was coming. And he didn't have a good answer, not one worthy of this fine woman. "Because I'm an idiot."

135

She gave him a look that said she thought the explanation was as lame as he did.

His heart hammering, he lifted his hand to her hair, stroking the near-black silk as he held her gaze. Then he slipped his fingers under her hair, grazing her neck, easing her a little closer.

"Evie?"

"Yes?"

He heard the breathlessness in the word, the need for him to give her a better reason than *I was a mess living in an emotional hole as dark and dank as a basement in an old house.*

"Oh wait." She reached into her back pocket and pulled out her phone, reading the screen. "Vestal Valley approved me to do Judah's surgery on Saturday."

"That's awesome."

She nodded, stepping back, out of his touch. "Let's take it one day at a time, Dec. We both need...time."

After twenty years? He didn't really need any more time, but maybe she did. Time and a hell of a better explanation.

She held up the locket and let it dangle between them. "We've already found a treasure. Who knows what else could happen?"

He knew. He knew exactly what could happen. If he could apologize for shutting her out for twenty years and be man enough to explain why.

And if that wasn't incentive enough, he didn't know what was.

# Chapter Eleven

Evie couldn't help letting him off the hook. Sometimes, all you can do for an animal in pain is let them curl into a ball and ride it out. She could sense Declan's walls coming down, if a little more slowly than she'd like. Maybe it wouldn't be the full-on detonation of the fortress he'd built, but she was getting through, one straight arrow and bad joke at a time.

And after twenty years, she was mature enough to know that being with him, even without getting the answers she wanted, was better than being without him. Plus, he was going to help her around Gloriana House, which was already a huge concession.

While he worked, Evie spent time with Granddaddy and Judah, playing an endless game of gin rummy with one and taking the other for slow walks to the grass.

It was nearly four when she walked Judah downstairs, grabbed a few bottles of water, and guided the dog to the garage building on the west side of the property, following the sound of an electric sander.

Outside the separate garage, which, in her lifetime, had never actually housed a car, but certainly had a century's worth of tools and random garden equipment,

Judah started sniffing and exploring some shrubs. Evie squinted into the building toward the workbench, catching sight of Declan in some afternoon light streaming through a window, his slightly damp T-shirt stretched over rock-solid muscles as he gripped the tool to shave a window frame.

*It's gonna be hard to be just friends.*

And imagine how complicated *making a baby* would be.

But what they had made was progress. From frozen to friends, and she liked that. She also liked how delicious he looked in a tight, sweaty T-shirt. Ripped. Solid. So damn masculine and easy on the eyes.

Her handyman.

When he'd mentioned that, her mind had slipped back twenty years to a cool Carolina mountain morning when a boy made...promises.

*I'll be your handyman...chauffeur...lover...husband.*

She couldn't remember the exact words he'd written on some random note card all those years ago, but she remembered the sentiment behind them. Sometimes, on her darkest nights, she'd dredge up that feeling of the last truly happy time they had together, less than an hour before their worlds and friendship imploded.

Yes, his father died, so it seemed fair to not hold him to promises he made when he was young and trying to get her back into his sleeping bag. But the fact was, Declan, for all his goodness and strength and loyalty and love, broke that promise so fast, her head spun just thinking about it. And he never even tried to fix it...yet.

"I bring water and a dog," she called when the electrical hum stopped, coming closer to offer a bottle of water. "Thirsty?"

138

Putting the sander down, he pushed the plastic goggles he wore up over his hair, sliding into a grateful smile. "Parched. Thanks."

He took the bottle and offered a casual toast, glancing past her to see Judah, snout-down in some bushes. "Look who's been sprung."

He took a sip and walked to Judah, crouching down to pet him. "How ya feelin', big guy?" Judah looked up at him, slightly interested, then returned to whatever smelled better on the ground.

At the workbench, Evie checked out his progress. "How's it going with the sixty-year-old window sashes?"

"Truth? Honey, you need entirely new windows in this place." After petting Judah some more, he rose and came to stand next to her. "This is a Band-Aid that will allow them to open and close again. Not sure how great the insulation will be this winter, or what one decent storm could do."

"All new windows?" She curled her lip. How much did she want to invest in making her family home beautiful when it wasn't…hers? Maybe she should let the wealthy new homeowner worry about that.

"It would cost a fortune if you wanted to match these," he said as if he could read her mind. "I think you'd need a real historic home specialist to do the job," he said after swallowing a deep gulp of his water. "Speaking of historic homes, do you ever get used to the tourists gawking and taking pictures?" He gestured toward the street. "I've seen half a dozen today."

"As long as they don't bother me, I take it as a compliment for the house my ancestors built."

He peered past her to the side of the house. "It needs work, but there's no denying this house is a stunner."

For some reason, hearing him say anything good about Gloriana House made her heart happy. "I'm so grateful for what you're doing," she said and wondered if he knew she meant so much more than helping with repairs. Being here, caring about this house, helping her…it meant the world.

"Then we're even." He pointed his head toward Judah. "He's so much calmer than he was at the station. You're like magic with animals, you know that?"

"He's a simple creature, to be fair. He's got a person and painkillers. Oh, I spoke to Dr. Rafferty," she added. "They're going to have a staff for me on Saturday, including an anesthesiologist and two nurses. They're even letting me bring Molly into the OR. In fact, she's on her way over now."

"Molly is?"

"She has to do one more physical on Judah and sign an online form for approval to be in the OR." At the sound of a car pulling into the long drive, she turned, seeing that old van that had been at Waterford. "Is that what Molly drives? I could swear that's the same dog van your aunt Annie used to drive."

He chuckled. "It is the same one. And not merely the make and model—it's the very same vehicle."

"Wow, it's in good shape."

"Molly never told you the story of how Trace found it and refurbished it? Ask her. And ask her why."

"I will—"

"But not when Pru's around, because she hates the story." He led her out of the garage into the sunlight as the doors of the van opened, and more than just Molly climbed out. "And speaking of Prudence, there she is."

A lanky teenage girl slipped out of the van, followed

by Gramma Finnie and Yiayia. Then Molly reached into the van and emerged holding Danny, her baby who probably wasn't even eighteen months old yet.

"Oh boy," Evie whispered.

"And not just any boy," Declan added. "Hide the china. That kid is a human tornado."

Sensing the new arrivals, Judah lifted his head and barked, starting toward the small group as they came up the driveway.

"I got him," Declan said, carefully stopping the dog without putting any pressure on his neck. "You go greet the guests."

She met the little party halfway down the long drive, waving and laughing when Molly put Danny down, and he toddled forward, arms outstretched toward the dog.

"Mmmbah! Mmmbah!"

"He thinks every dog is Meatball," Molly said, reaching for Evie with the same spark in her eyes as her little boy. "I travel in a pack," she whispered as they hugged. "And the grannies insisted, but points to me for making them leave their dogs at home."

"Oh, it's fine, I—"

"Is that Declan?" Molly asked with a soft gasp. "Brace yourself. Yiayia's gonna explode with high hopes."

"If her hopes are that the windows will open and close again, she's in luck." Evie added a squeeze and greeted the rest of them in a flurry of hugs and hellos, taking an extra moment with Pru, whom she hadn't seen in several years.

"Beautiful Prudence Anne," she whispered, making the teenager laugh and roll her eyes.

"Hi, Dr. Hewitt."

"Hey, I used to be Aunt Evie when you were a little bitty girl."

"I remember," she said, brushing back a lock of hair. "You used to play peekaboo with me. You'd say, 'Pru, where does the doctor play peekaboo?'"

"In the *I-C-U*!" Evie answered with a hearty laugh.

"That sounds like Evie," Molly joked. "The TA who could make a whole class groan at her animal puns."

Danny had reached the dog with more cries of "Mmmbah!" but Yiayia marched right up to Declan.

"My oh my, look who's here."

Declan nodded. "Nice to see you, too, Yiayia."

"Careful with that dog," Molly exclaimed, pulling everyone's attention to Danny as he zeroed in on Judah, who barked and backed up.

Molly scooped the child up before he could get his hands on Judah. But the surprise threw the dog off a little, and he lifted his head and howled.

"Upstairs?" Declan asked Evie.

"Good idea. You can take him up the back stairs to Granddaddy's room. Molly and I will come up and do the exam there in a minute."

He nodded, leading the dog around to the back of the house.

"I'm afraid we caused a wee bit of chaos, lass." Gramma Finnie patted Evie's arm as she walked them to the front door.

"I like a little chaos," Evie said. "We could use some around here."

"And I really wanted to see the house," Pru added. "I heard it's totally sick inside. Can I see the museum room?"

"Of course." Evie opened the front door and gestured

for them all to go first. "You can see the whole house."

Inside, Molly put Danny down, and instantly, he beelined for the stairs.

"Whoa, kiddo. No you don't." She launched after him, airlifting him seconds before he got to the first step. "He's unstoppable," she said on an exasperated laugh.

"He's gorgeous." Evie reached for the chunky baby boy with dark eyes and a shock of nearly black, Einstein-wild hair. "And he's a clone of Trace."

"Seriously, I just carried him," Molly quipped as she handed him over. "This kid is pure Bancroft, there but for the tattoos he'll probably get when he's twelve."

"Little Daniel Bancroft, do *you* want to play peekaboo?" Evie bopped his nose as he settled onto her hip in a way that felt insanely natural.

He gurgled in her face, giving a two-toothed smile and tugging at her hair.

"Oh, he's a lover," Evie cooed, easing her hair out of his hand right before it got tasted.

"And a drooler," Pru warned.

"Well, I adore a man who drools over me," she joked in a baby-talk voice. "Especially one this handsome."

"Can I show Pru the museum room?" Yiayia asked as they gathered around the baby.

Boy, they were eager to get in there. "Oh, yes. Be sure to look on the coffee table for a stunning locket that I discovered hidden in that newel." She pointed to the carved ball that now sat a little straighter and more securely on the stair rail. "Well, Declan discovered it."

A couple of meaningful looks passed between Yiayia and Gramma Finnie, and even Molly raised a brow.

"What was he doing looking in the banister?" Yiayia asked a little breathlessly.

"He was fixing it," Evie explained when yet another incredibly unsubtle look bounced between the older women. "He's helping with some maintenance and repairs in exchange for my help with Judah."

"Well, that's very nice," Gramma Finnie said. "He's such a thoughtful lad."

"And so handsome and responsible," Yiayia added with a smile.

Evie was half tempted to shoot back, *No kidding, and how 'bout those shoulders?* But she just rocked the baby on her hip and smiled at them.

"Now, can we…" Yiayia tipped her head in the direction of the museum room.

"Yiayia hasn't stopped talking about that room," Pru said.

"You guys go explore." Molly put her arm around Evie's back. "Evie and I will get this exam done. Upstairs?"

"Oh, do you want me to take Danny so you two can concentrate on the dog?" Pru asked, reaching for her little brother.

Evie inched back with a playful warning look. "You will not take this bundle from my arms and expect to live."

Pru cracked up. "Okay, but he does get heavy."

"Unless you think he'll go crazy when he sees Judah?" Evie said to Molly.

"He's calm now," she answered. "And you look, whoa, happy."

"Any day now, Prudence," Yiayia called.

"Coming." She blew her brother a kiss. "Be good, Dan the Man." She took off with the grandmas, leaving Molly and Evie with the baby.

"She's incredible, Molly," Evie said, looking after the coltish teen, whose black hair swung like a pendulum as she left. "Beautiful and sweet."

"She gets better every year," Molly agreed. "I'd say she's the light of my life, then along came her father and brother. Now my life is so much…brighter."

A twinge of something that might be considered envy tapped at Evie's heart. Not that Molly didn't deserve every happiness, but wow. She had *every* happiness.

"I can see why. And, uh, Yiayia's quite the character, isn't she?" Evie added on a whisper.

"You have no idea." Molly gave an exaggerated eye roll.

"I think I do." She laughed and stroked Danny's sweet little cheek. "Look up the word sledgehammer, and there she is, ready to smash."

Molly laughed. "Subtlety is not her strong suit."

"Ya think?"

"I guess you've figured out they're matchmakers."

"Not much figuring out involved. Yiayia mentioned Declan before she said hello to me."

Molly laughed. "It's kind of hard not to have the whole family rooting for you and Dec, Evie. You've known each other forever. Aunt Colleen said she always thought you two would get married."

Declan's mother thought that? "The whole family?" she whispered playfully to the baby. "Even you, little man?"

He replied with another drool-filled giggle, then dropped his head onto her shoulder and stuck his thumb in his mouth, his fine hair tickling Evie's jaw.

"Oh!" she exclaimed as they started up the stairs. "My poor heart."

"Your poor ovaries," Molly volleyed back. "My sister-in-law Beck is four months pregnant and totally blames Danny and my nieces, baby Annabelle and Fiona. We're pretty sure Darcy, Cassie, and Grace are hard at work on the next Kilcannon-Mahoney baby boom."

A Mahoney baby boom. Something slipped inside Evie's chest. Something that had been slipping around an awful lot lately.

"You sure look like a natural with him," Molly whispered with a jab of her elbow. "You know it's not too late for you. You and someone…right out there in the garage."

"Ouch. That sledgehammer hurts, Yiayia Jr."

"Come on, Evie. It's so nice to see you and Declan together again."

"We're not together. He's fixing my warped windows…" She narrowed her eyes. "Which is not a euphemism for what you're thinking. So, can we talk about the MRIs I emailed you, Dr. Bancroft?"

"Only because that topic is easier for you, and you're holding my baby."

"Much easier, and don't worry, I won't drop him."

Molly smiled. "Okay, yes, I did get the images, and is it wrong to be excited about standing next to you while you perform a ventral slot? Because this is probably a career highlight for little old small-town vet me."

On far more comfortable turf now, Evie shared the surgery plan, with Molly asking all the right questions. By the time they reached Granddaddy's room, Evie was certain she'd made the perfect decision asking for Molly's assistance.

"Hey, Judah," Molly whispered as they walked in

quietly, both noticing that Granddaddy was sound asleep. "How you feeling, buddy?"

Judah lifted his head from where it rested on Granddaddy's arm.

"He looks comfortable," Molly said. "Are you hanging with your pal, Judah?"

Evie stayed a few feet away with the baby, giving Molly a chance to establish herself with the dog who watched her warily.

"He's protective," Molly mused.

Danny's head suddenly popped up from Evie's shoulder. "Mmmbah! Mmmbah!"

The sound made Judah get right up on all fours, his gaze shifting to Danny with one quick bark.

"Not all dogs are named Meatball," Molly told Danny.

Evie laughed. "How do you get Meatball from that?"

"I speak Danny."

"Mmmbah!" He hit a higher, louder note, his hand outstretched to the dog, who immediately forgot Granddaddy. Judah took a few steps to the edge of the bed, tail flipping excitedly.

Granddaddy stirred at the disruption, then slowly opened his eyes, bringing them to focus on Evie and Danny. "Did I die and go to heaven?"

The dog reacted by putting his head back and letting out a monstrous howl, making Danny shriek in response.

"I couldn't agree more!" Granddaddy exclaimed. "Our prayers have been answered."

"Granddaddy, don't get Judah excited," Evie said with a light warning in her voice. "It can hurt him to move that way. You remember my friend from vet school, Molly? And this is her little boy, Danny."

"Hi, Mr. Hewitt," Molly said cheerfully.

But disappointment registered on every crinkled feature of his face. "Not yours?" he asked Evie.

"Nope. Did not go out and buy a baby while you napped. Sorry." She came a little closer to the bed while Judah stared at Danny with wonder and maybe a little uncertainty, then started to sniff his tiny sneaker.

"Let him smell you, Danny," Molly said. "Like all new dogs."

As the dog came a little bit closer, Danny's little fists grabbed at Evie's T-shirt, and his eyes widened in trepidation. "Mmmbah."

"This doggy is Judah," Evie said, vaguely aware she was rocking side to side to keep Danny calm. "Molly's going to help me in surgery with Judah," Evie reminded her grandfather. "So she needs to do a quick exam on him again."

He nodded, unconcerned about the dog, riveted on the baby. "He looks good on you, Evie."

She laughed. "He's not the latest accessory, Granddaddy, but I cannot tell a lie. He *feels* good, too."

Molly guided the dog to the other side of the big bed where she could look at him, starting the exam with a gentle hand on Judah's back.

While she did that, Evie bounced the baby and moved closer to her grandfather. "This is Granddaddy Max. Can you say Max, Danny?"

"Maaaaa."

Her grandfather laughed and clapped his hands. "Oh, this one does my heart good."

Molly smiled at the exchange, but her concentration was clearly on Judah's spine. "We had a Great Dane with Wobblers come in a few months ago," she said. "Didn't need surgery, but acupuncture worked really well, along with laser therapy, but as usual, we had to bring physical therapists in from Asheville and Charlotte."

"There's no PT here?"

"Oh, there is at the college, but they're booked solid. They're available for their vet patients, so Judah will get one for post-op, but the regular old vets?" She shrugged. "Really hard for us to get access to a lot of services."

"No mobile services?"

"I wish." She eased Judah's snout up to look into his eyes. "And you can forget a neurologist. I can never find one within twenty miles for referrals."

"Well, I'm here until after the holidays. Call me."

She looked up from Judah. "Seriously? Because I have a seven-year-old Lab with epilepsy, and he is not responding to meds."

"I can look at him this week."

"Oh, you're a godsend, Evie. Now, look at me, big fella."

While Molly continued checking out the dog, Danny shifted his attention to Granddaddy, reaching out a stubby finger to point at him.

Granddaddy playfully snatched it. "I gotcha!"

Danny giggled and tried to free his finger, but Granddaddy held on. "Might have to take a bite," he sang playfully, snapping at his finger. "Whoops. No teeth."

"Got...got...ga-ga-ga."

"He's trying to say 'gotcha,'" Evie exclaimed.

"He's got a brain under that mop," Granddaddy teased as his old watery gaze shifted to Evie, his look so full of abject longing she almost laughed. But it wasn't funny. She knew what he wanted, knew he ached for it, probably as much as she did.

"Granddaddy," she whispered in warning.

"What? I was going to say you look so much like my Penny right now." He gave her a big old toothless grin. "Could be her holding your father. He had a bunch of dark hair, too." He sighed noisily, the grin fading. "Ah, Evangeline."

"Please," she said softly, fighting the rush of emotions and praying he didn't go on a baby tirade right then.

"Okay, I'm officially done," Molly said, looking from one to the other.

"That was fast," Max said.

Because Molly was helping her out of an awkward moment like the true friend she was.

"Molly's already examined him at her office," Evie said.

"Yep, this is just for paperwork," Molly agreed. "Judah is all yours again, Mr. Hewitt. You can rest."

He reached his hand out to Danny's sneaker, giving it a playful tap. "I know what I'll be dreaming about…"

"Say bye-bye," Molly told Danny. "Can you say bye-bye?"

"Ba ba ba ba!" he complied, making them laugh as Molly and Evie headed back into the hall.

"No pressure or anything, right?" Molly whispered. "Sorry if Danny made things worse for you."

"Worse?" She shifted him in her arms because he was getting heavy, but the last thing she wanted to do was give him up. "The only thing Danny did was, you know…" She pointed down and made her fingers explode. "Ovaries have detonated."

"Oh, Evie."

"Hey, you sound like him now." She tipped her head in the direction of her grandfather's room. "'The family tree is dying, Evangeline,'" she said, imitating his gruff voice.

"And that makes you feel…"

150

"Like I'm disappointing him," Evie confessed, then slowed as they stood outside one of the guest rooms. "And myself," she added softly, grateful to be able to confide in a trusted friend.

"I know you wanted a baby, Evie," Molly whispered. "I remember when you went the academic route because you thought it would be better for your schedule and the possibility of getting pregnant."

"But donor insemination was a bust, as you know. Not to mention I'm forty now."

"Not too old, and you said you passed all the tests."

"With flying…eggs."

"Anyway, you could still adopt," Molly said.

"It's more complicated and scarier than adopting a pet." She stroked Danny's cheek and leaned in. "And to make matters worse, my grandfather actually suggested to Declan that he…" She lifted her brows. "*Help* me."

Molly's eyes popped. "Like…*impregnate* you?"

"Like DI, only no pesky pipette. I assume."

"Evie, that's…extreme."

"No kidding. I actually think your grandmother suggested it to him when she was here."

Molly shook her head. "Doubtful. We talked about her conversation with him on the way over here, and she didn't mention a baby. She said they talked about the things that usually come before that, like man-on-one-knee followed by something old, something new…"

"Well, Granddaddy heard something that cries and eventually goes to college. At least that's what he mentioned to Declan."

Molly searched her face, thinking and, Evie could tell, considering the possibility. Didn't anyone realize that wasn't something to casually do?

"It's...not the worst idea in the world," Molly said, almost on cue.

"Molly!"

"What? You two are great friends."

"We were."

"He's back in this house," she said. "That's huge, and you know it."

"I do."

"And you're mature adults who could probably work something out. It wouldn't be like, you know, medical. It would be..."

*Sexual.* Evie felt her color rise.

"Fun," Molly finished with a laugh. "Of course, maybe you shouldn't take advice from a woman who got pregnant in the back of her mother's dog van at nineteen."

"Is *that* why Trace bought the van?" She almost choked, but then a burst of laughter rang out from the museum room.

"The grannies and Pru." Molly rolled her eyes. "I swear they're like a clique of eighth-grade girls."

"Come on, let's go see what's so funny." She gave Molly's arm a squeeze. "And thanks for the help up there."

Molly winked. "Anytime. And were you serious about seeing patients this week?"

"Absolutely."

They headed into the museum room, and all the smiles immediately disappeared, and Evie felt very much like she had walked in on...something.

"This room is so stinking cool," Pru said suddenly. "So much history!"

"Did you see the new necklace?" Evie asked. "There

are pictures of Evangeline and Gloriana Bushrod as babies."

They spent the next few minutes looking at some treasures, while Danny got comfy in Evie's arms again. She told them some of the stories and recited the litany of generations of Gloriana House, a tumult of family pride spilling over as she shared the names and some life highlights with the same enthusiasm Granddaddy did when he told the stories.

"Your family is like something out of a Jane Austen novel," Pru cooed.

"They were, once." Evie rested her cheek on the baby's head, letting her eyes close as more emotion caught hold of her throat.

"I'd love to hear someone play that piano," Yiayia said, pointing to the Krakauer.

"I'm sure it's wretchedly out of tune," Evie said.

"So?" Yiayia lifted a shoulder. "You should still play."

"But that would mean I'd have to put down this sleeping baby." She stroked his head and smiled at Molly. "I'm so…" *Jealous.* "Happy for you."

"Thanks," she said, holding up her phone. "I emailed the form to Vestal Valley and…" She used the phone to point to Evie's chest. "And I'm afraid he got to you."

She looked down at her T-shirt, smiling when she saw the two-inch-diameter wet spot from baby drool. "Oh, he got to me all right," she said, finally giving him up to his mother. "And worth every minute."

After a bit, she walked them to the door, and everyone exchanged hugs goodbye. As they started down the walk, Pru turned back.

"Bye, Aunt Evie!" she called.

"Goodbye, Pru. Come back soon."

"Oh, we will. If we do, can you play that cool piano?"

"If you want to cringe at how bad I am."

"I do!" She giggled and waved, then darted away to slip each of her arms around one of Gramma Finnie's and one of Yiayia's to help them down the driveway, the three of them laughing over some secret joke.

As Evie watched them leave, she put her hand over her heart, pressing against the wet spot Danny had left, letting out a sigh of bone-deep longing.

# Chapter Twelve

When Declan came in through the back, he found Evie standing at the open front door, staring out, even though he'd seen Molly's van pull out a few minutes ago.

He cleared his throat, making her turn quickly, her expression distant. "Oh, hi. I...didn't hear you."

He pointed to the chandelier. "Want to give the cleaning a go?"

She followed his gaze. "It's a little tricky."

"I can handle tricky."

"Okay. You have to climb into the crawl space, which is part of the attic accessible from a bedroom closet. From there, you crank it down, assuming the winch is functioning as it should, then the chandelier will lower to about five feet from the ground. That way, I can clean the crystal and polish the brass, but I can't get that done in one day."

"Why don't I go up and check it out, and if the device still works, I'll lower it. If it's safe to leave it that way, you can take a few days with the cleaning, and we'll raise it up Friday after my shift. Would that work?"

"Perfect." She took a few steps closer, eyeing him carefully. "You're really sure about all this, Declan?"

"You know what I'm sure about?" he asked, reaching for her hand. "That I don't want you to ask me if I'm sure anymore."

She laughed. "Deal."

"Seriously, E. I wouldn't be here to help if I held some kind of grudge against the place, okay?"

"I know that, and it's remarkable." She waved him to the stairs. "So come with me to the attic, which is a thousand degrees, so you'll be…even hotter. If that's possible."

He smiled at the unexpected compliment, noticing she had a certain glow since Molly and the gang had been there. Was that because she held Danny? Or talked to Molly? Or could it be…him?

Whatever it was, it made her even prettier.

"Down here, to the other side of the house." At the top of the stairs, she led him the opposite way of her grandfather's room.

"This was your parents' room," he remembered.

"Yep. There's a crawl-through access that goes above the entryway." She gestured him toward the closet, but as he walked, he looked out the double doors to an upstairs patio wrapped with fancy wrought iron.

He stood for a moment, staring at it, realizing exactly where he was. This was the bedroom, that was the veranda, or deck. So, the patio was beneath it…and the sunroom was under where he stood.

And then he wondered if he'd spoken too soon about being okay. Because this whole wing…

"Hey." Evie was suddenly next to him, curling her fingers around his arm. "Wanna skip it? A dirty chandelier is not worth…"

"Shhh." He put his finger over her lips, realizing that the more they casually touched, the more he wanted to, well, casually touch. "I want to, Evie. It's…good to let go."

"That is not the face of a man letting go of anything."

"This is all new, right?" He gestured toward the room. "New downstairs, upstairs, and that deck, right?"

She nodded. "Completely rebuilt from scratch."

"Then there are no ghosts." He slid an arm around her, suddenly so grateful for her very presence. "Show me the crawl space."

She led him into the walk-in closet, obviously much more modern than any other closet in the house. The shelves were empty except for a few boxes stored in one corner.

"Pull that, and the ladder comes down," she said, pointing at a thin white cord hanging from a two-foot-square door built into the ceiling. He'd seen hundreds of these in his life while fighting house fires that frequently started in attics. It was nice to pull one and not get slammed by billows of black smoke.

He easily dropped a set of folding stairs that led to the rafters and started climbing. "What am I looking for, exactly?"

"I've never been up there, but my dad said it's like some kind of crank coming out of the floor above the chandelier."

He poked his head into the tight space, squinting into the darkness and pulling a flashlight from a clip on his belt to guide his way. The beam immediately showed dancing dust and snowy-white insulation. With his flashlight, he could see into the rafters, including a distinct burn pattern along the wooden beams that held up the roof.

So, not *everything* had been rebuilt up here.

As he crawled into the space barely high enough for him to sit up, he closed his eyes for a moment, letting the impact of what he was doing hit him.

For twenty years, he'd avoided this damn street, and now he was not only in the house, he was in the fire. At least, where the fire had been. It started downstairs, just outside the sunroom on the patio, but when the second floor burned, these rafters caught some flames.

Right? Sometimes, it seemed that the parts of his brain connected to his father's death had long ago…shut down. He hadn't had anything to do with the investigation— hell, he'd been checked out and didn't even show up for work for a few months after Dad died.

He sure as hell never opened a single page of the file to find out the details of what had happened. Braden had, but he handled arson dogs. Connor might have—he honestly didn't know. But Declan couldn't bear to read one word of the reports.

He shimmied on his belly another fifteen feet, then spotted the two-handled chandelier crank. It had wires wrapped around it, obviously installed when it was transformed from an antique oil light to the electric kind. He tugged at them, making sure they were to code, then placed the flashlight so the beam lit the winch.

Managing to sit up, he put both hands on the crank. "I got it, Evie," he called. "Just turn?"

"Yes. It'll stop when it reaches five feet. How is it up there?"

Freaking awful. He didn't answer, mostly because he didn't want to lie and say, *Gee, it's fine and dusty and not kicking me in the nuts or anything.*

"Can you turn it?"

He jerked back at the sound of Evie's voice not far behind him. "What are you doing up here?" He glanced over his shoulder to see her crawling closer.

"Backup."

"I don't need…" When her hand touched him, and the warmth of her body got close to his, he squeezed his eyes shut, stunned at how much he *did* need backup. "Thanks," he said gruffly, turning his full attention to the winch. "Let me get this thing."

Scooting into a sitting position, he twisted the lever, using all his strength to move the rusty old crank. Once he got started, it was easier, turning once, then twice, then finally feeling the weight of that massive lighting fixture begin to move as the chain slid through a channel.

"Another genius of Victorian design," he said, his voice tighter than he'd expected it to be.

Then he felt her fingers on his back, the lightest touch, a gentle stroke. "I realized while I was in the closet that the attic wasn't rebuilt," she said softly.

"Nope, this is original," he said. "It's okay." Even though it wasn't okay. Being in this airless, depressing place where the fire that took his father once raged wasn't okay at all.

"I wouldn't have asked you to come up here if I'd—"

"It's *fine*, Evie."

Her hand stilled. "No, Declan, it's not fine. And the sooner you actually acknowledge that, the sooner we can…"

The crank stopped turning, so the chandelier must be down. Still, he kept his hand on the metal handles, staring at the electrical cords, sweat stinging his temples and eyes.

"Declan." She added some pressure.

"Come on, E. I'm—"

"Going back to that place." Her hand moved to his shoulder, trying to turn him around.

Oh *man*. "What place?"

"Where you disappear behind some massive wall and shut me out and make me want to cry." Her voice cracked, and he had to turn around, meeting her gaze, which was damp with tears and dark with hurt. "I can take anything, Declan," she whispered. "I can take anger and guilt and shame and regret and even blame. I can take anything in the world, but you…disappearing into that place again."

*That place.* He knew exactly what she meant. The basement of his soul. His dark, dark, lonely, cut-off-from-the-world place. His personal hell, where he'd been a frequent visitor for the better part of twenty years.

He wet his lips, took a breath, and closed his eyes.

"Sorry," he whispered, the best he could do. Then he returned his attention to the crank, yanking on the lever to be sure it was locked in place. "You want to go downstairs and check the height? Make sure you can reach it?"

She didn't move for a long time, her hand still on his back making small circles, like she might on a wounded animal that needed nothing but compassion. "It was the worst hurt of my life." The words were so soft, not much more than a whisper. But they hit like she'd slammed him over the head with one of those charred attic beams.

He'd *hurt* her. Of course he had. He knew that. But he never let himself think about *how much*. He was too worried about his own hurt.

"I mean, it was one thing to endure…the tragedy of it," she continued softly. "The loss. The aftermath for my grandparents. And my parents' decision to up and leave the country, which really kind of sucked, even though I was in college."

He'd never even thought of that. He knew they moved away a few months after the fire, but her mom was always a little unconventional. Anyway, he'd been too wrapped up in his own grief to think about hers. Both her parents were alive—at least that's how he rationalized his lack of empathy.

"It must have hurt," he managed.

"But you…" She sighed, and her hand stilled. "Losing you was the saddest thing of all."

He turned to face her, the tight space, the heat of the attic, and the faint scent of decades-old smoke infusing every breath.

"I'm sorry." This time, the word carried a lot more weight than when he'd mumbled it a few seconds earlier.

As soon as he spoke, something shifted in his heart. No, it moved like a boulder, freeing up space he hadn't even known was there.

He could feel her next breath. "Declan, I—"

He put a finger against her mouth, suddenly, desperately needing her forgiveness. Needing it like air or water or…love.

"I'm really sorry," he said, a little louder. "Shutting you out was wrong and selfish and incredibly immature."

She didn't say a word, her eyes locked on him, the flashlight casting shadows on her face.

"I am so…" He put his hands on her shoulders to hold on, because it felt like a dam was breaking, and it might sweep him, or her, away. "Holy hell, I do not know what took me so long to say this. I was so wrong to do that to you, Evie. I shut you out and cut you off and…"

His eyes stung, and not from sweat. But he powered on, unafraid of the lump in his throat, because nothing, not one lousy tear, was going to stop this long-overdue apology. "I cannot believe I did that."

"Why did you?"

"Because…"

"Please don't say because you were an idiot. Please tell me the truth. I deserve the truth."

"Yes, you do." Sweat trickled down his temple, and a tear threatened at the corner of his eye. "But I'm not sure I can explain it without…a shrink."

"Try." There was so much plea and ache in the word, his heart twisted.

"Evie, I was in the blackest, ugliest place. For years, I barely made it through a day. I faked it half the time. It hurt so damn much to lose that man." He looked down, riding a wave of grief so familiar, he didn't notice when the waves came and went anymore. "I put all my focus on work and the family. I felt so responsible for…everything. My siblings, my mother, the whole thing became my job."

"Were you angry with me?"

"Angry?" He drew back. "With you? Why would I be?"

"Because I was the one who wanted you to change your shift with your dad so we could go camping on our birthday."

"I agreed to ask him. That wasn't your fault."

"You don't, way down deep inside, blame me?"

He searched her face, sweat rolling down his temples now. "No," he said.

"And you don't blame my mother?"

"No more than I'd blame the person who leaves the

Christmas lights on and there's a short circuit. Accidents happen."

"But if she hadn't put those rags in a bucket when it was so hot outside, maybe…"

"They probably smelled and she didn't want them in the studio. She didn't realize that the sun would move and bear down on them. I don't blame her, Evie."

She swallowed hard. "I feel like that and the fact that I made you go that night always stuck in your head and you blamed *me*."

Had he? Was that possible? He closed his eyes and marched down to that subterranean hellhole, trying to flip on the metaphorical lights so he could see the truth. Did he blame her? Did he shut her out because he felt like Dad would be alive if she hadn't been…

Maybe. Maybe he did. And that was another wretched thing he had to apologize for.

"Evie, if I did, I'm sorry for that, too. I'm really sorry. Because I know you can't backtrack and second-guess everything that leads to an accident. If you did, you'd never leave the house or get in your car. I asked Dad to take my shift, we went camping that night, your mom stored rags, and it was hot. That big porch collapsed, and a firefighter was in the wrong place at the wrong time. No one person is to blame."

She processed all that for a moment, her shoulders sinking under his hands. "Then…why? Why not call me? Why not talk to me, Dec? For twenty years."

He closed his eyes because the questions were fair…and the answers were unforgivable. But he ached for her forgiveness.

"Once so much time passed, it seemed futile. And in the beginning, for at least five or six years, I was so mad at...*everything*. I couldn't go back to where we were...that night. Going back to you would be like getting some kind of prize I didn't deserve."

She stared at him, confusion darkening her eyes.

"I loved you, Evie." His voice cracked with the admission, and he pulled her closer, feeling that she was as damp and shaky as he was. "I knew it that morning. I *loved* you. I was going to wait for you, marry you, have a family with you, and live like the happiest man on earth, and then...wham. Half an hour later, it was like God said, 'Uh, not so fast, son.'"

"Oh, Dec." She gave a sad, sad sigh. "So, you thought if you had reached out and...and loved me, then something bad would happen again?"

"I don't know if it was that cut-and-dried. Maybe. I did see you, and every time, I freaking froze up. Like, you don't bump into someone outside the hardware store and launch into 'Oh, by the way, about this last ten years?'" He shook his head. "I didn't know what to say or how to say it. I'm not good with words."

She stroked his arm. "You're doing okay right now."

The tenderness in her voice and gentle touch folded him in half. It was like she instinctively knew how to soothe and put a balm on the worst hurt and ease the pain. Just made it...go away.

"Look, we can analyze what went on in my head for twenty years, but I'd rather not." He put both hands on her cheeks, holding her delicate face, forcing their gazes to lock. "Only three words matter now. *I am sorry*. I'm so, so sorry."

She exhaled softly as if the apology hit somewhere deep inside, but then took his hands and brought them to her lips. She kissed his knuckles and closed her eyes, and

Declan felt washed with her forgiveness and a single tear that rolled down her cheek and onto his hand.

"You can't take all the blame," she whispered.

"Yeah, I can."

"I could have tried harder to get to you. I could have picked up the phone a dozen or more times in twenty years. I could have shown up at the fire station and demanded your attention. I could have done something more than stammer when I saw you outside the hardware store or stare at you after Rusty's surgery."

"I left the waiting room like an asshole." Why had he been so scared of talking to her?

"We were both afraid." Of course she knew it was fear. She knew him so well. "So, yes, you froze me out. But I didn't apply any heat to thaw you."

He let that sink in, feeling things slip and slide into place for the first time in years. "Why didn't you?" he asked.

"Because, deep down inside, I felt like I deserved your anger."

"No, you—"

"Declan." She quieted him with a squeeze of her hands. "My house and my family were saved, but your father was lost. And I *was* the one who insisted we go camping on our actual birthday, not you, which could have changed everything. And that fire started because my mother is just this side of flaky." Her throat thickened. "So I figured you hated me."

He choked in disbelief. "I couldn't hate you. It's not possible. I..." *Love you.* "Could never hate you. So, please, Evie. Forgive me."

She dropped her head and let her hair brush his hands. "I forgive you." The words were barely whispered air, but to him, it sounded like she sang them and trumpets blew.

"Thank you, E."

She raised her head and pressed a kiss to his forehead. "Now you have to forgive yourself and give life a real chance."

He wrapped his arms around her and hugged her closer, needing to express his feelings, but not trusting his lousy words. Instead, he held her so close he could feel her heart beat and each breath go in and out.

"Declan," she whispered.

"Evie." He smiled.

"Are we good now?"

"We're a hell of a lot better than we were." Inching back, he looked at her. "Thank you." He touched his lips to hers. "Thank you for being so…Evie."

He felt her smile as he kissed her lightly, tasting tears that could have been his or hers. It didn't matter.

After a moment, he opened his eyes and stared at the wall behind her…at the burn pattern of black in the brown wood.

She turned to follow his gaze, then blocked his view. "Don't look at it."

"I have to." He stared at the scorched wood. "I have to face that fire, because if I don't, it'll consume me for another twenty years. That fire took enough. It took all those years. All that possibility."

It wrenched his heart to think they could have been friends, lovers, partners, spouses…parents.

"Maybe it's not too late," she whispered.

Holy hell. Maybe it wasn't.

# Chapter Thirteen

Dogs. If anything had changed about Bitter Bark in the last twenty years, Evie realized, it had to be the number of dogs. And tourists.

There was an abundance of both in Bushrod Square, surprising for a Wednesday morning. This place had definitely grown from a sleepy small town in the foothills of the Blue Ridge Mountains to a bit of a tourist mecca, not unlike Asheville and Boone. But the difference here was that most of those tourists came with a four-legged companion, which only made the whole town even more appealing to Evie.

The change surely meant a huge boon to businesses that catered to animals, like Kilcannon Veterinary, where she was headed now to see two of Molly's patients. Since she was early, Evie took the time to stroll through the square and soak up an early autumn morning in what would always feel like "home" even if she lived in Raleigh the rest of her life.

In the middle of the square, she paused to look up at the statue that stood dead center. Thaddeus Ambrose Bushrod cast a mighty shadow—over the town and her life. Here she was, the last of her line facing the first.

"Sorry, Big Bad Thad," she whispered. "As a Royal Navy man, you can appreciate my favorite quote. That ship has—"

"Evie?"

She spun at the sound of a woman's voice, feeling a rush of warmth to her cheeks. "Oh God, I've been caught."

"Talking to your great-great-great-grandfather? There are few things I respect more."

Who would know how many greats there were? Evie studied the other woman, somewhere in her mid-fifties, with brown hair, glasses, and the look of a librarian. Of course—a librarian.

"Nellie Shaker?" she asked, remembering the woman known as Bitter Bark's top historian. "How nice to see you."

"And you, Evie." Nellie came closer to offer her hand, which turned into a quick hug.

"Yeah, I was talking to a statue," Evie admitted with fake sheepishness, pointing her thumb over her shoulder. "So, guilty as charged."

Nellie smiled up at the bronze giant. "He was a great man who started a great town. Nothing wrong with thanking him on the way past."

"Well, I wasn't exactly thanking him," she confessed. "How are you, Nellie? Are you still running the library and making sure the children of Bitter Bark pay their late fees?"

She laughed. "I am, and I've been the head of the Historical Society for almost a decade. So, that's why I share your love and respect"—she pointed at Thad—"for this man right here."

"Good for you."

"I heard you're going to be in town for quite some time," she said. "You know what that means?"

Oh God. Was this going to be yet another person encouraging a romance with Declan? They'd made huge progress on Monday, but by silent agreement, they were taking things slow.

"I'm not sure. What does it mean?"

"You'll be here for Founder's Day on October 22nd."

"I will be," she said. "Is there still a parade?"

Nellie's face fell. "Not since your grandmother died. Your grandfather seemed to lose interest."

"Oh, he doesn't get out much, I'm afraid."

"Well, we do a lot of dog-related events now," she said. "But that Founder's Day parade used to be quite the event."

"I remember," Evie said on a laugh, holding up her hand to do a queen's wave.

"You always looked like you were having fun. And how is Gloriana House?" Nellie asked. "I haven't been there for many years. The Historical Society wanted to do an event there once, but your grandfather…"

"I'm sorry. Granddaddy's getting up in years and hasn't been as involved as he used to be. But the house hasn't changed a bit, for better or worse."

"I'm glad it hasn't changed," Nellie said. "That room your grandmother created? It's an absolute treasure. And full of them!"

"The museum room? You're more than welcome to come and visit anytime, Nellie. I know you like to do those display events at the library. Why don't you borrow a few items for Founder's Day?" Her eyes widened. "We found a locket that belonged to Amelia Bushrod with baby pictures of Evangeline and Gloriana."

Nellie gasped. "Oh, I'd love to see that! And I might take you up on that offer, Evie." She thought for a moment, then got a little bit closer. "You know, I have a better idea."

"You do? I'm open."

"Well, wait until you hear it." Nellie searched her face as if trying to decide what to say next. "I used to talk about this with your grandmother, but we never did it. But maybe it's time."

Intrigued, Evie nodded encouragingly.

"How would you feel about opening up Gloriana House for a 'living museum' over Founder's Day weekend? Just the downstairs," she said quickly. "We could rope off rooms so any visitors would be limited to the living area and the dining room and museum room. If your grandfather's not up for it, he can stay clear of any people, but I think it would be so wonderful to show off some of that magnificent history you have in the house. Perfect for Founder's Day, and we've been looking for ideas to kick this year's up a notch."

Tipping her head, Evie considered that. "I kind of like that idea. There's so much beauty in the house that no one ever sees."

"I couldn't agree more. The whole history of Bitter Bark is woven into the fabric of that place."

The words reached down and twisted something in Evie's very soul. "Aww, Nellie. That's so true. I'd love to open up the house for people to appreciate it like you do."

"Really?" Nellie's whole face lit up. "I could help you stage and prepare the rooms so you don't have a ton of work."

"It really wouldn't be that hard since some of the front rooms haven't been redecorated in eons."

"How awesome is that?" she exclaimed. "And throughout the rooms, you could place items from the past, family pictures, that letter from Amelia." She pressed her hands to her chest. "Your grandmother let me hold it once."

"How sweet you are." Touched by the reverence in her voice and expression, Evie reached out to put a hand on her arm. "And I really think this is a fantastic idea."

"I've always loved that house. I'm so terrified that someday an out-of-towner will nab the hilltop lot, tear down the house, and build some McMansion in its place."

Evie sucked in a soft breath. Was *that* what James Bell had in mind? No. He had too much respect for the property. She hoped. "I'd hate that," she agreed.

"You know what else we can do?" Nellie asked. "Maybe we could have a private catered event on Friday night. Then an open house the next day, for the official Founder's Day celebration that Saturday? Oh, the entire Historical Society would simply explode with happiness."

Evie's eyes widened, swept up with the idea and Nellie's infectious enthusiasm. "Grandmama Penelope used to have costume parties when I was little. We have so many dresses and suits in storage."

"A costume party?" Nellie looked like she might burst with excitement.

"Yes!" Evie gave a little clap as the whole thing started to take shape in her mind. Not only would it be a wonderful way to honor the house and its history, Granddaddy might enjoy something like that. "I'm happy to lend some of the clothes, as long as everything gets returned. I have gowns from Evangeline and Gloriana, and my grandmother's, too."

"Evie, this is the best news! I'll tell the society at our

next meeting, and we'll start putting together a guest list. It'll be a night to remember! In fact, that should be our theme."

"I love that," Evie exclaimed. "Then we better start planning, since there's not much time."

They exchanged numbers and hugs and a few more ideas, long enough that Evie had to rush across the square to get to her appointment on time. But she was still on a Bitter Bark high when she made her way into a crowded vet office across the square.

"Oh, Dr. Hewitt." The receptionist beamed as soon as she walked in. "Dr. Bancroft is so excited to have you here today."

"You bet I am!" Molly called from an open doorway. "Grab a jacket, Evie. And don't kill me. I have four more patients coming in to see you."

Kill her? A zing of excitement Evie hadn't felt in a long time whipped through her as the woman behind the desk held out a turquoise lab coat.

"Here. You'll be covered in fur if you don't wear one," the young woman said.

"Oh, a little pet hair never hurt anyone." Evie took the jacket and slid it on like a comfortable pair of old shoes. "I'm coming, Molly."

She really couldn't wipe the smile from her face now.

She was needed in this town. She was wanted in this town. She was at home in this town. What exactly had kept her away all these years?

Or maybe the question should be: *Who* had kept her away?

"I'm used to you working past your shift, Big D, but now you're cleaning out the storage garage?" Connor came deeper into the fire station sweatbox, as they called the outdoor unit, where Declan was up to his elbows in cardboard boxes. "What are you doing in here?"

Declan lifted a paper. "Just looking at some old files."

Connor took a folder from an open box and blinked when he realized what it was. "What the hell, Dec?"

"I never read the investigation reports on the Gloriana House fire," he said, looking up at his brother. "Have you?"

"Skimmed," he admitted with a shrug. "Doesn't change anything."

Except it could change Declan. Maybe if he could finally understand exactly what happened that night, he could close and lock the door to that wretched emotional basement, never to be entered again. And that could mean...he and Evie might have a real chance.

"Did you know that fire was out so fast only one volunteer crew got called?" Declan asked.

"You know that sometimes the worst things happen at fires that don't seem that bad." Connor lifted his brows. "It's one of the first things you learn in this business."

Declan swallowed. "You also learn not to lose sight of your partner. Especially when you're in a hundred-year-old structure and under a wooden balcony."

"You think Dad caused his own death?" Connor's voice grew tight. "Dad? The original believer in 'we go in together, we come out together'?"

"He also knew better than anyone that there is always an element of the unknown in a fire." Declan's gaze skimmed one of the debriefing reports. "And something wasn't known in this fire. Why did he make that decision to go deeper and trap himself outside of that sunroom?"

"You think he should have known better? That he made a mistake?" Indignation colored every one of Connor's words.

"I think…" Declan squinted at a page, then flipped it. "That there must have been a compelling reason to go under the overhang and try to get inside the sunroom."

"He probably spotted the seat of the fire."

"But he was there early, and the rags combusted outside," Declan reasoned.

"Then maybe he saw someone inside."

"Everyone in that house was already out, accounted for, and standing in the street."

Of course, Connor had no comeback to that.

But there had to be some reason Dad broke protocol. His partner's interviews had been no help, since he'd stated repeatedly that one minute he could see Joe Mahoney, and the next he couldn't. And Lieutenant Rainey had moved to New York not long after Dad died and, sadly, was lost in 9/11, so they couldn't ask him now.

Connor put the file down and perched on a couple of boxes. "You think this'll make you feel better, or help you forgive Evie?" No surprise, his shrewd brother would cut to the quick.

"There's nothing to forgive," Declan said. "But could I feel better? I don't know. I do know that reading these is…long overdue."

"You took it hardest," Connor said simply.

Declan eyed his brother, remembering the brash teenager who'd emerged after Dad died. Work and maturity had toned him down, and Sadie Hartman had tamed the last of the beast in him, but still. "You didn't take it all too well, either."

He acknowledged that with a shrug. "So, what else are you finding in there?"

"One arson investigator didn't sign off on that final decision. A guy named Kirby Lewis, a specialist the NCBI brought in. He said there was more than one burn pattern, and the inside one wasn't consistent with the combustion of linseed oil in painting rags that started outside."

Connor nodded. "But read the whole report. The rags blew up in the heat. No one disputes that."

"It says here that Kirby Lewis found lighter fluid inside the house. I had no idea." Of course, he'd ignored every word about the fire at the time.

"But don't they have a lighter collection in that house? It made sense there would be lighter fluid."

"Yeah, and a sunroom that was adjacent to the covered patio was where Max cleaned his lighters. Still, I wonder why one guy didn't agree."

"Hang on." Connor pulled out his phone and touched the screen. "Braden knows the details inside out."

"He does?" Declan drew back with surprise. "How the hell did I not know that?"

"Because no one talks to you about this fire, Dec. You snarl like a ticked-off Rottweiler." He talked into his phone. "Hey. Come back to the storage garage for a minute." He waited a beat. "Eat later. Family business."

Not two minutes later, Braden walked in wearing his Bitter Bark FD T-shirt and department-issued khakis, carrying a half-eaten banana. "What's so important that I can't finish chow before a call comes in?"

"The fire that killed Dad," Declan said simply. "You've studied all these files?"

"I actually did a paper on that fire during my canine arson training."

Good God, did the whole family protect him from anything that had to do with Dad? A new shame crawled up Declan's chest.

"This is why you wanted to train arson dogs?" he guessed.

Braden's blue eyes flickered with a silent confirmation.

"So you think it was arson. You think this Kirby Lewis guy has a legit point?" Declan asked.

His youngest brother blew out a noisy puff of air, leaning on a stepstool. "First of all, you need to know who and what that guy was—a legend in arson investigation, but also cuckoo for Cocoa Puffs, if you get my drift."

"Was?" Declan asked. "Is he dead?"

"No. He's retired and so far off the grid, I doubt you could find him. More than one arsonist who managed to get paroled would like to."

Declan winced. "So he's really good? And he didn't buy the linseed oil as the origin?" He looked from one brother to the other. "Doesn't that bother you guys?"

"Not me," Connor said. "Read the Bureau report. The North Carolina State Bureau of Investigation is not cuckoo for anything. The cause was accidental. Or, as I like to say, human stupidity." At Declan's look, Connor shrugged. "Hey, just calling it as I see it. A lifelong painter should know better than to stick linseed oil rags in a container and put it outside on one of the hottest days of the year."

"Says here she snapped it closed."

"And then the wind knocked it over and opened it." Connor pointed at something he'd read on one of the pages. "Couldn't have been closed tightly enough."

Declan turned to Braden. "What else do you know about this Lewis guy, besides being nuts and good at his job?"

"He finds arson where it may or may not be," Braden said. "He also finds it where other investigators miss it."

"Which would be his job," Declan said.

"Yeah, and he cracked some big cases. But he also spent thousands of taxpayer dollars trying to prove some fires that were clearly accidental were really arson. He was a lone wolf, too. Not on anyone's payroll, but brought in by individual departments, usually when there's an LODD."

Because a line-of-duty death was the thing that made any department ultra-introspective and determined to find a culprit other than human error by one of their own. Especially one as respected as Captain Joseph Mahoney had been.

"Do you think Lewis was trying to find arson where others missed it in this case?" Declan asked, holding up a file.

"There was nothing else going on at the time to support arson," Connor said. "No suspects, no one unexpected at the scene, and no pattern of any other fires purposely set in the whole county at the time."

"I know," Braden said. "But I managed to get my hands on his notes when I wrote that paper, which aren't in the files. He made a pretty compelling argument that there was a lighter fluid spray in the burn pattern on the sunroom wall that was adjacent to the patio. Either somebody accidentally squirted the fluid all over the wall, or it could have been used as an accelerant to start the fire and the rags combusted from the heat of the flames."

A low-grade hum rolled through Declan's whole body. "And they…" He looked down at the report, seeing nothing—not a word—about that. "Ignored that?"

"They ignored Kirby Lewis," Braden said. "But I will say, they had canines in there the next day, and they did find the lighter fluid, but since the fire burned outside because of the chemical rags and inside near a desk with a bunch of lighters, they couldn't say with certainty that the lighter fluid was the cause. And the rags clearly combusted, so the most obvious conclusion was that they started the fire."

Obvious to everyone but Kirby Lewis.

"And no one else questioned the veracity of this investigation," Connor added. "It went on for months, was extremely thorough, and followed every protocol. That's why it hasn't haunted me."

But it sure as hell was haunting Declan, especially now as he read the report. "Any chance you could get this guy back *on* the grid so I can talk to him, Braden?" he asked.

"Depends on how he feels about the case, I guess. I can try. Let me see if I can scare up some intelligence on his whereabouts."

Connor turned a page of the file he held, nodding as he read. "This lighter fluid as possible accelerant *is* interesting, but the only fingerprints on the can they found were Max's, who handled the lighters all the time. Your eccentric arson investigator was soundly overruled."

"All the more reason to talk to him," Declan said.

Connor closed the file. "You sure you want to open that can of worms?"

Declan choked. "You're kidding, right? Our father died in this fire."

"If it was a mistake with the chemical rags, it's Evie's mother who carries that," Connor said. "But if it was set by someone spraying lighter fluid? Then you're essentially accusing someone living in the house of arson and, technically, homicide. Twenty years after the case was closed." He stared at Declan as that sank in. "You sure you want to go there, bro?"

Good God, did he? How far back would that set him with Evie?

Connor slid the file back in a box. "It seems to me that you two have enough obstacles to overcome without looking for some made-up ones."

Were they made up? Declan looked at Braden. "What do you think?"

"I have a lot of respect for Kirby Lewis, and I have always thought there might be more to this fire than some mishandled rags. But if you look really close, Dec, you'll see a subtext in that file."

"That says…"

"Dad broke protocol," he said softly. "We have no idea why, and we'll never know. But if you're looking to place blame, there's plenty for our family as well as Evie's."

"I'm not looking to place blame," he said. "I'm trying to get closure."

Connor huffed a sigh.

"What?" Dec asked, standing up to challenge his brother with a harsh look. "Is that so wrong?"

"Declan." Braden, ever the peacemaker between his two older brothers, put his hand on Declan's shoulder. "That fire…" He glanced at the file boxes, then back to Declan. "Makes you disappear. And as far as we're concerned, we lost enough that night."

"I'm sorry about that," he said, looking from one to the other. They had different ways of showing their love, but he respected them both enormously, as men and as firefighters. And he loved them as the true brothers they were. "It seems I owe a lot of people apologies for how I've acted for twenty years."

"Nah. Yeah, maybe." Connor laughed easily. "We don't hold grudges, Big D."

Braden lifted his brow in question. "So. Kirby Lewis? Yes or no?"

Declan didn't really have to think about it. "Yes. I'd like to talk to him."

He wasn't manufacturing obstacles, he told himself. He was trying to get rid of them. He had to face everything about the fire if he was ever going to escape the hold it had on him. Until he was free of that, he couldn't be all he wanted to be for Evie.

Or was he, as his sister suggested, looking for ways to sabotage this relationship?

Damn it. Did his whole damn family know him better than he knew himself?

# Chapter Fourteen

Evie was wiped out by late Friday afternoon. In addition to taking Judah in for his pre-op appointment, she'd ended up spending the better part of two days at Molly's office, seeing patients from as far away as Holly Hills and Chestnut Creek. Today, in between painstakingly cleaning the chandelier, she'd studied up on the CVS procedure, watching videos from around the world, including one of her performing the surgery on a Great Dane about five years ago.

Was that the last time she'd done the procedure? She wasn't sure, but she felt ready. And now, it was time to give Judah his last meal before the surgery in the morning. After she finished up with Granddaddy's dinner, she brought Judah down the front stairs, which he navigated easier than the back, for the chicken feast she'd prepared.

"You have to eat well tonight," she told him. "You have a very big day tomorrow."

But as she headed into the kitchen, a tap at the front door stopped her, and the silhouette that was becoming pretty familiar thrilled her.

That thrill only deepened when she opened the door to Declan.

"Hello," she said slyly, leaning against the doorjamb and crossing her arms. Her gaze dropped over the blue button-down and navy trousers, then settled on the simple badge on his broad chest. "Captain."

"Hello." He reached for her chin and tipped her face up to meet his gaze. "Doctor."

"Are you here to raise a chandelier, or are you just glad to see me?"

"Both." He laughed and came into the house, heading straight for the dog, who barked in greeting. "Hey, buddy. Is she corrupting you with off-color jokes?"

"Of course I am. And he thinks my bad humor is paw-some, right, Judah? It's keeping us both from getting nervous about tomorrow."

Declan straightened and turned to her. "I didn't think you got nervous."

"It's been a while. I've been studying the surgery and looking over his images, so I have a plan, but I want to be ready." She wrapped herself as if she were chilly, but the truth was she had to do something with her hands, or she'd reach out to grab hold of him.

Silent, he examined the massive chandelier that hung a little lower than eye level. "Sparkly."

She lifted her hands. "I have the Brasso under my nails to prove it."

He took those hands in his, examining her nails. "They look like surgeon's hands to me."

She wiggled her fingers. "They better be tomorrow."

For a moment, he looked over their joined hands and into her eyes, long enough to make her knees a little weak and her toes curl in her sneakers. She tried to come up with a joke—anything—but her brain went blank as she stared back at him.

The only thing she could think of was how good it would feel to kiss him. A lot of kisses. All-night kisses.

So where was her joke? She had…nothing. Just raging hormones sending blasts of heat low in her belly that somehow managed to fry her sense of humor.

"I can get it up," he said.

"Oh, I bet you can."

"I meant the chandelier, and that was cheap and easy, even for you."

She gave a playful laugh and poked his chest. "There's so much I could do with cheap and easy."

He rolled his eyes and snagged the finger pressing into him. "Remember I'm just off a twenty-four-hour shift, so I can't keep up with your mind, even when it's teetering on the edge of the gutter."

"Oh, you must be exhausted."

"Not at all, but I am starving, so let me get this chandelier up, and then I'll be back to beg for food like a dog." He tossed a look at Judah. "No offense, J."

"I'll make you dinner," she offered quickly.

"Or we can go out."

As appealing as a dinner date with Declan was, she shook her head. "Granddaddy was a little out of it, and I don't want to leave Judah. I'd love to cook for you, though. I made my grandfather spaghetti and can whip up some more with a salad. Yours won't even have to be cut in small pieces. Yes?"

"Are you kidding? Yes, please. Be right back." He took the stairs two at a time, leaving Judah at the bottom, panting as he watched him.

"Clearly, I know how you feel, bud." She guided the

dog with her to the kitchen to start dinner, and Declan was back in less than five minutes.

She glanced at him, knowing the impact the attic had had on him last time he was there, but he seemed cool, calm, and kind of sexy in his work clothes. God, not *kind of*. Just totally hot.

Oblivious to her hormone-infused thoughts, Declan leaned down again to get close to Judah. "Is he eating anything these days?"

"A little. And he has to eat something before six tonight, last meal prior to surgery. I'm cutting up some chicken for him." She turned with the dog bowl, and Declan took it, setting it down in front of Judah.

For a moment, the pure domesticity of it all hit Evie square in the gut, even more than her primal physical attraction. This was worse than hormones. This was…a physical ache.

The togetherness of cooking in the kitchen, with a dog, the late afternoon sun pouring golden light through the windows. What would it be like…

"He polished that right off," Declan said, crouching to gently love on the dog. "Good boy, Judah."

"Would you like wine?" she asked.

"Just ice water, thanks. I don't drink much."

"Really?" she asked, getting a glass from the cabinet while he washed his hands. "I remember that you liked to borrow your grandmother's Irish whiskey now and again."

"I'm famous for holding my drinks and not actually drinking them, if you ask my brothers. But don't let me stop you if you want some wine."

"Not tonight. I have surgery in twelve hours."

While she poured them ice water, he stepped close to

one of the antique oil lamps by the back door. "Please tell me you never light these."

"Of course not. I doubt they would work, but they do have to be polished, sadly."

"Want me to put that on the handyman list?" he asked, taking the glass she handed him.

"The list is getting longer, Declan."

He clinked her glass. "More reasons to see you, Evie."

She smiled and took a sip. "So you don't drink because you think you could lose control, or because you never know when you might get called in?" she guessed.

"I stopped drinking once I had my family to take care of." He angled his water glass and glanced at it thoughtfully. "Plus, once you have Jameson's in a paper cup with your best friend, every other drink after that is a letdown."

*Jameson's in a paper cup.*

A ribbon of emotion curled through her at the memory as she tapped the glasses again. "To good drinks we've had in the past."

She purposely let the conversation drop, asking him questions about work as she started the pasta water and pulled the salad fixings from the fridge.

Taking a serrated knife from the block, he started cutting tomatoes, all the while telling her about life at the fire station and all the administrative work it involved, while Judah snoozed under the table, satisfied and blissfully ignorant of what tomorrow would hold.

He stayed there when they set the table, barely moving during the hour or so they lingered over dinner and more conversation, mostly chatting about the Founder's Day event and how excited Granddaddy was for the party they'd have here that weekend.

By the time they'd finished, the glow in the room wasn't just from the setting sun. Dinner had been perfect.

"I have an idea," Declan said as they cleaned up together. "How about we take Judah for a slow walk? It's probably his last one for a while."

"That's brilliant. Let me run up and see if Granddaddy's awake, and I'll let him know."

But he was sound asleep, and a few minutes later, Evie grabbed a hoodie and met Declan and Judah in the driveway. "A walk through Ambrose Acres?" she suggested.

"He's okay without a leash?"

"A leash would be miserable for him. Even a harness. This is Judah. He won't leave our side."

He took her hand, which felt like the most natural move in the world, and they started toward the street, taking it slow for the dog, who sidled up next to Declan. "So you *do* still love me," he said, rubbing Judah's head.

"You talking to him or me?" Evie teased.

He gave a slow smile and slid a look sideways. "I already know the answer to that, E."

She laughed, so grateful they could fall back into easy jokes and the comfort of a lifetime of friendship.

"Hey, I know we missed a few, but how about a two-decade-long round of the Birthday Game?" she suggested.

"Wow, that's a blast from the past."

"A fun one," she said. "I'll start. Best movie?"

"In the last twenty years?" He narrowed his eyes, thinking. "Well, I did think of you when *Lord of the Rings* came out. We'd have liked watching any of those together, and I remember you devoured the books."

"Loved them," she agreed. "I took you for an *Avatar* or *Skyfall* guy."

"Oh, *Skyfall*. Close second. And you probably would vote for…"

"Don't guess, it's *Marley & Me* although…" She pressed her hand to her heart. "*Water for Elephants*. So good."

He laughed softly. "Animal movies, of course. Greatest personal accomplishment?" he asked, falling into step as easily as they fell into their old game.

"I guess earning the department head job," she said. "Although, like I told you, that's a blessing and a curse. You?"

He thought about it, then shrugged. "The family," he said softly. "Making sure Smella made it to thirty without falling off a cliff in some country we've never heard of."

"Smella." She sighed. "I can't believe you still call her that."

"Please, they call me Big D."

She chuckled. "Well, I would love to see Ella again."

"Drop by her store, or better yet, come to Waterford Farm on any Sunday."

"So Sunday dinners still happen every week? It didn't change after your aunt Annie died?"

"It changed, yeah, but it's never ended. And now Uncle Daniel is happy again and we have the Santorini Greeks, who bring food. Alex is a world-class chef, and John owns a restaurant. So that's a huge improvement over my uncle's cooking." He tugged her closer. "Plus, all the siblings and cousins are adults now, so the touch football game gets serious. Most of them are married, and there are scads of little Kilcannons running around. You could see more of your new pal, Danny."

"Oh." She let out a groan. "That kid is so stinking cute."

"They all are," he told her. "But I do get a kick out of that one. He's a freaking holy terror. And if you think he's cute, wait until you meet Shane's little girl, Annabelle. She'll steal your heart. And Liam has two kids."

"Molly told me. Christian and…Fiona?"

"Wee Fee, we call her. You should come on Sunday," he said. "I've got the whole day off."

"Oh, I don't know."

He slowed his step. "It's my family, isn't it? You're worried about seeing them."

Of course he knew the truth. "Not worried, but…" She sighed, stopping while Judah marked a tree. "I don't plan to avoid them, and I have seen them now and again. But not…your mom."

He drew back. "You're scared of my mother?"

"Not scared, but…" She blew out a breath. "I've never really talked to her since your dad's funeral."

"Well, it's time you do," he said. "And spoiler alert, Colleen Mahoney is pretty much the sweetest, most nonjudgmental person you'll ever meet."

"I know that."

"So you'll come?" he asked.

"We'll see. It all depends on Judah." She gave him a little nudge. "Back to the game. Whose turn is it?"

"Mine," he said. "Worst moment?"

"You know what it was, and it was the same for you. Let's skip that year," she suggested. "In fact, let's limit our worst moment to the last ten years. How about that?"

"Fine, but there are too many to pick just one."

"Cheery."

He gave a self-deprecating laugh. "Ask my family. The D in Big D might stand for *Drag*. What was yours?"

She hesitated for only a few moments, then went with the truth. "When you left your uncle's vet office after Rusty's surgery."

He sighed. "Yeah. Bad move."

"It's okay." She squeezed his hand. "We don't have to rehash the past."

He shot her a look. "I thought that was the whole idea of the Birthday Game."

"How about your biggest disappointment?" She squished her nose after she said that. "Gah. Why am I focused on the negative things?"

"Because that's when you find out the real truth," he said. "And mine was when I walked into Molly's wedding and…"

"I wasn't there," she finished. "I heard it was beautiful and wintry and full of dogs."

"All of the above. Were you busy?"

She looked up at him. "I made up an excuse because I couldn't bear to see you and not…"

He grunted and dropped his head back like he'd been smacked. "So many missed opportunities. So much time wasted." He swore under his breath.

"Don't, Dec." She looked up at him. "Don't dwell on what-ifs and what-wasn'ts."

He slid his hand under her hair, his touch gentle, his palm callused. "For smart people, we've been so damn dumb."

She gave a sad smile. "When I'm in Bitter Bark, I'm always dying to see you, but terrified I might."

"Then you walked into Linda May's…" He thumbed her jaw. "What did you think when you saw me?"

"Of all the bakeries in the world…" she joked.

"Seriously."

"I thought it simply wasn't fair that you are so damn good-looking and that I would have loved to have watched you change from a boy to a man and that I knew right then and there what my best moment of the year would be." She gave a smile, relieved to make the admission. "What did you think?"

"That this time, I wasn't going to let you slip away."

"And here I am. Unslipped."

He ran his fingers over the nape of her neck, sending a thousand chills down her back. "So, E. Can I keep seeing you while you're here? Can we pick up where we left off? Can I stop making excuses to come over and just…come over?"

She eased closer to him, still locked on the intensity in his dark eyes. "Yes."

He gave her that slow smile. "That was easy."

"All you had to do was ask."

He wrapped his other arm around her, pulling her closer. "One more Birthday Game question?"

"Keep them positive, like happiest moment or best meal?" she guessed.

"Best kiss."

She leaned into him. "I'm pretty sure it's the one I'm about to get."

"Yep." He was still smiling as he lowered his mouth to hers, but that smile disappeared as their lips met, very lightly at first, then with more pressure, more purpose, and more pleasure. She slid her hands up his shoulders, taking her time to appreciate the shape of him, the same way he coasted his hand up and down her back.

"Evie," he murmured.

"Declan," she echoed, making him laugh a little as he drew back to look into her eyes.

"It's been a long twenty years."

"No kidding."

Still holding her gaze, he rubbed his thumb along her lower lip. "Not one day passed that I didn't think about you."

The confession nearly collapsed her heart. "I tried to forget," she admitted.

"I never tried," he said with a sad smile. "Because I hate to fail."

She opened her hands and let her fingers slide into his hair, and even his head felt wonderful in her hands. She didn't want to think how good the rest of him would feel. "I'm here until the end of the year."

"Let's make up for lost time." He kissed her again, angling for a sweeter connection, opening his lips for a tender touch of their tongues.

She took the invitation, weak-kneed from the lightning bolts shooting through her, hot and fast and sudden while she kissed him again.

Then a big furry paw landed on her boot, and Judah let out a long, insistent howl.

"Is he in pain?" Declan asked as they broke apart.

"The pain of being ignored." She reached down to give him some love. "You're right, big boy. Let's get you home. Big day and an early-morning call in the OR tomorrow."

"We'll be there. In fact, would you like me to pick you up and take you guys in?" Declan slid his arm around her and reached down to rub Judah's head.

"I have to be at the hospital by five, and you just finished a twenty-four-hour shift. Judah and I can get there on our own."

"Or I could stay tonight."

She hesitated, mostly because of the heat that whipped through her. "Not the night before surgery," she said.

"Then maybe the night after."

She smiled, snuggling closer. "If surgery is a success."

"You hear that, buddy?" He gave Judah's head another pat. "Be good on that table tomorrow, and… and…"

She waited, watching, wondering where he'd go with that. "And?" she prompted.

"I was going to say I'll be a happy man, but I already am. You've forgiven me, and we have a second chance. What could be better than that?"

She knew exactly what could be better. Thank God he hadn't asked about her biggest regret as part of the Birthday Game. Because she might have told him, and knowing Declan, he would have offered right then and there to give her the one thing she wanted most.

And she might have said yes.

# Chapter Fifteen

Declan was only a little surprised at the number of family members who wandered into the Vestal Valley College Animal Hospital that morning. Yes, his immediate and extended family frequently showed up for any event that required "support," but this operation wasn't at Kilcannon Veterinary Hospital or Waterford Farm, and Judah wasn't exactly a family pet.

Still, a stream of women he knew and loved began to pour into the surgery waiting room shortly after eight. Gramma Finnie and Yiayia were first, followed by his sister-in-law Cassie and her mother, Uncle Daniel's wife, Katie. After they greeted him and found coffee and chairs, Pru came in with her father, Trace, walking Danny into the room.

"Let the games begin," Pru called out on a laugh. "Dan the Man has arrived." She slid into the chair right next to Declan. "Mom's so excited to be in on this surgery. She said watching Dr. Hewitt work is like taking a master class."

He smiled, proud of Evie, as always. "It's good to know Judah's in such talented hands."

Trace made his way over, his muscular, tattoo-covered

arms stretched down to let Danny grip his index fingers and toddle along, half on his own power, half by using his dad for balance. His dark eyes darted around the room with intelligence and curiosity, his mop of nearly black hair already a tousled mess, as if to announce this kid played hard.

"What happens if you let him go?" Declan asked, getting a wide grin from Trace in response.

"Well, looks like he's got his eye on you, so…" Trace straightened and slid his fingers out of Danny's hands, and the little guy's eyes instantly popped with the taste of freedom. In a flash, he started off on his own, waddling a little on fat, short legs, but headed right toward Declan at full speed.

He shrieked and slapped his hands on Declan's legs, fell down in a heap, and threw his head back with an infectious laugh, making the whole waiting room chuckle.

"Whoa, there, little fella." Declan reached down and scooped him up, setting him on his lap.

He giggled, then turned to Trace, arms out.

"You stay with Uncle Dec while I get coffee," Trace said. "Show him how you can stand on your head."

"He can?"

"New trick," Trace said.

Immediately, Danny slid down to the ground, folding in half, his diapered butt in the air. He turned to Declan with an upside-down, toothless grin, obviously waiting for praise.

"Good job, crazypants."

Pru clapped. "Way to go, Danny!"

Yiayia leaned in. "This is all very good if he wants to work at SeaWorld as a trained seal."

Laughing, Declan patted his lap. "Sit with me, young man, and I'll tell you how to be a firefighter. When we say stand on your head, we don't mean fold in half. We mean a headstand."

He climbed up on Declan's lap, suddenly fascinated.

"I'll take him, Uncle Declan," Pru offered.

"No, he's fine." With all the many hands in his family, it was rare that he got to hold any of the babies, and he kind of wanted to really pay attention to how it felt. "Aren't you, Danny boy?" He bounced his knee, giving the kid a ride and getting another giggle, this one complete with a slap on Declan's chest. "You like that?"

"He likes attention." Pru leaned in, tapping Danny's button of a nose. "Don't you, wild thing?"

He lifted both hands straight out. "Pwuuuuuu."

Declan cracked up. "I'm guessing that's Pru."

"Oh yes, his vocabulary is growing every day. He says cookie…"

"Coo-coo!"

"And Meatball."

"Mmmbah!"

"And there's Aunt Colleen and Ella."

Danny whipped around when he realized Declan's mother was coming into the waiting room with Ella.

"Smewwie!" he called.

"Even he calls her Smella," Declan said on a laugh, giving a nod to the new arrivals.

Ella and Mom came over to join the family that had essentially filled most of the waiting room, exchanging more kisses, hugs, and updates on when the surgery had started.

"How'd you both get out of the store?" Gramma Finnie asked.

"Darcy's covering," Ella said, bending over to greet the baby on Declan's lap. "Hi, Danny Fo-Fanny." She looked up to meet Declan's gaze. "Lookin' pretty natural with a kiddo on your lap, Big D." She leaned all the way over, slipping her hands around Danny to lift him up, whispering in Declan's ear while she did. "Does that mean you're considering the suggestion?"

He answered with a narrow-eyed warning that demanded silence.

But Ella laughed and hoisted the baby in the air. "Wanna take an airplane ride?" As she zoomed off with him and Pru followed, his mother took the empty seat next to him.

"You didn't have to come, Mom," he said after they exchanged a quick hug. "It's sweet that you did."

"I wanted to be here," she said, brushing back a lock of slightly graying brown hair that had escaped from the waist-long braid that she'd had since Declan was a kid. As usual, Colleen Mahoney wore a Bone Appetit T-shirt over jeans, the antithesis of glamour. "I don't get to see you that often, and you slipped out of Sunday dinner last week before we had a chance to catch up."

"True," he agreed. "But I promise I'll be there tomorrow."

"Will you bring Evie?"

He inched back at the question, remembering Evie's hesitancy last night, especially when it came to his mother. "It depends on how things go with Judah," he said. "But I'd like to." He put a hand on her arm, holding her blueberry-colored gaze. "Can we talk for a second?"

"Sure. Let's take a walk."

They stood and slipped out together, heading out the front doors of the animal hospital and down a few stone steps to find an empty bench under a tree.

"Is everything okay?" she asked as they sat down.

"Yeah, yeah." He settled back, stretching an arm over the back and giving her narrow shoulders a light squeeze. "Really good, actually."

A smile tugged. "That's nice. You know what your aunt Annie used to say. 'You're only as happy as your least-happy kid.' So hearing you say you're good makes my heart warm."

He eyed her for a moment, wondering how deep they could, or should, go. "You know why I'm happy, I assume."

"Pretty sure the reason is in the OR right now, and I don't mean the dog."

"I like the dog," he admitted with a wry laugh. "But yeah, I like the dog doctor even more."

"That's wonderful, Dec. You know I've always been fond of Evie Hewitt."

*Really? Even after the fire?* "There are no…hard feelings?"

She sighed softly, nestling closer as she plucked at an imaginary thread on her jeans. "There are feelings," she said matter-of-factly, in true Colleen Mahoney fashion. "And many of them are still hard to process, but not for one minute do I bear a grudge against Evie or her family or Gloriana House itself. Is that what you're asking?"

"I guess it is. I think she's a little…nervous? I don't know if that's the right word. Just worried that seeing you might bring back bad memories for both of you."

Mom shook her head. "No, I don't want her to feel that way. Especially now that you're together again."

"I don't know how together we are," he said on a laugh. "We're sharing responsibility for a dog, and I'm helping her around Gloriana House and..." *We're kissing.* He left that part out.

"I'm happy you're able to be in the house and let go."

He swallowed. "'Letting go' is a relative term. I'm...facing stuff." He threw her a look. "And I've been reading the investigation files."

"I heard."

Inching back in surprise, he frowned. "Connor or Braden?"

"Both," she said. "They think they're protecting me whenever anything comes up that has to do with your dad's death."

He nodded. "I guess they talk to you more about it than I do."

"You never talk about it," she said.

"That's why I'm reading the files and trying to, you know, come to terms."

"I've read those files," she said. "And the department kept me up to speed throughout the whole investigation." She gave him a questioning look. "Are you finding... contradictions?"

"Maybe. I'm trying to track down the arson investigator who thought the fire was suspicious, but if you've read the reports, you know that wasn't the official determination." He tried to read her expression. "What are you thinking, Mom?"

"I'm torn," she admitted on a sigh. "I've always had this nagging feeling that something wasn't right about that fire. It wasn't like your father to break a rule and take a risk, but something compelled him to that night."

"Did you ever talk to George Rainey? That was his partner on the call."

"You know he died at the World Trade Center?"

"I did know that," Declan said. "But before he left? You knew him, I assume?"

"Very well. He was never quite the same after that fire. He shouldered a lot of blame for losing a partner."

Declan nodded, totally understanding that. "He didn't say what was different that night? Why he thought Dad left his side?"

"Nothing more than what was in that report."

Which was that he got momentarily separated from Dad, losing sight of him in the smoke. Declan nodded, considering how much to share with her. "I'm trying to shed some light now on what happened. You don't mind, Mom, do you?" The last thing he wanted to do was ease his own pain, but cause more for his mother.

"I don't mind," she assured him. "But I do question the cost."

"The cost?"

She turned and looked hard at him. "Evie. It could cost you Evie."

He blew out a breath. "You sound like Connor."

"A man who knows firsthand how your life can be improved by the love of a good woman."

"Mom, if something happened that wasn't in that report—if Dad made a huge mistake or if the investigators did—we have to know."

"Yes, I get that," she agreed. "And honestly, I've always wondered what you'd think when you read the report, because you were already in the department. Maybe you'll see something that everyone else missed."

But what if he saw something that cost him Evie, as these people who loved him kept warning him?

"And then we worry," Mom added.

"About what?"

"About your happiness." She took both his hands. "That fire makes you..."

"Awful, I know." He didn't have to be told yet again how dark and miserable he got. "Get in line for my apologies, because they're coming fast and furious."

She laughed easily. "You couldn't be awful if you tried. You weren't just grieving the loss of your dad, and I know you two were close. But that fire cost you even more than that."

"Evie?" He shook his head. "That's all on me, not that fire. I built a wall two miles high and every bit as thick to keep her out. But..." He smiled at her. "You're right. Walls are crumbling every day."

"Then don't pick those broken bits back up again," she said.

But was that what he was doing by looking into the fire? "You know, Mom, she has a big job in Raleigh, and I have a big family here. It's...complicated."

"I have an idea." She leaned closer to whisper, "Bring her to Waterford and make her fall in love with all of us."

"You're scheming," he said on a laugh. "Just like your mother and her ruthless pal."

She laughed at that. "Not at all. My reasons are selfish. I want to talk to Evie."

"About?"

"I want her to know that no one blames her family for our family's loss." She sat back on a sigh. "And if that helps remove an obstacle for you? All the better. Nothing could make me happier than to see you in love, Dec."

*In love.* They'd barely kissed, and yet...he knew Evie so well. And she knew him better than anyone, including the woman sitting next to him.

"I like that look in your eyes," Mom said, patting his arm. "It reminds me of your dad."

"Yeah?" That made him smile, but just then the front doors of the building swung open and Molly stepped out, wearing blue scrubs and a big smile.

"Come on back in, you two," she called. "We're done and Judah is doing great."

They popped up from the bench and hustled closer. "Is Evie in the waiting room?" Declan asked.

"Yep. She's looking for you," Molly said. "Oh, and, Declan?"

"Yeah?"

"That woman is a beast with a scalpel. Hands down the most gifted surgeon I've ever seen."

He grinned, pride rolling over him. "She's something, isn't she?" He brushed by her and headed back into the building, turning into the waiting room where he stopped dead in his tracks at what he saw.

Evie, also in blue scrubs, holding baby Danny on her hip and talking with half his family. Nuzzling the toddler under her chin, she said something that, of course, made everyone laugh.

She smoothed Danny's wild curls with those long, beautiful fingers and absently pressed a kiss to his head.

In that moment, Declan saw everything he wanted in this world. All he had to do was figure out how to get it.

# Chapter Sixteen

"I don't want to leave you," Evie whispered in the darkened room. "But I have to take care of your best friend, who is home thinking about nothing but you. You know that, right?"

In the oversize crate, Judah didn't move. He lay perfectly still on his side, the stitches visible in the shaved ventral area over his trachea. Evie remembered each pull of the needle when she'd sewn him back up, utterly satisfied with how the procedure had gone.

"With the right PT, he's going to be a hundred percent."

Evie turned at the woman's voice, surprised she hadn't heard her come into the ICU area, immediately recognizing the physical therapist. "Oh, Christine. Hello. I didn't expect you to come in tonight."

"I had to check on him." The woman, an attractive brunette about Evie's age, came closer to the crate, but kept her eyes on Evie. "And you." She dipped her head to whisper, "You're all anyone around here has talked about today, Dr. Hewitt."

She smiled at the compliment, stepping aside so Christine could get closer to Judah's crate. "I'm hoping to take him home on Monday, assuming he's not in any pain we can't manage."

"If you do, I'll come and do the first two sessions with you," she said. "After that, you are probably more than qualified to take him through canine rehab, which, as you know, isn't technically PT. Or, if you want, bring him in here as an outpatient. It's up to you."

"Let's see how it goes," Evie said.

"You've had a long day," Christine noted, a familiar empathy in her voice. "You know that our vet techs are on duty all night. He's got the monitor and an IV, but they'll check on him every half hour, if not more often."

Just then, Valerie, the vet tech Evie had been working with for the past few hours, came in.

"You honestly can go home, Dr. Hewitt," Valerie said.

"I must look awful, since everyone keeps telling me that," Evie said on a laugh, making the other two women deny it. But she looked at Judah again as he stirred and let out a shuddering sigh. "I feel so close to this guy now, it's hard to take off."

"Happens when you've done an operation like that," Christine said.

"The whole hospital is buzzing about how you handled that surgery," Valerie added. "They filmed it, you know."

"I know."

"They're going to use it in some classes."

Evie reached a finger through the metal crate and stroked Judah's powerful paw. "I'm honored."

"They're lucky to have you at NC State," the vet tech said.

"Thank you, Valerie."

"The big schools always get the best people," she

continued, a sad note in her voice. "I didn't get in there, so…"

"Vestal Valley has a terrific vet program," Evie said.

"It's decent, yeah." The young woman lifted her shoulder, her gaze drifting from Evie to Judah and back. "But surgeries like you did today? Hard to get here. And I want to be a neurologist, too. Of course, I'm just a vet student now, so maybe I'll get into NC State for my specialty degree."

"I hope you do," Evie said, putting a hand on the other woman's shoulder. "But if you don't, I'm sure you'll get into a great school and make a fantastic neurologist."

She nodded her appreciation. "I hope so. Now, honestly…"

"Yeah." Christine gave Evie's shoulder a nudge. "Go get dinner, Dr. Hewitt."

Dinner. It was that late? Poor Granddaddy. "Yes, ladies. You have my number and can text me. Valerie? Progress reports throughout the night?"

"Yep. And you can knock on the back door anytime if you need a Judah fix before we officially open tomorrow. In fact, you should go out that way."

"Thanks." With one more stroke of Judah's paw, Evie headed out, grabbing her bag from a locker and feeling very…comfortable. This was like a second home to her—the late nights after a big surgery, the dimmed lights and soft snores of sleeping animals in recovery, the incomparable rush of a successful surgery.

She pushed the back door open and blinked into the early evening light, trying to remember where she parked her car about twelve hours ago.

"Right here, Dr. Dolittle."

She turned at the voice in the shadows, her heart

unexpectedly fluttering at the sight of Declan leaning against her car, arms crossed.

"Hey." And a whole new wave of comfort washed over her, dragging her back twenty years to that summer when she'd work late at Dr. K's office and Declan would be waiting for her to have dinner or watch a movie or hang out in the square and talk about life at the fire station and vet office.

Right then, all Evie wanted to do in the whole world was go back to those halcyon days, before the fire…and ice…that wrecked that friendship. To pretend twenty years hadn't happened and they were still kids, young and free and crazy about each other.

"How's my girl?" he asked as she walked slowly toward the car.

His girl? Well, she might not be young and free, but she sure was still crazy about him. "Hungry, tired, and high on…" *You.* "A great surgery."

"The front desk already called to give me the night report on Judah. He's resting comfortably. It's the surgeon I'm worried about. She wouldn't leave the patient."

She loved the fact that he didn't move, but kept his gaze pinned on her, that Mahoney smile tugging at his lips.

"I left him," she said. "But it wasn't easy." Just like it wouldn't be easy to leave Declan tonight.

Finally, as she stood in front of him, he shifted from one foot to the other and reached out to place his hands on her shoulders. "What do you want to do now?"

*Kiss you. Hold you. Fly back in time.* "Get my grandfather something to eat."

"Didn't you check your Granddaddy cam?"

"I haven't had a chance."

"Well, he had his 'linner' at four, got his dentures out, his meds in, and is probably sound asleep by now."

Her jaw loosened. "How…why…what did you do?"

He laughed. "How was easy. The back door was open. While I was there, I finished the last of the windows and worked on some floorboards."

"Oh." She slid her hands around to the back of his neck and pulled him into her. "Could you be any more wonderful?"

"At gin rummy, I could be. Your grandfather cleaned my clock."

"You played cards with him?"

"'Played' is a strong word. I tried to survive every hand."

She squeezed him in gratitude, folding closer when he wrapped his arms around her. "I swear he cheats, but thank you." She looked up at him, close enough for a kiss, but holding off because looking into his eyes was its own kind of pleasure.

"You're the one who should be thanked for all you did today. How can I? Dinner? A drink? Cry pie? That coffee shop is open. I checked."

"I was just thinking about what I wanted." She grazed his neck with her nails, getting a kick of satisfaction when his whole body seemed to tense in response.

"Anything," he said with such sincerity she knew he meant it.

"To go back in time," she whispered. "Twenty years, Dec. Before…it all. To that incredible summer when we were so stinking innocent and ambitious and…" She leaned into him, lightly pressing her body to his.

"Supercharged," he whispered into her ear, making her laugh.

"That was the young part," she joked.

"Speak for yourself. I'm pretty charged." He splayed his hands over her back, riding them up and down over her cotton sweater, making her arch into him ever so slightly.

Tipping her head back, she relaxed into him, looking up. "Can we do that? Go back in time?"

"'Fraid not. But we can…" He brushed her lips with the lightest kiss. "Be right here, right now, tonight, not thinking about all those roads not taken. Just the one that we're on this minute."

"Mmm. I kind of like this road." She lifted up on her toes to deepen the kiss, parting her lips to taste more of him.

"Me, too." He pulled her tighter to him, letting her whole body feel the cuts and slopes of his powerful chest and the sexy pressure of his hips. He slid his hands up her back, tunneling into her hair, giving her a million chills and shivers.

Angling his head, he intensified the kiss, letting their tongues touch and send electrical shocks of pleasure down her body.

"Evie," he whispered into the kiss. "I can't believe how much I've missed you."

She let out a light groan of agreement, lifting her chin to let him kiss her jaw and throat.

Heat rose from deep inside, a sweet, torturous burn that made her want to kiss him longer and harder and… everywhere.

The back door to the animal hospital clunked with the sound of someone coming out, automatically inching them apart.

"You want to leave?" he asked.

"I am hungry," she admitted. "So maybe some food is a good idea."

He eased her away, but held on to her waist. "Let's go."

They walked arm in arm around the corner, falling into an easy conversation when he asked for more details about Judah's surgery. Talking about the procedure helped her hormones settle down, but the buzzy, achy, thrilling feeling never really went away, still there when they ordered and ate and talked and laughed.

By the time they finished dinner and ordered their pie to go, Evie finally felt like that full-body hum was under control.

"So…" Declan wrapped his fingers around the coffee mug and leaned forward. "Can we make this official?"

She started humming again. "Like, Facebook official?"

He laughed. "Is that still a thing? Do you not see these gray hairs?" He pointed to his temples. "I mean family official." He inched closer and lowered his voice. "Will you go to Sunday dinner at Waterford with me tomorrow?" He leaned over the table. "My mother issued a very personal and heartfelt invitation."

She had no doubt that was true. She'd seen so many members of his family in the waiting room that morning—including Colleen Mahoney, who'd been warm and sweet and parted with, "We hope to see you tomorrow!" And the grannies, of course, who'd showered her with interest. They'd all been so welcoming and genuine.

"I'd like that," she said. "Not sure if it makes anything 'official,' but…"

He smiled. "I can't remember taking anyone to that dinner before."

"Not…what was her name? Bethany?"

"Not anyone."

"Well, hate to break it to you, but you took me there a lot of times."

"Anyone *else*," he clarified. "Not that there ever has been…" His voice drifted off, and he looked down into his mug.

"Declan, I'm sure there have been many other women in your life."

"None that mattered." Then he reached across the table and closed his hand over hers. "Have you been in love these past two decades, Evie?"

"I've been in like," she said. "I've wanted to be in love, almost talked myself into it a few times, but…" She lifted a shoulder. "It never happened."

"And that's why you've never had a baby?"

She dropped back and sighed, wanting to tell him at least some of her journey. "I tried assisted reproduction or donor insemination, as it's called."

He curled his lip.

"Exactly," she replied. "It's about as inviting as it sounds. And it failed twice, and I didn't want to go through it again. It was stressful and exhausting."

"You can get pregnant, though, right?"

"As far as I know, everything is working."

"And you really want a child," he said.

"More than life itself," she whispered, making him close his eyes as if she'd hit a bull's-eye. She squeezed his hand. "But the fact that I don't have one isn't your fault, Declan."

He looked at her, silent, obviously not agreeing with that.

"I also looked into adoption, here and overseas."

"How far did you get?"

"Not very," she admitted, shaking her head. "I didn't have whatever a person has to have to go that route alone. Time, energy, enthusiasm, unspeakable courage. None of it was there for me. If someone had handed me a baby and said, 'Here, this is yours to raise and love,' I would have been delirious. But the process is designed to weed out the weaklings, and I guess I was one of those."

He snorted. "You're anything but weak."

"I wasn't strong enough to do that alone. So maybe I'm not strong enough to be a single mother. Anyway, it doesn't matter. It's too late."

"Is it?"

She searched his eyes for a clue to what he was thinking. It wasn't hard to figure out, not when she could read his eyes as well as anyone on this earth. "You're not still thinking about that, are you?" she asked.

"I'm not...*not* thinking about it."

"Declan."

"Evie."

She smiled. "Step back and try to work out the logistics of that for a minute, will you?"

"A little complicated since you live in Raleigh and I live here, but..."

"Are you moving to Raleigh?" she challenged. "Because if I had a child that belonged to you, I know darn well you'd want to be with him or her every day."

"Probably."

"And your family would want to be..."

"Yeah," he said on a laugh. "Whatever a family could be to a kid, mine would be it on steroids."

"And what if you met someone, and you wanted a family with her?"

He stared at her.

"You could meet and marry a twenty-five-year-old or thirty-year-old, Declan. How would she feel about you having a kid with another woman who—"

He pressed his fingers against her lips. "Shhh. You're getting worked up about a hypothetical woman who, I can already tell you, would be exactly like every other woman I've ever dated."

"Which is…"

He tipped his head, looking surprised she didn't know. "Not Evie."

"Declan." She pressed his hands as an indescribable pleasure danced through her at the words.

"Sorry, it's true. Like you, I've tried and wanted and given things a chance, but in the end, I only wanted… you." He lifted their joined hands, drawing her fingers closer and stroking her knuckles. "And I don't know how to tell you how good it feels to admit that."

Holding his gaze, she nodded. "We sure did ruin each other for everyone else."

"Truth." He kissed her knuckles and pointed at her. "And you, sweet doctor, are dead tired."

She touched her face. "Can you tell?"

"Yep. I know you. I'm going to follow you home and make sure you don't fall asleep at the wheel, then pick you up tomorrow for Sunday dinner."

"Whoa, you have it all figured out, don't you?"

He laughed. "Tomorrow, maybe. After that? It's a blur."

"Okay. But one quick stop first?"

"Where to?"

She pointed in the direction of the animal hospital. "Let's say good night to Judah and make sure he's sleeping and comfortable."

"See that?" He dropped some money on the check and reached for her hand to bring her out of the booth. "It's like we have a kid already."

If only it were that easy.

# Chapter Seventeen

"**W**ait. What? Is that a legit Bloody Mary that just went into your mouth?" Connor leaned in and sniffed the drink. "I don't think I've ever seen you actually *drink* a drink, bro."

Declan shrugged, leaning against the kitchen counter, where he had a perfect view of Evie chatting with Molly, Ella, Darcy, and Pru, passing baby Danny back and forth and laughing at his antics. When Evie held him, he had to force himself not to stare.

"So you're losing control, huh?" Connor continued, then glanced over his shoulder to follow Declan's gaze. "Ahhh. Now it makes sense."

Declan narrowed his eyes. "Don't make me stuff this celery stick down your throat."

Connor laughed. "Man, I haven't heard you make a threat like that for years. You're *back*, dude."

"What's so funny?" Braden asked, sliding into the conversation.

"Declan is losing control and making jokes."

Braden's brows shot up in silent disbelief.

"I'm not losing anything. I'm in a good mood." He had been since walking Evie to her door last night, and making out with her in the entryway of Gloriana House until they damn near lay down on the curved steps. They somehow managed to say good night, still dressed but aching for more.

"Well, I'm either going to make things better or worse," Braden said, still not smiling. "I got a lead on Kirby Lewis, the arson investigator."

"Yeah?" Declan lowered his drink, interested.

"Rumor has it he lives up near Boone, but no one knows how to get in touch with him. I have a good friend at NCSBI who has a girlfriend who works in personnel, and she might be able to 'find' his address." He used air quotes.

"Which sounds 'illegal.'" Declan air quoted back.

Connor nodded. "Maybe get him a message that Declan wants to talk?"

"I'd be more comfortable with that than stealing his address," Declan agreed.

"I figured that," Braden said. "Let me see what I can find out. I should know something next week."

"Thanks." Declan looked from one brother to the other, a punch of gratitude hitting him. "And no news could ruin my day." He glanced at Evie. "Not much could right now."

Connor chuckled. "We can tell."

"Yeah, the whole family's talking about how chill you seem," Braden said.

Declan looked skyward with a half laugh, half snort. "Y'all need to get lives, then."

"We did," Braden said, holding up his ringed left hand. "And now you know what we're thinking."

"What are we thinking?" Cassie Santorini—well, now Cassie Mahoney, since she'd married Braden last year—

stepped into the circle, sliding a possessive arm around her husband.

"That Dec seems really happy," Braden told her, tugging her into his side. Naturally, his whole face lit up as he beamed at the woman who'd come into this family when her mother married Uncle Daniel, and now had the distinct honor of being a Santorini *and* a Mahoney.

"Oh, you do look happy," Cassie said, her dark Greek eyes dancing. "Everyone notices. Daniel says he hasn't seen you this animated since…well, for a long time."

"I'm *animated*?"

"Drinking vodka? Lookin' fly? And hey, I saw you kiss Yiayia when you walked in." Cassie tsked. "Pretty wild stuff, Dec."

"Fly? Seriously, Cass?" Declan snorted. "And I gave Yiayia a polite hello kiss. You're the ones who break into Zorba dances at the first note of a song."

Braden poked Declan's shoulder. "Don't fight it, bro. You're going down."

Who said he wanted to fight it? "I suppose there's money on the table."

"Oodles of it," Cassie assured him.

At the noisy laughter that comment caused, the group of women and a baby looked over and migrated across the kitchen.

"What's so funny?" Ella demanded, then pointed at Declan's drink. "Virgin?"

He pointed back at her. "I could ask the same thing."

While everyone laughed, Ella reached over and put a hand on his forehead. "Call a doctor. Declan must be sick 'cause he's cracking real honest-to-God jokes."

"He always makes jokes," Evie said, sweetly coming to his defense.

"Maybe with you," Connor said.

"Don't pay any attention to this crew, E," he said, draping his arm over her shoulders because it felt natural, and he couldn't care less that meaningful looks were bouncing around the group while they counted his drinks and jokes. "They're not to be taken seriously."

"So they weren't serious when they invited me to play touch football?"

"Oh yes, we were," Molly said. "I need you on my team."

"Then I'm glad you told me to wear jeans and sneakers, Declan."

He smiled down at her, loving every inch of those jeans on her. "Great. I'll be on your team."

Braden and Connor both threw their hands out in disbelief.

"*Now* you'll play?" Braden choked.

"Every other Sunday, you sit on the porch like the third grandmother," Connor said, balking.

Declan shook his head, laughing with them and at himself. "Most Sundays, I'm in uniform to start a shift at five."

Fortunately, Danny saved him from any more grief by shrieking to get down from his mother's arms.

"You want a tour of the property before we eat?" Declan asked Evie. "I know you want to see the kennels."

"I do." She lifted her own Bloody Mary. "Are these allowed?"

"Only, apparently, if you're fun enough to qualify." He slid a look at his brothers.

"You're gettin' there, Big D." Connor winked and stepped aside to let them go.

On the way, they stopped and talked to his cousin

Shane and his wife, Chloe, giving Evie a chance to coo over little Annabelle, born the same month as Danny, but way more docile.

Finally, he walked her out the kitchen door and into the afternoon sunshine.

"I don't remember Sundays at Waterford being anything like this. There are so many—"

"*Mavviiiiieeeeee!*"

Declan pulled Evie back just in time to avoid being mowed down by a tan Lab tearing across the driveway, followed by six-year-old Destiny, little Christian hot on her heels while his much younger sister, Fiona, stumbled along, trying to keep up.

"Kids," Evie finished on a laugh, then pointed to Destiny. "I haven't even met her yet."

"That's Destiny. You've met John Santorini, my step-cousin?"

"I think so." She nodded. "John and Alex Santorini, right? Twin brothers, Katie's sons, and Cassie's brothers?"

"You got it. Destiny is Summer's daughter. Summer and John just got engaged."

"Oh boy." She grinned up at him. "If there's a test…"

"The brain trust will ace it," he teased, tightening his grip on her hand.

"The brain trust." She laughed at that. "You used to call me that after every report card when we were young."

"Because you got A's, and I…didn't."

"Well, I want an A on your family names. I remember there were six Kilcannon kids and four Mahoneys, and I used to think *that* was a massive tribe when I'd come here on a Sunday. So is this everyone? Except Nick

Santorini, the son your uncle Daniel didn't know he had."
She shook her head. "I still can't believe that story."

"And Theo Santorini, Navy man, currently in San
Diego. Then that's it."

"Well, it's a phenomenal family." She let out a noisy
exhale and turned to look back at the house, spilling over
with kids and couples and two very happy-looking
grannies rocking on the porch.

Yiayia lifted her drink in their direction.

"You sure *everyone's* phenomenal?" he asked on a
laugh. "Because those two grannies can be a handful."

"They're precious and well-meaning." She responded
to Yiayia's cross-lawn greeting by lifting her own drink.
"I'd be lying if I didn't tell you I was green with envy
over this bunch. You know how I grew up. Alone in that
monstrous house with no siblings and no cousins. My
grandmother was lovely, but she couldn't compete with
Finnie or Yiayia for colorful and crazy. My mother hid in
her sunroom studio all day."

"I remember that house was always so quiet."

"So this is..." She glanced over her shoulder again,
then turned to the expansive pen where many of the
family dogs hung out during Sunday dinners. Without
finishing her thought, she headed toward the pen.
"Paradise for a person who loves big families and dogs."

"I didn't know you love big families," he said. "I
mean, you have the ultimate family. The founders."

"Yeah, but you have the actual living people." She
closed her fingers around the wire fencing and made a
few kissing sounds, immediately getting some of the
dogs' attention. "And four-legged furbabies, too."

Jelly Bean came trotting over, along with little Stella
and Lola.

"If you think learning all the people is challenging…" He leaned a little closer to feel her hair on his cheek when he talked. "They all come with dogs."

She laughed. "That's never a problem for me."

"Come on, I'll introduce you to all of them." He unlatched the gate, waving to his cousin Garrett, who was with his wife, Jessie, on the other side of the pen. They were working with a new terrier Declan didn't recognize, probably readying the dog for adoption.

"This beautiful Weimie is Jelly Bean, owned by my brother and sister-in-law Braden and Cassie."

"Oh, he is gorgeous." She knelt on the grass to get face-to-face with Jelly Bean. "What intelligent eyes he has."

"Yep, he's a genius," Declan told her. "Once, he ran all the way from Yiayia and Gramma Finnie's house to the fire station with an olive jar around his neck to let Braden know Cassie was stuck in the basement with a broken foot."

"No!" She gave Jelly Bean a kiss right on the nose. "You are brilliant!"

"And this is Lola, who once wouldn't eat a thing until Jessie Curtis"—he pointed to the couple across the pen—"came and brought Lola out of her shell. Then she brought Garrett out of his, and they're married and now have little Patrick."

"Hello, Lola." She feathered her fingers into the dog's pale gold fur.

"Go ahead, tell her you love her."

She slid him a sideways glance. "Really?"

"She'll say it right back."

"I love you, Lola."

On cue, the Aussie mix barked three times, delighting

Evie, who threw her head back with a hearty laugh. "Awesome! And who is this delicious little creature?" She reached for the tiny Chinese crested with a puff of white fur on her little head.

"That's Stella, and you'll love her story. She belongs to Darcy and Josh. She was blind, and Uncle Daniel got her into an experimental study at Vestal Valley for SARDS, and now she's looking at you."

"I heard about that study!" she exclaimed. "Those were groundbreaking results, and I was very proud of our little local vet school." She gave Stella's fuzzy head a rub. "You're a famous success story, Miss Stella."

The little dog climbed right onto her lap and curled into a ball.

"Dolittle is in the house." Declan could feel the goofy grin on his face as he sat in the middle of the grass, his whole being *falling* for this tenderhearted woman who stole the hearts of people and animals. Including his. Especially his.

"He thinks I can talk to animals, Stella," she whispered into the dog's ear, smiling at him as she did. "Can you understand me?"

Stella looked up and licked Evie's chin.

"Oh, you can? You, the little dog who was once blind but now can see?" She winked at Declan. "There's a lot of that going around these days."

"What does that mean?" he asked.

"That creatures change, you know? Sometimes all by themselves, sometimes with a medical intervention, sometimes with the help of..." She looked toward the house. "People who love them."

"You think I've changed?" he guessed.

She studied him for a long moment, stroking Stella's

head, thinking carefully before she answered. While he waited, he felt his heart kick up a little and his whole body inch toward hers.

"I think you're the Declan I've always known," she said softly. "But based on what I'm picking up from your family's comments? That man has been absent for a long time."

He blew out a breath. "Twenty years, E. Lost and blinded by a fog of grief and resentment."

"But you're back?" she asked.

"You are." He reached out to slide his hand under her hair. "Which seems to have made all the difference in the world."

For a long time, they didn't speak, but held each other's gaze, close and quiet.

"Are you going to kiss me or not?"

"We have an audience. A big, opinionated, pushy bunch of agitators who are right this minute putting money on whether or not we will."

"Well, someone should win that bet." She leaned in and kissed him, long and sweet.

He could have sworn he heard a response from the crowd. And he couldn't have loved them more at that moment.

Evie had sweat off her makeup and had two grass stains on her jeans, but the Terrible Terriers, led by Shane Kilcannon with Molly as his co-captain, beat the Bloodhounds by one touchdown, so she didn't care.

Grabbing a bottle of water that Destiny and Christian were handing out on the sidelines, Evie high-fived the opponents and realized the smile she'd been wearing most of the day wasn't going anywhere.

"There's a happy lass." Gramma Finnie came down the stairs from the porch, beckoning Evie closer. "Come and talk to the oldsters in our rocking chairs, will ya?"

"Of course." As if anyone could say no to the small but mighty Irishwoman. She followed Gramma Finnie to the back, a massive covered deck that looked out over an endless view of the foothills and mountains.

But her gaze wasn't on the scenery. Colleen Mahoney sat on a sofa, sipping tea, talking to Yiayia. The two doxies were stretched out in a patch of sunshine, while Rusty and Goldie snoozed under an empty chair.

"Nothing broke, and no one cried," Colleen said as Evie and Gramma Finnie joined them. "When the kids were young, that's what Annie Kilcannon and I used as our yardstick for a good game of touch football."

"I don't know," Evie said. "The Bloodhounds looked pretty dejected when Declan scored that last play. There might have been tears."

"Declan?" Colleen looked at Gramma Finnie, eyebrows raised. "Told ya, Mom," she said under her breath.

Evie took a sip of water and settled next to Colleen on the sofa, waiting for a little bit more of an explanation. But Yiayia leaned forward in her rocker and put a hand on Evie's knee.

"You're so good for him," she said. "Perfect, in fact."

Evie swallowed and smiled. "Declan and I've been friends for a long time," she said, sliding a look at Colleen. "I remember camping when Ella was so small you wanted to zip her in a tent so she didn't go flying into the lake."

"I've spent most of her life trying to zip that girl up so she didn't go flying…somewhere." Colleen's dark blue eyes danced, sending nothing but warmth to Evie. "And I remember Declan coming home from third grade mad at me because I didn't send cupcakes in for his birthday, and his name got added to your cake in glitter frosting."

Evie laughed, getting a jolt of pleasure that they had shared memories. She never wanted the tragedy of twenty years ago to come between them, but then, she never really had a chance to talk to Declan's mother about it. "That birthday was the start of a great friendship, Mrs. Mahoney."

"Please, call me Colleen." She reached over and took Evie's hand. "We've missed you," she said quietly. "And Yiayia is right. You're good for Declan."

"Like a tonic," Gramma Finnie added.

"Well, I'm glad…" She looked out toward the grass, catching sight of him joking around with his brothers. "And I've missed him—er, you all—too."

"Truth's out," Yiayia teased.

"Now how do we get you to stay, lass? What will it take?"

Evie blinked at Gramma Finnie. "To stay longer today or…in Bitter Bark?"

"Mom," Colleen chided Gramma Finnie. "You're not usually the one who's so blunt."

"Right? That's my job," Yiayia said, grinning at her friend and raising a hand for a high five. "Welcome to the dark side, Finola."

"Oh hush." The old Irish lady flicked her knotted fingers at Yiayia's palm. "I've known this lass since she was a wee girl, and her grandfather and my Seamus played cards together for years. Once, when he had no cash on him and owed Seamus money, your grandfather gave him a copy of Thaddeus Bushrod's *History of Bitter Bark*. Did you know that?"

Evie shook her head. "I didn't know that, but Granddaddy can be dangerous when it comes to cards. Do you still have the book?"

"You gave it to me, Mom," Colleen replied. "And my husband loved to read it. Then, when Connor and Sadie tied in the mayoral election, I gave it to him. It's quite a collection of lessons on how a man should live. Do you want it back, Evie?"

"Oh, no. We have one in the museum room. We'll have it on display for the Founder's Day event. Are you still planning to come over and get some dresses for that party?" she asked.

"We are," Colleen assured her.

"And what about the possibility of you staying in Bitter Bark?" Yiayia asked, clearly not willing to let the conversation go to the party and off the match they were so busy making.

"Well, I have a pretty great job in Raleigh," Evie said.

"NC State is one of the best veterinary programs in the country," Colleen added, getting a grateful smile from Evie.

"There are things I really love about my job."

"But there are also things you could love about Bitter Bark," Yiayia said, her sledgehammer out in full force.

"There certainly could be." Evie lifted her gaze to meet her dark Greek eyes. "I promise you'll be about the second or third to know if I decide to stay."

The older women laughed, but Colleen asked, "Will you keep Gloriana House as yours?"

Tension fluttered through her at the question. Not because it was a little personal, but mostly because… history. If Declan had to work to be comfortable with Gloriana House, then the subject couldn't be easy for Colleen.

"It's hard to say what we'll do with the house," she replied.

Colleen's eyes filled for a moment, the unexpected tears making Evie draw back.

"Oh, Colleen, I'm sorry…"

"No, you have nothing to be sorry about." She dabbed under her eye. "I'm emotional these days."

Evie swallowed. "It's never an easy topic."

"That's not why I'm emotional." Colleen put two hands around one of Evie's. "We've all let it go and come to terms with the past, dear. Well, all but one of us." She looked past Evie to the yard. "And today, I see a boy I remember like I remember you. Laughing, lighthearted, optimistic. No matter what happens, you've given me a gift simply by showing up and opening your heart to Declan. Thank you. I know he didn't make it easy these past few decades."

"Oh." The word slipped out of a knotted throat. "Mrs.…Colleen." She laughed, her own eyes filling up. "I love your family. I always have."

Colleen reached over and gave her a tight, long hug before easing back, still holding Evie, to say, "And we love you. And your family home is aptly named…it's glorious. You should always be proud of it and *all* of its history. The good, the bad, the happy, and the sad. It's what makes a house a home."

The words were so simple and heartfelt that Evie had to close her eyes and hug Colleen a little tighter, realizing only at that moment how much she'd needed this conversation.

"And one more thing, lass," Gramma Finnie whispered as Colleen and Evie parted.

"Not sure I can take it," Evie admitted, blinking back tears.

"Play that piano. Tonight."

"Oh…okay." Evie frowned, puzzled by the suggestion, but then Declan came up the stairs, wearing that smile that made her knees weak, and she forgot all about it.

# Chapter Eighteen

Evie and Declan left Waterford right after the game, laden with leftovers for her grandfather. Before Declan drove her home, they zipped by Vestal Valley to check on Judah, who was off his IV and quite alert. He seemed happy to see them and even was able to get out of his pen and take a short stroll around, so Evie confirmed she could take him home the next day.

On the way to Gloriana House, Declan rooted for a way to drag this perfect day out a little longer. But when he pulled his truck into the drive, Evie reached over and took his hand, her cheeks flushed from the sun and active day.

"Stay for a while," she said simply.

He exhaled and laughed. "So I don't have to manufacture a reason?"

She lifted his hand to her lips, holding his gaze. "I want you to. Is that reason enough?"

The words gave him a kick and the incentive to lean across the console and give her a kiss on the lips. "More than enough. Come on. Max's linner is officially dinner now."

She cupped his cheek, smiling into his eyes. "I love that you know that. And care."

After one more quick kiss, they took the food in, prepared a tray, and Declan put everything away while Evie went upstairs to spend some time with her grandfather. While waiting for her, he wandered around the downstairs for a minute, checking on his newel, testing a few of the windows, and admiring how clean the chandelier was.

After a moment, he stopped in the monstrous dining room, imagining all the dinners that had taken place over the years at the table that could easily sit eighteen people, maybe more.

They sure could have a Sunday dinner there, he mused, leaning against the doorjamb. What would it be like to see this room lit and lively again? He'd never noticed the details as a kid, but now he could really see the craftsmanship in the wainscoting and the beauty of the coffered ceiling.

"Looking for things to fix?" Evie came up behind him, sliding her arms around his waist and pressing against his back.

"Imagining this place full."

"You can see it for yourself at the Founder's Day event."

He placed his hands over hers to prevent her from slipping away, because even against his back, she felt good. "I bet there were some unbelievable dinners here."

"Two governors of North Carolina have dined in this room," she said.

"Really? I didn't know that."

"Family history says Amelia Bushrod went into labor with Evangeline in here, and Thad Jr. put her on the table until the doctor came and they got her upstairs for the delivery."

He laughed softly, finally bringing her to his side so he could put his arm around her. "How do you know all this?"

"It's all in the museum room. In journals and articles from the *Bitter Bark Banner*. In pictures and albums." She eased him that way. "Want to see the picture of Governor Cherry in 1946?"

"Sure. I haven't been in that room all that often. It was always off-limits."

"I remember one time you were in there, for my piano recital when we were in eighth grade." She grunted. "I hated that Grandmama made me do that every year. My mom put her foot down on the debutante ball, but dear old Penelope won the recital battle."

"You played a Beethoven symphony," he said as they reached the double doors. "I was blown away."

"'Ode to Joy,' Old Ludwig's Ninth Symphony. Please, it impresses, but isn't very difficult."

"Do you ever play now?"

"I haven't for years. But no one has asked me quite as frequently as your grandmother and Yiayia. I think they've suggested it every time I've seen them."

He turned to her, frowning. "Really? I wonder why."

"Who knows with those two?" She guided him toward a wall of gold-framed photographs, many sepia-toned and yellowed with age. "Here's the picture. That's my great-grandfather Montgomery Hewitt and Governor R. Gregg Cherry."

He studied it for a moment, more interested in her great-grandfather than the stuffy-looking governor. "Granddaddy Monty?"

She laughed. "Maybe privately with Evangeline. To the rest of the world, he was Montgomery Jasper Hewitt the Third, the man who started the Bitter Bark Bank, which he ran until Max did."

"Your father sold it, though, didn't he?"

"Yes, when Granddaddy retired. That's why it's a Wells Fargo now."

He stepped closer to the framed picture, squinting. "I can see your eyes."

"But I don't have the moustache."

"Thank God." He took a few steps to the right, his gaze drawn to a glass-covered display of close to fifty different lighters, some gold, some brass, some engraved, two shaped like cars, about seven shaped like various handguns, and one that looked like a genie's lamp with a small placard that said 1821 on it. "Wow, that's two hundred years old?"

"Worth a small fortune, too."

Some of them might be, he thought. The more modern Zippos weren't so impressive, though some had cool engravings, but even an untrained eye could see this collection was worth many thousands of dollars.

"Every man in the family has collected lighters," Evie said. "Starting with Thad the First. His son was a supercollector, and Montgomery picked it up when he married Evangeline. Granddaddy kept up the tradition, but my dad wasn't interested."

All these lighters and lighter fluid on hand twenty years ago...yet all but one of the investigators had dismissed the idea that lighter fluid had been used as an accelerant to set the fire. He stared at the collection, gnawing at his lower lip as he thought about all he'd read that week about the fire.

Could someone in the house have set it using the—

"Declan?" Evie's fingers curled around his arm. "What is it?"

He turned to her. "You always know when I'm thinking something, don't you?"

"It's my superpower," she joked. "Animals and Declan." She studied him for a moment. "What were you thinking just then?"

"Truth? About lighter fluid."

He saw her expression change and instantly regretted that truth. He didn't want to talk about the fire tonight. Didn't want to think about it. Today had been too perfect and so long overdue that he wasn't going to derail it by going…to *that place*, as she'd put it.

"Hey." He flattened his hand over hers, giving her fingers a squeeze. "How about some of that wine you offered the other day?"

"After a Bloody Mary today? You've gone straight off the rails, Mahoney."

He laughed. "I'm not on duty until tomorrow afternoon, and I enjoyed that drink."

"I know. Your happy glow was the talk of the town."

He rolled his eyes and walked away from the lighters toward the middle of the room. "They all act like I've been some kind of ogre. Someone had to take charge of that gang."

"Well, no one has to take charge tonight," she said. "I'll be right back with wine, and we can make toasting jokes like the old days."

"Perfect."

When she left, he took a steadying breath and one more glance at the lighters, then looked away. Not tonight.

Instead, he walked over to the giant, gaudy piano that looked like it had been rolled right out of the Munsters' house. Carved from dark wood with intricate designs and curlicues, the gold letters that said Krakauer above the keyboard were as shiny as he imagined they were the day this thing was built.

Which had to have been nearly a hundred years ago.

He grazed his finger along the key cover, noticing some very light prints in the fine, nearly invisible layer of dust. Had someone opened this recently? Evie said she hadn't played in a long time, so who would have done that?

Didn't she say Yiayia had been in here? And Grandma Finnie? So…

He put his hand over the fingerprints and lifted the keyboard lid, which weighed a ton and squeaked like a cat. The minute he did, he saw an index card between two keys. Were the keys broken, or was that a note, or—

He sucked in a noisy breath when he picked it up and stared at his own printing, distinct and familiar and…

Oh God.

*DECLAN'S PROMISE*

The words stared back at him, in screaming capital letters, raised like a dead man from the emotional basement, which was the only place Declan would expect the memory of this card to make an appearance.

*I, Declan Joseph Mahoney, being of sound mind and body…*

He closed his eyes, transported back, still hearing her voice as she teased. *It was pretty sound last night.*

The memory sucker-punched him, forcing him to open his eyes and read.

*Do hereby swear that I will wait for Evangeline May Hewitt…*

And what had she said to that? *There's nothing worse than a broken promise.* Good God, that's all he had done for twenty years. Break promises.

*For twenty years and anytime in between, I promise to be whatever she needs me to be. I will be her friend, lover, husband, confidant, partner, provider…*

That's when he'd caught her crying, he remembered, when she said, *You already are everything, Dec.*

Really? Because then he turned into a self-involved promise-breaker. He forced himself to read the rest.

*…chauffeur, chef, traveling partner, fellow camper, handyman, and father to our*

He'd never finished writing the sentence. The one promise he could still keep, and he hadn't written the damn words, but he did sign the promise with a flourish. And sometime after that, he'd lost this card. He'd remembered it only a few years later and assumed he'd thrown it away, like the rest of his life back then.

But someone had kept it. His grandmother, of course. And she left it here for Evie to find. To what end? To make her remember that he was the worst friend ever? To make her—

"You are *not* going to make me play 'Ode to Joy.'"

He stuffed the card into his jeans pocket without giving himself a nanosecond to consider why he was doing that. He had to think about it, had to reread it, had to take at least some time to wallow in self-loathing and thank God she'd forgiven him. He had to…

"Declan?"

Of course, Dr. Dolittle would read his thoughts and know everything.

He turned, determined not to give anything away. "Yeah?"

She frowned at him, coming closer. "Are you all right?"

"I was just…thinking."

"About your toast?" She handed him a glass of red wine. "Because I have mine all ready." She grinned. "It's a good one."

"I can't wait for this." He held up the wine and prayed his hand was steady.

"What did the grape do when he was crushed?" she asked, her eyes glinting with humor.

"He let out a little wine?"

"Oh, you know me too well." She dinged his glass. "Your turn."

"Evie…" He took a slow breath, not sure how to say what he had to say and definitely not sure how to turn it into a toast. He couldn't joke. This was too serious.

Her frown returned as she studied him. "What is it, Dec?"

"Let's have a baby."

# Chapter Nineteen

Evie barely clung to her wineglass. "Excuse me?"

"I'm serious."

"I can tell." She backed up, more from the sheer force of his expression than the words, which were...shocking. And kind of insanely beautiful. "What...made you want this?"

"You. Today. This house. Your family. And mine. Us." His voice was thick on the last word, and he tried to laugh it off. "I can't even form a sentence."

"Really? 'Cause I think 'Let's have a baby' is a pretty well-formed sentence." She lifted her glass and angled her head. "Can I even drink this, then?"

"So you'll do it?"

She managed a laugh at his enthusiasm, and maybe to cover the shock wave rolling through her. "I'll drink to talking about it. How about that?" She tried to take a small sip, and he did, too, holding her gaze with one so fiery and intense she couldn't look away.

"That's a start," he said after he swallowed, leading her toward the settee.

"Declan." She dropped down, happy for the support of something under her. "I don't know—"

"I do," he said, the words bathed in certainty. "I know. It's the right thing to do. And, Evie, before you launch into a laundry list of complications, hear me out. You call the shots. You make the decisions. You live where you want to live, and you're the boss on this. I'd love to be in our baby's life. Hell, I'd love to be in your life, in whatever capacity you think is right, but this would be for you."

"Wow. You've been thinking about this for a while."

"I guess I have, but it hit me. The rightness of it. And the…urgency."

Really? Was it right? Urgent? Or…terrifying? She lifted a brow, still as puzzled by this sudden change as the very topic itself. "I appreciate you saying it's for me, but let's be frank. A baby belongs to two people." And those two people belonged to each other, at least in a perfect world.

But was he offering a perfect world or a perfect solution?

"Of course," he agreed. "That's ideal, but what I'm trying to say is don't let that stop you. You want a baby. You said you want a baby more than life itself. I want to give you…everything you want. Why wouldn't we at least try?"

She took a slow breath and set the glass on the table, like he did, and probably for the same reason. The crystal would be much safer there than in her slightly trembling hand.

"I did try," she said. "I told you it didn't work." As excuses went, it was weak, but it was all she had in the face of this bombshell detonating in front of her.

"I'll go with you to a doctor or a specialist, if you like."

The offer touched her, making her squeeze his hand. "That's not necessary. The insemination didn't take."

His eyes flickered at the words. "So clinical."

"Oh, it was." She smiled and dropped back, sliding a look at him. "Cold and uncomfortable."

"Maybe that's why you didn't get pregnant."

She shot him a look. "Uh, sorry to go all doctor on you here, but that's not how it works."

"Really?" He lifted a shoulder. "I've heard stories of people who got pregnant only when they stopped trying. Or adopted a baby after years of infertility, only to find out they're expecting six months later. Maybe you didn't have your head in the right place."

She laughed. "The head's not involved in reproduction, darling."

"I know, but one thing I can promise, E." He lifted her hands and kissed them. "It won't be clinical or cold."

From way deep in her belly, something awakened and fluttered. Something like a thousand aching, dancing, hungry butterflies. There was no question they'd been on their way to the bedroom, but…a baby? "I guess it would be fun to try."

He smiled. "Understatement of the year."

For a moment, she didn't say anything, but blew out another breath, trying to control the whirlwind of emotions that whipped through her. Hope—*God, so much of that*—and joy and fear and gratitude, all exploding like a glitter bomb in her chest.

Finally, she reached for her glass and took a deep drink.

"Did something happen today?" she asked, still not quite getting this rather sudden shift. "One of your grannies talk you into this? Your uncle? I heard he's done a fair bit of matchmaking to get all his kids married off, too." Then she caught herself. "Not that you're suggesting that."

"What I'm suggesting is something I promised you a long time ago. You might not remember that once I wrote—"

She put her hand on his arm. "I remember."

"You do?" He looked a little stricken, like a man who wouldn't want to have made promises he didn't keep.

"But life happened, Dec." Actually, death. And they both knew it. "I'm not holding you to anything you wrote that morning."

"I'm holding myself to it, and damn it, Evie, it's not too late. It's what you want. A baby. You'll never find a better person for the job."

"Talk about an understatement."

"No, I mean in terms of giving you exactly what you want. The freedom to do what you want and live how you want…with your baby that I could make with you."

But without him right next to her every minute? She appreciated the wildly generous offer, but still doubted it would work out that way. "I don't really know what I want anymore," she admitted.

"Well, start with a baby. You know you want that."

"Yes," she answered without hesitation. "But it isn't even only the baby, because obviously, that only lasts a few years. But a child. A son or daughter. A friend. A person who'll be there when I'm old and care about the family treasures and take my advice and maybe give some of their own." Her voice cracked as emotion welled up.

He scooted closer, taking both her hands. "What I'm trying to say is you don't have to make it a package deal.

You don't have to take me to have my baby. I don't want that to stop you. And I know you don't want to wait. We're not kids, and it might not happen right away."

"I know." She bit her lip. "We might have to try over and over again."

"Multiple times." He gave a sly smile. "I can think of so many worse ways to spend a night."

"Of course, you're cheaper and way sexier than the nurse at the fertility clinic." She pulled him a little closer. "Declan," she sighed.

"Evie," he whispered back.

"Can I think about it?"

"All you want. Nonstop. I have been ever since your grandfather planted the idea, and then…" He caught himself.

"And then what?"

"I spent time with you," he said, pulling her closer to wrap an arm around her. "And I'm right back where I was that morning in the mountains."

"Oh yeah." She settled next to him, relaxing into him. "That was a good morning." Until it wasn't.

"I thought I knew how my life was going to go," he said, stroking her hair. "I figured we'd keep falling more and more in love, then we'd get married, maybe when you graduated from vet school, before you started neurology. Eventually, we'd live here and you'd have a practice, and we'd have kids, but…" His voice trailed off.

She didn't answer, leaning into him instead and closing her eyes to imagine that life. It wasn't the first time she had, but somehow tonight those fantasies felt bittersweet and beautiful and not so utterly out of reach.

"But it didn't happen that way," she finally said.

"It still can." He took her chin in his hand to turn her face to his. "At least a piece of it can. Before we're too old to think about it."

"Which is, you know, rapidly approaching."

"You've got a few good childbearing years in you, Evie Hewitt." He grazed her lower lip with his thumb, sending a shiver through her. "And the rest of those dreams? The part about getting married and living here… All I want to say is *everything* is on the table. And don't tell me there is no table. Whatever you want."

The totality of the offer nearly took her breath away. "Declan, I need to think about it."

"Okay, but thinking doesn't make a baby."

That made her smile, but the humor faded as she looked into his eyes, and all that hope rose up and clutched her heart. Was this even possible? In some ways, it didn't matter. Just that he offered was the sweetest thing.

"Declan Mahoney, you are the damn finest man I've ever known. You have such a good soul and a big heart." She touched his cheek. "And you're still so freaking hot."

He laughed softly, inching back to look at her. "And you are still the most beautiful, talented, sexiest, smartest, most empathetic woman I've ever known, Evie Hewitt. And you will make a stunning mother."

She inhaled as the compliments washed over her as he kissed her. She could taste wine on his lips and the sweet, sweet words that pressed on the innermost place in her heart.

Instantly, the kiss heated, and she wanted more, parting her lips and clinging to him with all her strength.

When they broke for breath, he narrowed his eyes at her. "Is this you *thinking* about it?"

"Yeah. Thinking hard." She slid her hands into his hair and pulled him down to stretch out on the sofa, which wasn't nearly big enough for both of them.

But right then, she didn't care. All that mattered was the weight of him on top of her, the strength and heat and pure masculinity of a man she cared deeply about. A man willing to give her anything and everything.

He kissed her throat and tunneled his fingers in her hair, making her weak and breathless.

"Evie," he murmured. "Once we start…"

"I know, I know." But she didn't care. She didn't want to stop. She wanted his hands on her breasts and his mouth on her skin and the full length of him right where she could rock against him. "This is helping me…think."

He laughed into the next kiss. "Really." He planted his lips down her throat, into the V of her cotton sweater, sliding one hand up to sear her waist and ribs with a callused, hot palm. "'Cause it's kind of making me lose my mind."

She moaned her response, arching and offering him an invitation to touch her. He took it, caressing her breast over the thin silk of her bra with one hand and cupping her cheek to angle her face for a deeper kiss with the other.

Denim rubbed denim as they rolled their hips against each other, each breath more strangled than the one before, her ears ringing as blood rushed between her legs and tortured her with sweet pleasure.

No, that wasn't her ears.

Declan broke away and rose up. "What is that bell?"

"Granddaddy," she said on a sigh. "He probably wants to be helped to the bathroom for the evening."

"He'd be really unhappy if he knew he interrupted this."

"Seriously." She kissed him one more time, knowing

that this particular interlude was about to come to an untimely end.

He sat all the way up and tugged her sweater back over her bare stomach, making her moan with disappointment. "It's better this way," he said.

"Says who?"

"Says the voice of reason. Evie. You do need to think about it and consider every aspect. Ask me a million questions. Make me sign something if you…" His voice trailed off.

"I will think about it. In fact…" She kissed him again. "I probably won't think about anything else."

"That makes two of us."

They stood slowly, a little shaky, but held on to each other. "I'm bringing Judah home tomorrow."

"Not without me you're not."

"You think I need you for everything?" she teased.

"For some things. Like Judah. And…a baby."

"A baby." She whispered the word, letting the possibility rest on her heart. "I can't believe we're even talking about it."

He put his hands on her cheeks and kissed her one more time. "It might have taken a long time, but I'm a man of my word, Evie."

She sighed against him, open to anything at all if he could be a part of it.

When Declan stepped outside a few minutes later, his head was still reeling. He took a few seconds to stand in the shadows of the front porch, looking out at the lights as they flickered to life and twilight fell.

He waited for a kick of second-guessing, but none came.

The suggestion might have been spontaneous and prompted by an old promise, but the rightness of it settled on his chest like a shiny new department badge.

He had no doubts. Questions, yes. Concerns, of course. But nothing he and Evie couldn't work out as adults who cared intensely about each other's well-being. Just as he was about to step off the porch toward the walk, something flashed in the street, making him stop.

Not lightning. Not a porch light in the neighborhood. A camera flash. Another flipping tourist.

On instinct, he inched back into the shadows, scanning the sloping driveway to the street beyond, empty but for one car parked in front of a house across the street. Wasn't it a little late to be sightseeing?

He stepped off the porch then and onto the walk, giving the evil eye to the interloper even though they probably didn't deserve it. Hell, the house was one of the prettiest things in Bitter Bark. And so was the woman inside it.

He turned back to look up the driveway, forcing himself to see Gloriana House for all its, well, glory. And not what it represented in the past, but...the future. For him and Evie. The two of them—oh, no, the *three* of them—making Gloriana House a happy home.

He almost choked at the thought. Not only had he made a compelling case for the most life-changing scenario imaginable, was he actually thinking about the possibility of...*living here*?

Yeah. He'd lost his mind. Or had he? What if there was a baby? What if Evie stayed in Bitter Bark? What if they raised a child here so Evie could carry on all her traditions and hold recitals in the museum room, and they could entertain a pack of cousins and aunts and uncles at that dining room table? Would that be so bad?

It might be tough sometimes, but if it would make her happy?

He reached his truck at the bottom of the driveway, glancing at a sleek silver BMW on the street, where a man sat behind the wheel, reading his phone. His window was open, and when he looked up, he caught Declan's gaze.

Oh, what the hell? Suddenly feeling magnanimous and even a little bit proud of the property that brought people from far and wide, Declan lifted a hand in greeting. "S'up, man?"

"Just admiring the house," he said.

"It's a beauty, isn't it?" Well, *there* were some words he never thought he'd speak, but they felt kind of good on his lips.

"Sure is," the man said. "Has she made any decisions about the sale yet?"

The sale? He slowed his step. "Are you the guy who made an offer?" he guessed.

The man stared back at him, not answering right away. "Depends on who's asking." He angled his head, showing a thin face under his wire-framed glasses. "Not sure I want the free world to know I made it."

"I'm not the free world," he assured the man. "I'm a friend of the owners."

He nodded, eyeing Declan. "Well, the offer was serious. Does she know that?"

"She mentioned it to me."

"I was thinking about asking again, but..." He shrugged. "I really don't want to be pushy or rude. I love the house." He laughed. "And I love the woman I'm marrying," he added. "She wants this house so bad, she begged me to take pictures of it in all lighting."

Suddenly, the thought of another couple living here kind of squeezed Declan in the gut.

The other man held up his phone as evidence. "But you know what it's like when you find a woman you'd do anything for."

He sure as hell did, and the fact that some stranger was echoing his thoughts? Gramma Finnie would say, "God can speak to you through anyone, lad."

"Well, she knows your offer was legitimate," Declan said, taking a few steps into the street and closer to the car, curious about this rich, generous man who might waltz into the life Declan could have had. "But I wouldn't bother her tonight or, really, until she's ready, which could be a while." Especially if she gets... pregnant.

"Oh, yeah, sure. Do not disturb. Got it, man. Thanks." He reached to turn on the ignition as if to underscore how he wasn't planning to disturb anyone. "I'm Jim, by the way. And you?"

"Declan Mahoney." He walked closer to the car and extended his hand. "Good to meet you, Jim."

He hesitated a second, then reached his right hand out, giving Declan a glimpse of a tattooed forearm. "I do not want to overstep my bounds," the man said. "But if it's ever possible to see the inside, I'd love to. I mean, I totally understand her situation and all, but when she's ready, maybe she'd feel more comfortable letting a stranger in if you're in the house, too. I could bring my fiancée."

And then he'd up his offer to *three* million, and Declan's stupid little fantasies would get buried in cash.

Not to mention that without the house, would Evie have any reason to stay here so they could get from where they were now to where they were destined to be?

"Or not," the man added quickly, obviously sensing hesitation.

Declan had zero right to try to stop this potential sale. It wasn't his house. It wasn't even Evie's, for crying out loud. "No, no. I'll ask her. She has your number, right?"

"Yeah, but you should have it, too." He reached toward the glove box, and out of habit and training, Declan followed his right hand with his gaze. It landed on black ink in the distinct shape of a bell on his forearm, the tattoo detailed enough to have been done by a real artist. "Here you go."

He handed Declan a cream-colored card with raised black letters. "Thanks, Jim. I'll, uh, put in a word for you."

"That's great, Declan." He nodded and slid the gearshift into drive. "And sorry to bother you."

"No, it's fine. Take your pictures." He stepped away and glanced at the card as he crossed the street. *James Bell, Consultant.* Bell…like the tattoo.

Declan tucked it into his pocket, and when he did, his fingers brushed another card. He pulled that one out and slid into the driver's seat of his truck, looking at the business card in one hand and his decades-old promise in the other.

"Sorry, Jimbo." He tossed the business card into the cupholder, where it would be trashed next time he washed the truck.

But he unfolded the index card with reverence, slowly rereading every word.

*Friend, lover, husband…and father to our*

"Children," he finished, trying to remember why he didn't complete that sentence when he was writing out his promise. Didn't matter. They both knew how it should end.

Then he glanced up at the house, seeing the lights on upstairs, imagining Evie chatting with her grandfather. "I promised you, E. I *promised* you."

Suddenly, he understood why his world had been all wrong for twenty years. He'd made a promise, and it was time to keep it.

# Chapter Twenty

"Look at him, E." Declan kept slowing down as they walked with Judah to the physical therapy room, marveling over the change in the dog. "He's different. Am I imagining it? I know he's sore and moving slow, but doesn't he seem different to you?"

"Definitely, but it's not that unusual." Evie had seen the transformation of thousands of animals after surgery.

"See that spark in his eye?" Declan asked.

Evie glanced up at Declan, seeing the spark in *his* eyes. "The chronic pain is gone," she said, taking his hand. "He instinctively knows that stiffness he feels is temporary."

"Wow." Declan stopped as they reached the door to the physical therapy room, pulling her closer by their joined hands to add, "You're magic, you know that?"

She laughed. "I'm a trained professional," she told him. "No different than when you put out a fire. It's what you do."

He studied her for a moment, then guided Judah into the room that was empty except for a tech working with a small cat on a ramp across the room. "I kind of feel the same as he does."

"You do?"

"Like the chronic pain got fixed." He held her gaze, his own so full of meaning she could practically read his thoughts.

"And that stiffness?" she joked.

He winked. "Pretty sure you can fix that, too."

She laughed as they walked in, her own step lighter than it had been in a long, long time. Was it possible? Had that discussion about a baby somehow surgically removed the cause of all their pain for twenty years? The thing that had made them both want to howl in pain like Judah?

Watching Declan drop to the floor and get in Judah's face, teasing and talking gently to the dog, she started to believe it.

"Hey, bud," he whispered to the dog.

Judah responded by leaning forward to swipe that humongous tongue along Declan's cheek, making them both laugh.

"He's thanking you," she told him.

"I didn't do it," Declan said to Judah. "It was all her. That one." He pointed to Evie. "The gorgeous one who changes lives with a knife."

"Actually, a drill."

"Even sexier."

The compliment sent a zing through Evie, who slid into a guest chair, kind of itching to pull out her phone and take a picture of Declan and Judah face-to-face on the floor. Suddenly, Judah got down on his belly and lifted his gaze up to Declan, swatting his paw on the ground.

"He's telling you he wants to play."

"Oh, you can't do that, big man." But Declan slid down to his belly, too, staying eye to eye. "Couple of weeks, maybe, and we'll have you running with the rest of the pack at Waterford Farm." He put a gentle hand on the dog's head, studying his eyes. "You happy, Judah? I think you're happy. I'm happy, too."

Her heart rolled around helplessly as she watched the two of them, hearing him admit to a change she could see in both of them.

Feeling the need to join in, Evie slipped off the chair and got down on her belly with them. Instantly, Declan reached for her hand, tugging her into his private space with Judah, pulling her close so the three of them were in a little circle.

"Here's your doctor," he said to the dog. "Dolittle. She gets you like no one else." He inched forward and let his nose touch Judah's. "Me, too, by the way."

Evie turned her head to look at him. "You think?"

"I know." He angled his head so his forehead touched hers. And Judah joined right in, sticking his snout between them.

"What a sweet little family." They all moved back at the woman's voice, turning to see Christine in the doorway.

"Oh, hi," Evie said, pushing up. "We're just…" What were they doing? Acting like a sweet little family. "Hanging out with Judah," she finished.

"Who is doing so well. I'm Christine, the physical therapist," she said to Declan as he pushed up to a stand.

"Declan Mahoney." He shook her hand.

"And after you get a little PT, Judah?" Christine leaned over to greet the dog. "You'll be running circles around these two parents of yours."

Declan and Evie shared a quick look, his expression matching the thrill that shot through her. *Parents*.

Every minute, the possibility felt more real and right.

"Okay, then, let me walk you through his program." Christine brought them over to a ramp. "This is where we'll do some puppy push-ups."

As she described the process, Evie tried to listen, but Declan's very presence distracted her. She stood next to him, asking questions and listening and feeling so very much like...parents.

And he was right. It felt so good and natural.

"Ideally," Christine said, walking them toward an incline ramp, "we'd get Judah on an underwater treadmill every day."

"For dogs?" Declan asked. "I've seen them in some firefighting training gyms."

"Absolutely," Christine said. "By submerging his lower body, the buoyancy of the water decreases gravity and really improves and hastens the training, but we can't do that. So I recommend—"

"Why not?" Declan asked.

"We don't have one," she said. "We used to, but it went kaput. There's an equipment request on file, but the budget won't be approved until next semester."

Evie certainly understood that. Budgeting and purchasing at a college were done on the semester schedule, so if it hadn't been approved for fall, it wouldn't be here until spring. Which sucked because she knew that was one piece of equipment that could really help fix Judah's gait.

"Where's the closest facility that has one?" she asked.

"That doesn't have a monthlong waiting list? Hours away, I'm afraid."

Declan threw a look at Evie, clearly not happy with that. "But if it's ideal, how does not having one affect his recovery?"

"It'll be slower, but he should be fine in six weeks," Christine told him.

"And with the underwater treadmill?" Declan asked.

"More like four weeks," Christine said. "But we can get him healed without it. And if you want to leave him overnight, he could get shorter, more frequent sessions which will also speed things up."

"I don't want him alone overnight," Evie said quickly. "Even with vet techs to check on him. He's completely alert now, and the pain is diminished, but he has deep attachment issues, and I don't want him to suffer with loneliness on top of his recovery."

"I get that," Christine said. "We'll work out a good schedule for him. Do you want to go do his post-op exam now, Dr. Hewitt? I'll go make sure room four is ready."

Evie nodded, and as the woman left, Declan put an arm around her as if he sensed she wasn't thrilled with the solution. "You okay?"

"Yeah, and so is Judah, which is the thing that's bothering me."

He frowned. "I don't follow."

"He's made such progress in such a short amount of time," Evie said, stroking Judah's head. "I know with advanced PT, he'd be living a normal life in far less than six weeks. I'm thinking about all the equipment we have at NCS. There must be six underwater treadmills on an entire floor dedicated to canine rehab."

"This isn't NC State," he whispered so that the cat therapist working a few feet away wouldn't hear.

"I know, and I'm disappointed."

"Don't be." He gave her a squeeze. "We'll take care of him."

Not as well as she could at a bigger, better facility, but she nodded. "I better go do the exam to get him released. We'll be back in a bit. Come on, Judah."

By the time she finished the exam, Evie had a strong sense of satisfaction—she'd nailed the operation—and still battled the disappointment that she couldn't do more for him and faster.

But she couldn't change that.

When she signed all the paperwork, she took Judah to the waiting room to find Declan talking on his phone. She guessed it was one of his brothers or a cousin, based on his casual tone.

He disconnected and gave her a quick smile. "Can we take our boy home now?" he asked.

There was that feeling again…like they were *parents*. And it only intensified on the way back to Gloriana House.

Evie sat in the back seat of Declan's truck, her arm over Judah resting on her lap. Declan was quieter than usual, driving slowly and carefully during the short distance to the house, easing into every stop like his precious cargo couldn't take even the slightest jolt.

He drove like he would…if they were bringing a baby home from the hospital.

As the thought hit her, she looked up and caught his gaze in the rearview mirror.

"What is it?" he asked.

"I guess I'm not the only one who can read minds, huh?"

He smiled and slowed at a light. "Gramma Finnie would say you look like someone just danced over your grave. Is everything okay back there?"

"Yeah." She held his gaze, staring at those eyes,

imagining…all the things. "I'm thinking about it," she admitted softly.

He laughed. "I told you. Once that seed gets planted…" He winked. "See what I did there? Seed?"

She laughed. "I've created a monster."

"Hey, our baby will not be a monster."

She laughed, an infectious joy rising up every time they slipped into their old banter…and at how easily they could discuss this new possibility. "Well, I was just sitting back here with Judah thinking that this feels like, you know, coming home from the hospital with a new baby."

His eyes flashed in response. "Only this baby is hairier."

"Much." She stroked Judah's fur. "And his tongue is bigger than anything we could produce."

He let out a slow breath. "You're joking about it. That's a good sign."

"You think?"

"I know." He started driving slowly, looking from the mirror to the road and back. "You make jokes when something gets really serious for you."

"Not always."

"Usually."

"You think you know me so well."

"I do," he said. "And I know you're not happy about the PT situation."

"We'll make it work, right, Judah?" She leaned over and pressed a light kiss on his head.

"What did he say?" Declan asked.

"He said…wait." She put her ear next to his snout and nodded. "Mmm. Uh-huh. Yeah, I think you're right. Declan is definitely that."

"Declan is definitely what?" he asked on a chuckle.

"A very good daddy."

He beamed at her. "Honey, you ain't seen nothin' yet."

The words made her whole body feel like she was floating on air, but she didn't get a chance to figure out a way to tell him that because they reached the driveway to Gloriana House, which was full of cars. She recognized Molly's van and Yiayia's Buick, plus a few others she'd seen the day before at Waterford.

"An impromptu Mahoney-Kilcannon party?" she asked.

"That's what my family does, E. They're here to support. Yiayia probably brought Greek cookies that Alex made. Gramma Finnie undoubtedly embroidered Judah his own pillow, complete with an Irish saying. Molly wants to check on him, General Pru wants to tell us all how to do it right, and Connor's here to keep things light. It's how we roll."

And it would be exactly how they rolled if she had Declan's baby. At least, if she had Declan's baby *and* stayed in Bitter Bark. The family would surround that child with love and support and humor and food and more love. A family like she never had and couldn't give a baby on her own.

"You are so loved, big boy," she whispered to Judah. And so was Declan.

That was abundantly clear as they brought Judah in the front door to find the welcoming committee—including Granddaddy, who'd dressed and put in his dentures for the occasion—gathered in the entryway to celebrate their four-legged hero.

As Evie greeted them all with hugs and hellos, answering questions and letting them gently and cautiously wish Judah well, she slipped over to her grandfather.

"You okay, Granddaddy? Did you get yourself all ready alone this morning?"

"Finnie helped me," he whispered. "She called, and I told her the back door is always open."

"Oh." She looked over to the little Irish woman, who was fussing over Judah along with the others. "How sweet."

"And the Greek one brought cookies that tasted like Zeus himself made them."

She smiled at him, taking in the flush in his cheeks and the gleam in his usually tired eyes. "I'm so happy to hear that."

"And she announced that something magnificent happened in the museum room." He leaned in. "Did it? Last night, maybe?"

A rush of blood warmed her cheeks. Something magnificent *almost* happened. How the heck did Yiayia know that? Had she planted a camera in the room?

"So it's true," Granddaddy said. "You wouldn't be blushing if it wasn't."

She felt her eyes flash wide. "Those ladies are crazy," she whispered. "And are you sure you're not too tired for all this?"

"Pffft. Listen, Evangeline. Just stop everything and listen. What do you hear?"

She took a breath for composure, then did as he asked. "I hear people talking. Laughing. Making the place echo with…" Her voice faded out as she deciphered his pleased expression and happy nod. "You like that, don't you?"

"I've missed it so much it hurts," he admitted. "The

only thing I'd love more is to hear my sweet Penny play that piano." He grinned. "You did, didn't you?"

"Play the piano?" She frowned. "No, I haven't."

He looked surprised, but just then, Molly came over. "I hope you don't mind that Pru and I found the only bedroom on the first floor and set Judah up in there. I know you're going to want to sleep with him, and he can't do the stairs."

"Molly, how thoughtful. You put him in the former maid's room?"

"That's a maid's room?" Pru sidled up next to her mother. "It's bigger than my parents' room."

Evie laughed. "Don't you go to school?" she asked with a teasing poke in her arm.

"I took the morning off to help, but I'm only missing social studies and PE."

Molly gave an apologetic look. "I know, worst mother ever. But she's number one in her class. Come on, let's take Judah back to his room. I think you're going to like what we did."

Touched and a little overwhelmed, Evie followed, but Declan snagged her arm as she passed. "I'm going to run out for a little bit, but I should be back in a few hours."

"Okay." She frowned. "Do you work at five today?"

"Yeah, but I have a quick errand to do, then I'll see you. You're in good hands."

"Many of them," she agreed, tempted to give him a kiss goodbye. But Molly urged her on and took her past the kitchen and around the back stairs to what Grandmama had called the "servant's quarters," but her own mother had referred to it as "that little room downstairs."

"Ta-da!" Pru said, leading the way. "We've created a suite for Judah and a place for you."

Under the window that looked out on the backyard, they'd placed a cushy new dog bed with blankets and a pillow embroidered with his name and the words *Your Best Friend Leaves Paw Prints on Your Heart*, all decorated with those very paw prints and hearts.

"Gramma Finnie?" she guessed.

"Who else?" Molly laughed.

His food and water bowls were inches away, along with a few new chew toys she didn't recognize. "You guys thought of everything."

Molly slid an arm around her and gave her a hug while Pru slowly led Judah to his new bed.

"Here you go, buddy," Pru said, gently encouraging him to lie down.

"Are you exhausted?" Molly asked Evie. "Hungry? Wish we'd all leave?"

A burst of laughter came from the kitchen, making Evie shake her head. "Granddaddy is so happy," she said. "And I'm glad you're all here."

"Well, this one does have to get to school before calculus starts." Molly gave Pru a nudge. "Let's move it, Prudence."

After she walked Molly and Pru out, Evie came back to the kitchen, poured some coffee, and joined the group at the table. Granddaddy was seated at the head, sipping tea, while Yiayia and Gramma Finnie flanked him, hanging on every word.

"Well, this turned into a party," she said.

"'Tis always a festive day when a dog comes home from the hospital, lass."

"Kind of like a baby," Yiayia said, making Evie nearly snort her coffee out her nose.

"You..." She pointed from one oldster to the next. "You *all* are nuts and unbelievably transparent." And, possibly, very effective.

"Are we?" Yiayia asked. "I think we're very smart. Although I have to say, the piano thing was Finnie's idea."

"What piano thing?"

The three of them shared a look so heavy with unspoken words she half expected an organ chord to play a sudden accompaniment. But Gramma Finnie shook her head, and Yiayia looked down, and Granddaddy was suddenly preoccupied with his tea.

"Have a cookie, lass," Gramma Finnie said, pushing a plate toward her.

"They're kourabiedes," Yiayia said. "And not your standard Greek cookie, but my grandson Alex's secret recipe."

"I heard he cooks like a god." Evie eyed the older woman, still not able to figure her out. Or her obsession with that damned piano. "So thank you."

"Did you know Finola and my Penny sang in the church choir together?" Granddaddy suddenly said.

"I think I did." Evie took a cookie, happy for the change of subject. "Tell me your best memory of her."

"Oh, lass, there are so many. Like the time she reached around Judy Logan and covered her mouth with her hand during her completely off-key soprano line in the middle of the ten-thirty service."

"Wait," Evie said. "My grandmother? Madam Proper?"

"Proper schmopper." Gramma Finnie slid a look to Granddaddy. "Not at the poker table."

Evie almost choked. "She played poker?"

"Choir poker is the best poker." Gramma Finnie gave a playful grin.

"Oh, let's play some cards now," Granddaddy suggested.

At the unanimous response, Evie got up and found a deck in a kitchen drawer, joining in on a few hands and checking on Judah every few minutes. She was barely aware of the time that passed while three people, whose combined age was more than two hundred and fifty years old, played cards, not one of them wanting to lose.

During the game, they shared snippets of their lives and filled her heart and mind with stories about her grandmother and each other. Tales that Evie hoped to sit at this very table and share with her grandchildren someday.

Was that possible? Could that dream—

She was pulled from her reverie by a text from Declan.

*Is the sunroom floor laid on concrete?*

What the heck? She stared at the question, so out of the blue she had to think about the answer. *Yes*, she finally typed back as she recalled seeing a concrete subfloor when they reconstructed that wing after the fire. She wanted to ask why…but wasn't sure she wanted to know. But his next text came in a second.

*Can you open one of the French doors in there for me?*

She pushed up, holding the phone and frowning. "I'll be right back," she said, heading to the other side of the house.

Walking into the bright, glass-walled room that had been redesigned as an indoor garden that had gone dormant after her grandmother died, she caught sight of Declan, Connor, and Braden standing out on the patio in a group.

Braden was pointing up to the second-story veranda covering the patio, and she suddenly slowed her step, imagining the conversation.

*That's where it collapsed on Dad.*

*Trapped him right where the fire was raging.*

*He never had a chance.*

Is this why they're here? Tracing footsteps, looking into the past, remembering...

Her heart dropped at the thought. When would he forget? Would he ever forget? How could they get anywhere if he slid back into the dark place?

Letting out a sigh and bracing herself for whatever they might say to her, she went to the French doors, only then noticing a huge wooden crate between the men. It had to be seven feet long and three feet high.

As she unlocked the door, her gaze fell on the words printed on the side.

*Aqua Paws.*

"Is that..." Words failed her.

"Underwater treadmill," Declan said with that crazy-slow grin. Only this time, it wasn't Evie's knees that went weak. It was her heart.

"How? It's so much, and...Declan." She literally didn't know where to begin to thank him.

"Waterford gets a massive discount at the canine equipment warehouse outside of Holly Hills," he told her. "The chief said the first responders' charity wanted to contribute, so we can donate it in the department's name to the vet school when we're done. And I covered the rest."

"Declan," she whispered.

"Evie," he echoed, coming closer to plant an unexpected kiss on her lips. "You didn't think I was going to let our boy not have everything he needs."

"Come on, Daddio, let's haul this thing in and get it set up," Connor said. "We're all on duty in two hours."

She stepped back and watched in stunned silence as the three muscular men carried in the heavy crate, then unloaded and assembled the treadmill and small pool. Braden dragged the garden hose in and connected it to a spigot long ago installed for watering plants, and voilà.

Judah had an underwater treadmill…and Evie had one more reason to adore Declan Mahoney.

When Connor and Braden left, Declan put his arms around her, cuddling her close for a kiss.

She looked up at him, her whole body humming with need. Not sexual need, not emotional need, but the need to make this decision.

"You know what this means, don't you?" she asked.

"That Judah will be better in no time?"

"No. Well, yes. But that's not all it means."

He frowned, waiting.

"That right there?" She pointed at the treadmill. "It's all the proof I need that you're going to be a wonderful, caring, generous, amazing…" She closed her eyes to whisper, "Father."

He sucked in a breath. "You've thought enough?"

"More than enough."

"You're sure?"

She nodded. "I am so sure."

"Evie." He pulled her close and kissed her. "I have a twenty-four-hour shift. I'll be back tomorrow by six, and then…"

"Let the games begin."

"We're gonna win this game, E. You and me and…" His gaze dropped to her belly. "Junior."

She put her hand over the spot where he looked, fully committed to the dream.

# Chapter Twenty-One

Declan was packing up at four fifty-seven on the nose when his phone buzzed with a text.

That couldn't be good. Either Evie was texting to tell him not to come over, or Chief Winkler wanted yet another freaking personnel form filled out so it would be on his desk when he arrived the next morning.

But it was neither. Instead, the text came from a number he didn't recognize, but the words seized his attention.

*You want to talk about the Gloriana House fire?*

Declan blinked at the screen and typed back, *Who is this?*

The answer came in seconds. *Kirby Lewis, former AI.*

The arson investigator Braden said was a retired legend. *When can we talk?* Declan asked.

*I'm waiting in the town square by the statue of the dead guy.*

The dead guy. Evie's great-times-three grandfather. Seriously? Come on, dude. He was on his way to Evie's for the best night of his life, for crying out loud.

Fine. What was another half hour after twenty damn years?

He grabbed his backpack, checked out with the night-shift dispatch, and headed out into the cool autumn air. He strode across the grass to the Bushrod statue looming high in the middle of the square. The playground was quiet at this dinner hour, and only a few dogwalkers were around as the first of the white lights started to sparkle on the trees.

An older man sat on the bench in front of the statue, alone, tapping a phone, a ball cap pulled low over his eyes. Declan approached slowly, waiting for him to look up.

When he didn't, Declan glanced around, then took a chance. "Kirby?"

He finally met Declan's gaze. His seventy-something face was weathered, his expression blank. "Captain Mahoney."

Declan nodded and sat down a foot or so away from him. "Thanks for coming out of hiding," he said. "I understand it's not easy to track you down."

"Exactly the way I want it. But for this case?" The man almost smiled. "I had to."

Something in the way he said it put Declan on edge. "Is that so?"

He faced forward, giving Declan his profile of a bulbous nose and soft jowls. "It's haunted me, that fire."

"That makes two of us," Declan admitted. "Why?"

"Because there was something there I couldn't see," he said. "And I can always see what others can't. But it was like I took months to put together a jigsaw puzzle, got to the end, and a piece was missing. Pissed me off, I tell you."

"Do you have any theories?"

He blew out a noisy breath. "Always got theories, son.

Starting with the fact that there were two burn patterns associated with different accelerants, and two possible ways that fire could have started."

"So your theory is that the seat of the fire *wasn't* the linseed oil-soaked rags?" Declan's mind went back to the files. "All the evidence was consistent with that."

"Not all the evidence," Kirby said. "Yes, there was a burn pattern consistent with combustion on the outside patio. Was that possible? Yes, but I saw the container. In person. You probably saw pictures."

He nodded, remembering them.

"The top snapped on," Kirby said. "And I didn't think that top could have been blown off unless the person who put it on didn't snap it in place before walking away."

Evie's distracted, erratic, artiste mom? "That's possible."

"Think about it. This woman is a painter, right?" When Declan nodded, Kirby continued. "A painter knows what linseed oil can do. She went to the trouble to put her rags in a container, cover it, and place it outside. She knew what could happen on a hot night, so of course she snapped the lid into place."

And it sure had been hot that night. He remembered the heat even in the mountains. And Mrs. Hewitt might be a bit bizarre, but she wasn't dumb.

"So what are you saying? The wind didn't blow the top off?"

He gave Declan a side-eye and raised a brow. That was exactly what he was saying. "That inside burn pattern was consistent with lighter fluid being squirted on the wall," he said. "That wall was directly adjacent to the patio where the combustion happened. So the question I couldn't stop asking is which burn pattern represented the accelerant and which happened because another fire had started? You get me? What was inside and what was outside? Were there two fires or one?"

"But there also was a lighter collection, so lighter fluid could easily have splashed on the wall."

"True," Kirby said. "There were a few lighters in that room, all being cleaned and polished that day, along with a very large tin of lighter fluid that was stored there for that purpose."

"All this was in the investigation files," Declan said. "The lighter fluid caught fire when the wall between the worktable and the outside caught fire."

"Uh-huh. Right."

"Which sounds more like 'not a chance,'" Declan noted with a dry laugh.

"All I know is that there were burn patterns of squirted lighter fluid inside," he said. "That doesn't happen from combustion."

"What do you think happened?" Declan asked, his chest tightening.

He was quiet for a long time. "I'm an arson investigator, Captain, not an accident investigator."

"So you think this fire was arson. Do you think someone could have broken into the house, where four people were sleeping, and set the fire?"

"Or..." He lifted a brow, and Declan knew exactly what he thought. "Someone already inside the house."

*A member of Evie's own family.*

"But none of those pieces fit, either," Kirby said. "I couldn't get the why, and if there isn't a why, then there isn't a case."

Exactly. No one in that house had a reason to destroy the property or risk lives.

Unless…someone did, and the investigators hadn't figured that out.

"So I had to ask myself why the lead investigators finally decided to ignore my rarely wrong gut instinct," Kirby continued. "And I hate to say it, but my instinct went to someone on the inside."

"Of the house?"

"Or the department. As a firefighter yourself, you know what a nightmare it is to lose a good man."

Declan stared at him. "What are you saying?"

"Maybe they didn't want to see the truth. Maybe someone in that fire department hid the last piece of the puzzle."

A hot, sickening burn started low in his stomach. "What piece? That my dad made a mistake?"

"Possibly." He nodded, mouth turned down. "Men do make errors, even ones you think should be up on a pedestal as high as that guy right there."

Declan didn't even look at the statue, but kept his eyes on the man next to him. "My father may have died because of his own error in judgment. It happens. But that didn't *start* the fire."

"True," he agreed. "So who else might they be protecting?"

"I have no freaking idea." Irritation snaked up his spine. "Why don't you spell it out for me?"

"Because my theories are just that—guesses. You were there."

"No, I wasn't," Declan shot back. "I was up in the mountains and not on duty that night." Otherwise, maybe they wouldn't be sitting here having this frustrating conversation.

"You were in the department, though. You had to hear something of the conversations."

Declan grunted, remembering the thick, soup-like fog he'd lived in. "I didn't go to work much after that fire. They gave me some time off to take care of my family." And hide in that emotional basement.

"Have you ever looked at the firefighter roster to see who was there that night? Including volunteers?"

"I didn't see that in the file for the investigation, but I could probably get my hands on it."

"Do that, because firefighters can be arsonists," Kirby said. "Some of the best, in fact. And the list of all the volunteers. Don't forget them."

"The fire was contained fast. Only one group of volunteers was called in." Suddenly, Declan's shoulders felt heavy with the weight of what he was doing. Did he want to reopen the investigation? All he wanted to do was *close* it—in his head and heart.

"So talk to them. Now that twenty years have passed, someone who wasn't willing to talk back than might be willing now," Kirby said. "And, of course, you have to look at the property owners to see what they had to gain."

"From losing a house that's been in the family for more than a hundred years?" He heard his voice rise with disbelief. "No amount of insurance could cover the treasures in that house."

"It's not always insurance," Kirby said. "Sometimes, they want to cover up some*thing*. In fact, covering past misdeeds is, in my experience, a far more common reason to start a fire than to get money. Especially for people that rich."

Declan considered that, but what would anyone living

in Gloriana House want to cover up? But then, how well did he know Evie's parents? Another sickening sensation spread through his chest. Was he really sitting here considering Evie's *parents* as suspects in the fire that killed his father?

God, maybe he really did want to sabotage this relationship.

"Or sometimes," the man said, flipping his phone over and over in his hands, "it's about money, but not in the way you think."

Declan looked skyward at the cryptic words. "What do you mean?"

His hands stilled, and he turned to Declan, looking him directly in the eyes again. "Max Hewitt donated thousands of dollars to the Vestal Valley First Responders Organization. Still does, actually. Did you know that?"

"Of course I know that." He shifted on the bench. "You think they could have protected him because he's a top donor?" His body hummed with the need to reject that idea, to rip it out of the universe and stomp on it. "The guy couldn't hurt a fly." The cliché was the best he could do, considering how his head was exploding from the conversation.

Kirby lifted his shoulders and made a face. "Just keep asking why, son. You'll get to the bottom of it."

"If there's a bottom to get to."

The other man exhaled and sat back. "Now it's my turn to ask you why. Why now? Why after twenty years? Why did this suddenly become your mission?"

"It's not a mission," he said. "I wanted to find out what happened, because I can't..." Let it go. "Because I want to know."

"Be careful what you wish for," Kirby said with a dry laugh. "And don't ignore the fact that the house was full of something that starts a fire…lighters."

"They're not going to tell me anything," Declan said.

"You sure? Find one that puts out the highest-temperature flame, and you'll have your lighter. That fire burned stunningly fast, probably at thirteen hundred degrees Celsius. That's a certain kind of lighter, a 1300, and it ain't what Grandpa used to puff on his pipe."

"Got it." Declan closed his eyes, remembering the array of lighters on display.

"Hope that helps, son." He pushed up to a stand.

No, it didn't help. It made things worse. "Can I call you if I have any questions?"

"I'd rather you didn't. I'm retired and would like to stay that way." He threw Declan one more look. "Just don't dig too deep. In my experience, the answer is right in front of you…if you want to see it."

He nodded once, pulled the ball cap low, and walked off, leaving Declan staring up at Thaddeus himself.

He sat there for a long, long time, letting it all play out. Could Max have set that fire? Or was there a skilled arsonist? And was the fire inside the house the reason Dad had powered through to the sunroom and got trapped when the burning veranda above him collapsed?

Or was this just the ramblings of an eccentric old man who liked to find arson where there may have been none?

All he knew now was that this was keeping him from the one person he wanted to be with.

Not to mention that if Evie had any idea that he'd had a conversation like this—about her own family—it would break her heart. And God knew he was never going to do that again.

No. He was going to have a baby with her, and if everything went according to the plan he was still formulating, he was going to spend the rest of his life with her.

He'd already let this damn fire ruin half his life. He wasn't going to let it ruin the rest.

# Chapter Twenty-Two

Wen six o'clock came and went, Evie started to wonder if Declan wasn't going to show. But his delay gave her a chance to get Granddaddy situated for the night, then feed Judah and run him through a short rehab session.

With both her patients exhausted and in their respective beds, Evie showered, put on some makeup, and picked out a tank top and soft cotton skirt, taking more time selecting lace undies than the actual outfit. She'd made Declan's favorite sandwich, opened wine, and lit candles on the farmhouse table in the kitchen, but it was after seven when she heard Declan's truck door in the driveway.

Curious why he hadn't texted he was on his way, she took her wine to the front door in time to see him climb out, grab a backpack, and take a minute to look up at the sky and sigh.

She stepped out onto the porch. "Are you having second thoughts, Captain?"

He turned, stared at her for a long moment, then let his gaze roam over her the way he used to that summer when they knew where they were headed, but didn't know when or where.

"The only thoughts I'm having…" he said as he walked toward her, cracking that unhurried Mahoney smile. He reached her, took the wine, sipped it, then leaned over to kiss her. "Are kinda dirty."

A sexy hot tendril curled around her insides. "I was starting to feel stood up."

"I had…business."

She searched his face, more because of his tone than what he'd said. "Everything okay?"

He studied her for a moment, sliding a hand under her jaw, giving her chills when his palm grazed her skin. "It is now."

"I made us hoagies," she said. "Your favorite Italian with extra cheese and no onions." She led him into the house. "Are you hungry?"

He nodded, still sort of staring at her.

"Yeah, I'd call that hungry," she joked. "Ravenous, in fact. So why don't we—"

He stopped her with a kiss, hard and hot, wrapping his arm around her and drawing her into his body. "Food can wait," he said. "I can't. I honest to God cannot wait another minute for you, Evie."

She folded against him, looking up. "Then don't."

He kissed her again while he closed and locked the door, then ushered her toward the back, somehow knowing exactly where they were going. He stopped to lean against a wall to intensify the kisses, his whole body so hard and powerful she felt like she was melting into the board-and-batten panels.

"Not bad for post-twenty-four-hour shift," she murmured.

"And I didn't sleep five minutes." Tunneling his fingers into her hair, he lifted her head to get to her throat.

"A lot of calls?"

"Very few."

"Then why didn't you sleep?" she asked.

"'Cause I felt like a kid on Christmas Eve." He glided a hand down her neck and slowly caressed her breast. "Presents waiting to…"

She bit her lip and looked up at him, dragging her hand down the front of his T-shirt. At the bottom, she let her fingers graze the button of his jeans. "Unwrap," she finished for him.

He chuckled into the next kiss, his whole body responding against her. "Ho, ho, ho," he teased, caressing her back and angling her hips against his. "It's Christmas in October."

She kissed him again, a whimper escaping as their tongues touched like the opening notes of a long, beautiful symphony.

Still holding each other, still kissing, he stepped her back like they were dancing. "Hope Judah sleeps heavy, or else…"

"He's sound asleep. Come." She walked him to the little suite of rooms behind the back stairs.

It was dark and got even darker when she closed the bedroom door, but she easily guided him to the bed. He set his backpack on the floor, very carefully, glancing at Judah.

"I don't want to wake him," he whispered.

"Listen to that dog snore," she said. "He's underwater-treadmill tired."

He smiled. "It works?"

"Like a charm. Christine was mightily impressed. Do you need a light?" she asked.

"Only if you want me to find protection."

She'd thought so much about this moment, this question, this issue. "How's your health, Captain?"

"Flawless. Checked constantly. Yours?"

She gave a dry laugh. "I've been celibate since my last doctor's appointment."

With a moan, he leaned down and kissed her, guiding her to the bed. "Gotta change that situation, stat."

"Yes, please." She fell onto the comforter with him, wrapping her legs around him so her skirt slid up, gasping at the way his body fit against hers. They rolled once, then again, refusing to break the kiss as he worked her top over her head, and she did the same with his.

He took a moment to appreciate the pretty lace bra, or maybe what was in it, then easily unhooked it, taking a much longer moment to admire her bare breasts. His gaze seared her, and then he touched her skin, and that burned hotter. He dipped his head to plant a kiss on her breast, nearly taking all her breath away.

"And the protection?" He lifted his head to look into her eyes. "Because, Evie, I want to make love to you with or without…consequences. I want you. Before anything or anyone else, I want *you*."

"So, are you saying this is not about a baby?"

"It can be, but…" He stilled his hand, giving her a serious, smoky look. "First and foremost, it's about us."

"Declan." She stroked his cheek, feeling the stubble from a long shift and the face of a man who couldn't be better, on any level. "I never dared to dream this could happen. Well, that's not true. I dreamed it a lot. Awake and asleep dreams."

His eyes shuttered at her words. "Same."

"And in my dreams, we were always in love." She couldn't stop now. She had to tell him the truth. He had to know before they made love. "Not trying to make a baby and not trying to make up for lost time. But you and me...in love." She sighed against him, kissing him with her lips parted and eyes open. "I wanted that more than I wanted sex."

He looked at her for a long time, his heart hammering so hard she could feel it.

"Then let's start this the right way," he whispered.

She stared back, silent.

He curled his arms under her, elevating her a little bit as he looked into her eyes. "I love you, Dr. Evangeline Hewitt. I loved you then, and I love you now. I might have stopped living for twenty years, but I didn't stop loving."

"Oh." She exhaled the word on a whispery sigh, feeling like she could float on the happiness of that. "You love me."

"I knew it in the mountains that morning when I woke up," he whispered. "I knew I loved you and that we'd always..." His throat grew thick, and she quieted him with a kiss.

"I knew it, too," she murmured against his mouth. "Always you, only you."

They got lost in another kiss, while everything in the world faded away.

"So, last time. Protection?" he asked when they parted.

"I have all the protection I need right here in my arms."

"Then let me love you, E."

Declan was as tender and gentle as he'd been the night she'd given him her virginity. Every touch, every stroke, every delicate exploration was done with the sole purpose of making sure Evie felt safe and pleasured.

Of course they laughed and whispered, like they had on that blanket under the stars. And he slid the rest of her clothes off with the same crazy-slow care he'd used on her jeans that first time, pressing his lips to her as if every new inch of exposed skin was a glorious discovery that he had to taste and inhale and explore.

He let her finish undressing him, then eased them both under the covers with the same confidence he'd rolled out that sleeping bag and cocooned with her inside it.

He left her breathless with kisses, taking his time to let her whole body wind up and grow needy and tense as they rolled and rocked and touched and teased.

"I'm having déjà vu," she whispered into his mouth.

"If you make a pun now…"

She laughed, turning them over so she was on top for a moment. "I'm serious. I keep thinking of that night in the mountains." She planted a few kisses on his chest, letting the hair there tickle her lips. "Only you have more muscles now."

"And I bet I can last longer than two minutes."

"That was only the first time." She looked up and smiled as she slid farther down his body. "Plus, it was the best two minutes of my life." She closed her hand over him and drew her tongue along his abs. "Until tonight."

He groaned as she stroked him, then pulled her up and turned her on her back, kissing her until she could barely breathe, holding her with those big strong hands. "It was worth the wait," he said. "Worth every minute of twenty years for right now."

She wrapped her legs around his hips, so ready to feel him inside her. "Declan."

"Evie."

"Now?"

He touched her lightly, making her hips rise, feeling how ready she was. "Now."

He held her gaze, then lowered to kiss her, connecting their mouths as their bodies did the same, a sweet trick that made her whole being quiver with pleasure.

He moved slowly at first, making her writhe and moan, then they found a perfect rhythm that seemed to match her heartbeat, increasing every second, pleasure lapping at her body, tightening her limbs, but making her feel utterly boneless and lost.

She forgot about the world, the past, the icy years. There was only right now, this very minute, this blissful, intense, perfect connection of two people who had never known anything but love for each other.

New and remembered sensations zinged over her body, hot sparks when he caressed her skin, dreamy waves of pleasure rolling inside her, and tight knots of need that threatened to unravel with each stroke.

He seemed to somehow hold her poised between the most beautiful elevation and a crashing out-of-control spiral that made her giddy and dizzy and free.

And just like that, he kissed her again, held still for two or three heartbeats, and her body gave in. She clung to him, pressing her lips against his powerful shoulder, squeezing her eyes shut as she quaked with satisfaction. She'd barely caught the next breath when he took the same ride, murmuring her name over and over again as he lost every shred of some rather impressive control.

With one last groan, he fell against her, their bodies damp and shaky and sticky and spent.

"So, are you supposed to lie really still or put up your legs or something?" he asked after a moment.

"I don't know," she said. "I've never tried getting pregnant this way."

He laughed a little. "How'd you like this new, conventional method?"

"You're no nurse with a syringe, Mahoney, but you'll do."

He managed to lean up on one elbow to look down at her. "Was this the right time of the month?"

"Close enough."

"But we'll still have to try again." He kissed her. "And again. And…"

She put her hand on his cheek, stopping the next kiss. "I don't care, Declan."

He searched her face, a frown forming. "Did you change your mind?"

"No, I don't care if I get pregnant or not. I only care about you right now. About us. About finding our way back to each other and not letting anything ever get in the way of us again."

A shadow crossed his expression, fast and gone before anyone who didn't know him as well as she did would ever have noticed. "There's going to be an us?" he asked.

"There *is* an us."

"What about…life? And where we live? And how we live?"

"Can we figure that out as we go along?" she asked. "I'm drunk on Declan and can't think straight."

That made him smile. "E." He whispered the single letter, tracing her lips with his finger. "E is for everything. Excellent. Electrifying."

"Big D," she teased. "For delicious and darling and…" She bit her lip. "Daddy."

With a moan that sounded like it came from somewhere

deep inside, he squeezed her in a full-body embrace. "I can't remember the last time I was this happy."

"I remember it. I just remembered every moment of it."

He closed his eyes and rested, wrapped together, not moving for a long, long time. And Evie finally, finally felt as if twenty years had never passed.

Something wet and heavy scraped Declan's face. Hot breath puffed against his ear. And a hairy paw landed on his chest, making him grunt and open his eyes.

"Whoa…" He groaned the word, eyeballing the dog trying to get onto the bed.

Next to him, Evie stirred, flipping her head on the pillow and opening sleepy blue eyes. She gasped and popped up. "Judah! No." In a flash, she was out from under the covers and rolling over Declan and using both hands to keep Judah down. "I know you feel good, honey, but you can't climb onto beds yet."

Judah let himself be eased back to the ground, his brown eyes locked on Evie's bare breasts.

"Annnnd I'm naked," she said, sliding a slightly shy look at Declan.

"And the problem with that is…" Smiling and not able to take his gaze from her, Declan reached down to the floor and grabbed the first article of clothing he found. "Fine. But she looks good without her fur, right, Judah?"

He barked twice.

"What'd he say, Dolittle?"

"He said you're a dirty dog." She pulled the top over

her head, which was a waste of time since he'd have it off in a minute anyway. Like he had last night when they'd slipped into the kitchen at midnight to devour hoagies and potato chips and each other up against the counter.

As soon as she scrambled back under the covers, Declan wrapped himself around her. "God, you're the best thing I've ever opened my eyes to see first thing in the morning."

She kissed him lightly, then pulled back. "What time is it?"

Declan slid deeper into the bed, rolling onto his side to line up their bodies, curling his leg over her bare thigh. "Time to try again."

"Mmm." She bent into his body, warm and silky. "But I have to get Granddaddy's breakfast at seven. Is it past seven?"

He eased back to break the news. "It's past eight."

"Dang it." The covers flipped again. "He'll be starving. Where's my phone? I need to check to see if he's still in bed. Oh, and Nellie Shaker's coming over at noon with some of the ladies from the Historical Society, but I invited your sister and cousins and mom and the grannies to come at eleven."

He drew back, confused. "Why?"

"To pick out some dresses for the Founder's Day Living Museum party. I want your family to have the first choices. And this afternoon, I have some patients to see at Molly's after I take Judah over to Vestal Valley for a session with Christine. What are you doing today?"

"I thought I was making a baby, but it seems that Mom is way too involved in other stuff."

She smiled as if the name had given her a genuine kick

of pleasure. "Then rest today and store up for a big night."

"Nope. We're going to baby-make before anyone shows up before eleven." He pushed out of the bed. "You stay here, and I'll get Max's breakfast."

"And explain your presence how?"

Snagging his boxers, he threw her a look. "First of all, if he knew the truth, he'd dance down those stairs and throw a party. Second, I could have shown up here to work. Or to check on Judah. Or to see you. Do I need a reason for being here?"

"I guess not. But I can take him tea and applesauce and avoid the whole discussion altogether."

"You'll be up there for an hour tending to his every need," he said. "I'll take him breakfast. You stay here and rest up for the next attempt. I'll tell him you're very busy with Judah."

Judah sat up at the mention of his name, his look hopeful.

"And while the water's heating up for tea, I'll take our boy out to the back for a trip to the grass," he added.

"Declan," she sighed.

"Evie." He mimicked her tone perfectly.

She smiled up at him, a lock of dark hair falling over one eye, her lips pink from all that kissing. "Is this how you'd take care of me if I was pregnant?"

"If? Think positive. Maybe you already are."

"Nah, they're still swimming around on an egg hunt." She tapped her tummy. "You can do it, guys. It's waitin' for you." She smiled up at him. "Like I've been waiting for you, Captain."

He studied her for a moment, wanting to run his fingers through that hair, or brush his knuckles over her well-kissed mouth, or fold her into his arms and tell her that she would be the most pampered, protected, and loved expectant mother on earth. But he stared at her and let the moment wash over him. "I still can't believe this."

"That we're trying to get pregnant?"

He traced a line along her jaw, careful not to move that strand of hair because it made her look so sexy. "That you forgave me," he whispered. "That you trust me again."

She closed her hand over his. "Don't dwell on what wasn't, Dec. Think about what's going to be. Like how loud that bell upstairs is going to be ringing any minute."

"On it. Wait for me. Do not move."

"Bathroom?"

"In and out and back in bed so we can try one more time before your day explodes with activity." After he pulled on his jeans and T-shirt, he bent over to kiss her again.

She fisted his T-shirt and pulled him closer. "By the way, Declan Joseph Mahoney, you have been working on your technique for twenty years."

He gave a quick laugh. "Not that much."

"Well, last night was a-freaking-mazing."

"Hold that thought, E." One last kiss. "I hear the bell."

He didn't even try to wipe the smile off his face when he walked into Max's room, carrying a tray with hot tea and applesauce, a few minutes later.

"Room service," he called out when he saw that Max was awake and sitting up.

"That's a different delivery person," the old man said, turning to catch sight of Declan. "What are you doing here at this hour?"

He zipped through his options and settled on Judah. "I wanted to—"

"Oh, never mind. I can see exactly what you've been up to."

"You can?" He set the legs of the bed tray on the comforter, suddenly wondering if she'd left lipstick on him or, God, a hickey. Things had gotten a little wild in the middle of the night.

"She could have at least told you your shirt's inside out."

Declan choked a soft laugh, looking down to see the seam of his T-shirt. "My bad."

Max gave him a fully toothless grin, reminding Declan of one of the Kilcannon babies. "No, you're good." He looked down at the tray, then back up at Declan. "Thank you."

He nodded, uncertain if he was being thanked for breakfast…or how the shirt got inside out.

"Will you open my drapes?" Max asked. "And maybe stay a moment?"

As much as he wanted to get back to Evie, sympathy for the old man won out. "Sure." Kneeling on the window seat, he slid the heavy curtains along the rod, letting morning light pour into the room. Turning, he perched on the edge, thinking how lonely it must be up here, especially without Judah.

"Your buddy Judah's doing great," he said. "The biggest challenge is keeping him from being too active."

He nodded, spooning some of the applesauce. "He's a good dog."

"A great one."

"He can live here with you and Evie."

Declan blinked at him. "Wow, you have things more figured out than we do," he confessed.

"I have it all figured out," he said. "Me and the grandmothers. I might join their little matchmaking club."

Declan chuckled at that. "Just what they need, encouragement."

"That Greek one is nice-looking." He sipped his tea. "Doesn't mince words and plays a good game of gin rummy. And she makes a helluva cookie."

Declan was pretty sure her grandson made those, but who was he to argue with this happy man? "Good to see you in such high spirits, sir," Declan said, wondering if this was the right time to maybe ask a question or two, maybe dig a little deeper into the things he'd talked to Kirby Lewis about. "So, I was looking at your impressive lighter collection the other day."

"Oh, those things." He lifted a bony shoulder. "I rarely even pick one up anymore. I was just thinking about the Dunhill Alduna, though. Nice piece of workmanship there."

Declan shifted in his seat, not quite sure he wanted to take the conversation where it could naturally go, but when would he get another chance? "I know a little bit about lighters."

"I guess so, in your line of work." He sipped his tea and looked at Declan over the rim.

"Do any of those in your collection burn at 1300 degrees? I know that's unusual."

"The Ronson Whirlwind," he said without a second's hesitation. "There are two of them down there. One's gold with a blank engraving spot. The other's a petrol lighter with a map of Scotland on it. And yes, there's another one, too. Newer model."

"And you remember them all?"

"Mostly." He tapped his temple. "My memory is the only thing left that works at full speed." He gave in to a wide grin and looked down at his body. "Although, if I spend more time with the Greek goddess, I think a few things might come back to life."

Declan gave a soft snort, kind of wishing he didn't have that particular image in his brain. "Careful what you tell Finnie, then. She'll have you and Agnes Santorini on a honeymoon before you know what hit you."

He gave a throaty laugh and spooned some more applesauce. "You know who'd hit me? Penny, when I got up to the pearly gates. I'm blowing off steam. But the memory's sharp. Go ahead, test me."

Shifting on the window seat, Declan thought about all the things this man might have stored in that still-functioning memory of his. Like…the truth about what happened that hot August night.

He leaned forward, bracing his elbows on his knees. "Do you remember the fire?" he asked.

Putting down the teacup, Max let out a long sigh. "Of course I do. I remember what pajamas I was wearing. I remember what I ate for dinner that night. And I remember that my daughter-in-law isn't the sharpest tool in the shed and maybe shouldn't have been allowed to play with chemicals."

"You know, Max, there are actually two schools of thought about what happened that night."

His watery old eyes suddenly looked very, very sharp. "You want to clear Evie's mother's name?"

"Her name doesn't need to be cleared," he said. "She did everything right with those chemicals, including putting the container outside. The official report said it was a wind gust that knocked the container over."

"Hmmm." Max lifted his spoon, studying the applesauce like it held the answers to life.

"Do you have any reason not to believe that assessment?"

"Not really." He stared into his teacup for a minute. A long minute. Then he looked up at Declan. "Do you?" he asked.

Declan eyed the other man. "I'm looking into it," he said quietly. "Considering all aspects of the investigation."

"They closed the investigation," Max said, a tiny bit of defiance in his voice. "Called it an accident after a good long time and a lot of money and interviews."

"I know that."

"But you don't agree?"

He rubbed his hands over his jeans, not entirely sure how much to share. "I met with an arson investigator who thought maybe the accelerant was lighter fluid, not combusted rags."

Max stared at him.

"And it's his opinion that the fire might have started inside the sunroom, not outside on that patio. Maybe that's the reason my father tried to get into the sunroom, which is something no one seems to understand."

Max still didn't say a word, but Declan could see something in his eyes. Hurt. Fear. Maybe regret. He didn't know.

"Do you have any idea why he would have done that?" Declan asked.

"I was out in the street when the upstairs veranda collapsed."

"Yeah, I know. But that day? Do you remember, maybe, spilling lighter fluid when you were cleaning your collection?"

Old gray brows drew together, and his gaze grew narrower. "You want some advice, son?" He didn't wait for Declan's answer, but pointed an arthritic finger at him. "You go looking for trouble, you know what's going to happen?"

"I'll find it?" he guessed.

"You'll lose...*her*."

Declan stared at him.

"Is it worth it to you? To turn over stones that were long ago pressed into the ground and meant to stay there? Is it?"

He wasn't sure. "The truth is always important," he managed.

Max pushed the tray away and fell back on the pillow. "I'm tired now."

Declan sat very still for a moment, letting the conversation sink in and not particularly liking any of it.

After a moment, he stood, took the tray, and headed down the back stairs to the kitchen, stopping when he saw Evie leaning against that same counter where they'd kissed like teenagers the night before, staring at her phone.

"Hey, you're supposed to be waiting in there for me." He angled his head toward the bedroom.

She looked up from her phone and walked toward him, her expression blank, actually humorless.

"He's right, you know."

He inched back, frowning.

"You would lose me." She turned the phone so he could see the screen, a camera shot of Max sound asleep. "I thought it would be fun to check out what you two were talking about."

*Damn* it. Silent, he put the tray on the island, thinking

about the advice he'd just been given. When he turned, she'd already gone back into the bedroom. He followed her, finding her sitting on the floor, petting Judah.

"He remembers things," he said. "He might be able to shed some light on what happened that night."

She looked up at him. "I didn't know it was in darkness."

"It is for me, Evie. I'd never cracked a file on that fire. Never wanted to get that close to it. But after I was up in the attic, I realized I had to. I have to face it in order to get free of it."

"Then face it, but don't try to re-investigate it. Do you have any idea what that will do to you?"

Yes, as a matter of fact, he did. He closed his eyes, knowing where a good dive into the cause of that fire would send him.

"I mean, now you're looking for lighters that burn a certain way and asking about spilled lighter fluid?" She stood up, her eyes steely as she pinned her gaze on him. "Do you think my grandfather set that fire on purpose?"

"No, of course not."

"My mother? My father? Someone in my family?"

"I don't," he said. "None of them had a motive, and there's only thin evidence that contradicts much stronger evidence."

"Then why are you looking for trouble?" she asked. "To sabotage us? Like your sister said? Maybe that *is* what you do, Dec."

He sure hoped not. "I wanted to talk to him about what he remembers from that night," he said, coming closer to her.

"Why?"

"Because somebody made a mistake. It *might* have

been my dad. It might have been…someone else. And I feel like I should know."

"You do know. My mother put rags in a bucket, and they combusted."

"That's what we think, but…" He couldn't finish the sentence, because the look of fear and sadness in her eyes took his breath away.

"Why would you ask Max about his lighters?" Her voice was taut and her eyes fiery with emotion. "Why would you have secret conversations with an arson investigator?"

"It wasn't secret."

"Well, you didn't tell me."

He huffed out a breath. "Evie, I want to know what happened."

"I get that, I do." She wrapped her arms around herself. "But ten minutes ago, you were marveling that I trust you again. Can I? Or will you go back to that dark, cold, shut-off place?"

"I won't—"

"You might. You very well might. And I honestly don't know if I can take that again." Hurt hung on every word, slicing him in half.

"Evie." He reached for her hand, but she stepped back. "I swear I don't want to let anything wreck this again."

"Then don't." She stared hard at him. "The case was investigated and closed. *Thoroughly* investigated. Can't that be enough for you? Can't you move on and live in the present…with me? Isn't that what you want?"

"More than anything," he said. He finally got her hand and held it tight, bringing her knuckles to his lips and holding her gaze. "It's all I want, Evie."

"I need to trust you," she whispered. "I need to know that you won't go back there, Dec. That you won't freeze me out, that you won't go…"

Down. Way down to the basement of his soul.

"I won't." He pressed another kiss on her hand. "I'm going to let it go. I promise."

She gave him a sad smile, reminding him that he'd made—and broken—promises in the past.

Well, he wouldn't break this one. He would not.

# Chapter Twenty-Three

A few hours later, Evie finally put the conversation behind her as she escorted the Mahoney, Kilcannon, and Santorini women into the "turret room" to enjoy the explosion of silk and satin in every color of the rainbow. Dozens of dresses hung from the shutters and the doors of a massive antique armoire, and more were spread out over the bed.

Chloe and Andi squealed with excitement, while Cassie and her mother, Katie, linked arms and gushed over two gowns Evie thought they might like.

"I don't know what's cooler," Pru exclaimed, twirling in the circular bedroom. "This room or these clothes!"

"The room is cool," Jessie agreed, lifting a deep green empire dress that set off her strawberry-blond hair. "But this dress is a dream. Do you think it'll fit?"

Gramma Finnie tucked at the material. "I can make it fit, lass, if Evie doesn't mind a few stitches in the dresses."

"As long as they hold their integrity," she said. "I wouldn't want anything to be cut."

"You wouldn't have to cut this to fit me." Yiayia held a bright blue satin tea dress. "If I squeeze into it, I'll claim it as mine."

"Oh, Yiayia." Evie put a hand on her shoulder. "That belonged to my Grandmama Penelope. You would look striking in it."

"Look at this one!" Ella exclaimed, sliding a black-and-white ball gown from the 1950s from a hanger. "Just call me Doris Day!"

"Oh, honey, you'll be a princess in that dress!" Colleen fluttered the material, fussing over her daughter.

"Did you find anything you like, Colleen?" Evie asked. "I was thinking of you for that elegant rose-colored 1920s number. It would really look beautiful with your hair."

Her eyes lit as she studied the dress. "I don't think I've ever worn anything that...exotic."

"Then it's time."

Colleen slid her arm around Evie's waist. "What about you, dear? Have you picked a dress?"

"I have." Several of the women in the room stopped their examinations of the dresses to listen to her. "My great-grandmother Evangeline's engagement dress."

"An *engagement* dress?" Yiayia and Gramma Finnie said the words in such perfect high-pitched unison that everyone burst into laughter.

"Well, that's...promising," Yiayia said.

"No promises." Evie tapped the woman's shoulder playfully.

"Oh, the Dogmothers want promises," Pru said, sidling up to Evie. "We basically live for them." At Evie's look, she shrugged. "Yes, we. They made me a Dogdaughter for my sixteenth birthday."

"What we want are happy endings," Gramma Finnie said, getting a wide-eyed look from Evie and several others in the room. "What? Agnes has convinced me that subtlety is for younger people. We don't have all the time in the world to ring those wedding bells."

Evie bit back a laugh and looked from woman to woman. "No one's going to give me an assist here?"

"Of course they won't," Ella said, sliding her fingers into her tousled short hair. "Because they've all been wooed to the dark side, and I'm the only one of this lot who hasn't been helped down the aisle by a well-meaning family member." She leaned in to wrinkle her cute nose. "But in this case, I'm going with the majority. I've never seen my big brother so happy. Well, yes, I have. And so have you."

Yiayia clapped. "Then bring on the engagement… dress."

Gramma Finnie's face crinkled into a smile. "You're a good sport, lass. We usually don't have to try this hard."

"You don't have to try at all," she said softly.

"So everything is right where it should be?" Gramma Finnie asked. "There's hope?"

Evie sighed. "There's always hope." Once Declan let go of the past for good and kept his walls down.

"Do you know what my mother says?" Colleen asked, pointing to Gramma Finnie.

"I think I do," Evie said. "I think I've heard this one…"

"With hope, anything is possible." The words were spoken in unison by every woman in the room, except Gramma Finnie, who beamed like a conductor who'd gotten her orchestra to play the perfect note in unison.

"'Tis true, lassies" she said on a sigh, her gaze dropping to Evie's stomach. "*Anything* is possible."

Evie bit her lip and smiled at her and Colleen, feeling her eyes fill with the emotion of the moment and the aftermath of her argument with Declan this morning. Was anything possible? Could she trust Declan not to spiral into that darkness, where she'd lose him again? Would he ever be able to let go of that pain once and for all?

"What is it?" Colleen asked, taking her hand.

The gesture was so genuine and motherly that Evie nearly blinked out a tear. "Oh, it's…nothing like…"

Every woman in the room stilled and looked at her.

"Nothing like being the center of attention," she tried to joke.

"Come on, Evie." Molly slid an arm around her. "Do you need some advice? A shoulder? Some insights from the family who knows him best?"

Colleen squeezed her hand. "I'm pretty sure you'll never have this many advice-givers in one room."

She let out a sigh and leaned into Molly, looking from one loving, beautiful face to another. "I never had sisters," she admitted, her throat thick.

"Well, here we are." Molly beamed at her. "Ready to advise and…sister."

"I've never even had cousins or in-laws or steps," she added, smiling at Andi and Chloe, who were clearly dear friends, and Cassie and Katie, who had an enviable mother-daughter relationship, and Darcy and Ella, always next to each other. The grannies, of course, and Beck, who rubbed her barely showing baby bump, next to Pru, who had her arms around Grace and Sadie.

"Whatever you need to know or understand about Declan," Colleen said, "this is the group to ask."

She held Colleen's gaze, as warm as any of them in the room. "You've all noticed that he's changed."

There was a chorus of agreement.

"Do you think it's a lasting change?" she whispered. "It was a long twenty years. And this has been a short week or so. I'm scared. I'm an…attacher."

"So true," Molly agreed. "She almost wouldn't give Danny back."

"I don't want to get hurt."

For a moment, no one said a word. Then Gramma Finnie stepped closer and joined the small group in the center of the room.

"Lass, what you are is a *nurturer*. Pure and simple. You have a magical touch with animals and…" Gramma smiled. "Declan Mahoney. The person you need to trust is yourself and your glorious healing power."

"Oh." Evie put her hand to her chest. "Thank you, Gramma."

Yiayia took a step closer, the blue dress in her arms. "Everyone in this room will tell you Declan's heart is gold. You know that."

She nodded. "Pure gold."

"And real gold is tested, refined, and purified by fire," Yiayia said. "Believe me when I say people can and do change after they've been through the worst of times. But sometimes it takes some intervention. And I don't mean us. It's *you*."

"That's so sweet, Yiayia."

The older woman looked skyward. "I've made Finnie blunt, and she's made me sweet. Kind of."

As they all laughed, Colleen took Evie's hands. "I can tell you this, honey. Joe always thought our son would marry you. And he—and I—very much liked that idea."

Evie bit her lip as if that could stop the tears from welling. It didn't, so she reached out and hugged Colleen, breaking contact only at the sound of the doorbell chime.

"That's Nellie and company," she said, reluctantly letting go.

"So I guess we can all back off this poor woman." Ella threw an arm around Evie. "Hold off the Historical Society long enough for us to pick our dresses."

"I'll mow down anyone who tries to take my periwinkle silk," Yiayia announced, clutching her dress.

Feeling light and loved, Evie started out, but Sadie snagged her arm. "Um, I meant to warn you about something."

Was one woman in this room going to try to talk her out of a relationship with Declan? "Yes?"

"I'm speaking in my official capacity as the co-chief of staff and de facto mayor," Sadie said. "The Historical Society petitioned the town council to reinstate the Founder's Day parade." She inched closer. "With you and Max in the lead convertible. So, please say yes when they ask you."

Evie let out a soft laugh of surrender. "How could I say no?" She looked past Sadie to the room full of women. "To any of you?"

The cheer echoed in the hall and followed her all the way down the stairs.

"Declan! I didn't think you'd be here today." Owen Winkler's booming voice reached into Declan's office and made him swear silently. He wanted to get in and out, with one goal—to return the complete set of investigation files and put the matter to bed.

"Yep, I'm here. Do you need anything, Chief?"

Without being asked, the big man took a chair, cringing as he sat. "New knees."

"Spoken like a true former linebacker." Declan stuffed the last of the files into the brown cardboard box. "Plus, I think you can buy those now."

Chief chuckled. "I might have to." He pointed to the box. "Gloriana House?"

Nodding, Declan dropped into his desk chair, because conversations with this man were never brief or casual. "Yes, sir."

"I saw you signed them out." His ebony eyes slid over Declan's face. "What brought that on?"

"If you don't know that I've been hanging out with Evie Hewitt and spending time at her house, then you would be the last person in Bitter Bark to have heard the news."

He laughed and pointed a meaty finger. "Just checkin' to see if you'd be real with me, Mahoney."

"Always, Chief."

His smile faded a little as he rubbed a hand over his shiny dome. "What'd you find out?"

"Nothing," he said. "Case is closed, as it should be after an investigation that thorough."

Owen leaned back, crossing his arms. "I'm sorry I never met your dad, Declan."

"So am I. You'd have liked each other."

"I certainly like his sons," he said. "If they tell me anything about the man, my guess is he was wise, kind, and a skilled firefighter."

Declan nodded his thanks. "He was all that and more."

Chief leaned forward and tapped the box. "I've heard he wasn't one to make mistakes on the job."

The comment reached down and twisted Declan's gut. Forget the lighter fluid. Not knowing what had caused his dad to make a decision that cost him his life was what really unsettled him. He'd get over it—he had to—but it was like a low-grade hum of discomfort now.

"But as we all know, it only takes one mistake," Declan replied. "And you can never know what's going to happen in a fire."

Chief nodded, as if he knew Declan needed to make the statement.

"You know what might help you?"

He didn't know he needed help, but leveled his gaze at his boss. "Six more personnel reports on your desk by tomorrow?"

Chief gave a hearty laugh. "Well, other than that, of course. You should talk to some of the men who were there."

"I have, the ones that are still around. Dad's partner on that fire is also gone, as you know."

"But there are others. Have you reviewed the list to see who's still in town, or who you could call?"

No, and he didn't want to. He'd made a *promise*. "I haven't."

"I can get a list for you."

"That's all right, Chief, I—"

"It could help you."

Again, he honestly didn't need help. "It's fine."

"No, it's not fine. You're doubting your father, and that is never fine. I say that as a man with three kids."

Actually, he was doubting the investigators— including the eccentric one—but maybe Chief was right. Maybe part of his need to look further into this case was so Joe Mahoney's halo could be restored.

"I'll get you a complete list." Chief said it the way he said anything that left no room for negotiating.

Declan fought a sigh. He wasn't going to go off and interview guys who'd worked here twenty years ago. If they knew anything, it would have been included in the reports. Unless…someone was hiding something, like Kirby Lewis had suggested.

*Damn it.* "Okay, thanks."

"Now, let's talk about something else." Chief locked his hands behind his bald head, his huge biceps bulging. "My knees."

"Oh yeah. I know they've been killing you." He eyed the other man, knowing there was more to this part of the conversation than him moaning about his knees. "Are you going to get the surgery? I can cover for you if—"

"Oh, I know you can. But I don't want you to cover for me, Dec."

"Oh, okay." He'd give that role to one of the other two captains?

"I want you to take over my job."

Declan stared at him for a moment. "For…good?"

"For as long as you want it."

"You're quitting?"

"They call it retirement, son, and it's a fine-sounding word." He held up a hand to stave off arguments. "I know I'm only fifty, but Lizzie wants to live at the beach, and the retirement package is good, and the kids are getting older, so…" He leaned forward. "You're the only man in this department I'd consider, and if you mention that to the two other captains, well…" He shrugged. "You won't have to, because they'll know when it's announced."

Declan fell back in his chair. "Whoa. I didn't think it would be quite this soon."

"Neither did I, to be honest. And I might have hung in there ten more years if I didn't know such a good chief was waiting in the wings."

"That's...wow. Thank you. I'm honored. I'm ready." He added a laugh as an unexpected zing shot through him.

"It's a big change, you know. Way less action, and I think you'd miss the action. I mean, for a single guy, no responsibilities, no wife, getting into a fire can be a big thrill."

Out of respect, Declan didn't snort a laugh. "I don't think of firefighting as a thrill. It's a calling."

"Absolutely. And so is leadership, which is *your* calling."

Declan fought a smile. "Thanks, Chief."

"Hey, thank your old man. He was the one who trained you, whether you realize it or not. I know he was in line to be the next chief. He'd be proud of you."

A kick of satisfaction hit him hard. "I hope so." He stood when Chief Winkler did, taking the hand his boss extended.

"We'll announce it in a few weeks," Chief said after they shook, then he walked to the door. Before he opened it, he turned back to Declan, who probably had a stupid grin on his face. "Oh yeah, contrary to what you think, I'm not the last person in Bitter Bark to get the news. I can't wait to dance at your wedding, Dec."

That stupid grin got stupider. "I can't wait to see you dance, Chief."

With that thought in his head, dumping the files back into the storage garage and officially signing off on their return was the easiest thing Declan had done in ages. He'd glance at the firefighter list when he got it, but his life was exactly where he wanted it. Evie in his arms, a baby in the making, his career reaching a pinnacle.

Right now, he couldn't remember what that moldy old emotional basement even looked like, which was exactly as it should be.

# Chapter Twenty-Four

"It's today," Evie whispered before her eyes were even open. "Today is...the day."

Declan turned to her, his hard, warm body familiar after a few weeks of falling asleep next to him every night that he wasn't on duty at the station.

"The Living Museum extravaganza wherein I don a black suit that looks like I am about to be buried in it?"

"Wherein?" She poked his shoulder. "Who says that?"

"The guy who wears that suit."

"You look like my great-grandfather Montgomery Hewitt, a very dashing man." She snuggled closer, loving the feel of him from head to toe. "But that's not what today is." She gave him a squeeze. "I'm due today...or not."

His eyes grew wide. "Really? Do you know? Now? Can you tell if you're getting it?"

"Let me go to the bathroom." She kissed him on the lips, then reached to the floor to grab a T-shirt that happened to be his navy BBFD shirt. "Wait here and say good Irish prayers."

"When will you be able to take a test?" he asked, pushing up on his elbows.

"Once I'm a few days late. Hang on." She tugged the T-shirt over her hips and stepped out of bed completely.

Instantly, Judah barked at her, his head up at the first sound of talking, an abject plea on his remarkable face. "Okay, I'll help you up, Judah. Easy does it."

"I got him." Declan sat all the way up and gently assisted Judah onto the bed. "When do you think he can do steps, Evie?"

"Well, it's only been a few weeks. I'd say two more weeks, and he'll be able to get up and down the stairs and even jump on this bed." She rubbed the dog's back and gave Declan a look. "Careful what you wish for, Dec. There'll be three of us in here."

"Or he'll go up and keep Max company."

Judah made his way up the bed to snuggle with Declan, giving him a massive tongue bath.

"Oh!" Declan laughed, backing away. "Is that necessary?"

"Can't say I blame him," Evie joked.

"Your tongue is different. Your tongue is—"

Judah barked once, then sat up, put his head back and let out a huge howl.

Declan rubbed his head. "Are you sure he's not in pain anymore?"

"Nope. That's a happy howl. Eyes on you, tongue out, body quivering with joy." She came around the bed to give him a kiss. "Like I was last night."

As she stepped away, he got a hold of the T-shirt, pulling her back, holding her gaze. "That was incredible."

She inhaled deeply and let it all out with a sigh. "Yes, it was." She gave him one more kiss, then headed into the en suite. There, she gave a little fist pump of joy when there were no signs of her period, then brushed her teeth and stared into the mirror.

Did she look pregnant? She was…glowing. But that might be because she'd spent so much time with Declan, making love, laughing hard, eating well, and falling…

Oh yeah. She was in love. Deeply. Totally. Crazily in love. And it was time she tell him her news. Not the news he was hoping to get, but something that might make him happier. She hoped it would.

She leaned toward the mirror to whisper, "You are never going back to Raleigh, Dr. H." The decision to move back to Bitter Bark and open The Hewitt Veterinary Neurology Clinic had been shockingly easy, which Grandmama Penelope would say was a sign that it was the right decision. She'd made it the night he told her about his impending promotion to chief of the BBFD.

She just hadn't told him yet.

Baby or not, she didn't want to leave Declan or this town or this house or the family that felt like it had adopted her. Hell, she was actually entertaining Nellie's suggestion that she be the newest member of the Bitter Bark Historical Society. She could even teach a few classes at Vestal Valley, too.

She looked down at her belly, touching it lightly. And, God willing, she'd be raising a baby with Declan, too. And if that didn't happen, then they could adopt, or even look into being foster parents—of a child and dogs. Whatever happened, they'd be together.

She came out of the bathroom and crossed her arms, leaning on the doorjamb with a big smile and a heart that was as light as she could remember. It was time to tell him.

"Well?" he asked, so excited that Judah barked.

"I'm not *not* pregnant. So far, anyway. And I usually start in the morning."

"Judah!" He growled the dog's name and gave his big head a vigorous rub. "Did you hear that? Not *not*. That's a double negative, which means…"

"Nothing yet," she told him, coming closer to the bed, that light heart suddenly kicking up a few levels as she tried to think of exactly the right words to tell him about her decision.

He looked over Judah's head at her, that smile she loved so much pulling at his lips. "Look at you, E," he whispered.

"Look at me what?"

"My girl. My best friend. My…" He sighed and shook his head as if words eluded him.

"Lover," she finished for him, reaching hungrily for his bare chest and letting him pull her onto the bed.

"Among other things."

"Possible mother of your children?"

"Here's hoping." He leaned over and kissed her nose and dragged his hands over the T-shirt. "This is mine. Take it off."

She laughed into the next kiss. "With Judah on the bed?"

"He needs to go." Declan drew back, looking at her, his hands on the T-shirt and her bare legs. "You know, you look exactly like you did that morning in the mountains. Wearing a BBFD T-shirt and nothing else. Same shirt, same girl."

"Hardly a girl," she said, managing to wedge herself between him and Judah. "But I do remember that before you woke up, I was down on the dock, looking out over the lake and mountains."

"Do you remember what you were thinking about?" he asked, his voice as low and husky as it had been in the sleeping bag that morning.

"I was thinking what the hell would I do if I got pregnant." She laughed softly. "Oh, the irony. We'd have a nineteen-year-old now."

He gave her a hard look. "And she would never, ever spend the night at the lake with her boyfriend, that's for damn sure. At least not without us. And Judah. And all her uncles."

She giggled and got closer to him. "So you're going to be that kind of dad."

"I'm going to be any kind of dad you want me to be." He kissed her hair. "But you do look the same, Evie. You are the same."

"Not even close," she said. "I'm twenty years older and so much wiser."

He stroked her hair and cheek. "What do you know now that you didn't know then?"

"I know..." She looked up and into his eyes, the words bubbling up. "I love you."

"You do?"

"You can't be surprised."

"You hadn't said it before."

"I was waiting." She kissed him.

"For what?"

"For now." She moaned a little and hugged him tighter. "I love you, Declan Mahoney."

"I love you, Evie Hewitt." He grinned at her. "Now there's a good echo for us."

Judah tried to climb between them, barking.

"Yeah, we love you, too," Declan said. "But you have got to get off this bed, because we have to celebrate."

But Judah barked again, pawing at her. "Oh wait. He's telling me my phone's ringing."

"He is?" Declan snorted. "Now we've gone too far."

"He always tells me when you're calling during your shifts. He licks my hand so I don't sleep through your call." She rolled over and reached past Judah's head to get her phone, but Declan held her tight.

"It's not me, so ignore it." He punctuated that with a kiss and managed to get his hands all the way under the T-shirt.

She eased away. "It could be Nellie Shaker. I promised her we'd touch base first thing this morning. Caterers are coming soon. She hired history specialists who are obsessed with every single thing being authentic to the Victorian era, including the dishes and food and...*oh*."

Evie forgot what she was saying as he coasted his hand over her body.

"I'm obsessed, too. With..." He cupped her breasts. "You."

"One second. I'll tell her I'm busy." She grabbed the phone, squinting at it. "Oh shoot." She straightened right up. "Holy heck, it's Joan Whitfield. Why is she calling me?"

"Who is she?"

"My boss, *Dean* Whitfield."

He gave her a *not a chance* look and pulled the T-shirt higher. "You're on sabbatical. And I'm on a mission." He kissed her belly.

"She wouldn't call unless it's important. Hold that..." She brought the phone closer. "Oh. Yeah. Hold *that*."

She cleared her throat and tapped the phone. "Evie Hewitt," she said in her most professional voice, despite being one hot kiss from naked and completely horizontal.

"Joan Whitfield," the dean's familiar voice came through the phone. "How is your sabbatical going, my friend?"

She smiled at Declan, who was tracing a line on her leg. "It's..." His finger disappeared under the edge of the T-shirt. "Incredible. That's...I mean, it's...been perfect." She glared at him, but he chuckled and tortured her by inching his finger higher.

"Good, good. Well, I'm not calling to cut it short, so you can relax about that."

She couldn't relax about anything when his hand was...there. "Glad to hear it, *Dean*." She emphasized the title to remind him this wasn't a run-of-the-mill girlfriend calling.

He dipped his head to kiss the very skin he'd been touching, using his tongue to make her crazy.

"So things in your little town are going well?"

"Really...well." She bit her lip as he nibbled her thigh. "The whole experience has been simply... breathtaking."

She fisted some of his hair, tugging lightly.

"Oh, really?" Joan laughed, and Evie tried to picture the silver-haired sixty-year-old who loved patterned scarves and red wine. But she failed. The only silver she could see were the threads at Declan's temple when he turned his head to kiss the other thigh. "And here I thought you were just taking care of your grandfather and his house."

His lips pressed on the most tender part of her, making Evie want to drop her head back and whimper in delight. "I'm doing a lot more than that," she said, working to keep her voice steady.

He peeked up with a question in his eyes. Evie smiled and pushed his head down. "I can multitask," she told her boss...and her boyfriend, whose shoulders moved with a silent laugh.

"I know you can," the dean said. "Better than most. Which is why I'm calling with some very big news."

"Oh?"

Declan stilled at the sound of that single syllable, as if the interest in her voice piqued his.

"I'm taking the job as head of the College of Vet Med at Cornell."

Evie gasped and not because Declan found another sweet spot. "Joan! Congratulations. Cornell has an amazing program! And their teaching hospital is one of the best in the world."

"I know, and I'm stoked for the job, but I wanted to call and tell you personally."

"Thank you for that," she said, vaguely aware that she'd inched away from Declan. "You'll be missed," she said. And, if she'd already told Declan her news, she'd probably spill the beans to Joan right now. But she didn't want him to find out that she'd decided to stay like this.

He paused and watched her, taking her cue to slow down the fun as she got more serious.

"Cornell is lucky to get you," she said, thinking of the strong and fair hand that Joan used at NC State. It was no wonder she'd go to Cornell, one of maybe three schools in the country ranked better than their own for veterinary medicine. "Do you start in the fall?"

"Actually, I'm going this spring, which has the powers that be in a tizzy around here."

"I can imagine," she said, holding Declan's gaze as he abandoned his teasing to let her finish the conversation.

"Be right back," he mouthed, pointing to the bathroom.

She nodded and blew a kiss. "What do you think they'll do?" she asked Joan, her mind whirring through the school's options. "Interview from outside?"

"Nope."

Evie switched the phone to her other ear as she watched Declan disappear into the bathroom. "Oh?"

"Come on, Evie. You know what I'm going to say."

A tight tendril of something like twisted hopes and fears wound around her chest. "I'm not sure…"

"You're the first choice. Would you consider taking the dean position? You'd need to come back a few times before January to pound out the details, but you don't have to end your sabbatical."

"Me." It wasn't a question. It was the way her career had gone from day one. Every promotion, every time.

Then why didn't her heart soar with success like it had with all the other steps up the career ladder? Because she was about to jump off that ladder and land in Bitter Bark. But…dean of the vet school?

*It's different for women.*

She could hear Declan's comment and remembered her gut-level reaction to that. But *was* it different for women? For this woman?

"Oh, they'll go through the usual hoops and contracts and lawyers," Joan continued. "But you've been a good friend, Evie, and I wanted to let you know your name is at the top of the list. And it couldn't happen to a more deserving person. You have earned the rich rewards and lovely perks of being a dean. And quite a young one, at that."

A very young one. Young enough to still be…trying to have a baby. Young enough to still be practicing medicine. Young enough to start a whole new life with the man she loved.

"Listen, don't commit to me," Joan said on a laugh, as if she sensed Evie's hesitation. "Make them throw scads of money at you and get the big house off-campus. I know they want you, Evie. You've been nothing but a boon to the whole school since the day you arrived."

"Joan…" She couldn't think of how to respond. "That's really kind of you to say."

"Um, I'm not sensing a but, am I?" The other woman gave a dry laugh. "Because you'd be out of your blasted mind not to take this job, Dr. Hewitt. You were born for it."

Was she? Or was she born for Bitter Bark and Gloriana House and a family line she loved and being hands-on with the animals? She stroked Judah's head. Not to mention Chief Declan Mahoney and the job *he'd* worked for throughout his whole career.

"I'm a little speechless," she said. "But thrilled for you and…the opportunity. Thank you for letting me know."

"Let's talk after you've had a chance to let it sink in. But be warned, you should be getting that call any day now."

"Okay, I'll be ready. Thank you." After another moment, she hung up and sat perfectly still except for the hand she moved over Judah's head, holding his gaze. "What am I going to do, J?" she whispered. "What the hell am I going to do?"

If she took the job, would Declan be willing to give up his dream? Of course he would. He'd do anything for her. But would that make him happy? Would it make her happy? And what would be best for a baby? Would they want to leave the family and Bitter Bark and—

Declan opened the bathroom door, wearing nothing but boxers. "Done?" he asked around the toothbrush in his mouth.

She stared at him. "Yeah."

He frowned and slipped the toothbrush out. "You okay?"

"I'm…fine. Yeah. Are you coming back to bed?"

He held up one finger, then turned, and she heard the water running in the sink. He returned and put both arms around Judah. "Down you go, bud. This bed belongs to me. And this woman is…" He set the dog in his own bed, then turned to her. "Upset."

She blinked at him, a little surprised that he could figure that out so easily.

"No, I'm not," she said quickly. She wasn't ready to have this discussion. Because she imagined there wouldn't be a discussion, that Declan would immediately offer to give up his job for her. Was that what she wanted?

She didn't know. She didn't know what she wanted at all. Until he knelt on the bed and kissed her, tasting like peppermint toothpaste and possibilities.

At least she knew she wanted…*that*.

And for right this minute, that was all she wanted.

# Chapter Twenty-five

"**W**ould you beautiful ladies like an escort?" Declan held out both arms, one for each of the well-dressed grandmothers who'd arrived just as the Living Museum party was starting to come alive. "I can take you on the grand tour before the crowds arrive."

"Or we can stand here and gawk, lad." Gramma Finnie, decked out in a silver dress with more ruffles than he'd ever seen her in, paused in the entryway and looked around. "'Tis magnificent."

"Didn't Evie do a great job?" he asked. "Each open room represents a different era over the last hundred and twenty years. You're standing in the Roaring Twenties right now."

Yiayia stretched her neck and looked straight up. "And I see the chandelier was cleaned for the first time *since* the Roaring Twenties."

He laughed. "Please, I had to fight with the Historical Society not to change it back to an oil-burning lamp for the night. They actually suggested that. To a *firefighter*."

He looked from one to the other, then settled on his own grandmother, dying to get an answer to a question that had been haunting him for weeks. "So, Finola Kilcannon, how did you get it?"

She drew back and raised a white brow, feigning innocence.

"Oh, come on," he said. "I know it was you who hid that card in the piano keys."

"I don't know what you're talking about," she said. "Sounds like Gloriana House has a wee leprechaun about the place."

He snorted and looked at Yiayia, who looked a little too proud of herself.

"A leprechaun named Agnes Santorini?" he guessed, making them both laugh and give it away.

"Gramma, how did you even get it?" he asked. "I thought it was lost."

She put a hand on his arm. "You don't remember the morning, lad. You dropped your bag on the lawn, and when you went into the house, I gathered it, and some of your belongings fell out. I happened to glance down and read the words."

"My promises."

"I tucked it away, for the right time. You know the Irish say, 'Death leaves a heartache no one can heal, but love leaves a memory no one can steal.'" She leaned her head against his shoulder. "I knew you had to handle your heartache before you were ready for love."

"How did you know I'm ready now?" he asked, curious how his grandmother knew him better than he knew himself.

"I was in the waiting room the day Evie performed surgery on Rusty."

He dug into his memory banks. He'd been vaguely aware that the room was crowded with Mahoneys and

Kilcannons. And one beautiful neurologist.

"I saw the look that passed between the two o' ye." Gramma's voice grew low and her brogue thick. "And then Darcy said a couple of weeks ago that she'd seen Evie in town, and we cooked up the excuse we needed."

"Why not give the card to me if you thought I needed a push?" he asked.

"Good question," Yiayia interjected, hanging on every word of the conversation. "That was exactly what I wanted to know. But this one had me sneaking around this house, looking for a hiding place."

"I felt Evie should find it," Gramma Finnie said. "I hoped it would have her come to you because, honestly, I didn't think anything would get you out of your ways."

"But…the croissant run? Were you covering all your bases?"

She chuckled. "Truth be told, while Agnes was planting that in the piano, I had a conversation with Max, and we decided to help things along with a little Sunday morning visit to the bakery. There was always the chance Evie wouldn't take the bait."

"That's *all* you and Max discussed?" he pressed.

"Well, the wedding plans, of course." She adjusted her bifocals. "And he was yammering about great-grand-children, but sweet Saint Patrick, Declan, I'm not *that* much of a busybody."

"He is," he said on a laugh.

"That's part of his charm," Yiayia said, gesturing toward the stairs. "And so is the fact that he needs an assist and is too proud to ask." She pointed to the top of the steps, where Max Hewitt stood, wearing a dark suit very much like the one Declan had on.

And Judah was already at the bottom, looking like he might attempt to be the one to help Max.

"Excuse me, ladies," Declan said, heading across the entryway to stop the howl from one and the possible tumble from the other. As he got to the bottom of the steps, Pru came up next to him.

"Let me take Judah, Uncle Declan," she offered. "You can help Max."

He shot her a grateful smile and headed up the stairs, his gaze on the old man who apparently *was* more of a busybody than the so-called Dogmothers. Thank God.

"Well, someone's looking quite dapper," Declan said when he reached Max.

"We both are," he said, his eyes looking suspiciously damp as he scanned the scene below. "And will you look at this affair?"

Declan stood next to him and looked out over the large entry as more people filled it and spilled into the dining room and parlor on either side. Dresses swooshed in every imaginable color, an array of fashions from eras gone by, while waiters in footman's outfits carried trays with champagne and hors d'oeuvres, and a small string quartet filled the oversize hall with classical music.

"Pretty cool to see Gloriana House like this, isn't it?" Declan asked.

Max put one hand on the railing and the other on the arm Declan offered. "I never thought I'd see this again in my lifetime," he mused. "Penny would simply burst with joy if she were here. It's what she always wanted, you know. To open the doors and show the place off, always celebrating the history and generations who've lived here."

Declan peered out at the massive space, hearing the

echo of laughter and the clink of crystal, once again seeing the unique beauty of Gloriana House.

"And would you look at that?" Max nodded to the parlor entrance where Evie, dressed in a cream-colored gown with a deep blue satin belt, welcomed another guest. The dress was like something out of a movie, with layers of sheer silk like a cloud around her when she moved.

Her distinct and musical laugh floated up the stairs as she linked an arm around Ella's and his mother's, and they all cracked up at something Connor said.

"I could look at that all day, Max," Declan admitted. And for the rest of his life.

"She brings something special back to this house," Max said. "Respect and reverence, and she has a way of sharing it with others."

"I've noticed that."

Max looked up at him and gave a slow grin. "Made you kind of love the place, didn't she?"

"The place and the people in it," he admitted.

Max gave his hand a squeeze. "So, the plan worked, huh?"

"The plan." He snorted and jutted his chin toward Gramma and Yiayia. "Your cohorts are right down there waiting to gloat with you."

"Waiting to drink with me, more like."

"Even better." As Declan escorted the old man slowly down the grand staircase, he was aware of a lot of eyes on them. On him. And he knew what they were thinking...

How could Declan Mahoney look so happy, here in the house that took his father?

Because of that woman, there. The woman who healed him with the same skill that she used on Judah.

The woman who loved him with the same urgency she had as a young girl. The woman who was going to be by his side—in this house—for the rest of their lives.

"Who's she talking to now?" Max asked.

Evie's back was to him as she spoke to a man who held both her hands and leaned close. A jolt of jealousy rocked him momentarily, but then he recognized the reddish-brown hair and wire-framed glasses of the... potential buyer.

Bell? James Bell. With the BMW and the seven-figure offer?

"Some nitwit who has the audacity to think he can buy this house."

"Ha!" Max choked. "Over my dead body." Then he grinned. "Literally."

"Nope. Over mine, Max. Over mine."

"Oh, wait one second." Max squeezed his arm and stopped their progress. "I gave a little thought to that conversation we had a few weeks back and took a look at my lighter collection." He reached into his pocket and pulled something out, slipping whatever it was into Declan's pocket, adding a bit of weight to the jacket. "That one's not mine. Penny found it during construction and insisted it was part of my collection, but I never saw that lighter before. Wasn't until you mentioned another possible way it could have started that I even thought about that one, but it was still in the collection. Maybe it'll help with your quest."

Or maybe it was lost by a construction worker and was nothing more than something that could send his happiness...up in flames. He had no intention of digging into this new piece of "evidence" and his *quest* was over.

But he nodded his thanks to Max.

"And now, if you don't mind, I think I'll go charm that Greek lady in blue." He headed toward Yiayia the minute they reached the bottom of the stairs.

"Declan, there you are." Behind him, Evie put her hand on his arm. "I want to introduce you to—"

"Jim." Declan extended his hand and forced a smile. "Nice to see you." *Now take your money and leave our house.*

"Oh, you know each other?" Evie asked, surprised.

"We met briefly on the street," Bell said. "Declan. Nice costume."

Declan let the compliment—which didn't exactly sound like one—pass as he looked beyond the other man. "Is your fiancée here?" he asked. "The one who's in love with the house?"

"I didn't dare bring her," he said on a laugh. "Because, trust me, she wouldn't leave until this woman right here signed a contract." He jabbed Evie with a playful elbow. "You still have my offer. I can have a deal drawn up by tomorrow."

"Mr. Bell, now is not the time," Evie said gracefully. "But please, I know you wanted to have a look around, so you should enjoy our Living Museum." She turned when someone called her name.

"I really wanted to see it all," he said, undaunted. "Could I just—"

"I'll show you around," Declan said, easing the man away from Evie.

She gave him a grateful look and mouthed, "Thanks."

And just to let this rude guest know what's what, Declan leaned down and added a light kiss on her lips. "I got this, E."

She slipped away, and he turned to the man who might have missed the whole exchange as he gaped around.

"We can start in the dining room," Declan said, aware of a burst of laughter that came from some members of his family, making him really hope this diversion didn't last long so he could get back to people he'd rather be with.

But he wasn't going to let this guy ruin Evie's big night with talk of offers and contracts.

"The dining room?" Bell sounded less than enthused.

"Where two governors dined."

"Hmm." His gaze still scanned the area quickly, his interest in the dining room was pretty low. For all his money, he probably couldn't even appreciate the unique beauty of that ceiling or the finishings or the history.

He didn't deserve this house.

"Folklore has it that Amelia Bushrod almost had a baby on the table," Declan added, waiting for at least a surprised look, but getting none.

"I heard there's quite an art and jewelry collection." Bell leaned in. "You think she'll sell it all with the house? Because, I'm telling you, I want it all."

Annoyance slithered through Declan with every word the guy spoke. "I can only tell you that she isn't selling the house in the foreseeable future, so if I were you, I'd seriously think about finding another."

"Mmm." Bell seemed to ignore the warning as his gaze darted around the dining room again, then back into the crowded entry. Across the hall, Declan saw his uncle and Katie had joined a growing group of family, and Evie was right there with them. Irritation kicked again, because that's where he wanted to be.

"So, enough of a look?" Declan asked. "Can I get you a drink?"

"No, no, I'm not nearly done." Bell headed around the stairs. "I want to see every inch I can. I've waited a long time to get back…" He pointed. "There. To the museum room? Is that what they call it? I saw an article in an old issue of *North Carolina Living*."

Declan blew out a breath and tipped his head. "Follow me."

As they rounded the steps, Bell inched closer to whisper, "What's it going to take, you think? I mean, you're obviously her main squeeze. More money? Some kind of guarantee that I'll keep everything as is?"

Declan had to dash some hopes, and fast. "Look, you want me to be honest?"

"Yeah, man. Help me out here." They stepped into the double doorway of the museum room, and Bell's eyes widened like a kid's in a candy store. "Are you kidding me?" His gaze lingered on some paintings, a display of necklaces, the large shelf full of lighters, then slid to the piano. "Would you freaking look at that thing?"

That *thing*…where a sweet old lady hid a twenty-year-old piece of paper that meant the world to him. That *thing*…that Evie played during a recital he sat through because he already loved her when they were kids. That *thing*…that maybe his own little girl might someday play Beethoven on and impress a boy.

"That's not for sale," he said quickly.

"Anything? That big portrait?"

Of Glory Bushrod herself? Was he kidding? "No."

"That settee?"

Where he and Evie made out for the first time as adults? "No."

"That lighter collection?"

"*Nothing* is for sale, Mr. Bell. Not anything in this room, and not this house." He kept his voice low and steady, aware that there were other people in the room. "And if you don't mind, I'd like to…"

"I don't mind." Bell practically dismissed him, taking a few steps toward the lighters, his whole face looking…hungry. As he reached for one, part of the tattoo that matched his name peeked out from his cuff. "I can look."

And *steal*. Who'd stop this lunatic from slipping one of Max's beloved Ronsons into his pocket? Or sneaking off with the locket *that Declan found*. He didn't trust this clown, not one single thing about him. And he didn't like him salivating over the house and heirlooms that belonged to Evie's family…*their* family.

He gracefully stepped between Bell and the lighters. "So, Jim, can I introduce you to anyone? Who did you know to get on the coveted invitation list?"

His eyes flickered for a second. "Nellie's an old friend."

"Really? Because she's right there, and you haven't said hello."

"Oh, yeah." He glanced around and nodded to a woman…who was *not* Nellie Shaker.

What the hell?

"I'll talk to her later. Could I see those—"

"No." Declan glared down at the man. "You can leave."

"Excuse me?" He choked a laugh. "Do you have a problem with me or something?"

"I kinda do, Jim. You see, you're not picking up on the not-so-subtle cues that say this house isn't for sale and neither is anything in it. Evie and her grandfather live here, and a Hewitt or a Bushrod has lived in this house for one hundred and twenty years. So a Bell isn't going to be next."

A Mahoney might, but not this guy.

The man's pale brown eyes narrowed. "What are you saying?"

Did he not speak English? "That the house isn't for sale, so you can stop salivating over it."

"You want me to leave?" He gave Declan a challenging look, holding it long enough that for one minute he could have sworn he knew the guy. Or maybe it was just that Bell cockiness reminded him of someone.

"I do." Declan tipped his head to the side. "In fact, I'll walk you out. Through the back." Because the last thing he needed was a scene at Evie's party, and he did *not* trust this pushy guy.

The other man seared him with a look. "Fine," he said. "But if you think I'm done going after—"

"You're done." Declan put a hand on the man's elbow and steered him toward the kitchen. In there, the place hummed with caterers and clanging dishes, the low lights casting the whole room in odd shadows.

*Very* odd shadows.

As he walked to the back door, Declan slowed his step when he saw the flickering kerosene lamps on the wall.

"Who lit these?" he demanded.

A black-clad waiter stepped next to him. "For authenticity," he said. "It puts us in the mood."

"Turn them off," he demanded.

"Who the hell are you?"

"The next chief of the fire department," he said, catching a glimpse of Bell going right up to the brass fixture to examine it like the lights might be part of the house purchase he was never going to make.

"But they work fine," the waiter said.

Declan glared at him. "You do not light kerosene lamps in a hundred-and-twenty-year-old house. Do you understand how easily they could start a fire? Catch one bit of oil on one of these outfits, and someone could be engulfed in flames."

The man drew back at the force of the words. "I'll turn them off."

"And leave them off." Just then, he saw Bell disappear out the back door.

He waited a split second, then decided to follow, standing on the back step to watch the man skulk through the shadows to the other side of the house.

Where he crossed the patio to stand outside the sunroom.

The son of a bitch was going to come right back in, wasn't he? Declan marched after him, the low-grade annoyance fully amped up to pissed-off now.

He found him on the patio, hands cupped against one of the French doors, peering inside the sunroom.

"Can I help you find the front of the house?" Declan said in a voice that left no doubt how he felt about the encounter.

"Gotta say, Mahoney." He inched away from the glass and turned to Declan. "You're the last person I thought would care about this house. On the contrary, I'd expect you'd like to see it burned to the ground."

Some heat fired through his veins, but he didn't say a word.

"I mean, if my study of Gloriana House's history is right, then…a man named Joseph Mahoney died right on this spot. Wild guess—your father?"

Declan swallowed, tamping down a temper that rarely showed its face. "If you keep going to your right, Mr. Bell, you'll see the driveway. Come on, I'll take you."

As he got closer, the other man stepped back.

"But think of it like this," Bell said. "Sell me the house, and you marry the woman who owns it, and you get a nice big payoff for your grief."

"Who the hell are you?" Declan demanded through a clenched jaw.

"I'm a history buff," he said quickly. "And I'm a man madly in love with a woman who wants this house and everything in it. And I happen to be rich enough to get it for her. And I know you don't want to live where—"

Declan got right in his face. "You don't know anything."

"I know people," he said, undaunted. "And I suspect you can't walk into that room…" He gestured toward the sunroom. "And not wonder what happened. I doubt you can stand under this overhang and not think about the moment he died. I'm sure you can't sit in that sunroom on a nice day and not think about your father."

Declan's hands fisted into such tight balls he could feel his nails dig into his palms. "What is *wrong* with you?"

"I want this house."

So he'd do and say anything to get it?

Declan took a quick step closer, grabbed the guy by the collar, and shoved his fist under his chin. "What you are is so far out of line, your head could snap. Or I might help it."

"I want the house," he mouthed the words. "And you want to be free of it. Why are you fighting it, my friend?"

"You're *not* my friend. And you're not welcome here." Declan pushed him away. "Leave. Now."

"Fine. But get this straight, pal. I get what I want, one way or another." He started off in the direction of the driveway.

Digging deep, Declan forced himself to stare straight up at the overhang and imagine the sound and sight of it collapsing. The flare of sparks. The flash of fear. He could smell the smoke and feel the pressure on Dad's gear. Did he burn? Did it crush him? Break a bone? Kill him instantly?

He took a slow, steadying breath, erasing the sensations.

*It's not the same. It's not the same building.*

But *could* he ever forget that? Could he so cavalierly say he'd *live* here with Evie?

For a long moment, he stood there, adrenaline dumping like a waterfall into his blood, his chest rising and falling with each pained breath. He could feel himself falling and falling...down to the dank, dark, awful place that consumed him.

The *freaking* basement.

He dropped his head back and rooted for the strength to grab hold of something, anything, and kick that door shut once and for all. For Evie. For the baby they would have. Yes, for this house that meant so much to her, her family, and his hometown. He needed to keep this house so dimwits like Bell couldn't ruin it.

But the questions still echoed.

What *had* his dad seen that night? Why would he make a move without his partner? There were still so many unanswered questions. Questions he needed to at least try to answer.

He pulled out his phone, tapping the contacts to find Chief Winkler.

"Declan," he answered with warmth in his voice. "I thought you were at the big party."

"I am, but I want to take you up on your offer, Chief. I'll take that list of everyone who was at the fire that night. I want to talk to them. I want to talk to them all. I have to know…" He swallowed hard. "I'll take that list," he finished.

"Will do, Dec."

He hung up the phone and turned to head back to the house, but he didn't get five steps before he froze at the sight of Evie in her gossamer gown.

"I had to get rid of him, E. Sorry, he…" His voice trailed off at her stricken expression.

"Is he right, Dec?"

"Is who…what?"

"Can you ever forget it, really?"

How much of that conversation had she heard? "I can damn well try."

She closed her eyes. "You promised, Dec. You promised you'd let it go."

The impact of her whispered words was as bad as if she'd screamed them. Would this be another one of his unkept promises?

"Evie, I'm trying, believe me."

"But you're *failing*. I saw your face just now. You had that same look you had twenty years ago…when you left me." She hugged herself. "You're going back to that…place."

Damn it. Even she knew when he was about to fall into the basement. "Look, that guy—"

"That guy put into words what we all know," she said. "Every time you doubt, every time you miss him, every time you come near here…you'll be plagued."

"No, I won't," he insisted. "I'm just now beginning to appreciate this house. And it's a part of you. Why do you think I was fighting so hard to get rid of some jerk who wants to buy it?"

"And calling for investigation files and lists of people who were here that night?"

"I want to find out why my dad made the choice he made, that's all."

She let out a sigh, soft enough to draw him closer.

"Please, Evie. Please." He reached for her. "Were you looking for me?"

"I went back to my room for a moment, and when I came out, I saw you leave, and I was curious, and…I heard your conversation. Enough of it, anyway."

"You heard the words, Evie, but you don't know what I'm thinking."

She looked up at him, sighing. "I'm not pregnant."

He felt his jaw loosen as a sucker punch of disappointment hit, but he hit it right back. "That's okay. We'll try—"

She shook her head, tears welling. "And I've been offered the job as dean of the vet school at NC State."

Now his jaw actually fell open. "Holy…wow. Evie. That's…huge."

"It is," she acknowledged. "And kind of what I've been working for my whole life."

"Yeah." He nodded, disappointment rising up like bile. "I know it is."

"Actually, you don't know, because…you weren't there for the last twenty years."

"Evie." He could practically feel his heart break. "I told you how sorry—"

"I know you are. And I believe you, Dec. I do." She

pressed her hands to her cheeks as if she wished she could stop herself but couldn't. "But can I give you my life and my heart and my soul and live in constant fear that one day you'll just…disappear? Can I subject a child to that kind of emotional rejection? I'm scared, Dec. I don't want to relive that pain every time you relive yours."

The words sliced right through him. Because on some deep level—as deep as that emotional cellar he liked to avoid—she might be right. He didn't respond, but just stared at her, paralyzed as he'd been for the most of the past twenty years. Words once again all sounded pathetic and hollow. Instead, he stood frozen, falling into the abyss.

"I'm going back to the party," she said on a sad sigh, turning to head to the back door.

"I'll go with you." He took a few steps, then paused, watching her cloud of silk float toward the door. "I'll go with you anywhere, E," he added on a whisper, but she didn't hear him.

# Chapter Twenty-six

From the moment Evie woke the next morning, one single thought echoed in her head: *I am a flipping idiot.*

Yes, she'd overheard bits of a conversation that upset her. And yes, the tone in Declan's voice had dragged her back to the dark days, when she couldn't get eye contact from him, let alone honesty about his feelings. And yes, stress from the job offer and the party, combined with the bone-deep disappointment from discovering she was indeed *not* pregnant...all had had her off in search of comfort from Declan.

Then she'd watched him outside the sunroom, reliving his father's last moments, fighting tears...and all her fears swamped her. But now, in the light of day on the morning of the parade, common sense prevailed. She wasn't taking that job. She wasn't living in fear. She wasn't giving up on their dreams.

And she *had* to tell him that.

She even changed the plan of having the parade convertible pick her and Granddaddy up at home, in case she needed her car to drive around to find Declan.

She huffed out a sigh, getting a look from Granddaddy

as she walked him from the parking lot behind the bookstore, where she'd been more than mildly disappointed not to see Declan's truck. It was a short stroll across Bushrod Square toward the parade staging area, but maybe not short for her ninety-two-year-old grandfather.

"Too much, Granddaddy?" she asked when he slowed a bit. "I should have gotten Grandmama's old wheelchair."

"In front of the whole town? I told *you* we should have brought Judah, and then no one would notice how slow I'm going."

"He's not ready for an outing like this," she said. "And now I'm starting to worry that maybe you aren't, either."

"I'm enjoying myself." Granddaddy adjusted the angle of his Navy vet ball cap and waved to some passersby. "I'm regretting that third shot of Jameson's last night, but I had too much damned fun with those women. Are the Dogmothers going to be here?"

"I'm sure they're with the whole clan." Which she hoped to God included Declan.

"The Irish Mafia of Bitter Bark I used to call those Mahoneys and Kilcannons," he mused. "And now there's a Greek goddess."

Where *was* the Irish Mafia? Her heart dropped a little as she remembered how she'd teased Declan about the same thing. Where was *he*? When they'd said goodbye last night, it had been cool and quick, all they could manage with people around and his family urging him to join them all for a nightcap at Bushrod's.

He'd asked her to go, and she'd said she'd try to make it, but by the time she got Granddaddy in bed and the caterers had cleaned up and left, she collapsed on her bed with Judah in a pool of tears, emotionally and physically wiped out.

And Declan hadn't texted or called—not that she could blame him.

But he *had* to be here today. She scanned the crowded square, peering between groups of families, tourists, dogs, and past the fiery trees that exploded in the reds and oranges of autumn, but she didn't see a single member of his family. But then she spied the bleachers and recalled someone referencing the "family viewing section" in the square.

They'd all be there, she guessed. But would Declan? Because once, a long time ago, he told her he used to get here early to sit on the steps of town hall.

She'd find him, one way or another. But she couldn't drag Granddaddy around on that mission. "Let's go this way, toward those bleachers," she said. "You can sit with your friends for a while, since we're early." An hour early because she wanted to see Declan so bad. "And I can…" Apologize to the man she loved.

It had been tempting to call him, but what needed to be said had to be done in person, holding his hand, looking into his eyes, asking his forgiveness and assuring him they could make it through anything.

As she rounded the bleachers, she spotted the distinctly silver hair of Daniel Kilcannon, one arm around Katie, the other holding one of his grandbabies. Her gaze darted over rows of family members, all of them laughing, animated, and talking in groups.

But no sign of Declan.

"Evie!" Molly stood and waved.

"Let's go join them," she said to Granddaddy. Before he had a chance to respond, Connor and Braden both shot up and jumped off the side of the bleachers to come help her grandfather. The people in the front row, including Gramma Finnie and Yiayia, started clearing some space, and Pru headed over to greet her, holding little Danny's hand as she helped him walk on unsteady baby sneakers.

Suddenly, they all looked very much like...family. And her throat grew thick with regret for the things she'd said and the need to talk to Declan.

"Aren't you supposed to be going to the staging area?" Connor asked, reaching them first.

"We're early, and we thought Granddaddy could rest here a minute."

"Sure," Braden said, taking her grandfather's other arm. "I know a couple of ladies who haven't stopped talking about taking shots with you last night."

Granddaddy adjusted his cap again and grinned. "Wait till they see me in the convertible."

As Braden helped him toward the bleachers, Evie turned to Connor.

"Where's Declan?"

They asked the question in perfect unison, making Evie draw back.

"I thought you'd know."

Connor lifted his brows. "I thought he stayed with you last night."

"Didn't he go to Bushrod's?" she asked.

"He never showed." A frown pulled. "I called him about an hour ago, but it went straight to voice mail."

"Could he be at the station?" she asked, knowing how often he popped in there to check on things even when he wasn't on duty.

"I'll go check."

"No, I will, Connor." She couldn't wait one more minute to see him. And maybe he was on the town hall steps. Just for old times' sake. "Let me go," she insisted. "I need to."

"Everything okay with you two?" he asked. "'Cause he was kind of quiet during the party last night."

"Everything's fine." Or it would be. "I'll find him, Connor. Keep an eye on…" She leaned around him and caught sight of Granddaddy sitting between Yiayia and Gramma Finnie. "Never mind. He seems fine."

Connor laughed. "Yeah, he found his drinking buddies."

With a quick wave to Granddaddy, she headed out of the square toward town hall, her heart rate increasing with hope as she searched the crowds already seated on the wide front steps.

But there was no sign of him, no handsome firefighter waiting in the spot where he used to perch at every Founder's Day parade when she was a kid.

Biting back her disappointment, she hustled through the crowd, turning onto the street that led to the fire station. He told her once that he slept there sometimes, or went in to work on admin.

Hope growing, she pulled open the glass front door and smiled at an older woman at the front desk. "Is Declan Mahoney here?" she asked without even a hello first.

The woman frowned and shook her head, turning to glance at a board behind her. "He's not on duty until tomorrow."

"Oh. And there's no chance—"

A tall, bald man stepped into the reception area, looking up from some papers in his hand. One look at his uniform and badge, and Evie knew exactly who he was.

"Chief Winkler?" She extended her hand. "I'm Evie Hewitt."

"Evie!" His face brightened. "Well, I bet you can help me out. I can't seem to get a hold of Declan."

"Oh." The word slipped out. "I was hoping he was here."

Dark brows furrowed as he shook his head. "No. I haven't heard from him since he texted me in the middle of the night with his bad news."

"Bad news?"

"For me, but not for you." He winked and leaned closer to whisper, "I think he'll like Raleigh. I'm crushed, but I totally get his decision."

His decision? To go to Raleigh? He was giving up his dream of being chief so she could follow hers? Her heart almost burst with love and the need to hold him in her arms and tell him—

"You'll see him before I will." Chief held out the packet to her. "Will you give him this? He called last night and asked for it, and I was about to scan it in to email it, but this is easier."

"Sure." She closed her fingers around what she already knew was a list of firefighters who'd been at Gloriana House the night of the fire. "You don't have any idea where he might be?"

"Somewhere out in that mess in Bushrod Square, I suppose." Then he gave her a curious look. "Aren't you supposed to be in the parade?"

"I am, but I have an hour." An hour to find him, but where could he be? "I'll get this to him, I promise."

As she stepped away, she glanced down at the papers before she could slide them into her bag. Her gaze landed on the third name on the alphabetical list.

*Jamie Bell***

Wait. Could that be *James* Bell? The guy who wanted to buy the house and was being such a jerk to Declan last night?

She turned as Chief Winkler was headed back in. "Excuse me, Chief?" She pointed to the list. "This Jamie Bell? Who is he, and why are there asterisks next to his name?"

"One means he was a volunteer. The other means he was not at the fire, just on the vol roster. I don't want Declan wasting any time going to talk to him."

The James Bell she knew had said he used to live around here.

"Why? Do you know him?" the chief asked.

"I think I've met him." She tipped her head, not even able to picture the thin man as a rugged firefighter. "I actually think he was in my house last night."

"Oh, that's a coincidence." He shrugged. "Well, then I assume Declan talked to him already and knows he wasn't at the fire that night."

"No, they didn't talk about..." She shook her head, thinking. "Would Declan know him for sure?"

He lifted a thick shoulder. "If the volunteer hung out at the station, but if he wasn't called in much? Maybe not."

"Would he know Declan?"

His eyes widened. "More than likely, yes."

Then maybe the name was just a coincidence. It was common enough.

She thanked the chief and tucked the papers into her bag, but couldn't shake the unnerving sense that crawled up her chest when she thought of the things that man had said to Declan. He knew the history of the house...and about the fire.

Was *that* a coincidence?

No. And Gloriana House was open right this minute—open and empty. They'd left the back door unlocked so the Historical Society ladies could get in to host the open house after the parade.

She needed to lock that door, and fast. She checked her watch and made a quick decision to head back to the bookstore, get her car, and zip up to the house right now. On her way, she broke down and called Declan, but it went straight to voice mail.

Where *was* he?

When Declan had parked his truck at the old campsite last night, the lights shining on the dock and lake, he'd braced for a long, ugly trip to the place he hated most. As he walked down the dirt path that he once ran before cannonballing into the lake with Evie, he imagined himself crawling into the old subterranean hellhole, ready to unpack some pain.

But when he sat down, the only thing he could unpack was the sound of Joe Mahoney's voice.

All night long. In the chilly mountain air, he barely heard the lake waves splash against the wood pilings or the cool breeze through the pines. No, he heard a steady stream of Joe Mahoney's life advice, from midnight until he finally crashed. And maybe even after that, Joe kept talking in Declan's head.

And his message was loud, clear, and pointed. It started with, *I didn't raise you to waste your life wallowing over stuff you can't change*, and ended with a simple, *Get your ass back to that woman, and don't ever leave her again.*

Now, Declan finally pushed up from the dock, squinting into the now bright sky over the mountain lake. A good night, he decided, even if it was hard, cold, and a little bit miserable at times.

He guessed by the sun that he had exactly enough time to drive back to Bitter Bark and get to town hall to stand on the steps to wave to his girl in the parade.

He made a face at the crick in his neck. Oh hell, his whole back was destroyed by a very long, chilly night with only Judah's blanket from the truck and a wool jacket, once worn by a Bushrod, to keep him warm.

Both were covered in dog hair, but they'd done the job.

Now, he had to do his and get to Evie. He needed to tell her that he would leave his life, job, and family to follow her wherever she went. And they could keep or sell Gloriana House, whatever her family wanted. All she needed to do was understand that, and she'd believe he'd left the dark days behind.

As he walked to his truck, he reached into his pocket and pulled out his phone, swearing softly at the black screen. His battery had died, but not before he'd sent a text to Chief Winkler telling him he wouldn't be taking the job.

He snagged his keys, opened the truck, and tossed the blanket in the back. Stretching again, he slipped off the jacket, but folded it carefully, knowing it was valuable to Evie.

When he did, something fell out and clunked to the ground, making him inch back to see what it was. Damn. The lighter Max had given him to "help on his quest."

He bent over and scooped it up, almost tossing it into the center console when an engraving on the front caught his eye. He stared at it for a moment, the outline vaguely familiar in the shape of a…

Bell.

He'd seen that…tattooed on the arm of James Bell, the asspain who started this. Was it the same design?

He angled the lighter into the light to study the engraving, which could simply be another bell, but it was a strangely unique shape, and he could still vividly see it on that man's arm.

*Penny found it on the grass while we were doing construction and insisted it was part of my collection, but I never saw that lighter before.*

Maybe it wasn't dropped by a construction worker? Maybe it was accidentally left behind by someone…

His chest tightened as he stared at the lighter. He turned it over and sucked in a breath at the sight of a completely different engraving on the back. The four curved rectangles with a circle in the middle might not be immediately recognizable to most people, but to a firefighter?

The Maltese cross formed the insignia for thousands of fire departments around the world. So yes, this could have been dropped during S&O by any firefighter… except for the name *Jamie* etched in the middle.

Jamie? Like James? With a bell on the front?

The tightness in his chest squeezed so hard he couldn't breathe for a second. James Bell…the man who wanted Gloriana House so bad that he'd get it *one way or another*?

No, no. He hadn't said that. He'd said, *I get what I want, one way or another.* What if what he wanted was this lighter? Because, oh *hell*. It *was* evidence.

Declan mumbled a rough curse as he threw a look at

his phone, furious that he didn't have a charging cord in the truck, but then, he was a guy who never let his phone battery go below twenty percent. And his radio was at home on his dresser.

A fresh jolt of adrenaline took all the aches out of his body. Who the hell was James—or Jamie—Bell, and why was he so desperate to buy Gloriana House?

Because he'd left his lighter there one hot August night? Was he on the roster back then? Had he been at the fire and dropped it? Did he know something about Dad's death?

He twisted the key and hit the accelerator, not entirely sure where he needed to go first. The sheriff? The parade to find Evie? The fire station?

Or maybe he'd better haul ass to Gloriana House, because everyone in Bitter Bark knew the house was empty while its occupants were in the parade. And James Bell wanted something there…and Declan wanted *him*.

# Chapter Twenty-seven

Evie barreled up the driveway, grateful to see it was empty, so no open house guests yet. She tried to reach Declan a few times, anxious to share with him the name she'd found on the roster, but the calls again went straight to voice-mail.

He'd been right to have it out with that guy, she knew now. There was something weird about James Bell. He *had* to know Declan if he'd been a volunteer twenty years ago…but had he mentioned that last night?

No doubt James Bell would be the first in line at an open house, even though Declan had summarily booted him out the night before. Well, they'd handle that later. For now, she wanted the back door locked.

She rounded the side yard, looking around, peering into the sunroom as she passed, but everything looked empty and quiet. When she reached the unlocked kitchen door, she stepped inside, listening for Judah's bark of greeting. But he must be sound asleep.

She walked past the back stairs and headed toward what she now thought of as her bedroom. The door was open, and Judah's fuzzy dog bed was empty, the pillow

Gramma Finnie had embroidered for him resting against the side where his head usually was.

Had she left this bedroom door open? Had she left those drawers open? She frowned at the dresser, trying to remember even accessing those drawers this morning. For underwear, yes, but the dress she was wearing had been hanging in the closet.

She shook her head. Her memory of this morning was a blur because she'd gotten ready with the single-minded determination to find Declan and set things straight. She walked back into the kitchen, glancing around, noticing some open cabinets. She'd been certain the caterers had left it spotless last night, but again, she'd been in a fog.

Rounding the corner, she headed down the wide corridor toward the front of the house, which still bore evidence of the big party the night before. The staff had cleaned up glasses, but the area rugs looked a little askew on the hard wood, and the museum room...was a hot mess.

"Wow," she whispered, pausing at the double doors. Had her guests been so rude they'd opened the drawers of Grandmama's secretary desk and looked through the lighter collection?

She took a few steps toward the display, blinking in surprise at how many were knocked over, and...could some be missing? She couldn't remember how many there were supposed to be.

Did she have time to get this back in order before the open house and still make the parade? She pulled out her phone to check the time as she walked back into the hall, stopping completely when she heard a sound.

Was that a…growl? From upstairs?

Judah? He shouldn't have gone up the steps yet.

Instead of taking the time to get to the front and up the massive staircase, she returned to the kitchen to head up the back stairs. They were closer to Granddaddy's room where, she had no doubt, Judah was not so patiently waiting for his favorite person.

Just as she passed the landing and made it up a few more steps, Judah let out a massive howl, making Evie freeze in stunned surprise.

"Shut up!"

The man's voice nearly took her breath away. Someone was up there. With Judah. She took a millisecond to think through the best course of action, then pulled her phone out of the pocket of her dress to call 911.

She turned and tiptoed down to the landing, blinking as the camera app on her phone flashed to indicate movement in Granddaddy's room. She tapped the icon, and the image opened, the camera angle locked on the bed, of course.

But the angle was enough to see some nightstand drawers had been opened, and she could hear someone yanking at dresser drawers now. What the hell was he doing up there?

Judah started barking.

"Shut up!" the man yelled. "Unless you ate the damn lighter! Did you?"

Ate the…*lighter*? Why would he be looking for a lighter? She couldn't answer that, but the voice was familiar enough that she knew exactly who it was—exactly who she'd suspected.

She tapped to her keypad to call for help, but as she did, she heard footsteps crossing Grandaddy's room. If he came this way, he'd see her. And if Judah heard or smelled her...

Swallowing, she started to run down the rest of the stairs as Judah's barking got louder. He was coming this way. Straight down these steps.

She had seconds to decide what to do. Try to make a run for it, or...she looked down. Hide in the hole.

Without a second's hesitation, she leaned over, grabbed the tiny handle that few people even knew was in the floor, flipped the latch, and yanked up the door. In a flash, she scrambled down, pulled the door over her head, and rolled into a ball in the complete darkness.

She heard footsteps right overhead, followed by the slap of Judah's distinctive paws. Poor guy, following this jerk around hoping for love and getting told to shut up.

James Bell wouldn't *hurt* Judah, would he?

The thought sent a shot of horror through her, making her push the door up, her fingers pressed against cold metal. She lifted it about an inch, peering right into big brown eyes.

Oh God. Judah.

Instantly, he pawed at the wood, pushing it down, followed by a series of noisy barks and one long, loud howl.

*Stop, Judah! Don't let him know I'm here!*

She bit her lip, forcing herself not to lift the wood and try to quiet the dog. That would only make him more worked up than he already was. Bell didn't want the dog. He wanted a lighter.

Why?

She tapped her phone, the light spilling out over the tiny basement-like space. It wasn't very deep, really meant to store food for the winter, and it sure was cold.

Would he hear her voice when she called 911, or would he be gone by then? She had to get help before he got off the property and could deny the whole thing.

She angled the light to the ceiling right above her head, surprised to see the bronze glint of copper. God only knew why those Victorians would line this space with copper, probably to keep it freezing, but…

*Copper.*

Shoot. Would she even be able to make a call? She tried tapping 911, but nothing happened. The Wi-Fi signal, never the best in this house, was flat. And she had no cell service, either.

Judah was still barking and pawing at the floor, so she waited a minute and then pushed the floorboards again. This time, the copper-covered wood wouldn't move.

"Hey," she murmured, shoving a little harder. Damn it! Judah must have bumped the latch and locked her in. With no Wi-Fi or cell signal. Seriously?

He was smart, but not smart enough to undo the latch. Right overhead, he barked and growled and howled in frustration.

And then she heard a crash. What was that? She pushed again, a low-grade desperation growing from the eerie sound of glass breaking. What did Bell do? How long would she be down here until someone heard her?

She stopped pushing for a moment, tried the phone again, then slowly lowered it to think.

But all she could do was…smell. Something pungent and unpleasant. One of the oil lamps?

*Kerosene?*

Was he setting the house on fire?

She pushed again with all her strength. "Judah! Judah! Get out of the house and get help!"

But all he did was howl in panic, echoing exactly how she felt.

Declan broke a few speed limits on his way to Gloriana House, but he had enough time to put some puzzle pieces together. Some fit, some didn't. But he saw enough of the picture to suspect James Bell wasn't who he said he was. Without a phone, he couldn't find out more yet, but he'd charge it when he got to Evie's. He'd have time to plug his phone in to make a few calls, hang around for a while in case Bell showed up, and then get to town to meet Evie at the end of the parade route so he could tell her what he'd decided.

He bypassed town, which would be a traffic mess, and powered up a back route to the top of Ambrose Acres, reaching Evie's street in record time. As he neared the house, he caught a glimpse of Evie's red car, which didn't surprise him, because he knew she and Max were going in the parade car with Nellie.

But then he saw the BMW on the street and, one second later, the now familiar scrawny figure of a man hustling down the drive, his head down as he walked.

Declan whipped his truck into the driveway and damn near mowed the guy down.

"Whoa, whoa!" He held up two hands. "I know you don't like me, but—"

"I knew I'd find you here." Declan said as he climbed out of his truck. "What are you doing?"

"Uh, there's supposed to be an open house." He smirked up at Declan. "Which, by its very name, means it's *open*."

"Not to you."

"Not to anyone, since the door's locked." He stepped away. "Relax, man. I was only coming by to tell Evie I changed my mind about wanting to buy the house. It's cool."

Cool? Nothing about this man was cool.

"So no need to beat me up, Captain. I'm out." He hustled away, toward the street.

"Jamie?" Declan called.

He spun around, eyeing Declan. "I go by Jim."

"Do you? Your lighter says Jamie." He held up the lighter, and Declan saw all he needed to in the flash of shock on the man's face.

"Never saw that before," he said.

"Really? Because this engraving here matches your tattoo."

"A drawing anyone could find on the internet if they google 'bell images.'" He snorted. "Not a family crest, sorry. Now if you'll excuse—"

"I won't excuse you. We're not done with this conversation."

"Yeah, we are. And now I have places to be. And don't you? There's a parade in town, right?" He tipped his head back, and when he did, he reminded Declan of someone again, but he couldn't quite nail who. "She's not here if you're looking for her. I knocked for ten minutes when I saw her car."

Bell jogged down the drive, but this time, Declan followed.

"What's your deal, Jim?" he asked.

"We're finished here." He almost reached his car, pulling out a set of keys.

"No." Declan put a hand on his shoulder and turned

him around. "I know you." The words spilled out the moment they hit his brain. He *did* know this guy. But from where? "How?"

Beads of sweat formed on Bell's upper lip. "I have no idea."

"No. No. I've met you before." He rooted through his brain, back in time. Twenty years. The station. A training session. Dad was there. "*Jamie* Bell. You were a volunteer." But not a very well-regarded one, he remembered. Some of the guys had called him *Lamie* Bell.

"A hundred years ago," he said, reaching for the door handle.

"*Twenty* years ago," Declan corrected. "Were you *here*? Did you work the fire that night?"

He yanked the door open and threw Declan a look. "I was not at the fire, and that is not my lighter, and I'm done."

Then there might have been a completely different reason for why he'd lost his lighter here.

"Then why was this on the grass after the fire?" He flipped the lighter. "Catch!"

He whipped his hand out and snagged the air, just missing the toss. But before he could bend over and pick it up, Declan grabbed his arm, twisted it back, and got right into his face, hearing the man's keys hit the ground. "What the hell was your lighter doing in the yard?"

Blood drained from the other man's face, leaving a dusting of orange freckles over pale skin. "I don't know," he ground out. "I lived in this town briefly a long time ago, and I was on the vol roster. Maybe one of those blowhard guys in the department stole it from me. You ever think of that, Mahoney?"

"Nice try. Then why do you want to get inside this house so bad that you cooked up some stupid story about buying it for your fiancée? To find something you *lost*?" Even as he said the word, things started to make sense. Sickening sense.

Bell wouldn't be the first firefighter to start a blaze. And a volunteer who never got called?

The other man looked down, his gaze on the lighter on the ground. "Are we done?"

"No. Not even close." Declan backed him up against his car. "Were you here for another reason that night? Because what better way for you to get called in for work than to start a fire at the town's favorite landmark?"

At Declan's question, whatever blood was left in the guy's face drained. Declan grabbed his chin and forced him to face forward.

"Were you at this house that night?" he demanded.

Bell stared at him. "I just told you. I wasn't called to that fire."

"But you wanted to be," he ground out.

Terrified eyes narrowed behind his glasses. "I see where you're going, but the fire started because chemical-soaked rags left behind by the lady of the house exploded. No arson, big shot."

"Is that how it started? Or did it start because someone squirted lighter fluid in the sunroom?" He pushed him harder against the car, adding a hand to his throat for emphasis. "Were you in the house that night?"

He could feel Bell's Adam's apple rise and fall with...guilt.

"Tell me what happened, or I will squeeze it out of you." He added enough pressure to his throat to make good on the threat.

"He saw me." The words came out in a rough whisper as Bell's voice cracked.

"*What?*"

"He saw me trapped in the sunroom and..." Tears pooled behind his wire frames, askew on his face. "I wanted to buy the house and raze it to wipe away the memory."

"Are you talking about my father? That's why he..."

Bell dropped his head on a sob. "Yes, I wanted to be called in. I went in to start the fire. Not a big one and not where people were. The door to that garden room wasn't even locked."

"What happened, Bell? Start from the beginning." It took everything Declan had not to shake the guy until his bones rattled.

He shuddered. "I squirted the lighter fluid, and before I could even get the fire started...wham. The damn rags blew up, and I was *stuck inside*. If I left through the house, I'd be caught. The engines came and got people out, and they didn't know I was back there. Until...he saw me."

"Dad saved you."

"Yes." He sobbed the word. "His partner moved away for some reason, and he saw me and...walked through the fire to get to the door. I ran out. Got away. Dropped the lighter. And the balcony collapsed on him."

Declan barely understood the garbled words, but he got enough. He was standing here with his hand on the throat of the man who walked this earth because his father died saving his life. Yes, Dad had broken protocol by leaving his partner. But to save someone's life?

Joe Mahoney would do that.

"It wasn't on purpose," Bell cried out. "I got in over my head, and it really was an accident, but I can't forget. I can't...forget..."

Declan loosened his grip as an unexpected bout of sympathy hit him. "Hardly an accident."

"It was!" he insisted, finally lifting his pathetic head to look at Declan. Past Declan. "And so was that. I swear to God. I accidentally broke the oil lamp and—"

Declan whipped around and looked at the house just as a smoke alarm started to shriek loud enough to be heard through the windows. At the back of the house, the first billow of smoke rose.

Swearing, he let go of Bell, and the guy used the moment to try to get in his car, but Declan grabbed him and threw him to the ground, slamming a knee on his chest to pin him. "Give me your phone," he demanded. "Now. Or I *will* kill you. Joyfully."

"Pocket." He fumbled reaching for it. Declan ripped it from his hands.

"What's the passcode?" He spat the demand.

"3336."

As Declan took off for the house, he scooped Bell's car keys and lighter off the ground. This asswipe could run, but he wouldn't get far. Declan had to get Judah out of the house.

As he shot toward the back, he called 911 as he ran, cursing the fact that he didn't have a radio to call dispatch directly.

"911, what is your emergency?"

"It's Captain Mahoney. There's a fire at 32 Ambrose Court. Gloriana House. Need a full crew."

"Dispatching now, Captain. ETA under five minutes."

They could make it in three...except for the parade. Shit!

"Send the sheriff. An arsonist is on the street, probably running. Male. Fortysomething. Leather jacket. Red hair and glasses."

352

"Contacting sheriff's office immediately, Captain. Same ETA."

"There's a dog inside the house. I'm going in." If he wasn't visible when the trucks arrived, he wanted them to know he was in there.

"They'll be there shortly, Captain. I advise you not to go in without gear."

He snorted into the phone and hung up, already hearing Judah howling as he got to the back door.

"I'm coming, boy!" He ran into the kitchen, the smoke smacking him in the face, then he saw the flames on the drapes next to the broken oil lamp. He *knew* those freaking things were a hazard.

Flames licked up the wall, already burning one bank of cabinets. He hoped to hell his guys were here in three minutes.

"Judah!" He turned left, following the howl, finding the dog on the flat landing of the back stairs, no doubt trying to get away from the smoke and unable to get any higher with his not-yet-healed spine.

"Come on, come on." Declan got to the landing and wrapped his arms around Judah, the smoke alarm overhead screaming only a little bit louder than Judah was howling in his ear. "Let's go."

But the dog seemed to make himself heavier, pressing down so Declan had to work to get him up. His constant barks, mixed with the shrieking alarm, deafened Declan.

*"Come on."* Using all his strength, Declan hoisted him up, and immediately Judah turned and snapped at him, no doubt in fear. "It's okay, it's okay," he shouted, sure that the dog couldn't hear him, either.

He got him down the steps and rushed to the open

door to put him outside. But the minute he set him down, Judah bolted right back in, so fast Declan couldn't snag him. With a stream of freaked-out barking, he tore right back to the stairs.

"What the hell?" Frustration and anger and all the agony of what he'd just learned outside battled with years of training. He knew how to stay cool with flames licking behind him, and he knew how to do the only thing that mattered, which was protect this dog.

But he wanted to howl, too.

Judah flattened himself on the landing, lifting his head to howl and bark, pounding his big paw in fear. Of course, he smelled the smoke, he sensed the danger, and he could be in excruciating pain.

Once more, Declan reached down to get him, and as he lifted the dog, he thought he heard the first siren over the smoke alarm and howling.

"Here they come." He grunted as he picked up Judah and marched him downstairs. But the pounding he'd thought had come from Judah's paw continued.

What the hell?

He spun around and stared at the steps, trying to block out all the other sounds to concentrate on one that was coming from…inside the stairs? The hidey-hole? Where Ella had gotten trapped that time?

Judah howled one more time, this time right in Declan's ear.

*Was someone down there?*

"That's what you're trying to tell me." He put the dog down and dropped to the ground, smoke already burning his throat and eyes as he flattened his head to the wood to try to hear.

"Help me! Please!"

Holy crap. *Evie.*

He fumbled around, looking for a handle or a lock or something, just as he heard glass explode in the kitchen.

"Hang on, E! Hang on!" Sliding his hand around the wood, he felt every inch. Where did those damn Victorians hide their secret latches? And what the hell was she doing down there?

Hiding from Bell, no doubt. Had the son of a bitch locked her in there?

Fury and smoke nearly blinded him, but he finally found the metal latch, popped it sideways, and the door flew up, practically hitting him in the face. He reached down and scooped her into his arms, pulling her out of the opening.

"Is Judah okay?" she asked before she took her next breath.

"He is now."

The dog instantly stopped howling, staring at them both with his tongue out, panting in relief.

Then she gasped as she realized the kitchen was burning.

"No panicking." He hoisted her into his arms and over his shoulder, grabbing Judah's fur. "Out! Now!"

"It's him," she cried. "It's Bell. He did this."

"I know, I know." He hauled her out of the house through the back door, reaching the driveway just as Chief's Suburban came screaming up the street. He parked at the bottom of the drive to leave room for the engine and pumper that were scant seconds behind.

As he put her down, Evie clung to him, crying silently as he ushered her out of the way of the action and onto the grass with Judah, getting a satisfying jolt when he saw the Vestal Valley sheriff's deputies surrounding James Bell, already in handcuffs.

"Declan, that Bell guy—"

"Is being arrested. Did he hurt you?"

"I hid. He didn't know I was there." A sob escaped. "I was so scared. He started this fire."

"Shhh." He pulled her close, watching the crew move into action under the chief's direction from the incident command system he and his driver had set up from the back of the SUV. "I know. I know."

As much as he wanted to scare up some gear and get into this fight or at least back up the chief at command, he couldn't leave her.

She inched back and finally looked at the house, horror registering again.

"It's not bad, E," he assured her. "Kitchen fire. They'll have it out in a few minutes. Minor damage, I promise."

She held on to him, both of them watching the crews in action. "Declan, I need to tell you something," she said, reaching up to put her palms on his face to make him look at her. "It's important."

"What is it?"

"I was so wrong last night. I love you. I trust you. I'll be with you through good times and bad." She squeezed him tighter. "I cannot and will not live another moment without you in my life."

He held her tighter, his eyes stinging from tears and smoke, the words like a balm that made them disappear. "That's…everything, Evie."

She pushed back, insistent. "No, no, you have to hear me, Declan. I want forever. Together. I don't care about a job. I don't even want to be a dean. I want to be a neurologist. And I want to be with you…and whatever family we have. Whether or not there's a baby, I don't care.

We can adopt. We can foster kids. We can have a dozen dogs, I don't care. I just want…my best friend."

He squeezed her against him. "Then we want the same thing."

"Except this house?"

"If you want to live here, we will," he said without a second's hesitation. "I love the place, Evie. I see everything it is and was. And I want you to be happy and where you belong."

"No, no, no." She shook her head, vehement. "While I was in that cellar? I had a better idea."

"You were down there, only minutes from death, having better ideas?"

She managed a smile. "Sometimes when you're in the worst moments of your life, you get clarity."

He closed his eyes and dropped his forehead to hers. "And sometimes it takes twenty years and a few grandparents to give it to you."

"Declan!" Chief Winkler called from the command post. "I need you over here!"

"Go." Evie pushed him. "I have Judah. I'm fine. You go do what you do best, future Chief. Save this house. I have big plans for it."

"Evie, I love you."

She closed her eyes and whispered, "I love you, too."

With one kiss on her forehead, he took off toward the command post.

# Chapter Twenty-eight

Declan climbed out of his truck so he could go around to the passenger's side to help Max out, scanning the many vehicles in the drive and on the street in front of his mother's home. A full house for the major family meeting today.

As Evie got out of the back seat with Judah, she did the same. "Déjà vu all over again?" she asked with a sad smile.

"It does feel like that morning," he said, reaching for her hand. "We just spent the night together, and the future looks bright."

"So bright." She squeezed his fingers. "And tonight…"

"A standing ovulation?"

She laughed. "Egg-zactly."

He cracked up. "All right." He tipped his head as he got to Max's door. "Hang on to that mood, E, because this could be tough."

Once he helped Max out, they all walked up to the two-story brick house where he grew up, not surprised when the door opened and Colleen stood there, waiting.

"Welcome, everyone." Declan's mother reached for him, and instantly he could tell something was different with her. For the first time in decades, Colleen Mahoney looked…relieved. Like the weight of the world was off her shoulders. He knew exactly what that felt like. He'd been feeling it for two weeks now.

"Sorry we're a little late," Declan said. "We all met with the construction crew."

"Everything on schedule?" she asked.

"They said the new kitchen and downstairs bedroom will be done by Christmas," Evie said.

"Which I have a hard time believing," Max said, adjusting his Navy ball cap. "But I don't care since Judah and I are comfortable at Declan's house and happy to stay there."

Colleen beamed at him. "Max Hewitt, your spirit is an inspiration to everyone in this town. You know people are still talking about how brave you were during the parade, riding alone like the hero you are, when the fire trucks were flying up to your house."

"Ah, I loved the attention." Then he leaned in to ask, "Are my girls here?"

Laughing, Colleen led them toward the back. "Yes, Max, Yiayia and Gramma Finnie are waiting for you."

They headed into the large addition that Declan's dad had built with his own hands, including a bar, a wall of bookshelves, and a stone fireplace where a portrait of Captain Joe Mahoney sat on the mantel.

The entire family was here to greet them, including his brothers, sister, uncle, cousins, and, of course, the grannies, who lit up at the sight of their new best friend and, if family rumors were true, drinking and card-playing buddy.

Declan greeted Deputy Jerry Hanson from the sheriff's department, along with Chief Winkler, a woman who wore an NCSBI polo shirt and carried a clipboard, and an older man who'd taken off his ball cap and settled on a barstool who Declan immediately recognized as the arson investigator who'd helped him.

"Kirby Lewis," Declan said, greeting him with a handshake, then introduced Evie and Max.

After a moment, everyone settled to let Sharon Baker, who represented the North Carolina State Bureau of Investigation, walk them through the new report, which confirmed that the first fire at Gloriana House had indeed started because linseed oil-soaked rags combusted in the heat.

In addition, she confirmed that the second fire, two weeks ago, had started because an oil lamp in the kitchen had been tampered with by James Bell, who had taken them apart looking for his lighter.

After answering their fire-related questions, Deputy Hanson took over to fill them in on the suspect, a former volunteer firefighter who'd confessed to attempting to start a fire at Gloriana House twenty years earlier on August 28. He'd failed in that effort, but only because the rags combusted on the other side of the wall that he'd squirted with lighter fluid, starting a fire that trapped him in the sunroom. He also admitted he'd taken the lid off the container of paint rags because he'd planned to use it to fan the flames, so Evie's mother hadn't done anything wrong. However, the chemical's exposure to the heat had started the fire.

From the best they could tell by Bell's memory, Joe Mahoney and his partner had been momentarily separated as they'd begun to enter the sunroom. Joe had spotted Bell inside and had to make a split-second decision to try to save him. He did, getting Bell out just before the porch collapsed and the flames made their way to the second floor, even touching the attic.

"How did Bell get away that night?" Evie asked.

"He knew enough about the controlled chaos of firefighting," the deputy said. "He blended in and disappeared, but lost his lighter in the process."

"And lived for twenty years with no price to pay," Declan murmured, holding Evie's hand, but turning to Max. "Until this man provided us with the missing piece of evidence. Without that, we could never have proved his role in the fire."

"You were the one that made me think of it, son," Max replied with a denture-filled smile.

"Bell didn't escape unscathed in those twenty years, though," Deputy Hanson said as he glanced at his notes. "He's been treated multiple times for depression and has attempted suicide on more than one occasion. His lawyer will no doubt plead insanity for this last fire, especially if the DA levels homicide charges for the first fire, which is possible, but don't worry, he won't walk."

"He better not," Kirby Lewis said, crossing his arms and leaning back on the barstool, his gaze on Declan. "Because I wouldn't be surprised if he started a few other fires in the ensuing years."

"He doesn't seem to have the profile of an arsonist," the sheriff said. "But he was on the scene for two fires at the same place, claiming both were accidents. He did spray the lighter fluid in an attempt at arson, we know that. And the rags combusted outside, and he got stuck."

Kirby nodded. "That finally makes sense of everything I saw."

"We also know he managed to gain entry to Gloriana House on two different occasions, one during a historical event, but he couldn't get to the lighters. Also, he tried again by convincing Penelope Hewitt that he was an electrician. Mr. Hewitt confirmed the incident," Deputy Hanson added. "His goal was always to find the lighter that could pin the fire on him."

"He got into the house?" Evie choked. "Oh my God, that's terrifying."

"And now that whole electrician thing makes sense," Max added. "Penny walked in on the guy poking around the museum room and read him the riot act. She got him out of there, but she was upset. She must have caught him before he found his lighter."

"So his offer to buy was a hoax?" Declan asked. "Just a ruse to get inside?"

"Actually, no." Deputy Hanson flipped a page. "His grandmother passed away and left a large amount of money."

"And he decided to use it to buy the house?" Evie asked. "Just to find the lighter?"

"A man'll go to great lengths to get away with a crime," Kirby said.

"He kept his eye on the place by blending in with the tourists out front," Deputy Hanson added. "He confessed that when he spotted Declan coming out of Gloriana House, he renewed his efforts to get inside."

"Well, he won't need that money in jail," Max said.

"Especially because a whole bunch of it could be yours," Shane, Declan's cousin, interjected. "Speaking as a former attorney, you have a rock solid civil suit, if you're interested in pursuing it."

"Hell, yes," Max said. "Just the idea of that gives me a new reason for living."

Evie beamed at Declan then, giving his hand a squeeze.

An hour later, the room was a little emptier, and Declan could swear he heard a collective sigh and unloading of a few decades of emotions, especially from the Mahoneys.

"Thanks, bro." Connor looked hard at Declan, his eyes suspiciously damp. "You did this for us."

He shook his head, not wanting any credit.

"Seriously." Next to Connor, Braden's look matched his brother's. "This has always bugged me. I couldn't find the missing piece, so I figured it wasn't there."

"I'm sorry I didn't put two and two together sooner," Max said. "I never gave that lighter a moment's consideration until Declan asked about the collection in light of the fire. He deserves the credit."

"Dad would be proud of you." Ella put her arm around Declan's waist, wiping tears from her eyes. "We all are so happy to know this. You realize that, don't you? Somehow it changes everything to know he gave his life to save someone else, no matter how awful that someone else turned out to be."

"It was so like Joe," his mother said on a sigh. "I should have always known it."

Declan reached for her. "You feel better, Mom." It wasn't a question.

"I feel light and free," she whispered. "I don't know how to explain it."

"You don't have to," he replied. "I already know."

Uncle Daniel leaned forward from his seat on the sofa. "Dec, he used to tell me that you were the finest firefighter he knew. He said you'd be chief one day. He had no doubt."

Declan just smiled, but Evie looked up at him. "One day soon," she added. "*Very* soon." At his look, she shrugged. "What? You said there are no secrets in this family."

"True." As they all stared at him, he laughed. "I'll be named chief early next year," he announced.

A cheer went up, taking the whole room from somber to celebratory as they congratulated him on the promotion.

As that quieted down, Max slowly pushed himself to a stand and glanced at Evie. "Can we make this announcement now?"

At the question, a new hush fell over the room, except for Ella's little squeak of excitement and Gramma Finnie's gasp.

"An announcement, you say?" she asked, adjusting her glasses to look at Declan and Evie. "'Tis about time."

"'Tis about something else," he teased her. "You tell them, Evie."

Still holding Declan's hand, she reached for her grandfather's with the other. "We, the three of us, have made a big decision. And my parents are in one hundred percent agreement with this plan."

After a chorus of interest, she continued, "The work being done on Gloriana House is going to be a little more extensive than you might realize. With Granddaddy's approval and support, we are completely restoring Gloriana House to a perfect replica of the Victorian era. And…" She glowed as she took a breath to announce the rest. "We'll be working side by side with the Bitter Bark Historical Society to transform the mansion into the Gloriana House Museum, which will not only display our family's treasures, but the whole history of Bitter Bark. It'll be open to the public, with all proceeds going to the first responders' charities of choice."

This time, the whole room gasped, and another cascade of questions and cheers rained down. As the family celebrated, Declan pulled Evie and Max in for an embrace, almost overwhelmed by how great Evie's idea was and how enthusiastically Max had agreed to it.

Gloriana House was meant to be appreciated...by everyone.

"Nellie Shaker is going to run the day-to-day operations of the museum," Evie added as the chatter died down. "She's also planning to open the first floor for special events like fundraisers, parties, and weddings."

"Did someone say *weddings*?" Yiayia interjected.

Declan shot her a look. "Would you calm down?"

"But where will you live, Max?" Colleen asked. "I think it might get crowded in Declan's house."

"It better get crowded," Max said. "If these two could get on with their real purpose in life and add to the line."

Declan rolled his eyes, but couldn't help laughing. "Tell them the rest, E."

"There's more?" Gramma asked with unabashed hope.

"Declan and I are building a new house, with a view of our favorite lake in the foothills, on land I had no idea that the Hewitt family owned, but..."

"I was going to leave it to her anyway," Max said with a shrug. "But I can't seem to die."

"You better not." She gave Max a kiss on the cheek. "Because we're going to build a beautiful house and start a whole new family history there, all of us, together. With Judah, of course."

From the sofa, where he'd jumped up when Max stood, Judah swished a tail at the sound of his name.

"You're staying here?" Molly's voice rose with

excitement as she reached excitedly for Evie. "Please work with me. Please."

Evie laughed. "Bitter Bark needs a vet neurologist, and I'll need an office, so yes. And I might teach some classes at the college, too."

That got a huge reaction, but Gramma Finnie narrowed her gaze at Declan. "*Live* together?" she asked in a harsh whisper. "I mean, I know that's fine nowadays, but, *lad*, not what I expected."

"Can I please do this my way, Gramma?"

She relaxed a little. "Of course." She turned to Yiayia. "Don'chya be worryin', Agnes. He's doing it his way, so our work is essentially done."

"It's not done," Yiayia said. "We have three more grandchildren."

"Uh-oh," Ella said, lifting her hands and pretending to back up. "I feel a sudden long trip coming up. Madagascar? Maybe New Zealand…"

"Don't run off, Smella," Yiayia said, cracking everyone up with the name only Mahoneys used. "It's time for a Santorini next."

"But Theo's in San Diego, and Nick's in Africa," Daniel reminded them.

"No matter," Yiayia said. "The Dogmothers are unstoppable."

As everyone laughed about that and Colleen announced that Santorini's Deli had a lunch all set up in the dining room for them, Declan wrapped Evie in a hug and whispered, "Let's sneak out."

"And leave Granddaddy?"

He tipped his head to where the octogenarians were already in a tight group, and holy hell, Gramma Finnie had a *flask* out. "I don't think he'll miss us. And I want to

finish this morning by going full circle, E." He put his lips
to her ear. "Let's go up to the mountains. To our campsite.
I can't wait any longer."

"You want to start tonight's party early?"

"I want to make good on a promise I made a long time
ago. Bring Judah. This might not have happened if he
hadn't done the talking for me that day in the bakery."

Evie hadn't been to the lakeside campsite in more than
twenty years, but that feeling of déjà vu swamped her again.
In the first week of November, it was deserted, with the
blue autumn sky turning the water near navy and plenty of
trees still showing off shades of crimson and fiery orange.

Judah had fallen asleep on the way up, but he barked
happily as soon as Declan stopped the truck, eager to
jump out and explore.

"When was the last time you were here?" Evie asked
as Declan helped Judah out.

"I spent the night of the Living Museum party here."

"Really?" She blinked in surprise. "You never told me
that."

"I forgot." He reached into the back and gathered up a
blanket. "Slept under this, not that I slept much."

Judah bounded off, then suddenly slowed, as if he
remembered he didn't like to be alone. Turning, he came
back to walk between them down to the dock.

"What did you do, if you didn't sleep?"

"Talked to my dad."

"Aww. About?"

"You, of course. And I planned…this. Today. Coming
back here."

She slid her arm around him. "Do you think we can come back on our birthday?"

"Every year. And bring…Judah." He inched closer. "And whoever else happens to tag along in a stroller."

She bit her lip and wrapped her arms around him. "So is that why you brought me here? Thought the mountain air might make those swimmers even more eager to get egged?"

"Nope." He took a step away and reached into his pocket. "I wanted to give you this."

For a moment, her heart leaped, expecting…the little black box. But that wasn't what Declan held out to her, and he certainly didn't get down on one knee.

He flipped open a small index card that had handwriting on it, making her gasp and press her hand to her chest when she realized what it was.

"You found it?"

"It was never lost." He put the card in her hand. "Gramma Finnie had it for twenty years."

"So she really was our matchmaker." She sighed softly, reading the words that she remembered so well.

*DECLAN'S PROMISE*

"Oh." A shiver ran over her entire body. "Declan."

He put his hands on her shoulders. "I know I said I'd wait twenty years, which I think technically gives me until our next birthday, so…"

"How did Gramma get it?"

"She picked it up from the grass that morning. It fell out of my backpack. She kept it, and the grannies planted it in your piano. For you to find, actually, but I beat you to it."

"Why…oh wait. *That's* what Yiayia was doing that day in the museum room. She called it subterfuge. I call it…" She lifted the card to her lips. "Magic."

"I finally finished writing out my last promise," he said. "Go ahead and read."

She skimmed the words, the promises, all the roles Declan wanted to have in her life.

"Friend, lover, husband, confidant, partner," she read in a whisper.

"Chef, traveling partner, fellow camper, handyman," he added. "See how I'm already working on some of these?"

She laughed and read the last line. "And father to our..." One more word was written, in a different-colored ink. "Children."

"That's what I wanted to say, but you made me sign it, and I never wrote the word."

"Children? I'd be happy with one."

"Who knows, E? We can adopt or foster and have as many as you want."

"You know, Dec." She folded the card. "Somewhere deep in my heart, I always knew you'd keep these promises. I knew that morning that you made them that I would marry you. I just didn't know it would take all these years."

"And speaking of that..." For a long moment, he just looked at her, then he took one step back and *then* lowered himself to one knee.

"Oh, Dec."

"Oh, E."

She laughed, her eyes filling as he reached into his pocket, and...there it was. The little black box. "Really? Now? You don't want to wait for..."

"I don't want to wait another minute. I don't want to wait until Christmas. I'd marry you this afternoon, but let me ask first." He took a deep breath and reached for her hand. "Evangeline May Hewitt, my best friend, my sweet lover, and my favorite person on earth. Will you marry me?" He opened the box, letting the sun glint on a gorgeous solitaire.

But she really only had eyes for the man on one knee in front of her, the love in his eyes taking her breath away more than any diamond ring. "Yes," she managed to say, spreading her fingers so he could slide it on. "I will marry you and love you and cherish you and never, ever leave you for the rest of my life."

As her voice rose with the pronouncement, Judah came closer, got right between them, and howled as they kissed.

"What's he trying to tell us?" Declan asked.

"This *mutt* be love?"

He laughed. "Yep. He's our dog *fur* sure."

# Epilogue

*Six Weeks Later*

When Evie reached the top of the Gloriana House stairs wearing her great-great-grandmother's wedding gown, carrying red roses that matched the holiday decorations around the house, and stood with her arm linked with her father's, Declan decided that he couldn't get any happier.

But then he remembered yesterday's news, and yeah, he got happier. They'd kept it a secret, even from her parents, who'd arrived last night for the rehearsal dinner. But knowing what he knew and looking at the woman he was about to spend the rest of his life with...wow. He *couldn't* get much happier.

"I hope someone just got a picture of that," Connor muttered from right next to him.

"Of Evie?" he whispered.

"Of your face." Connor put a hand on Declan's shoulder. "Man, this is the stuff, huh?"

"You have no idea, Connor."

His brother just laughed. "Uh, yeah, I do. You beat me to the altar, but not to love."

Declan relaxed into another grin. "Thanks." Then he caught Braden's eye, his youngest brother standing next to Connor.

He never dreamed the day would come that he'd stand next to his two brothers…as the groom. He sure never dreamed it would happen in Gloriana House. And then he looked at the little old man on his other side. He'd also never dreamed he'd have a ninety-two-year-old best man.

Max winked. "She's a beauty, eh? Just like my Penny."

"She is a beauty, Max," he agreed. "And I hope we're as happy as you and your wife."

"Oh, you will be," he proclaimed.

The musicians played the first few notes of a familiar song, not a wedding march but…Beethoven. The Ninth Symphony. *Ode to Joy.*

The song he'd heard Evie play on an antique piano for a childhood recital, and a lifetime of love, came rushing over him. From that glitter-frosted cake to the spelling bee to the camping trips…to this moment, right now. When his best friend would become his wife.

He took a deep breath as MJ Hewitt, Evie's father, glided his daughter to the bottom of the grand staircase, where Declan stood in front of the small gathering of family and friends who'd come to Gloriana House for its first official wedding.

"Declan," MJ said. "Take good care of her."

Declan gave him a hug and assured him that he would.

And then she was by his side, her eyes glinting with love, her color high. She gave a nervous touch to the gold locket that hung around her neck, the family heirloom of Amelia Bushrod's that she'd chosen as her something old.

"You look beautiful," he whispered.

She gave a shaky smile, and then he could see that the color in her cheeks was makeup, and she was shockingly pale underneath it. He reached for her hand and gave her a reassuring squeeze before guiding her toward the pastor. That man nodded to them and opened a Bible that Declan knew had come from Ireland and once belonged to his grandfather, Seamus Kilcannon.

Declan barely heard the words, though he tried to concentrate, tried to hold on to the moment. He remembered the vows, though. Was there a way to say he'd more than love, intensely cherish, honor her every feeling, and give this woman his heart and soul until he breathed his last breath? Because that was the vow he wanted to give.

When it was Evie's turn, she stumbled over a word or two, and her hands were damp and trembling when he slid the wedding ring on.

He searched her eyes, silently asking the question, *Are you okay?*

She silently answered, *Barely.*

Poor thing. He rubbed the knuckles of her hand, listened to the last prayer, and they finally got pronounced husband and wife.

As he pulled her close for a kiss to seal the deal, she let out the softest moan. "Outside?" she whispered. "I need air."

"Can you make it through the crowd and out the door?" he whispered.

"Hold me and I will."

He gave her the support of his arm as they turned, and dozens of overjoyed faces greeted them, cheering, clapping, looking as satisfied and happy as he felt.

But not Evie. She looked…like she might collapse any second. Maybe this no-wait wedding hadn't been a good idea. The Gloriana House transformation wasn't done yet, but they'd wanted to get married before Christmas. Before…it was obvious that more than two people stood before that pastor and vowed to become a family.

As they crossed the entry and stepped out into the late afternoon sunshine, Evie sucked in some air and held on to his arm with both hands. "That was rough."

He laughed. "Not what you expect to hear from your brand-new wife after exchanging vows."

"Sorry." She put her hand on her stomach. "I'm better now."

"Not gonna blow?"

"Not…yet."

Suddenly, the guests poured out to be with them, his immediate family closest, including Evie's mother, Dawn, concern on her face.

"Evie." Dawn scooted closer. "I thought we said you were going to head right into the living room for pictures. It's freezing out here."

"In a second, Mom." She fanned herself. "I need the cold air."

"Dear lass." Gramma Finnie took her hand. "You look a wee bit peckish."

"She looks greener than the leaves in her bouquet," Yiayia added.

"Which I have right here." Molly said. "You doin' okay?"

"I'm fine," Evie assured everyone, but clung a little tighter to Declan's arm. "Just…"

"You need water?" Ella asked. "Nerves get you?"

"Nerves and…" Evie laughed a little. "Other things."

"Other things?" Molly stepped closer.

"What other things?"

"Are you sick?"

"Do you need to sit down?"

"What's wrong?"

The questions came so fast and furious that Declan held up both hands to rein in the whole lot of them. "Whoa. Back off my wife." He threw her a grin. "I like the sound of that."

She gave a tight smile, nodding. "It's fine, Dec. I just needed air."

"Just like you, Mom," Pru said, sidling up to Molly. "And a Christmas wedding, too. Remember how dizzy and hot you were even though it was cold?"

"Because I was preg—" Molly froze.

And so did everyone else.

Except Declan and Evie, who just looked at each other and laughed.

"I'm telling you," he murmured. "There is no such thing as a secret in this family."

"Secret?" Ella exclaimed. "Why would you keep that a secret?"

"Because we were waiting for this." Declan held up Evie's left hand.

"Oh, nonsense, lad," Gramma Finnie said. "'Tis a rare woman in this family who does things in that order."

Trace put his hands over Pru's ears. "You did not hear that, Umproo."

"Oh my gosh!" Pru exclaimed. "Really?"

Declan and Evie shared a look and another laugh. "Tell them everything?" she asked.

"Why not?"

"Everything…what?" Colleen inched into the group, between Yiayia and Gramma Finnie.

"The reason…" Evie said, nervously toying with her necklace again. "I'm wearing this."

"The locket with the baby pictures in it," Pru said. "Right? Your great-great-grandmother's locket?"

Evie looked up at Declan, her natural color returning. "There are baby pictures in it, but not Gloriana and Evangeline." She flipped it open and turned the inside of the locket toward the group so they could see the teeny-tiny ultrasound images Evie and Declan had tucked inside the night before. "Unless our twins are girls and that's what we name them. It's too soon to know."

*"Twins?!"*

The noise that rose up from the group was loud enough to wake Gloriana and Evangeline, wherever they were buried. Questions got fired, jokes were flying, and more than a few tears flowed as the celebration took on a whole new level of frenzy.

Somehow, they all managed to get back inside, and Pru hurried over with two champagne flutes for Declan and Evie.

"Yours is sparkling cider," she whispered as she handed the glass to Evie.

"Perfect for making a toast," Evie said, holding her glass high. "To Declan Joseph Mahoney, my husband, who is…"

"A banana?" he whispered, cracking her up as they got a few strange looks.

"The man of my dreams," she said. "And that's no joke."

He lifted his glass. "To Evangeline May Hewitt Mahoney…" He swallowed as his throat tightened. "My wife, my partner, the mother of my *children*…" The lump in his throat nearly strangled him. "And my best friend."

As their crystal glasses dinged softly, he could have sworn that was the sound of a basement door closing and locking, forever.

Christmas is right around the corner in Bitter Bark… and that means it's time for a holiday novella! Don't miss *Feliz Naughty Dog,* book seven in The Dogmothers series.

Want to know the minute it's available? Sign up for the newsletter.

www.roxannestclaire.com/newsletter-2/

Or get daily updates, sneak peeks, and insider information at the Dogfather Reader Facebook Group!

www.facebook.com/groups/roxannestclairereaders/

The Dogmothers is a spinoff series of
# The Dogfather

*Available Now*

SIT…STAY…BEG (Book 1)

NEW LEASH ON LIFE (Book 2)

LEADER OF THE PACK (Book 3)

SANTA PAWS IS COMING TO TOWN (Book 4)
(A Holiday Novella)

BAD TO THE BONE (Book 5)

RUFF AROUND THE EDGES (Book 6)

DOUBLE DOG DARE (Book 7)

BARK! THE HERALD ANGELS SING (Book 8)
(A Holiday Novella)

OLD DOG NEW TRICKS (Book 9)

Join the private Dogfather Reader Facebook Group!

www.facebook.com/groups/roxannestclairereaders/

When you join, you'll find inside info on all the books and characters, sneak peeks, and a place to share the love of tails and tales!

# The Dogmothers Series

*Available Now*

HOT UNDER THE COLLAR (Book 1)

THREE DOG NIGHT (Book 2)

DACHSHUND THROUGH THE SNOW (Book 3)

(A Holiday Novella)

CHASING TAIL (Book 4)

HUSH, PUPPY (Book 5)

MAN'S BEST FRIEND (Book 6)

*And many more to come!*

For a complete list, buy links, and reading order of all my books, visit www.roxannestclaire.com. Be sure to sign up for my newsletter to find out when the next book is released!

# A Dogfather/Dogmothers Family Reference Guide

**THE KILCANNON FAMILY**

**Daniel Kilcannon aka *The Dogfather***
Son of Finola (Gramma Finnie) and Seamus Kilcannon. Married to Annie Harper for 36 years until her death. Veterinarian, father, and grandfather. Widowed at opening of series. Married to Katie Santorini (*Old Dog New Tricks*) with dogs Rusty and Goldie.

**The Kilcannons (from oldest to youngest):**

• **Liam** Kilcannon and Andi Rivers (*Leader of the Pack*) with Christian and Fiona and dog, Jag

• **Shane** Kilcannon and Chloe Somerset (*New Leash on Life*) with daughter Annabelle and dogs, Daisy and Ruby

• **Garrett** Kilcannon and Jessie Curtis (*Sit…Stay…Beg*) with son Patrick and dog, Lola

• **Molly** Kilcannon and Trace Bancroft (*Bad to the Bone*) with daughter Pru and son Danny and dog, Meatball

• **Aidan** Kilcannon and Beck Spencer (*Ruff Around the Edges*) with dog, Ruff

• **Darcy** Kilcannon and Josh Ranier (*Double Dog Dare*) with dogs, Kookie and Stella

## THE MAHONEY FAMILY

**Colleen Mahoney**

Daughter of Finola (Gramma Finnie) and Seamus Kilcannon and younger sister of Daniel. Married to Joe Mahoney for a little over 10 years until his death. Owner of Bone Appetit (canine treat bakery) and mother.

**The Mahoneys (from oldest to youngest):**

• **Declan** Mahoney and Evie Hewitt (*Man's Best Friend*) with dog Judah

• **Connor** Mahoney and Sadie Hartman (*Chasing Tail*) with dog, Frank, and cat, Demi

• **Braden** Mahoney and **Cassie** Santorini (*Hot Under the Collar*) with dogs, Jelly Bean and Jasmine

• **Ella** Mahoney and…

## THE SANTORINI FAMILY

**Katie Rogers Santorini**

Dated **Daniel** Kilcannon in college and introduced him to Annie. Married to Nico Santorini for forty years until his death two years after Annie's. Interior Designer and mother. Recently married to **Daniel** Kilcannon (*Old Dogs New Tricks*).

**The Santorinis**

• **Nick** Santorini and…

• **John** Santorini (identical twin to Alex) and Summer Jackson (*Hush, Puppy*) with daughter Destiny and dog, Maverick

• **Alex** Santorini (identical twin to John) and Grace Donovan with dogs, Bitsy, Gertie and Jack

• **Theo** Santorini and…

• **Cassie** Santorini and **Braden** Mahoney (*Hot Under the Collar*) with dogs, Jelly Bean and Jasmine

Katie's mother-in-law from her first marriage, **Agnes "Yiayia" Santorini,** now lives in Bitter Bark with **Gramma Finnie** and their dachshunds, Pygmalion (Pyggie) and Galatea (Gala). These two women are known as "The Dogmothers."

# About The Author

Published since 2003, Roxanne St. Claire is a *New York Times* and *USA Today* bestselling author of more than fifty romance and suspense novels. She has written several popular series, including The Dogfather, The Dogmothers, Barefoot Bay, the Guardian Angelinos, and the Bullet Catchers.

In addition to being a ten-time nominee and one-time winner of the prestigious RITA™ Award for the best in romance writing, Roxanne's novels have won the National Readers' Choice Award for best romantic suspense four times. Her books have been published in dozens of languages and optioned for film.

A mother of two but recent empty-nester, Roxanne lives in Florida with her husband and her two dogs, Ginger and Rosie.

www.roxannestclaire.com
www.twitter.com/roxannestclaire
www.facebook.com/roxannestclaire
www.roxannestclaire.com/newsletter/

Made in the USA
Las Vegas, NV
07 September 2022